EX LIBRIS

VINTAGE CLASSICS

WESTWOOD

Stella Gibbons was born in London in 1902. She went to the North London Collegiate School and studied journalism at University College, London. She worked for various newspapers including the *Evening Standard*. Stella Gibbons is the author of twenty-five novels, three volumes of short-stories, and four volumes of poetry. Her first publication was a book of poems *The Mountain Beast* (1930) and her first novel *Cold Comfort Farm* (1932) won the Femina Vie Heuruse Prize for 1933. Amongst her works are *Christmas at Cold Comfort Farm* (1940), *Westwood* (1946), *Conference at Cold Comfort Farm* (1959) and *Starlight* (1967). She was elected a Fellow of the Royal Society of Literature in 1950. In 1933 she married the actor and singer Allan Webb. They had one daughter. Stella Gibbons died in 1989.

STELLA GIBBONS

Westwood

or The Gentle Powers

WITH AN INTRODUCTION BY
Lynne Truss

VINTAGE BOOKS
London

Published by Vintage 2011

4 6 8 10 9 7 5 3

First published in Great Britain by Longmans, Green & Co. Ltd.

Vintage
Random House, 20 Vauxhall Bridge Road,
London SW1V 2SA

www.vintage-classics.info

Addresses for companies within The Random House Group Limited
can be found at: www.randomhouse.co.uk/offices.htm

The Random House Group Limited Reg. No. 954009

A CIP catalogue record for this book
is available from the British Library

ISBN 9780099528722

The Random House Group Limited supports The Forest Stewardship
Council (FSC®), the leading international forest certification
organisation. Our books carrying the FSC label are printed on FSC®
certified paper. FSC is the only forest certification scheme endorsed
by the leading environmental organisations, including Greenpeace.
Our paper procurement policy can be found at
www.randomhouse.co.uk/environment

Typeset in Bembo by Palimpsest Book Production Limited,
Falkirk, Stirlingshire

Printed and bound by CPI Group (UK) Ltd, Croydon, CR0 4YY

To
Peggy Butcher

Philippians iv. 8

Introduction

This is what everyone knows about Stella Gibbons: she wrote only one book, but it was a very, very good one. *Cold Comfort Farm*, published in 1932 when its obscure female author was thirty years old, was a brilliant, perfect comic novel, satirising the 'loam and love-child' genre of English fiction. It was a huge success on publication and is rightly regarded as a classic eighty years later. But what about its author? What did Stella Gibbons go on to do? Did she ever write anything else? Did she perhaps renounce the literary life and devote herself to bee-keeping? Was 'Stella Gibbons' perhaps not even a real person in the first place? After all, how can someone write a huge debut book like *Cold Comfort Farm* and then not become a literary celebrity?

In fact, Stella Gibbons went on to write more than twenty more novels, one of which was the 1946 novel *Westwood* you are currently holding in your hand. Like all the others, it has been overshadowed by the success of *Cold Comfort Farm* (rather than helped by it) which just goes to show the rotten unfairness of things sometimes. I first read *Westwood* about ten years ago, when I was in the habit of suggesting nifty ideas to BBC radio, and had come up with an intriguing literary hypothesis on which I proposed to build an ambitious season of programmes and adaptations. Was it true, I wondered, that funny women writers are generally allowed only one success in their careers? Wouldn't it be interesting to examine this rather clever insight in relation to (say) Anita Loos, Stella Gibbons and Betty MacDonald – and then dramatise one (each) of their less well-known books or novels? A quick look through the reference materials told me that Stella Gibbons had published over two dozen books between 1930 and her death in 1989, including a couple of collections of poetry. Just as I had suspected, none of these books, apart from *Cold Comfort Farm,* was even in print.

So I thought I should probably read some of these neglected books of hers – for one thing, I needed to check they weren't rubbish. I picked up *Westwood* under guidance from my frighteningly widely-read friend Deirdre, and it occurs to me as I write this that I still haven't properly thanked her for the recommendation, because *Westwood* is a book I loved deeply on first reading and have loved deeply ever since. It is a wise and truthful novel which makes me laugh, and also makes me weep. If *Cold Comfort Farm* is Stella Gibbons's *Pride and Prejudice*, then *Westwood* is her *Persuasion*. Sadly, the BBC rejected my idea about the female one-hit-wonders. However, they did let me rescue one element from the wreckage. They allowed me to dramatise *Westwood* as a two-part 'Classic Serial', and it remains one of the most pleasurable things I've done.

Westwood makes an interesting companion to *Cold Comfort Farm*, being concerned just as much with the eternal struggle between romantic illusion and common sense; however, it expresses that struggle much more sympathetically. Set in wartime north London (specifically the Hampstead Heath and Highgate beloved of its author), it concerns the 23-year-old Margaret Steggles, an emotionally earnest, plain, loveless young English teacher who reveres, above all things, poetry, art and drama. 'I've got such frighteningly strong feelings,' she tells her old school friend Hilda in the first chapter. 'I think you imagine a lot of it,' is the matter-of-fact reply. Through the bathetic agency of a dropped ration book recovered on Hampstead Heath, Margaret gains entry into an exciting world of north London intellectuals – the fashionable painter Alexander Niland, his spoiled wife Hebe, and above all, his eminent father-in-law Gerard Challis, a deeply unfrivolous playwright of high renown. Margaret is overwhelmed by this opportunity to share a more intellectually elevated way of life – ignoring the obvious fact that these people are ghastly. Not only do they quite openly mock her sincerity (and high-handedly foist their small children onto her), but they disappointingly sit about discussing mundane things such as the scarcity of matches, just like anyone else. How confusing this all is for an intelligent girl like Margaret. She wants to worship Gerard Challis; she can quote his preposterous plays; she dreams of his beautiful blue eyes. And yet she can't help it: she still instinctively quibbles with every lordly generalisation he deigns to confer on her.

> Margaret's nervousness was as keen as her delight as they walked together across the faded carpet to the door. As [Challis] opened it, he turned to her once more with his grave searching look, and she experienced a delicious tremor . . .
>
> 'There is a helpless quality, don't you agree, about a room that is prepared for a party,' he observed. 'The silence and flowers are like victims, awaiting the noise of conversation and the cigarette smoke and dissonant jar of conflicting personalities that shall presently destroy them.'
>
> Margaret had been thinking that the hall looked perfectly lovely and wishing with all her heart that she was going to the party too, but she hastily readjusted her point of view, and answered solemnly, 'Yes, I know just what you mean.'

Challis is a terrific character. Pompous, vain, self-satisfied, humourless, he speaks as if from a mountaintop, and refuses to compromise with real life, even in a time of war. By way of everyday conversation, his high-minded characters say things like, 'Suffering is the anvil upon which the crystal sword of integrity is hammered' – which fits in with the way they quite often step outside and kill themselves on the flimsiest pretext as well. In his play *Kattë* (written and premiered in the course of the novel), the Viennese heroine's lover shoots himself offstage; then her father shoots her mother for having borne him such a daughter; he then jumps into the Danube. And in the end, of course, Kattë shoots herself for bringing so much misery on everyone else by her sheer cursed attractiveness.

> 'He knew that his plays were good; each one better than its predecessor. *Mountain Air*, the one about six women botanists and a male guide isolated in a snowstorm in a hut on the Andes, had been surer in its approach and handling than his first one, *The Hidden Well*, which concerned the seven men and one female nurse on the tsetse-fly research station . . . while *Kattë* dealt with an Austrian woman who was bandied about by the officers of a crack regiment in Vienna, and was, he felt convinced, his masterpiece.
>
> He was for ever thinking up new permutations and combinations.'

Challis was rather transparently modelled on the writer Charles Morgan (1894-1958), whose play *The Flashing Stream* had been a big hit before the war. Morgan had annoyed Stella Gibbons in two significant ways: first, by arguing that a sense of humour was overrated in writers (the great Shakespeare had managed without one, he claimed); and second, for writing exasperatingly dreadful female characters along the lines of Kattë. In *Westwood* (Chapter 20), Challis's cut-glass wife Seraphina is devastatingly frank about his lack of realism in this important area:

'I don't mean to butt in or be rude, and I do know everyone *says* you're such a *marvellous* psychologist and I'm not highbrow or anything, but honestly you *don't* know much about women. The women in your plays are such *hags,* darling; absolute witches and hags, if you don't mind my saying so. I don't know *any* women like them and I've known *hordes* of women.'

Or, as Gibbons the narrator more drily explains, 'Like most seekers for an ideal woman, [Challis] did not really like women, believing that they disappointed and failed him on purpose.'

Gibbons punishes the humourless misogynist Challis brilliantly: by making him fall in love with Margaret's down-to-earth (but very attractive) old school friend Hilda. He is thus placed in an infatuation quite as miserable and hopeless as Margaret's – but much, much funnier. 'You look like a painting by Signorelli, in that cap,' he tells her, ardently. 'There we go again,' harrumphs Hilda. Of the three main characters in the book, it is Hilda that is *Westwood*'s greatest creation. A girl who takes nothing seriously and keeps her service boys 'everso cheery,' Hilda is a life force; every line that drops from her mouth is worth its weight in gold. When Challis tells her that a 'friend of his' has written a play, she can't imagine what for. When he tells her what the play is about (serial Austrian suicide), she flatly refuses to see it. Even the sublime work of Leonardo da Vinci doesn't impress her. 'I don't know how you can bear to have that fat pan looking at you when you wake up in the morning,' she says, indicating the tasteful *Mona Lisa* poster Margaret has proudly hung on her bedroom wall. 'It would brown me off for the day.'

What a modern young woman might find hard to swallow in *Westwood* is the rather pitiless, matter-of-fact way Margaret's lack of sex appeal is dealt with. But Stella Gibbons was a doctor's daughter and she never believed in sugaring the pill. Margaret is described as having 'tiny ears, fine dark eyebrows, and good ankles – all minor beauties and not in themselves enough to make a woman attractive.' Naturally it hurts Margaret to be aware of her shortcomings (and to be reminded of them quite so often by her unhappily married mother). But facts are facts: Margaret's plainness ultimately rules out the possibility of *Westwood* being the twentieth-century *Persuasion*, after all. Stella Gibbons is just too honest about the realities of life to provide a happy romantic ending. Men are drawn to attractive women, and they don't select partners according to any other measure of their worth. In the real world, Captain Wentworth does not reclaim the plain and ageing Anne Elliot; he marries someone else. But that doesn't mean Gibbons is unsympathetic. Not at all. In fact, re-reading *Westwood*, I suddenly remembered one of Gibbons's best-known poems, 'Lullaby for a Baby Toad', in which the little, ugly creature is lovingly told that, because it carries a precious gem in its forehead, its looks are actually its protection:

> *For if, my toadling,*
> *Your face were fair*
> *As the precious jewel*
> *That glimmers there,*
> *Man, the jealous,*
> *Man, the cruel,*
> *Would look at you*
> *And suspect the jewel.*
>
> *So dry the tears*
> *From your horned eyes,*
> *And eat your supper*
> *Of dew and flies;*
> *Curl in the shade*

Of the nettles deep,
Think of your jewel
And go to sleep.

I am so pleased *Westwood* is finally coming back into print. I'm quite sure that if it hadn't been written by the author of *Cold Comfort Farm*, it would have fared a great deal better in the world. Stella Gibbons's nephew Reggie Oliver, who wrote an excellent biography of his aunt, told me he was sure she felt more proud of *Westwood* than of any of her other books. This is a rich, mature novel, romantic and wistful, full of rounded characters and terrific dialogue, with a pair of pleasingly intertwining plots, and great comic scenes. It is beautifully written by an author whose precision with idiom was unerring. It deals with heartbreak and hope, longing and disappointment; and is underlined by a genuine poetic love for natural beauty. And it teaches us that integrity does not always have to be forged on the anvil of suffering, whatever the Gerard Challises of this world might think. Sometimes integrity is the cause of suffering, rather than the result of it.

Lynne Truss, 2011

1

London was beautiful that summer. In the poor streets the people made an open-air life for themselves under the blue sky as if they were living in a warmer climate. Old men sat on the fallen masonry and smoked their pipes and talked about the War, while the women stood patiently in the shops or round the stalls selling large fresh vegetables, ceaselessly talking.

The ruins of the small shapely houses in the older parts of the city were yellow, like the sunlit houses of Genoa; all shades of yellow; deep, and pale, or glowing with a strange transparency in the light. The fire-fighting people had made deep pools with walls round them in many of the streets, and here, in the heart of London, ducks came to live on these lakes that reflected the tall yellow ruins and the blue sky. Pink willow-herb grew over the white uneven ground where houses had stood, and there were acres of ground covered with deserted, shattered houses whose windows were filled with torn black paper. On the outskirts of the city, out towards Edmonton and Tottenham in the north and Sydenham in the south, there was a strange feeling in the air, heavy and sombre and thrilling, as if History were working visibly, before one's eyes. And the country was beginning to run back to London; back into those grimy villages linked by featureless roads from which it had never quite vanished, and which make up the largest city in the world. Weeds grew in the City itself; a hawk was seen hovering over the ruins of the Temple, and foxes raided the chicken roosts in the gardens of houses near Hampstead Heath. The shabby quietness of an old, decaying village hung in the streets, and it was a wonderful, awe-inspiring thing to see and to feel. While the summer lasted, the beauty was stronger than the sadness, because the sun blessed everything – the ruins, the tired faces of the people, the tall wild flowers and the dark stagnant water – and, during those months of calm, London in ruin was beautiful as a city in a dream.

Then the autumn came with mists. They began early in September, and the beauty lingered while the leaves came slowly down through the still air. On Hampstead Heath the young willow trees growing on either side of a long hilly road did not turn until late October, and they were still in their long full leaf one evening at sunset, when a young woman was the only person in the road, which she was crossing on her way to the open Heath.

She glanced up the road's length, and gasped as she saw the willows; the scene about her was all gorgeous in deep colours softened by the mist, but each willow tree looked like a streaked fountain of yellow and green and fire-colour hanging down in a blue haze, while, under some large, motionless, yellow and dark-green trees on her left, there spread away a broad lustrous lake of golden water, glowing not on its surface but in its depths. The dim blue sky was streaked with grey and scarlet mist, and the damp grass was blue in the shade.

The air smelled of fog. There were other people hurrying home in the distance, but they were only dark figures against the general gorgeousness and glow.

She looked at her watch. It was nearly five o'clock, and she set off quickly across the Heath in the direction of Highgate, whose church spire looked out at the spire of Hampstead's church across the intervening small valleys and hills. Her shoes quickly became soaked in the long grass and the masses of black and yellow leaves, and the air grew cold, but she was so absorbed in the beauty of the scene, richly coloured as some dream of a Brazilian garden, that she noticed nothing else. She was a thin young woman of medium height in her early twenties, with a strong dark face, and untidy dark curls hanging about her shoulders. Her mouth was too full, and her brown eyes had an eager look.

Presently she came out on the path below Kenwood that leads directly down to Highgate There were allotments here with giant cabbages of a rich blue-green colour; the mist, and the dim blue of the sky, and the green of the grass caught up the colour and repeated it again and again almost as far as she could see, and the leaves were huge and beaded with water, for rain had fallen that afternoon. She hurried on with her hands in her pockets, still looking about her, but the colours were quickly fading now, and the greyness of evening was creeping over the fields.

As she was leaving the Heath, between two wide lakes reflecting the last colours in the sky and the clumps of dark roseate osiers, she saw two tall men coming towards her through the mist. The elder wore a closely fitting dark coat and a black diplomatic hat, and carried a leather brief-case, and had eyes of so deep a blue that it was noticeable even in the gathering dusk. The younger wore looser clothes, and a black sweater with a turtle neck, and had no hat.

'But Henry Moore isn't —' the younger was saying as the two passed her, and then he took a handkerchief out of his pocket and the rest of the sentence was lost. Both were walking fast, and in a few moments they had passed out of her hearing.

But she turned once to look after them, attracted by their distinguished appearance and unusual height, and, as she did so, she noticed something lighter than the path lying a few yards away; a small, square, cream-coloured object. She approached it, and on stooping to pick it up saw that it was a ration book.

'Oh dear,' she said aloud, looking first at it and then after the two gentlemen, who were by now almost out of sight across the misty fields. Her voice was deep, with a decisive note.

It was no use running after them, she thought; besides, she was late now. She looked down at the name on the book. It was such an odd one that for the moment she thought it was foreign:

> Hebe Niland,
> Lamb Cottage,
> Romney Square,
> Hampstead, N. W. 3.

Oh well, I can drop it in the post to-morrow, she thought, and put the book in her pocket and hurried on.

It was almost dark by the time she reached Highgate Village. A figure in a mackintosh and beret rushed out from the shade of a shop door, crying reproachfully:

'Well, you're a nice one! I've been here for ages! What on earth happened to you? I'm frozen and now we won't be able to go; Mother doesn't like me out in the blackout, you know that as well as I do. You are the limit!'

'I'm awfully sorry, Hilda. I walked over the Heath and it was so gorgeous, I didn't notice the time. But we *must* go; come on; if we hurry we'll just be there before blackout,' and she put her arm through Hilda's, and strode away across the road towards Southwood Lane.

'Oh well, p'raps we'll just make it, and I don't expect Mother'll mind, as there's two of us. Have you got the keys?' said Hilda, pacified.

The dark girl nodded and jingled them in her pocket.

'What've you been doing all the afternoon?' Hilda went on.

'I went to the concert at the National Gallery, and then I walked about.'

'Walked about? You are dopey. I say, Margaret, have you thought – there'll be no blackout, so we shan't be able to shine a torch.'

'We shall be able to see all I want to see – if there's a proper place for coals and all that sort of thing.'

'Of course there'll be a proper place for coals! Those houses have only been up about ten years. You're very lucky to get the chance of one.'

'I know we are, and I don't think it's right,' said Margaret, grimly.

'Why ever not?'

'Millions of people all over the world have lost their homes. Why should *we* have a new house?'

'I don't see that! It wouldn't make it any better for them if you didn't have one.'

'People in England haven't suffered enough.'

'If you're going to start about Russia I'm going straight home!' cried Hilda, standing still in the middle of the road.

'I wasn't going to say anything about Russia *particularly*.'

'That's a wonder. Here, is this it?' and she darted forward and shone her torch on the gate of a house which was one of a row. 'Yes, number seventeen. Well, it's still got a gate. That's something.'

She pushed the gate open and walked up the narrow crazy-paving path. The dim light of the torch shone on the tall weeds, fluffy with withered seedlings, that brushed against her skirt. Margaret followed, and the gate slammed after them.

'Are all these house blitzed, I wonder?' went on Hilda. 'No, there's a chink in your next-door neighbour's blackout. Phew! Doesn't it smell of bombs! Got the key?'

Margaret was already shining her own torch over the narrow

front door, which badly needed painting, and fitting the key into the lock. It was nearly dark. Something so enormous, round and red that for a moment it was hard to realize what it was, was rising slowly between the black houses. Hilda glanced over her shoulder and exclaimed:

'What a gorgeous moon!'

'Ominous,' said Margaret quietly, pushing open the door, which was stiff on its hinges. A little hall and a narrow staircase were revealed in the faint light. The floor was covered with a white substance.

'So what? Whatever's all that muck on the floor?'

'Plaster,' said Margaret, stepping inside, 'I expect the ceiling is down.'

'Never mind, ducks; you said we haven't suffered enough; you'll be able to have plaster every day in your powdered egg. Shall I shut the door?' And she did so, with a bang. Some more plaster came down, but when Margaret flashed her torch upwards the light revealed only a small hole.

'It could easily be repaired,' she muttered.

'Oh, I shouldn't bother,' said Hilda blithely. 'What's this? The dining-room? Oh, the ceiling *is* down here, Margaret!' and she flashed her torch over a dismal mass of white on the dusky floor. 'Gets better and better, doesn't it?'

'But it's a nice little house,' said Margaret, flashing her own torch over walls and fireplace. Her serious voice had a slight accent that was not London, nor completely southern.

'Isn't it wicked, though, ruining peoples' places like this?' demanded Hilda, going out into the hall again. 'Look, here's the drawing-room – oh, it's got French windows into the garden – rather nice.'

The increasing moonlight shone faintly upon canes of dead golden-rod, and clouds of feathery willow–herb gone to seed. A stone bird-bath stood up in the middle of the rank little lawn.

Beyond the garden's end a hill, covered in dim buildings and trees, ran up to a line of houses that were dark against the misty moonlit sky.

'Let's go upstairs,' said Hilda, leading the way. Their footsteps echoed all over the house.

There were two fairly large bedrooms and a little slip-room over the front door.

'One for your father and mother, and one for you, and a spare room,' said Hilda, going from room to room and flashing her torch into corners and cupboards.

'Mother and Dad have separate rooms and we shan't be having anyone to stay,' said Margaret, going into the bathroom. Hilda made a rueful face to herself in the darkness, as if she were sorry she had spoken, but the next instant said half defiantly, 'People can be quite fond of each other even if they do have separate rooms; my Auntie Grace and Uncle Jim do, and they're quite a pair of old love-birds.'

'Be careful how you flash that torch or we'll have the wardens after us,' was all Margaret said.

'There's a separate bathroom; good,' said Hilda, opening a door and shutting it again. 'Oh, Margaret – the kitchen! We must look at that; Mother says it's the most important room in the house.'

They went downstairs again. Moonlight was now shining in squares on the bare, dusty boards. The kitchen looked dismal, for the gas cooker had been removed by the outgoing tenants, and the ceiling was down, but there was a large larder (in the coolest part of the room, Hilda pointed out to the silent Margaret) and the sink was actually under the window.

'Like they always have them in American films,' said Hilda. 'Oh, what an enormous spider!' and she peered into the sink. 'Do look, Margaret, I've never seen such a huge one. I suppose it *is* a spider?' looking about for something to poke it with. Margaret made a shuddering noise.

'Oh, I rather like *them*,' said Hilda. 'The only creepy-crawlies I can't stand are earwigs. When we were at Bracing Bay the year before the war there was a boy always trying to put earwigs down the back of my bathing costume; honestly, I used to scream so you could hear me all over the beach!'

'Listen!' said Margaret suddenly. Far away to the east over the river's estuary a faint ululation was beginning, and even as the two girls listened it was taken up close at hand.

'There!' said Hilda. 'Oh dear, Mother'll be having fits. What shall we do? There isn't time to run home, I s'pose?'

'Of course not,' said Margaret decidedly. 'We'll go and sit on the stairs,' and she led the way back to the hall.

'Gosh, isn't it hard!' said Hilda, sitting down gingerly.

Margaret took out a packet of cigarettes and lit one, and Hilda produced a paper bag.

'Last of my sweet ration,' she said, holding up a large round greenish object. 'Sorry I can't give you half.'

'Can't you bite it?' suggested Margaret, with a reluctant smile in her voice, and they both laughed.

'Oh, you are a dear old stick!' suddenly said Hilda, looking up at her friend, as she sat on the stair above. 'Doesn't it seem ages since we were at school?'

'Years,' and Margaret sighed.

'You're different, you know.'

'How do you mean, different?'

'I don't know. Just different. When I saw you at the station, the first thing I thought was, she's different.'

Margaret was silent.

'As if something had happened to you to make you – sort of miserable,' concluded Hilda.

Margaret's cigarette glowed in the dusk.

'Is that guns?' she said.

'I expect so. Never mind them. What I mean is –'

'Aren't you frightened?' asked Margaret seriously.

'Me frightened?' cried Hilda. 'Whatever do you mean, Margaret Steggles?'

'Well, how should I know? I've never been in a raid with you before.'

'I'm not frightened of anything,' announced Hilda. 'And if you went about with as many Service boys as I do, you wouldn't be either.'

'Yes, I should,' said Margaret in a low tone, staring across the dim hall to the pale square that marked the front door. 'I'm not so frightened for myself − though that comes into it too, of course. It's all the other people I think about, all over the world, when I hear *that*,' and she jerked her head in the direction of the distant barrage that sounded like giants rapidly and furiously stamping.

'They're all right in South America,' said Hilda.

'Oh −!' Margaret moved impatiently.

'I mean, they don't have air-raids.'

'That doesn't make it any better. You don't understand.'

'It's you that doesn't understand. It *does* make it better. I *like* to think of them having cocktails and all the chocolates they want and silk stockings. It cheers me up to think that *someone* can.'

'I can only think about all the people who haven't enough food, let alone cocktails and silk stockings.'

'Well, don't think about them. It doesn't do any good. You always did take everything so seriously at school and now you worry about your old Russia all the time, and you're always moaning about reconstruction. Honestly, Margaret, you get me down.'

'I'm sorry,' said Margaret, politely and bitterly. 'You make me sound a complete bore.'

'I didn't say anything about being a bore,' cried Hilda

remorsefully. 'You're ever so much cleverer than I am; I couldn't be a teacher to save my life, and you know how fond I am of you, you old mutt! It's only that I don't like to see you so browned-off and different.'

Again Margaret was silent.

'I'm sure something's happened,' said Hilda. 'I do wish you'd cough it up, then you'd feel better.'

'Do you always cough things up?'

'Well, nothing ever happens to me. I mean to say, only with boys, and I can manage them. Mother and me often have a good old laugh about my boys. She says it makes her feel young again. Isn't she a scream, though?'

'You're happy, aren't you?' asked Margaret suddenly.

Hilda gave such an emphatic nod that all the smooth blonde curls on her shoulders danced, but all she said was:

'I s'pose so. Can't say I've ever thought about it.'

'Well, I'm not,' said Margaret, feeling in her handbag for another cigarette. 'I never have been, and as I get older it just gets worse and worse.'

'Your father and mother don't get on, do they?' interrupted Hilda, bluntly.

Margaret shook her head; her friend could just see the little movement in the dimness.

'I always thought so, and so did Mother and Dad (of course, we didn't chew it over a lot, but you can't help noticing little things). Well, that's enough to make you miserable – your parents not getting on.'

'I suppose it was that to begin with,' said Margaret slowly, 'but it isn't only that. I've just got an unhappy nature, I think. I take everything so seriously, and I mind it so much when things are ugly, and I worry about the mess the world's in, and the war. And the year before last –'

'I should think the All Clear'll go in a minute,' interrupted

Hilda, 'and the sooner the quicker; I'm starving, aren't you? Go on, sorry.'

'That time you came up to stay with us – I don't suppose you remember a boy called Frank Kennett, do you? He was a friend of Reg's.'

'Short fair boy. Rather quiet. Nice manners,' said Hilda at once, as if quoting from a private file. 'He danced with you nearly all the time at that dance we went to with Reg's crowd.'

'That's the one. But he isn't short, Hilda, he's a bit taller than I am.'

'Well, you're no giant,' retorted Hilda, 'and I distinctly remember thinking of him as a short fair boy. Never mind, go on. What about him?'

'We used to go about together a good bit at one time. Boys never did take to me much, you know, I'm not like you' – there was a smile in her voice again, and this time it was a loving one – 'and we liked all the things – music and poetry and pictures – that the rest of Reg's crowd didn't like. Well, it wasn't so much that they didn't like them; they never thought about them; all they cared about was the pictures and dancing and getting enough money to have motor-bikes or cars of their own. They didn't *know* about anything else; they were all as ignorant as pigs and as common as dirt, and I loathed and despised the lot of them,' she ended savagely.

'They didn't seem too bad to me.'

'I dare say. You aren't like me; lucky for you you aren't. Frank and I used to go to the concerts at the Corn Exchange, and that winter there was a repertory company at Northampton and we never missed a week; they did some really good plays, too; Shaw and Ibsen, and Shakespeare and O'Neill. That was the nearest thing to happiness I've ever had.'

'Did he kiss you?' interrupted Hilda.

'Sometimes,' said Margaret, without much expression in her voice. 'Not very often.'

'I said to a Raf boy I was out with last Sunday, "It's a good thing I don't want to kiss you as often as you want to kiss me," I said, "or we'd never have time for anything else." "Oh, Hilda," he said, just like that. "*Oh, Hilda!*" with a kind of a sigh. I had to laugh. But he was a nice boy; I gave him one of my new Polyphotos for luck. "You be careful not to drop it over Berlin," I said, "I don't want to be one of Goebbels's pin-up girls." Go on, sorry.'

'He worked in Sintram's; you know, that big wireless factory outside the town; he was something to do with the research they were doing there on short-waves and he was clever. I *did* like him!' she burst out resentfully. 'We were friends.'

'Were you sort of in love with him?' demanded Hilda.

'I don't know. I just liked going about with him and having a friend who liked the things I did. It was all – kind of quiet and happy. And then Mother started.'

'How do you mean?'

'Oh, worrying me about getting married. She's always been crazy about that; you won't believe it, but she started dinning it into me how a girl *must* get married when I was a kid of twelve. I don't know why, because she doesn't think much of men really, or being married, but she's very down on old maids.'

'No pleasing some people, is there? You should worry.'

'I don't expect *you* would have, but she kept on moan, moan, moan, about it until she absolutely got under my skin. I got so embarrassed about it that I made excuses to keep Frank from coming to the house. I think Mother must have spoken to Dad about it, too, because he said something to me once about young Kennett having a good job.'

'Did she ask you if he'd proposed?'

'Not so much that. She took it for granted I should tell her if he did. But asking me every time I came in after I'd been out with him if he seemed to be *cooling off* and giving me hints on how to *bring him up to the scratch* . . . it was simply disgusting!' she burst out again, writhing at the memory.

'Silly, too,' said Hilda. 'And I think all that sort of thing's so common, don't you? Besides, it never gets you anywhere. Mother doesn't know *what* she feels about me getting married. One minute she's dying to see me sailing down the aisle in white satin, and the next minute she says she doesn't know how she'll ever get on without me. Well, I laugh at her. Go on, sorry.'

'I felt worse and worse about it. She never gave me a minute's peace. It was almost as if' – she hesitated – 'she wanted to drag me into the worry and sordidness and pettiness of being married.'

Far away, in the silence that had followed the barrage, the All Clear began.

'Goody!' cried Hilda, springing up. 'Come on, you can finish telling me on the way home.' She opened the front door. The moon was shining brilliantly but a cold, still mist crept among the leafless trees and lightless houses. Hilda thrust her arm through Margaret's and with the other hand slammed the door of the little house.

'If I were you I'd decide on that one, Margaret,' she said, as they hurried down the path.

'It's certainly the most suitable one I've seen yet.'

'And it's so nice and near us!' cried Hilda with a skip, already planning to introduce Margaret to the most bookish among a multitude of decidedly non-bookish boys who frequented the small house where she lived with her parents.

'Oh, you must have that one! Go on about Frank, we'll be home in a minute and I shall be too busy eating to give you my full attention.' She pressed Margaret's arm and lifted her small face, with its delicate aquiline features, to the moon whose light sparkled in her blue eyes. 'Gorgeous night.'

'So, at last,' said Margaret heavily, her face and voice unlightened by the haste of her footsteps and the refreshing night air, her whole personality sunk in unhappy memories, 'I – I asked him outright.'

'Gosh!' muttered Hilda. Then, recovering herself, 'Well, why not? If he was really your friend, he'd have understood.'

'That was what I thought, you see. I *told* him how Mother had been worrying me, and how awful it made me feel, and I said I was only asking him about – about how he felt – so that I could have *something* definite, one way or another, to tell her and shut her up. I – I made a kind of joke of it, you see, really.'

Hilda squeezed her arm again, in silence. Margaret was silent for so long that Hilda at last peeped round at her dark brooding face and said more quietly than usual:

'And what did he say?'

'He was very quiet and – and nice, really,' said Margaret in a low tone that barely concealed her agony of shame. 'I don't think he did understand. He seemed surprised that I took it all so seriously. He made a kind of joke out of it too – not unkindly, of course – he was two years older than I was and much more sensible. And he explained – he said – he told me – that he didn't love me . . .'

'But that was all right, because you didn't love him,' interrupted Hilda, 'so you needn't feel bad about that.'

'No, I didn't love him when I told him. But afterwards when I'd had a frightful scene with Mother and she'd told me I'd messed up my chance and I'd probably never have another, then I got thinking about how kind and quiet and sensible he was and how we liked all the same things, and I – I thought I did love him and that made it worse than ever. I was so miserable I wanted to die.'

'You take things *to heart* so,' said Hilda at last, in what was for her a depressed tone.

'I know. I always have. I can't help it.'

'What *will* you be like when you're old?'

'Perhaps I shan't live to be old.'

'Go on, that's right, be really cheerful.'

'Well, I don't want to be.'

'Yes you do; we'll live together in that little house when I'm old too and all my boys have deserted me.'

'You'll be married.'

'Well, so will you.'

Margaret shook her head. 'No, I shan't. I'm not the type.'

'You aren't' – Hilda hesitated – 'you don't still care about him, do you?'

'I'm not still in love with him, if that's what you mean. I still like to remember what friends we were. You see, I think of him as two people really; the real person who was so easy to get on with, and kind and sensible, and the person I was in love with, who was all romantic and marvellous because he was unattainable.'

Hilda could only shake her head.

'Did you see him again after you'd told him about your mother?' she asked presently.

'No. He did want to, but I said not. We wrote to each other once or twice, at Christmas; just ordinary letters, not long ones. After I'd got over being in love with him I didn't want to see him again.'

'Wouldn't you like to see him again now?' suggested Hilda.

Margaret did not answer for a little while. Then, when they were nearly at the gate of Hilda's house, where she was staying, she said:

'No. I still feel too bad about it. It absolutely did something to me, Hilda. That's what's made me "different," as you say. It was such a shock to me, telling him like that — and then falling in love with him after he'd *told* me he wasn't in love with me — and feeling so despairing. I've got such frighteningly strong feelings — you don't know.'

'I think you imagine a lot of it,' said Hilda firmly, pushing open the gate of a tiny house whose wintry garden had not a dead leaf in sight or a grass blade out of place, and whose blackout showed not a cranny or chink. The front doorstep was snowy in the moonlight and the metal letter-box glittered.

'No, I don't. I wish I did.'

'Well, never mind now. You're quite bats but I love you,' and she gave her a quick hug and tapped out the Victory tattoo on the knocker, 'and it's lovely that you're coming to live in London.'

2

The town of Lukeborough, to which Margaret returned in a few days, was in Bedfordshire.

Before the Second World War Lukeborough had a population of some seventy thousand, being smaller than Northampton and larger than Luton, its nearest comparable neighbours to the north and south. Evacuees from London and war-workers drafted into its new factories from the Midlands and the North had increased its numbers to nearly eighty thousand by the fourth year of the War, and its natural ugliness and dullness were enhanced by overcrowding in its streets and shops and cinemas, and a chronic shortage of those small delicacies that make life in war-time a little brighter. As a result, the pre-Second World War inhabitants of Lukeborough were bitter about the town's new population, and the newcomers swore that it was the last place God made and were only anxious to get away from it for ever as soon as possible.

Lukeborough's growth during the last forty years had been due entirely to its commerce; all its large new buildings were factories, and its small ones were bungalows or rows of neat, boring little houses built to house the factory workers. There was not even a core of gracious country-town architecture buried in the heart of the place, for it had only been a sprawling village with a strong Dissenting tradition, and all that was left of the village was one or two weather-boarded cottages in the High Street which had been turned into cafés and wireless shops, and the Corn Exchange, a hall built in 1882. The sky seemed to be grey for five days out of the seven above

Lukeborough, and when it was blue it only stirred in the hearts of the few romantics in the town an echo of loveliness, an aching longing, as they glanced away over the low, mean houses and unpicturesque streets towards the clear, ethereal turquoise heaven.

But although nine out of ten of the inhabitants of Lukeborough were permanently cross and on the defensive, this does not mean that they were discontented with their lot, and pined to make Lukeborough the Athens of North Bedfordshire, flashing with concrete mansions and gracious with gardens where civic pride grew like flowers. So long as buses ran regularly, and the electric light and gas worked properly, and the streets were kept moderately clean, and there were up-to-date films at the Roxy and the Lukeborough Plaza, they did not ask for much else; and if the evacuees and the war-workers could have been removed overnight, their pipkin of happiness would have been full. Life certainly did run on a very low voltage in Lukeborough; we pride ourselves on being able to perceive romance and beauty in the common scene, but even we are bound to admit that at Lukeborough the streets were usually covered with a thin greasy paste that was not quite mud, the air was usually windless and muggy, and the rise in the ground from one end of the town to the other was about half an inch in five hundred yards.

Margaret came out of the station on a typical Lukeborough afternoon, grey and moist, and walked along to the end of the road to catch the bus. It was exactly half-past three. She would arrive at her home – which was on the outskirts of the town – in time for tea at four o'clock.

Her mind was still full of pictures of London, and she felt half-enchanted. She had been there before, but this was the first time that she had been able to wander about by herself and let the spell of the capital sink into her heart. She had stood for half an hour on Chelsea Embankment and watched the sullen pearly river running roughly past the Egyptian massif of the Battersea Power Station, the only beautiful modern building in London; she had seen the rows of ruined houses with their blind windows of black paper, and the charred wood in the doorways of Soho that was like quilted black satin. For a week she had wandered about, searching for a house for her parents to live in, and conscientiously doing what she had been sent by them to London to do; but she had also dreamed more, and found richer food for her imagination, than she had ever found before. London had changed her. The knowledge that in a few weeks she would be returning to London, to live there, was full of wonder and delight.

The bus was entering a road with small detached redbrick houses standing at the end of long narrow gardens. At the next stop she got down.

The houses, which were fairly new and three-storied, had names like Coombe Dene, and Wycombe, and Fiona. Margaret pushed open the gate of one called Ilsa, and walked up the path. The windows were draped with soft curtains of pale yellow, frilled at the edges and crossed, and the doorstep was as white as that of Hilda's home and the metal-work on the front door as gleaming. Clumps of yellow chrysanthemums stood in the narrow beds on either side of the path and the lawns were neatly mown. Beyond the house could be seen flat fields and elm trees with houses here and there; this was a main road leading straight to Northampton, and provided an excellent example of ribbon development.

She rang the bell, and in a moment her mother opened the door.

'I thought it would be you, dear,' she said, and gave her daughter a pecking kiss. 'Come in and shut the door; the damp makes the oilcloth look so dull, and I've only done it this morning. Well, I hope you've found somewhere nice for us; you didn't say much in your letter. Better go up and put your things away; tea's just on ready. Reg will be here any time after five; he's got forty-eight hours again. It's nice having him, of course, but I do wish they'd give you longer notice. I've just sent his eiderdown to be cleaned, and Mrs Burrows and I were going to do his room to-morrow. But it can't be helped. Margaret! You've dropped this.'

Margaret came down the stairs again to take the glove her mother was holding out.

'I can't say your holiday seems to have done you much good; you look half asleep,' said Mrs Steggles, glancing at her sharply and discontentedly. 'Sitting up half the night talking with Hilda, I suppose. Well, hurry up and get washed; I want my tea, and I want to hear all about the house. How we're going to get everything packed up and ready in three weeks I don't know. Still, it's got to be done, so I suppose it will be. Don't leave the bathroom untidy, dear, it was only done this morning.'

Margaret went upstairs, and Mrs Steggles hurried into the dining-room, where a little electric fire was burning on one bar, and tea was laid. The room was decorated in light, cold colours, and the furniture, made of pale wood in angular shapes, gave an impression of flimsiness and sparseness. Every object, from the frilled curtains to the yellow tea-cosy, was exquisitely clean. A faint odour of furniture polish and freshly made tea hung in the air. Mrs Steggles sat down at the head of the table and stared out of the window, waiting for her daughter. The worried look faded from her face as she gazed, and it was possible to see that she had once been unusually pretty, though now her complexion was marred by the settled reddish hue of middle age and her abundant dark hair was waved stiffly and unbecomingly against her head. Her teeth were not her own and her figure was spare and taut. Deep lines of worry ran down on either side of her mouth and across her forehead. Her large brown eyes were suspicious, and, when she sat quietly as she was doing now, very sad. Her full mouth, that was like Margaret's, was ill-tempered and her voice edgy. Rage, rather than mere irritability, lurked in that voice and mouth. She wore a pale satin blouse with elaborate embroidery at the neck, and a dark skirt; and although her hands were worn with housework some attempt had been made to preserve their softness.

Margaret came in, pushing back her hair from her forehead. She had tiny ears, fine dark eyebrows, and good ankles; all minor beauties and not in themselves enough to make a woman attractive.

'I expect you want your tea,' said Mrs Steggles, beginning to pour out. 'Was the train very crowded? I had a letter from Mrs Miller this morning; she said they had a terrible journey down; they had to stand all the way, and Ella was sick. I'm sure I hope it won't be like that when we go. Well, now, about the house. It's near Hilda, you say?'

'Yes, in the next road but one. It's almost the same kind of house. There's a hill at the back of it –'

'Oh dear, I hope we shan't be very overlooked!'

'It's all hills round there, so we shall have to get used to it. Hilda said I was to tell you the kitchen sink is under the window.'

Mrs Steggles nodded. 'And you say they promised to get the ceilings done by the end of this week. Are the rooms much smaller than these?'

'They said they'd try. No, about the same size. Mrs Wilson was awfully kind, Mother; she promised to go round every day and see how the men are getting on.'

'Yes, that was kind of her. How is she? Is Hilda any nearer being engaged yet?'

'She's very well. No, I don't think so; she never said anything about it.'

'If she's not careful she'll miss her market; those very popular girls with crowds of boys so often don't marry; I've noticed it.'

'Mother, she's only twenty-two!' exclaimed Margaret, colouring.

'Oh, yes; I know you think there's all the time in the world to get married, and Hilda's the same; but time goes quicker than you girls realize, and you'll both be twenty-seven before you can turn round. Is it a light house, should you say?'

'Not quite so light as this because the road isn't so wide, but it is light. I think you'll like it, Mother. It's in a nice road, and the shops are only just round the corner.'

'Well, that's something. Is it near the bus for your father?'

'About five minutes' walk from a new Underground station.'

'And how long does it take to get into London?'

'I found it took me nearly three-quarters of an hour; everything was so crowded.'

'How did you get on? Did you like the look of your new school? I don't expect so!' Mrs Steggles vigorously helped herself to jam.

'It's in a neighbourhood that's gone down a lot, and the school itself is very knocked about; they've been evacuated, as I told you, and the school has been used as a British Restaurant. The headmistress, Miss Lathom, seemed quite nice.'

'Is it far from Stanley Gardens?'

'About twenty minutes by bus.'

'Well, it all *sounds* very convenient; we'll hope it's as nice as it sounds. Another cup, Margaret?'

'Yes, please, Mother. How – is Dad all right?'

'Yes, of course. Why shouldn't he be?'

Margaret did not answer, and they went on to talk about the house again and to discuss plans for the move in three weeks' time.

Mrs Steggles was not daunted by the prospect of a move in

war-time, for her restless unhappiness found relief in a domestic upheaval, and she enjoyed moves. The Steggleses had had six homes in their twenty-eight years of married life, and each one a solid little provincial house filled with good plain furniture from attic to kitchen; not a series of three-roomed flats sketchily equipped with a few sticks. Mr Steggles earned a comfortable income as Chief Sub-Editor on the *North Bedfordshire Record*, an old-established weekly newspaper, and his particular weakness was not improvidence with money. He indulged his wife's liking for movement and change. She was an excellent manager and a superlative housewife. There had always been every amenity in those six little houses during the past twenty-eight years except laughter and love. There was not much laughter left in Jack Steggles at the age of fifty-six, and as he went to other women for love, he felt vaguely that Mabel must be allowed her fits of discontent with a perfectly satisfactory house and her feverish search for a better one, and her purchase of new rugs and curtains to equip it when she found it. She was neither socially nor financially ambitious; he granted her that. She did not nag at him to earn more money or get a more important job. She was only driven by some inward passion for perfection; some deep dissatisfaction that made her scrub and polish and rub and dust and clean until their home, wherever it was, glittered and shone like a museum.

After tea, Margaret unpacked and put her clothes away. She sighed as she looked at her untidy curls in the mirror, and decided that a neater way of wearing them must be found before she joined the staff of the school in London at half-term. A style that had been indulgently over-looked at Sunnybrae School, Lukeborough, where she had had her first post as a teacher, would not do for London. The few members of the staff whom she had encountered on her visit to the Anna Bonner School for Girls had been noticeably neat.

She drew her hair behind her ears and gathered the curls at the back of her neck with a black velvet bow. It looked too striking, but it was certainly neat, and it made her seem older and taller. She brushed her hair smoothly on the top and noticed that her mind, usually so full of dreams, actually felt more orderly. She remembered the passage in Keats's *Letters* in which he describes his own recipe for calming his wandering thoughts and over-excited nerves; washing his face and hands and re-lacing his shoes and then sitting down to write. She looked up the passage, and stood dreaming over it.

Her mother called angrily up the stairs:

'Margaret! Put that book away and come down here at once! Reg'll be here any minute and I want the cloth set and some potatoes done, and he's sure to want a bath, the boiler'll want making up. Come along, get a move on, now!'

Margaret reluctantly returned to the present, put the book back among the many others that crowded her room, and went slowly downstairs.

'Whatever have you done to your hair?' demanded her mother at once, looking round with a flushed face from the open oven. 'It makes you look about forty. Is that one of Hilda's notions?'

'It looks so untidy the other way. How many potatoes shall I do?'

'About ten – he's sure to be hungry. I should think what was good enough for Miss Lomax at Sunnybrae was good enough for anybody.'

'I don't want to go looking untidy; it'll reflect on Miss Lomax, as she recommended me there.'

'Well, you've made yourself into a proper school-marm, if that's any comfort; you only want your horn-rims and the picture will be complete. *I* think you look a sight, but I've given over expecting you to do anything to please me. Margaret, *Margaret*, do be careful what you're doing; I only scrubbed that table this morning, and there you go putting a greasy spoon down on it. Can't you put it on a saucer? There! There's Reg now!'

Mrs Steggles was not one of the mothers who lavish all their affection on their sons. She gave Reg a kiss but she also noticed that his great muddy boots were making marks all over her clean linoleum, and she nearly told him so, but controlled herself: once, years ago, she had been an ordinary pleasant girl with a quick temper and a pink complexion, and the ghost of that girl, puzzled and bitterly unhappy, sometimes looked out from her face. She looked out now, and with a real effort Mrs Steggles did not mention the linoleum.

'Hullo, Mum!' said Reg, grinning and kissing her. 'Hullo, Margaret, what've you done to your hair; you look a proper school-marm. I say, something smells good! I'm starving. Is Dad home yet? Can I have a bath?'

He winked at his sister, who gave an unwilling smile in response, while unloading himself of his heavy Service respirator and tin hat. 'Can I have that bath now, Mum? I've got a date this evening!'

'Dad'll want to see you,' was Mrs Steggles's only protest as she moved his kit to the side of the hall.

'I shall see him when I come in; I'm not going to be late. A crowd of us are going to the Luna. Like to come, Margie?'

'No, thanks.'

'You surprise me! An old pal of yours is going to be there.'

'Who's that?' Mrs Steggles glanced curiously at her son, and then at her daughter's face.

'Frank Kennett. He's got a spot of leave, too.'

'How do you know?' demanded his mother, going to Margaret's rescue even while she despised her for her stricken look.

'The blonde at the Luna told me. I 'phoned up to see what

25

was doing there this evening, and she said there's a dance and Frank and most of the crowd would be along.'

'How thrilling!' said Margaret sarcastically, and went back into the dining-room to finish laying the table. Her brother stamped upstairs in his heavy boots, whistling, followed by Mrs Steggles.

The news that Frank Kennett was in the town had set Margaret trembling, and as she arranged the knives and forks her one hope was that she would not accidentally encounter him during the next few days. She had a morbid horror of meeting him. They had never seen one another since that painful scene by the Canal, when she had been so anguished and he so embarrassed and so eager to make her take the situation lightly. She had long ceased to weave romance about him (and with Margaret this meant that she no longer loved him) but she still could not endure to meet him face to face.

She imagined the Luna Café and Dance Hall as it would be about nine o'clock that evening; full of smoke, and smelling of fried food, and noisy with the wireless music and voices and loud laughter. Before the Second World War it had been a meeting-place for Lukeborough's rowdier boys and girls with money to spend, and since the war it had become even rowdier, for there were American soldiers, lonely and craving for pleasure, quartered in the neighbourhood and they had soon found the Luna. The place was licensed and was attached to the Luna Cinema, one of a big circuit. Its walls, which were shaded in colour from sickly orange to an arsenical green, were now faded and peeling, and its gilt basketwork chairs were battered and tarnished; all its appointments were depressing as only modernist furnishings which have deteriorated can be; yet at night, when its curtains shut out the black silent streets and the damp silent countryside, and if you were young, the Luna was better than the Naafi or your own home. But Margaret wondered how a boy with Frank's tastes, as she remembered them, could want to go to the place. To calm herself, she began to think about the school in London where she would shortly be teaching.

She had not a vocation for teaching, but she was clever and could impart her knowledge to others, and at Sunnybrae she had done so well that, at the end of the year when the head-mistress of the school had heard of a vacancy at a private school in London, she had recommended Margaret for the post. She herself had formerly been on the staff of a famous London girls' school, and her recommendation carried weight. At twenty-three years old, Margaret would have a post on the staff of an old-established and prosperous London school. Had she been ambitious, the future would have seemed full of promise.

She heard her father's key in the front door and went out into the hall.

'Hullo, Margaret!' he said, pleased and surprised, shutting the door after him and turning to give her a kiss. 'I didn't think you'd be home yet. Well, so you've found a house for us. Are we going to like it?'

When he was cheerful, which was not often, Jack Steggles had a teasing, laughing note in his voice, but usually he was moody and quiet. It was not a neat, depressed quietness; it matched his wife's air of suppressed ill-temper and seemed as if it might explode into acute irritation at any moment. He wore his clothes with a carelessness that clung to him from his reporting days, and he seemed to belong to a background of bars and newsrooms rather than to the neat conventional little house in which he lived. He was a handsome sturdy man looking much younger than his years, a very heavy smoker and fond of drink.

'I hope so, Dad. Mr Wilson, Hilda's father, think's it's a bit of luck our getting it,' answered Margaret.

'How far is it from Fleet Street? That's all I want to know. Is Reg here yet?'

'Yes, he's upstairs having a bath. It's about three-quarters of an hour, I should think.'

'All right; I'll go and get my slippers and then you can tell me about it.'

He went upstairs to his bedroom; Mrs Steggles did not encourage people to keep their slippers in the living-rooms.

Her mother's confidence in Margaret had been destroyed by the girl's failure to land a husband at twenty; she had thought her daughter a queer, sulky little thing when she was a child, and had increasingly resented her reserve and artistic tastes. Now, she had an impatient affection for her and was resigned to seeing her settle down into an old maid; but Mr Steggles was clever, in the quick natural way that never earns much money or wins fame, and he not only knew that Margaret 'had a good head on her shoulders' but trusted her. It was he who had suggested that she should go to London, combining a visit to the Wilsons with business, and find (if such a thing were possible – the Steggleses all doubted it) a house for them to rent.

Mrs Wilson had written that of course they would be ever so pleased to have Margaret for a week, but as for the house – well, London was as full as it could be, *and Herbert* (that was Mr Wilson) *is afraid you will be unlucky* (Mr Wilson, a minor Civil Servant employed at Mount Pleasant, was always afraid people would be unlucky, and Hilda and Mrs Wilson had a job for life persuading him that the sun did sometimes shine.) So Margaret had gone to London, and there, after four days' hopeless search, she had been told by Mrs Wilson of the house in Stanley Gardens which an old lady, who had fled into the country to escape bombs, was willing to let.

At the same time that Margaret's headmistress had recommended her for the post in London, her father had heard from a friend, a former reporter on the *North Bedfordshire Record* who had gone to the capital some years ago on the invitation of a newspaper baron who liked to encourage talent from the provinces. The reporter had prospered, and now wrote that there was a forthcoming vacancy at the sub-editorial table of his own London daily, and much talk of getting a man from the provinces to fill it. He saw no reason why Jack Steggles, whom he held in gratitude and affection, should not get the job.

Mr Steggles did not care much whether he got it or not, for he was without ambition and he knew what he enjoyed and how to get it, and he hoped for nothing more than these pleasures until the day he died. But the pleasures he enjoyed would be equally easy to get in London, and his wife had said that she 'would not mind' going to the capital and that it was time that they found a more suitable house: this one was too far from the shops and there was a draught under the front door fit to cut you in half. This meant that she wanted to move. So he allowed his reporter friend to make representations on his behalf, and they were both surprised when he got the job. The many and complicated business arrangements were set in hand as soon as the house was found, and in three weeks the Steggleses would move to London.

The first part of the evening passed less dully than was usual, for Margaret must give her parents every detail she could remember about the house, and before he went off to the Luna Reg had supper with them, and for nearly an hour there was something resembling ordinary family life about the dining-room table, with Reg saying how good his mother's cooking tasted after the Army, and making them laugh with his stories of the camp some twenty miles away where he was stationed. But after he had gone, and Margaret had told all that she knew about Number 23 Stanley Gardens, and Mrs Steggles had settled down with some fancy-work and Mr Steggles with the early edition of the London *Star* which he had brought from the office, the telephone bell rang.

Mrs Steggles continued to draw her silk evenly through her work and Margaret did not look up from her book: Mr Steggles went out into the hall and shut the door after him. A deeper flush slowly came into his wife's face as the moments passed and he did not return, and Margaret felt miserably apprehensive. Presently her father half-opened the door, saying heartily, 'I've got to go out, Mabel, don't wait up for me, I may be late.' Her mother looked up quickly, her lips pressed tightly together, but he had gone. They heard the front door slam.

The mother sewed and the daughter read in silence. A great dreariness filled Margaret's heart. The neat, pretty room, the silence, the upright figure of her mother sitting embroidering, seemed unreal, and she felt she was a prisoner, and must sit there for ever. She was so sorry for her mother! and she could not comfort her because they must pretend that nothing was wrong. Yet she could understand how her father must get away from his home; out and away into something more real, at which she could only guess. Oh, surely, she thought wretchedly, there are homes where the evenings aren't so miserable as they are here!

3

The move to London was as complicated and exhausting as most moves in war-time. On their first night there, as the furniture had not arrived, the Steggleses had to ask hospitality of the Wilsons and Mr Steggles's reporter friend, who both proved friends indeed; Margaret and her mother going to the Wilsons and Mr Steggles to the reporter's bachelor flat in Moorgate.

It was a time of strain for Margaret because of her mother's awkwardness as a visitor; Mrs Steggles was unsociable and suspicious, and disliked paying visits unless it was to relations, and although Mrs Wilson and Hilda were born hostesses, able to make the shyest people feel at home, they were not successful with her; she determinedly made conversation and was anxious every ten minutes about giving so much trouble. After she had gone, Mr Wilson said that he felt as if she had been with them for three years. Mrs Wilson and Hilda rebuked him (for he was not encouraged to express opinions likely to lessen their social activities) but when alone they agreed that for once Dad was right; Mrs Steggles was not easy to get on with. The two families had only met briefly before this, and had known next to nothing of each other's lives. Now Mrs Wilson and Hilda understood a number of things which had puzzled them about Margaret.

So Margaret was greatly relieved, on the evening of their second day in London, to stand for a moment at the window of her own room at the back of the new house and gaze up at the hill, where lights were shining just before blackout time, and to know that all the bedrooms were ready to be slept in, and their new life fairly begun.

How lustrous, how golden and clear, shone out the evening lights! She rested her hands upon the windowsill and gazed pensively out into the dusk, and thought that before the war they had never looked so beautiful. We had got into the habit of taking them for granted, she thought, and yet a light shining at night is one of the oldest and most beautiful things in human life, and poetry and folk-lore are full of them; the light in the forest that guides the lost traveller to the witch's hut, and the lamp shining between the trees in *The Merchant of Venice, like a good deed in a naughty world,* and the Lights of London in all the old novels –.

'Margaret! Have you seen the spoons your Aunt Chrissie gave us anywhere? I believe those wretched men have lost them. What on earth are you doing up there?' Her mother's voice, shrill and irritable, came up the stairs.

'I'm just doing the blackout, Mother; I'll be down in a minute,' she called, and pulled the curtains across her window.

If I couldn't get five minutes to myself sometimes to think of things like that, I'd get as bad as Mother and Reg, and almost everybody else I know, she thought, running downstairs. The only person I've *ever* known who sometimes thought about things in that way was Frank; even Hilda – who's a darling – never does. I suppose I'm just different, that's all.

'I seem to remember putting those spoons in a corner of the knife-box,' she said, going into the kitchen and glancing critically about her.

'You *seem* to remember! That's helpful, I must say. Mrs Wilson telephoned while you were round at the shops to see how we were getting on, and said she might look in with Hilda this evening. Why people want to come round and see you on the first night after a move is more than I can make out.'

'She meant it kindly, Mother.'

'I expect your father got something solid for his lunch in town,' went on Mrs Steggles. 'What are you having?'

'Oh – bread and cheese – anything,' said Margaret indifferently, going into the dining-room, where the pictures were still leaning against the walls, to lay the cloth. She was not interested in food, and regarded people as rather low if they were; she herself ate quickly and without comment anything that happened to be provided.

After supper, to which Mr Steggles did not return, the front-door bell rang and Margaret answered it, as her mother was annoyed and slightly worried by her father's absence, and did not want to leave the sorting and tidying with which she was working off her feelings.

Two romantic figures stood there in the starlight, with smiling faces and lace scarves over their heads. Mrs Wilson was as slim as Hilda, and almost as pretty. She had a good deal of innocent coquetry, and carried on running verbal flirtations, some of which had been in progress for years, with the better-looking among the tradesmen where she shopped.

'Hullo, Margaret! Why, haven't you got it looking nice! Are you nearly straight?' she exclaimed, stepping into the hall and gazing round.

'Looks a bit different from that first evening, doesn't it?' said Hilda, unwinding her scarf.

'Mother, here's Mrs Wilson and Hilda,' said Margaret, opening the drawing-room door. 'We aren't quite straight in here yet,' she added.

Mrs Steggles was on her knees in front of a large box by the electric fire, and gave her visitors a brief smile as she got up.

'Good evening. We're still at it, you see,' she said.

'Well, it's a shame to come in, really, and I expect you're calling us all sorts of names!' cried Mrs Wilson, tossing the scarf away from her clear pink face, 'but we really came to see if we could do anything for you – you know, tell you anything about the neighbourhood, and that.'

'Do you want a reliable doctor and a good dentist?' interrupted Hilda, waving a piece of paper. 'Dad wrote you down the names and addresses of two – oh, and the chemist's telephone number in case you wanted some Sloan's or Aspro. Isn't he a scream, though!'

'Well, he thought it might be useful,' explained her mother, laughing too. 'You know what he is – prevention is better than cure is his motto.'

'I'm sure it was very kind of Mr Wilson,' said Mrs Steggles reprovingly, taking the paper from Hilda.

'Margaret, will you write down these addresses in the book straightaway, before we forget it. Please sit down, Mrs Wilson, and Hilda; make yourselves comfortable. I'm afraid we're still in a bit of a muddle in here.' She moved books and boxes to make room, thinking the while what a mad thing it was to come out in the cold with those bits of lace round their heads.

'Are you admiring our headdresses?' asked Mrs Wilson cheerfully, catching her look. She was a kind and happy woman, but neither she nor Hilda let themselves be disapproved of without showing fight. 'I expect you think I'm getting on a bit for this sort of thing!' (As this was exactly what Mrs Steggles was thinking, she looked conscious.) 'Hilda looked so nice in hers, I thought I'd try how I looked too!' and she gave a gay little nod, smiling steadily at Mrs Steggles.

'I think they're lovely,' said Margaret, too emphatically.

'Rather cold, I should think,' said Mrs Steggles, in whom old dreams and pains had been revived by the sight of the scarves. 'But they are pretty,' she added, and Mrs Wilson's smile grew less steady. Poor thing, she thought.

'How about a cup of tea, Hilda?' said Margaret. 'Mother? You'll have one, won't you? Mrs Wilson? I'll go and put the kettle on.'

'I'll come and help you,' and Hilda followed her out of the

room, leaving their mothers to carry on a conversation about the neighbourhood's amenities and disadvantages, which, considering their differing natures, was not too awkward; but Mrs Steggles's manner was constrained, and as she talked she listened for the sound of her husband's key in the lock.

The first cups of tea had just been poured out when she heard it, and set her own down with an exclamation to Margaret – 'There's your father at last! I wonder whatever's kept him' – turning to Mrs Wilson, 'I've been expecting him this last two hours.'

Poor man, thought Mrs Wilson, but she said comfortably, 'Oh, I expect he's found the journey back took much longer than he expected; I always think you do, in a strange place,' and turned her bright eyes towards the door. Her flirtatiousness did not extend to the husbands of her acquaintances, but she enjoyed masculine society, to which her daughter's admirers had accustomed her, and saw no reason to subdue her smile because Mrs Steggles was a jealous wife.

Mr Steggles came into the room with the litter of half-unpacked boxes and tea-drinking, and smiled with pleasure at the sight of two pretty faces. Mrs Wilson was too good a woman to make her a dangerous one to him, but he liked to look at her and make her laugh, and he suspected Hilda of being the type known in his youth as a little devil. Hilda was not; but the illusion gave zest to his exchanges with her.

'Hullo, what's all this, a party?' he said, looking round and blinking his handsome eyes because they were still dazed from the blackout. 'I'm very late, I'm afraid, Mabel,' putting his hand for an instant on his wife's shoulder, and feeling her shrink, without any change of expression: 'I went in for a quick one with some of the boys afterwards, and we got talking.'

'How did you get on, Father? Tea?' asked Margaret.

'Please.' He moved some books from a chair next to Mrs

Wilson, and sat down. 'Well, I feel a bit as if I'd been running the quarter-mile all day, but I shall get used to it, I expect. The work is so much –'

'Did you find somewhere nice for lunch?' interrupted Mrs Steggles.

'I went to a pub; quite good. A bit expensive, but I was –'

'Well, I hope you had a good one, because there isn't much for your supper,' and Mrs Steggles glanced at Mrs Wilson with a little laugh. 'What did you have?'

'Steak and kidney (otherwise sausage and spam) pudding and –'

'Isn't it disgraceful the way they take people in?' demanded Mrs Steggles, peering into Hilda's cup. ('More tea, Hilda? Really? Sure?') If everybody refused to pay the fancy prices they ask for the rubbish they give you, they'd soon change their tune. I expect Mr Wilson finds it the same, doesn't he?'

'Oh, Herbert has been to the same comic little old place for about twenty years now. They know him there and don't try any tricks on him,' said Mrs Wilson.

'They must have seen Mr Steggles coming,' and Mrs Steggles laughed again. Her husband laughed too, and held out his cup for more tea. *If I was Margaret's dad I should sock her mother one,* reflected Hilda, sipping her tea and looking like a pensive aquiline angel.

'Is it a very big building, Dad?' asked Margaret.

'The *Gazette* offices were blitzed; I saw it in that list they gave of the newspapers that were bombed out,' said Mrs Steggles. 'More tea, Mrs Wilson?'

'No, thank you. Have they got temporary offices, then?' said Mrs Wilson, smiling and shaking her head.

'Yes, in Thames Street. They aren't very big by London standards, I should think, but they're much bigger –'

'Than he's been used to,' said Mrs Steggles. 'Well, they say

London always rubs the corners off people from the provinces, so we shall see what it does to Mr Steggles,' laughing.

Mr Steggles put his hand into his coat pocket for an instant. When it came out again it was holding an old pipe, and he glanced smilingly round at the ladies for permission to light it, which he received. But during that instant he had deliberately crushed in his hand a thick letter in a violet envelope scented with violets and signed, 'Always – always your Bettie.' The brief contact comforted him with the memory of a real woman as he sat among these four, who did not seem to him to be real women at all.

'Oh, when Mr Steggles lights up that old pipe I know he's really settled down, like a cat licking the butter off its paws!' exclaimed his wife.

'Yes, I don't expect anyone does that to the cat when they move nowadays. When do you start at your new school, Margaret?'

'Next Monday, Mrs Wilson. Mother,' said Margaret abruptly, 'I'm going to show Hilda my room – coming, Hilda?' and with murmurs the two escaped.

'Doesn't it look nice!' exclaimed Hilda, looking round Margaret's domain.

Margaret laughed. 'Bless you, you know you don't like it a bit,' she said, and Hilda laughed too.

'Well, it is rather sort-of-monk-like, if you know what I mean.'

'The most highly bred Japanese, with the purest taste, never wear any colours, only shades of grey.'

'Japanese!'

'Why not?'

'Margaret, they're *awful*!'

Margaret shrugged her shoulders. 'No worse than any other nation.'

'You ought to go about with some Service boys,' was all Hilda could say, examining her curls in the mirror.

Margaret sat down on the bed, which had a coverlet of pale brown patterned with large brown leaves, and gazed about her with satisfaction. The only pictures were a pastel of some grazing deer in the same soft tint, and a large monochrome of the Mona Lisa, and the grey curtains were stencilled by herself with a conventional design in darker grey.

'Then I s'pose you think *my* bedroom is lousy?' said Hilda, turning away satisfied from the mirror.

'All pink, and calendars, and photographs of boys. No I don't; it's just like you.'

'Thanks. You know,' stopping in front of the Mona Lisa and gazing up at her, 'honestly, I don't know how you can bear to have that fat pan looking at you when you wake up in the morning. It would brown me off for the day.'

'It's beautiful,' said Margaret, but even as she spoke a faint doubt assailed her. Was it?

'It's a fat, awful pan,' repeated Hilda vigorously. 'Now, I'll tell you a picture I saw once (by an Old Master too, so you see I'm not so low-brow) that I simply adored; it was the Virgin Mary in a blue cloak on a cloud, holding the Baby, and some old saint, and a sort of angel in one corner, and a cupid –'

'A cherub.'

'Cherub then – it's all the same thing – leaning on his elbow at the foot of the picture looking up at them. It was *lovely* – she had such a beautiful face, and her hand coming right round the Baby, holding Him tight – it was so lifelike. Now that's my idea of a *picture*. It was on a Christmas card Iris Morrison sent me. You wouldn't think she'd have such good taste, would you, though?'

'It sounds like the Sistine Madonna.'

'I don't know what it was, but it was lovely. Do you really

like all these Japanesy colours?' she demanded suddenly, staring at her friend. 'This room isn't a bit *like* you, you know.'

'Of course, or I shouldn't have them,' answered Margaret decidedly, but suddenly she thought of the flowers she loved best; rich old-fashioned pansies, wall-flowers like sombre velvet, crimson roses, and Sweet Williams of so dark a red that they were almost black; she seemed to breathe their summer scent in the chill of autumn, and the colours in her room seemed cold and pale.

'Well, sooner you than me. Got any new clothes to show me?'

Margaret shook her head.

'Eaten all your sweet ration?'

Margaret nodded.

'Then I think I'll be going. Walk down the road with me?'

'Yes, I've got some letters to post.'

She put on a coat which she had not worn since she had house-hunted in London, and as they went downstairs she slipped her hands, as was her habit, into the pockets.

'Oh!' she exclaimed.

'What's up?'

'How awful! That ration book – I never sent it back!'

'What ration book?'

'The one I found on the Heath when I was staying with you.'

'But that's nearly a month ago!'

'I know, that's what makes it so awful.'

'Wasn't the address on it?' asked Hilda. They had paused in the hall outside the drawing-room door and both had lowered their voices.

'Of course.' Margaret handed her the book. 'I meant to send it back at once, only I didn't wear this coat again and there were so many things to see to that I forgot.'

'Hebe Niland,' Hilda read aloud. 'What an extraordinary name. Is it a girl or a man?'

'A girl. Hebe was the cupbearer of the Gods in Ancient Greece.'

'Sounds like a refugee,' mused Hilda. 'N. W. 3 – that's Hampstead. Probably is a refugee, then; Hampstead's alive with them. What'll you do about it?'

'I don't know. I can't just send it back with a note after all this time; it looks so rude. I expect it's given them a lot of trouble, too.'

'Given me a lot, you mean,' said Hilda, who worked in a Food Office. 'Why don't you 'phone her up?'

'If she's a refugee (but I don't believe she is, somehow) she won't be in the book.' Margaret stopped and her eyes grew wider. 'There's a famous artist called Niland,' she said. 'I suppose she couldn't be anything to do with him?'

'Might be. It isn't a common name. Why don't you walk over to Hampstead and see?'

'Oh, I'd love to!' Then she hesitated, and went on: 'Only it might seem – it's rather a queer thing to do – going to see someone you don't know.'

'Whereabouts did you find it?'

'On the path down by the lower ponds – it was a man who dropped it, I'm almost sure. I noticed two men walking past, and then I saw it on the path.'

'Perhaps it was him – the artist.'

'It might have been. Alexander Niland,' she repeated to herself, 'the Modern Renoir, the papers call him. I don't know, I've never seen a photograph of him.'

'Well, if it is his wife it will make it more of a thrill for you,' said Hilda, slightly bored. 'I'd certainly walk over; you might get another peek at him.'

'Perhaps I will.' Margaret put the book carefully away in her bag. 'Don't say anything about it —' she jerked her head towards the drawing-room door.

'I get you,' murmured Hilda, and opened the door and inquired dulcetly:

'Mum? Are you staying the night? Pardon me, Mrs Steggles, if I collect my parent.'

'I'm just going out to post these, Mother,' said Margaret, holding up the letters. The three elders were sitting in silence with flushed faces, and Mrs Wilson looked slightly embarrassed and relieved when Hilda entered.

'Yes, we *must* be going,' she said, getting up quickly. 'Well, good night, and thank you for that welcome cup of tea, and mind you give us a ring if we can be of any help in any way.'

'That's very kind of you, thank you, we won't forget,' said Mr Steggles heartily, following her out of the room. Mrs Steggles said clearly, 'Good night, and thank *you*. You and Mr Wilson must come round to tea properly one Sunday after we're straight,' and knelt down once more in front of the box. Mr Steggles shut the door on the visitors and came back into the drawing-room. He stood by the mantelpiece looking down at the pipe he was refilling in silence for a few moments.

'Well?' said his wife, without looking up.

'Well?'

'Aren't you going to tell me how you think it looks?'

'Yes, of course. I think it looks fine, old girl,' glancing round the room. 'Of course, it's all a bit strange at first, but you've got it quite home-like already. I like the old ship over the mantel-piece; it shows her up.' (The old ship was a reproduction of a painting of a vessel with very white sails on a very blue sea, which had been painted to please the thousands of people who think that a sailing-ship on a blue sea is one of the most beautiful sights to be seen in this world — as, Heaven knows, it is.)

'Well, there's a lot to be done still,' sighed Mrs Steggles, carefully lifting some book-ends in the shape of Highland terriers from the box and putting them down beside a statuette of a girl tennis-player, 'and it's been the worst move we've had yet for losses and breakages. There's the glass clean gone out of our wedding group, and that green vase with the red spots on smashed to atoms, and I can't find Aunt Chrissie's teaspoons anywhere and the green and yellow tea-cosy is missing too.'

'Perhaps some of them will turn up to-morrow. Do you think you're going to like it here, old girl; that's the main thing?'

'I can't possibly tell yet, Jack. We haven't been here twenty-four hours. The house *seems* all right. I wish we hadn't got that great hill at the back, it makes me feel overlooked, but I expect I shall get used to that. It seems a nice quiet road.'

He nodded. He had sat down in an arm-chair and was watching his wife as she slowly and carefully unwrapped each treasure, and thinking that now they were alone she was natural again; no longer talking him down and interrupting him and making the spiteful little jokes at his expense that had caused Mrs Wilson, at last, to look embarrassed, and an uneasy silence to fall. Now the devil of jealousy had gone, and his wife was Mabel again; complaining, not very happy, but giving the brighter side its due and enjoying in her own way the anxieties and adventures of the move. At this moment, she hasn't a thought in her head except what's happened to the tea-cosy, he thought, and made the best of that brief peaceful moment.

At least he can't go out anywhere this evening, Mrs Steggles was thinking as she worked. Thank God, that Bettie creature and that other wicked devil are left behind in Lukeborough.

'Well,' she said at last, leaning back with a sigh and rubbing her hands on her overall, 'I shan't do any more to-night. I'm tired. I shall go up. What about you?'

'Oh – I've got some letters to write,' he said, taking the evening paper from his pocket and unfolding it without looking at her, 'and I want to finish this; I didn't get a seat in the train. I shan't be long.'

She went slowly out of the room without answering, and in a moment he was reading through the news-stories he had sub-edited that day, and had forgotten her. It did not seem strange to him that she had not asked him more about his first day's work on a London daily, because he was used to the mixture of genuine indifference and conventional respect for 'your dad's job' which she felt towards his work; and besides, he did not want any woman, let alone his wife, bothering him about his work. That was not what he wanted from women.

'*Whatever* was the matter with you all? Sitting in a row exactly like Madame Tussaud's,' burst out Hilda the instant Margaret was out of ear-shot. 'Had he been getting fresh with you or something?'

'That's not a nice way to talk, Hilda,' said Mrs Wilson firmly, but spoiling the reproof with a giggle. 'Of course not, but she's so dreadfully jealous, poor thing, she can't bear him even to be polite.'

'*Poor thing!* I like that.'

'Oh, but she is, Hilda. Jealousy's a real disease, you know; it's wrecked many a marriage. You and Dad and I are so happy; we never think of homes where there isn't any happiness.'

'What would you do, Mum, if Dad was to get jealous of you?'

'Laugh,' said Mrs Wilson briefly.

Mother and daughter, arm-in-arm in the starlight, laughed delightedly at the mere thought.

'No, but it's ever so sad,' said Mrs Wilson, sobering. 'It makes me feel quite bad to see them; I don't think I shall go there much.'

'It gets me down too. Never mind, we'll have Margaret round to our place and find her a specially nice boy. Oh, there's Dad.'

As they approached the house a dim figure could be discerned in the porch, making shooing movements towards a smaller and motionless form.

'He's putting Geoffrey out,' said Hilda. (Geoffrey was the cat, named after the rear-gunner who had given her to Hilda as a kitten three years ago.)

'Hullo, Dad! Gorgeous night!'

Mr Wilson, abandoning the attempt to get Geoffrey to move on, glanced up at the brilliant stars and observed that he thought it would freeze before morning.

Margaret walked quickly homewards, absently noticing the beauty of the night while her excited thoughts played about the idea of going over to Hampstead on the following afternoon, and trying to recall everything she had ever heard or read about Alexander Niland. She had seen a reproduction in colour of his best-known picture: a soldier and a woman lying embraced in long grass full of clover, under a dark tree whose branches hung down against the evening sky. The popular press had called its greys and greens and purples daring, while praising it. She herself had thought it beautiful, but it had shocked her. She had felt while looking at it as if she were spying on the kisses of those closely embraced figures, and it had made her remember every pair of twilit lovers she had ever seen.

This feeling was not peculiar to Margaret. The common denominator was felt in all Niland's paintings, and it was this, apart from their beauty and his genius, which gave them their popularity. For they were popular. Thousands of reproductions of them had found their way into homes all over England and America, and the strange, simple juxtaposition of their colours, unexpected yet immediately felt to be inevitable, had helped thousands of ordinary people to look at ordinary yet beautiful objects with refreshed eyes.

Somerset Maugham has written of 'the animal serenity of

great writers.' Niland possessed the visual serenity of the greatest painters. His work was untormented, and charged with his pleasure in the world he saw about him, and while there was no deliberate rejection of pain and ugliness in it, both were transmuted as they passed from his vision to his canvas. His paintings were not old-fashioned in the slighting sense of the words, but they resembled those of the painters of three or four hundred years ago, in that they were created in an age full of horrors and violence, yet breathed a calm loveliness which was timeless. In those medieval paintings the best of earth and the vision of the celestial were blended; on Niland's canvases, his feeling for life penetrated the countenances and limbs of his happy mothers, his sleeping children and laughing girls, and made them glow. To an indifferent public, long confronted by a surfeit of guitars and swollen legs depicted either singly or in determined conjunction, the result was as refreshing as it was surprising.

He had no political views, and therefore in certain circles his name was mud.

The possibility of going to his house and perhaps catching a glimpse of him greatly excited Margaret, and she thought far more about that than about her first day at the new school on Monday. She planned what she would wear, and what she would say if he himself should open the front door (for Lamb Cottage did not sound like the name of a large house with many servants) and even prepared a little speech that was humble or casual or provocative as her mood varied. The Anna Bonner School for Girls seemed a dull place when she at last spared it an impatient thought, and as she opened the front door of her new home, it seemed an ordinary dull little house that needed painting, standing in an ordinary dull little road.

4

The next day there was of course a great deal to do and Margaret was busy all the morning, but she announced firmly that she was going for a walk in the afternoon, and although her mother grumbled she afterwards admitted that it was a nice day and a walk might do Margaret good; she wouldn't get much time for walks once school started.

Margaret observed with mixed feelings signs that her mother was about to start upon one of her famous lightning friendships. This time it was with their neighbour on the left, who had come in with a delicate tray of tea and thin bread and butter an hour or so after the Steggles's arrival. Mrs Steggles could not say enough of such kindness, so thoughtful, so neighbourly! Mrs Piper must come in and have tea with them the moment they were settled; she seemed such a nice woman, quite their sort, not a bit like a London woman, and had Margaret noticed how nicely her home was kept? Quite the neatest garden in the road, and the only other house with frilled curtains. It was quite a coincidence, being next door to each other and both having frilled curtains.

Mrs Steggles's jealous and irritable temperament made her unconsciously desire the friendship and affection which it kept at bay, and occasionally her loneliness drove her to make violent friendships with women she hardly knew, whose acquaintance she had made in a teashop or a queue. At first all would go well, and no praise could be too high for the new friend, but soon her nature would assert itself, and she would begin to find fault and give unwanted advice, and the friendship would rapidly cool until it was extinct. Each failure added to her bitterness, for it never occurred to her that it might be her fault, and she accused everybody of being jealous and spiteful and two-faced. Mrs Piper of the tea-tray seemed a pleasant enough person, and Margaret hoped that living next door as she did she might prove to be more lasting than her mother's other flashes-in-the-pan, and provide her with companionship and an interest outside her own home. But the omens were much as usual, and not good.

However, she had forgotten all about it when she set out at two o'clock that afternoon to walk across to Hampstead. She had been perplexed about what time to start, for at all costs she must avoid arriving at Lamb Cottage anywhere near tea-time, in case they should think she was trying to get herself invited to the meal, and she finally decided to present herself at exactly three o'clock.

The villages of Highgate and Hampstead confront one another across a mile or so of small valleys and hills and copses, the whole expanse of some six hundred acres of open land raised upon two broad and swelling hills which look over the immense grey expanse of old London on their southern side and the ever-growing red and white expanse of new London upon their northern. Each village upon its hill is marked by a church spire, and both are landmarks for miles. Both villages are romantic and charming, with narrow hilly streets and little two-hundred-year-old houses, and here and there a great mansion of William and Mary's or James the First's reign, such as Fenton House in Hampstead and Cromwell House in Highgate; but their chief charm dwells in their cold air, which seems perpetually scented with April, and in the glimpses at the end of their steep alleys of some massive elm or oak, with beyond its branches that abrupt drop into the complex smoky pattern (formed by a thousand shades of grey in winter and of delicate cream and smoke-blue in summer) of London.

The afternoon was fine and windless, and many people were working on the allotments which since the Second World War had spread over the southern slope of Parliament Hill and the sunny valley lying between there and Kenwood. The latter was all that was left of the mighty forest that had once extended over the whole countryside; there were magnificent beech trees there, and a mansion which Margaret had seen between the trees, with an unusually large bomb-crater in the green sloping lawn immediately in front of the house. Now the mild sun beamed on the water in the crater and there were prints of children's shoes in the soft mud round its sides. Those moonlit nights when the air had rung and quivered for hour after hour with the roar of guns and the horrifying whine of falling bombs, and the hot reek of explosives had stifled the sweet damp scents of autumn, seemed like a nightmare and were half-forgotten. Only in the hearts of the quiet cheerful people working on the allotments the memory was still alive, and when two or three of them got together for a cup of tea or a drink, the talk would sooner or later turn on The Blitz, and there were many of the women, with young children, who would never be the same again.

Margaret walked quickly, wondering if her clothes were suitable, and then scornfully telling herself that even if she did see Alexander Niland he wouldn't notice what she was wearing, and then remembering that he was a painter and would naturally notice everything. She had tied her hair with the velvet bow and put on a dark-brown suit with a yellow and crimson handkerchief knotted under her chin, and her shoes and stockings were heavy and good, as were the shoes and stockings of most girls in England in those days. Her heart beat faster than usual and she was almost trembling; so much of her craving for a more beautiful and satisfying life took the form of wanting to meet interesting people that the possibility of meeting one,

48

however briefly, excited her painfully. During her morning's shopping she had found time to look up his name in a telephone directory and had found that he did live at Lamb Cottage! So this Hebe must be his wife, or perhaps his sister? No, she seemed to remember that he had painted several portraits of his wife. Hebe Niland. It was a strange name and Margaret thought it a beautiful one. Someone with that name started with an advantage lacked by someone named Margaret Steggles. I wonder what her name was before she was married? – thought Margaret. One thing, if ever I do marry I shall get rid of my name – though of course I might get landed with something even worse! But I shan't marry, so why worry?

Her feeling for nature was the common one of sensitive temperaments which have suffered a blow; she found spring flowers and autumnal woods too beautiful to be borne, and a splendid sunset reminded her of Frank Kennett and made her want to cry. Now, as she ascended the last slopes leading to the Spaniard's Walk, she was reminded, by the sight of a little wood of pine trees with a grey stone fountain at its edge, of a walk she had once taken with Frank. The dark-green branches kept up a soft solemn sighing against the cold blue sky, for the wind was rising. Unmistakable sound, never to be confused with that made by any leaf-shedding tree, as lonely and mysterious when issuing from this ragged and shabby little copse as when it sighs in the thin clear air above an Alpine precipice! That was the time he said I had a nice voice, thought Margaret, sighing in her turn. In a few moments she was walking down Hampstead High Street.

Hampstead was less picturesque than it looked from a distance. Like the rest of London, it needed painting; it had been bombed; its streets were disfigured by brick shelters and its walls by posters instructing the population how to deal with butterfly or incendiary bombs; most of its small shops which had sold antiques or home-made sweets or smart hats before the war were empty; and its narrow streets were crowded with foreigners, for the village and its lower districts of Belsize Park, St John's Wood and Swiss Cottage had been taken over by the refugees, and their population almost doubled. But there was a heartening note among all the sad sallow faces and unfamiliar accents; there were many young mothers with ringing voices, each pushing a pram with one fat baby in it like an acorn in its cup; hailing each other cheerfully across the turbaned heads of the aliens and asking each other what luck they had had with the biscuits or the fish.

Margaret asked several people where Lamb Cottage in Romney Square was, and at last an old gentlewoman with a stick, who was wading through the refugees with the air of one traversing a malarial marsh, crisply informed her that it was the first turning on the left, up – and she pointed with the stick. Margaret thanked her carefully, and turned up the hill on the left. The clock on the tower opposite the tube station said three o'clock.

Romney Square was not a square; it was a number of old houses and their gardens, grouped irregularly about a triangle of grass, and standing of course on the slope of a hill. Beyond one of the houses, a charming one made of white weather-boarding which prolonged itself into long galleries and little towers, Margaret saw an avenue of ancient lime trees leading on into the blue distance. She looked about her, and at once saw Lamb Cottage: it was directly opposite to where she stood. It was a cottage; it was unimposing, and built of small bricks that were darkened by age, but it had a wonderful scarlet front door, and behind it, rising to three times its height, was a lofty building with three long uncurtained windows which admitted the full light of the autumn day. Margaret's heart beat faster. It was a studio.

She decided to knock at once, because it would look odd if anyone shold see her loitering and staring at the house; so, clasping the ration book firmly in one hand, she crossed the road and approached the brilliant door (it had surely been freshly painted) and rang the bell.

Her sensations as she stood waiting there were as confused as they were strong; she was nervous, hopeful, defiant, and expecting wonders to befall even while assuring herself that in another moment she would see the door opened by a maid, make her explanation, hand in the ration book, be thanked and told that Mrs Niland should be given the message, and then turn away, and the whole incident would be over.

But even as she waited a child began to cry loudly in the house, and then she heard footsteps hurrying down a passage, and the next instant the door was opened violently and a voice exclaimed 'Grantey! Thank goodness you've come! Wherever –' and a young woman stood there, staring at her, with a child in her arms and another standing crying at her feet.

'Oh –' she said blankly, looking very cross. 'I thought you were someone else. What is it, please? (Barnabas, *darling*,' to the crying child, touching him sharply with her knee, 'do you think you could stop making that ghastly and hideous noise for just one *instant, please?*)'

'I'm sorry,' stammered Margaret, holding out the ration book and bewildered by the suddenness of the young woman's appearance, and the noisy crying of the little boy, 'I think this must be yours. I found it nearly a month ago on the Heath and I'm so sorry, I forgot to send it back to you. I'm very sorry. I –'

'Oh, my ration book,' and suddenly she smiled and the cross expression vanished as she gave Margaret a full look from her beautifully shaped light-grey eyes. 'I'm always losing it – though actually this time it was my husband. Where did you find it?'

Margaret explained, and the girl listened, moving the child

51

in her arms on to her hip as she did so, and still keeping Margaret fixed with that soft, amused, attentive stare. What with that, and a similar stare from the eyes of the baby which were identical in shape and colour with those of its mother, Margaret felt her cheeks slowly growing hot, and hastened to end her story. The little boy had stopped crying and was drying his face in a business-like manner with a dirty handkerchief, but when she glanced down at him with a timid smile, Margaret was disconcerted to meet the upward stare of yet another pair of beautiful eyes, this time of so dark a grey as to suggest violet. She was so confused that she only received a vague impression of the young woman's appearance, but gathered that she was soon to have another child; even her wonderfully elegant black and white clothes could not conceal the fact.

'Where's Grantey?' the little boy suddenly interrupted Margaret. 'You thought it were Grantey at the door, Mummy, didn't you? Who's that lady? You thought it *were* Grantey this time, didn't you, Mummy?'

'Yes, Barnabas, I did.' She glanced down at him. 'We're waiting for my mother's maid to come,' she explained to Margaret. 'I'm going out and she's going to look after the brats.'

She seemed in no hurry, standing there with the baby (who was about two, and dressed in a romper-suit of brilliant cotton) perched on her hip. Her eyes still studied Margaret.

'I'm sure,' she said at last in an amused voice, 'that you'd like to do something to make up for having kept my ration book for such ages, wouldn't you?'

Margaret laughed awkwardly. The familiarity of the tone delighted her, but she was not sure if she were being laughed at.

'Oh, yes, of course. It was awful of me –' she stammered.

'Well,' said Mrs Niland, suddenly but gently thrusting the baby at her, 'will you be an absolute *Teresa* and keep an eye on these two for me until Grantey comes in? She'll be here any minute now, I can't think what's kept her, and they'll be good if I tell them to, and I'm hideously late now. That's right. She goes to anyone, don't you, my honeybunch?' And she added to Margaret, 'Do come in.'

The latter had grasped the baby clumsily but not weakly, for she was so alarmed by the responsibility suddenly thrust upon her that all the resourcefulness she possessed came to her aid. She settled the child in her arms with a confident and yet gentle touch that the little girl evidently liked, for she said some unintelligible cooing words, and suddenly smiled, showing two teeth.

'I adore your little Mozart bow,' said her mother carelessly, going ahead of Margaret down a passage. 'Barnabas, lamb, shut the door. Yes, you may slam it. Here' (she bent over a wide divan and shook up some cushions), 'do sit down. Here's her tin with a bead in it (isn't it sinister, but she adores it), and Barnabas is making a house with the coal; he'll do that for hours, only when Grantey comes she won't let him, of course. It is angelic of you,' she added, smiling at Margaret in an old, dim mirror on the wall as she tilted over her eyes a hat that was nothing but a huge black and white flower.

Margaret smiled and murmured something, trying to seem at ease. Her cheeks were burning. She had put the baby girl beside her on the divan, and still kept a hand on the child's back as she plunged about. She was longing to look round the room and yet she wanted to go on looking at Mrs Niland, and she was also aware that there was a little staircase at the far end. Did it lead up to the studio?

Mrs Niland picked up an outsize handbag and some gloves and a mink coat from the floor. 'Good-bye, Barnabas.' The little boy gave her an absent kiss.

'Have a nice party, Mummy,' he said graciously, evidently repeating a formula and not taking his eyes off the coal.

'Thank you, I'm sure. Tell Grantey there's some dripping with lots of goobly in the frig, for your tea.'

'Goobly – boobly,' cried Barnabas, but still not looking up from his house.

'Gooby – gooby –!' echoed the baby, butting Margaret with her smooth fair head and chuckling.

'What's your name?' demanded Mrs Niland, pausing at the door with the mink coat swinging from her shoulders. The light from the window shone on her brown hair where it was swept up from her white nape.

'Margaret Steggles,' said Margaret. She thought that her own voice sounded self-conscious and dull, and hated her name more than ever.

'Good-bye, Margaret Steggles, and don't murder my children. Good-bye, honeybunch,' said Mrs Niland, addressing the baby. Margaret smiled and tried to sound gay as she said, 'Good-bye!' A second later she heard the front door slam. At the same instant the baby burst into tears.

'Oh, good heavens – this won't do – come here, darling –' muttered Margaret distractedly, picking up the shaking little body. Tears were literally spurting from the tightly shut eyes. Margaret put her own cheek gently against the wet warm one, but the baby only roared the more.

'She hates Mummy going out,' observed Barnabas in a detached tone. 'She always does that.'

'What's her name?' demanded Margaret.

'Emma.'

'Emma, don't cry – here –' Margaret picked up the tin and rattled it. 'Has this got a name?' she demanded of the unforthcoming Barnabas, holding up the tin.

'It hasn't got a name, *really*.' For the first time he glanced across at her. 'It *were* called Weeny.'

'Emma – look, darling, here's Weeny. It hates to see you crying. Love Weeny, then.'

Emma hiccoughed, and was suddenly silent. Her wet grey

54

eyes gazed up solemnly and reproachfully at Margaret while two tears ran slowly, slowly down.

'Oh, you darling –' whispered Margaret, gazing into the tiny face, red as a japonica flower.

'Her nose is running,' remarked Barnabas, and scrambled to his feet and came across with the handkerchief. 'It's all right. She hasn't got a cold. It's crying.' He wiped Emma's nose, and she gave a loud short snarl and wriggled away from him. 'She hates having her nose wiped,' he added, and wiped his own. 'It's all right. I haven't got a cold, really. It's only a snuffle, Grantey says,' and he returned to his coals.

Emma now scrambled briskly off the divan and crawled away across the floor. Barnabas watched her warily until she had shuffled past his house and established herself amid a pile of bricks in a far corner; then he returned to his building with a quiet sigh of relief.

'Bick!' crowed Emma, smiling radiantly and holding up a brick to Margaret.

'Yes, darling. Lovely!'

Emma was silent for a little while, burrowing in the box, and Margaret, breathing more freely now, took her opportunity to look round the room.

A little indignation mingled with her dazed admiration for the surprising Mrs Niland. She would have liked to say to some imaginary listener: 'The poor little mites; she just walked out and left them like that with a total stranger and the room hadn't been dusted for days and the fire was nearly out' – but in fact the few pieces of old furniture gleamed like satin, and the red carpet was well brushed. The panelled walls were painted a strange bluish-green, and instead of pictures there were vases of white Italian pottery hanging at intervals, filled with bouquets of violets and white hyacinths which deliciously scented the warm air. A low fire burnt in the basket-grate, but Margaret thought that the house was centrally heated. The one small window, at which hung curtains of yellow Chinese brocade, looked over a gravel yard with a fountain in the middle and some bushes of Portugal laurel in blue tubs, but beyond this, as is often the case in Hampstead, there was a dismal view of blank walls and ugly roofs. The red carpet, on which toys were scattered, fitted closely to the wainscoting, and there were no draughts; the children, the many books on their white shelves, and the luxurious flowers silently breathing forth their perfume seemed enclosed in a hushed, warm cavern hollowed from some deeply coloured jewel, while the chilly world of autumn sunlight outside seemed unreal. Margaret remained quite still, relaxing and forgetting her nervousness as she reclined among the cushions and gazed about her.

'We went on the Heath this morning,' suddenly remarked Barnabas. 'With Stephen and Barbara.'

'Oh. Er – was that nice? Don't you go to school?'

'I'm going when I'm six.'

'Oh, that *will* be fun, won't it? And when will you be six?'

'Fourteenth of January. I'm going to have a trike, too.' Then there was silence once more. Emma fortunately seemed contented with her bricks and Barnabas's house now had three storeys. Margaret wondered if she ought to tell him not to make marks on the carpet, but decided not to say anything; Grantey would attend to that when she came. Margaret hoped that she would not come just yet, for she was enjoying the beauty about her, and impressing its details upon her mind so that she could recall them when she was alone. She could not get over the flowers; those large dark violets curving on their nacreous stems among broad green leaves; and, more amazing still, the delicate, pale double blossom of Parma violets! She had not seen Parma violets for years; she had not known that there were any still to be had in the whole of the British Isles!

They must have cost a small fortune, she thought, and even with money they wouldn't have been easy to get, but *she* looks as if she would always get everything she wanted. She could vividly recall every detail of Mrs Niland's face; satiny hazel nuts and the white petals of wild flowers seemed to have been translated into her hair and cheeks. I never saw anybody like her, thought Margaret, and yet she isn't all that striking. It's just that you can't help watching her.

Suddenly there was an agitated knocking at the front door.

'That's Grantey,' said Barnabas, scrambling up. 'I'll go.'

'Ar goo,' repeated Emma instantly from her corner, scattering bricks in every direction and getting purposefully on to her feet and tottering towards the door.

'No, Emma lovey – I don't think –' began Margaret, hastily going over to her and gently taking hold of her little arms.

'Ar goo – ar goo!' cried Emma, pulling herself away.

'All right, then, let's go together,' said Margaret, holding out a hand instead; but Emma ignored it and hurried down the passage to the front door, which Barnabas had just opened.

A small severe-looking woman in a raincoat and felt hat stepped into the hall, exclaiming, 'Well, Barnabas, and did you think Grantey was lost? The naughty old bus wouldn't wait for me, so I had to wait for the next one. Come and give Grantey a kiss, then.'

Barnabas obediently held up an unenthusiastic face.

'And where's my Emma?' cried Grantey, advancing down the passage and giving Margaret – who was lurking by the sitting-room door – a very keen glance. She caught up Emma and kissed her. 'Where's Mother, Barnabas?' she demanded more quietly, still looking at Margaret.

'She's gone out to her party,' piped up Barnabas, before Margaret, who was feeling awkward, could begin to explain. 'You were *awfully* late, Grantey, and that lady came to the door with Mummy's ration book. She found it on the Heath. So Mummy asked her to stay and be with us until you came.'

'Yes, I – I – that's about it,' said Margaret, coming forward with an affected, nervous laugh, 'Mrs Niland did ask me to. I was scared stiff; I'm not used to such small kiddies, but we managed all right, didn't we, Barnabas?'

Barnabas gave her a long stare. 'Don't know,' he said at last, humping his shoulders, and put his hands in his pockets and strolled back into the sitting-room. Margaret thought what an unpleasant little boy he was.

'Oh, that was how it was, was it?' said Grantey, and she gave a slight grim smile which indicated both pride in Mrs Niland's odd ways and a refusal to comment upon them. 'Well, I hope they were good.'

'Oh, yes, they were both very good,' said Margaret eagerly, hoping to delay the moment of her departure. 'Emma did cry a little after her mother – Mrs Niland – had gone, but she soon cheered up and she's been playing with her bricks as good as gold ever since.'

'And what's Barnabas been doing? Playing with the coal?' playfully demanded Grantey as she moved towards the sitting-room, but in such a tone as to suggest that not for an instant did she believe such a breach of the conventions could have been taking place.

'No,' said Barnabas instantly, and Margaret's quick glance towards the corner revealed only the neatly filled scuttle and an expanse of carpet from which every trace of black dust had been removed. Her respect and dislike for Barnabas increased.

'Oh no, of course not,' said Grantey ironically, also surveying this picture. 'Believe it or not, as they say.' And Margaret, like Barnabas, was left uneasily wondering whether she did or did not know the truth. 'Well,' she went on, addressing Margaret, 'you'll feel like a cup of tea after looking after these little beings for all that time; I'm going to have one and I'm sure you won't say no.'

'It's very kind of you,' began Margaret, 'but –'

'Now come along, it won't take a minute, and the children'll be having theirs, too,' said Grantey. 'We always have it at half-past three or a quarter to four because they have their lunch at twelve.'

Her tone was not effusive, but Margaret received the impression that she would be welcome if she did stay. In fact, Mrs Grant was fond of society and a new face, and one of these long afternoons alone with the children at Hampstead (though they were a part of her work that was pleasant to her) would be all the pleasanter for a little company. Miss Hebe would not have asked this young woman to stay with the children if she had not liked the look of her, and Grantey herself approved of Margaret's quiet clothes and obvious admiration for the Niland establishment.

'Well, it's very kind of you, if you're sure I shan't be eating up your rations,' said Margaret, delighted at the invitation. Grantey took no notice of this remark, for she ignored the war as far as was possible, regarding it as a tiresome interruption of the activities of the two households which she served.

She made Margaret take off her scarf and gloves and leave them in the little hall, and soon they were getting tea in the kitchen, which was a mere large cupboard at the back of the cottage but painted white and equipped with every contemporary device for making housework harder because they will go wrong. Grantey took down a large tray and began to put cups and plates on it.

'We'll have tea in the nursery; it gets the last of the sun,' she said. The children had already gone up, taking their toys with them. 'That's right; you cut some bread, and we'll make them their dripping toast upstairs.'

Margaret had not been so happy for months. There is a soothing quality in the presence of a person who is absorbed in what they are doing at the moment; who does not ask questions of life or comment upon its more striking strangenesses, and Grantey possessed this quality in a high degree. She was without imagination and humour, those troublers of our peace here below, and to the passionate and self-conscious Margaret, already thrilled at being in the beautiful little house of a genius, her personality was both calming and pleasant. Margaret was not the only one who had been thus pacified by it. In the first night of the blitz on London, Alexander Niland had been steadied by overhearing Grantey admonishing the wakeful Barnabas – 'Go to sleep now, like a good boy; it's only bombs.'

Grantey did not talk much while they were preparing the tray; but when they were seated round the table in the unexpectedly large and sunny nursery, and Barnabas and Emma were silently eating their dripping toast with every appearance of enjoyment, she made it clear that she was going to hear all about that ration book. Margaret was more than willing to tell her, for a little sore feeling lingered in her heart at Mrs Niland's casual acceptance of the situation. A lost ration book was very important in Margaret's circle; indeed, she could not, upon careful reflection, think of any circle in which it would not be considered important. It must either be that Mrs Niland never bothered about anything, or else she had everything that was tiresome done for her by other people. But she needn't have been *quite* so casual about it, thought Margaret.

Grantey wanted the story from the beginning, and she also asked interested but inoffensive questions as to why Margaret was on the Heath that evening, and seemed interested in the story of the Steggles's move.

'Stanley Gardens; why, that's just down at the back of us,' she said, wiping Emma's fingers. 'Mr and Mrs Challis, Mrs Niland's parents, live in that big house I expect you can see from your back windows. Westwood, it's called.

'I can see it from my bedroom,' said Margaret, and then, hardly believing her ears, she added, 'Do excuse my asking, but it's such an uncommon name; is Mr Challis any relation to Gerard Challis, the dramatist?'

'That is Mr Challis; he is a play-writer,' said Grantey, wiping Barnabas's fingers in their turn. 'I expect you've heard of him, haven't you?'

'Oh, yes!' breathed Margaret. The circle was even more charmed than she had supposed.

Grantey said no more, but firmly put two wedges of cake, made by herself, first upon Emma's plate and then upon Barnabas's. No living soul had ever heard her express an opinion upon Mr Challis and his works.

Margaret felt this reticence in the air, but she naturally assumed that Grantey was silent because Mr Challis's plays were immeasurably above her head. And she herself did not want to speak just at the moment. She was too moved; almost awed. Gerard Challis, the writer of those beautiful, beautiful plays, lived on the hill that overlooked her back garden! And she was sitting at the same table with his – yes, of course, they were his grandchildren; but he was still young, she had seen a photograph of him. That striking face; so intellectual! Oh, what a lucky, lucky chance had led her to the Heath that evening! Oh what a marvellous place was London, where famous painters dropped their ration books at one's feet, and one's bedroom windows were unconsciously viewed every morning by the spiritual eyes of famous dramatists! Why, there are people who would give a year of their lives to be sitting where I am now, thought Margaret.

'Grandpa's going to give me a trike for my birthday,' observed Barnabas.

'Ganpa?' said Emma, looking questioningly at Grantey.

'Granpa; yes, that's right, dear. Eat your cake,' said Grantey, and just then the telephone began to ring downstairs.

'Excuse me a minute,' said Grantey, going off to answer it. 'Now you show Miss Steggles how nicely you can behave.'

5

'Grantey? Oh, you are there, then; goody,' said Mrs Niland's voice. 'Listen, is Mr Alex in?'

'Not yet, Miss Hebe; at least I haven't seen him.'

'Well, I'll be back about half-past six and I'm bringing Earl and Lev. You can stay and bath the children for me, can't you?'

'If I can be back by seven, Miss Hebe.'

'Oh, ring up Mamma and explain. And Stubbles'll help you; she'd adore to. Listen, don't forget to tell Mr Alex I'm bringing Earl and Lev. Good-bye, Grantey dear.'

'Good-bye, Miss Hebe.' Grantey replaced the receiver and went upstairs.

There is a certain class of mother who cannot go out on an hour's merry-making without finding upon her return that some disaster has befallen her children. If she goes out to stand in a fish queue or to hunt for long woollen stockings, all is well, and she returns to be greeted only by the customary remark, 'Have you brought anything exciting?' But should she dare to lunch with an old friend or go to the pictures, she invariably opens the front door to be met with the dreaded words, 'Now don't flap, but I've got a sore throat,' or 'I fell down at netball and my knee absolutely poured with blood,' and even as she gobbles down the lunch or feverishly watches the picture with one eye on the clock, her revelling is darkened by forebodings which invariably turn out to be too well-founded.

But Mrs Niland did not belong in this category.

'There!' said Grantey, reseating herself at the table. 'That was

Mrs Niland. How'd you like to be nurse again after tea, Miss Steggles, and help me bath these two little beings?'

It was said with gracious condescension which a less infatuated person would have found intolerable, but Margaret felt only grateful pleasure.

'I'd love to,' she exclaimed, smiling affectionately at the children, who remained unmoved, 'if I might just 'phone up Mother and say I may be a bit late.'

'Oh, you'll be back by seven; I've got to leave here myself sharp by half-past six and we'll catch the bus outside Jack Straw's Castle; it only takes about ten minutes,' said Grantey decidedly. 'We'll go together; two's better than one in the old blackout.'

'I've been in the blackout,' boasted Barnabas, 'when I went to Robin Campbell's party. It wasn't over until *seven o'clock*, and me and Stephen were the *very last*. Robin had to push us out of the front door.'

'You'll be asked there again, I should think,' observed Grantey. 'Now, Miss Steggles, if you're sure you won't have any more, I'll just get these few washed up and then we'll have a quiet game before bedtime. That'll be nice, won't it. No, thank you, I can manage; you just stay here and keep an eye on them.' She had been packing the tray while she talked, and now went out of the room with it. Barnabas was pulling Emma along the floor on a rug, and both seemed to be enjoying it, so Margaret went over to a little window at the other end of the room. It overlooked the small paved garden. She felt peaceful as she stood there, gazing out at the roofs and chimneys whose dull colours were warmed by the red light of the winter sunset. The rays poured into the nursery and gave its miniature blue and white furniture the special, charmed look that belonged to this house, and the slightly uneven floor and ancient sash windows possessed the same glamour.

Suddenly a door opened in the wall and a hatless man came

through into the garden, shutting it after him. She recognized him as one of the two she had seen on the Heath that evening; it was Alexander Niland himself! He was unusually tall, and had a high round forehead and his dark hair was thinning on the top. He looked up even as she was staring down at him, but immediately glanced away again, and she could see that his mouth was deeply dimpled at the corners. He crossed the garden and went through another door immediately under the window. He's gone up to the studio, she thought, and slowly released the fold of the curtain which she had been grasping.

She was disappointed. His baldness was disconcerting enough, but an appearance of slight oddness and of deficient health, which was noticeable even at that distance, was more so. She had been unconsciously anticipating something like the disdainful leonine beauty of Augustus John, of whom she had seen photographs in *Vogue*, and she was still inexperienced enough to expect famous makers of beautiful works of art to be themselves physically attractive. But she had no time to think any more about what she had seen, because the door opened and he came into the room.

'Hullo,' he said, smiling and looking round on them all. His voice was pleasant but in no way striking.

'Hullo, Daddy,' said Barnabas, 'come and give me a ride.' Emma, whose face was red with excitement and pleasure, looked up at her father and laughed as she waved her legs above her head.

He glanced at Margaret, who was standing awkwardly by the window, but without curiosity; he seemed to take her for granted. In fact he supposed that she was some friend of Grantey's who was spending the afternoon there, but Margaret, flustered at being in the presence of a genius and anxious to do the right thing, at once came forward and said in a voice which nervousness made overemphatic – 'How do you do?' (She hesitated for a second, too nervous to say his name.) 'I suppose I ought to introduce myself. My name is Margaret Steggles and Grantey – I'm afraid I don't know her other name' (with a little laugh) 'asked me to stay to tea. I found your wife's ration book' (*oh Lord, that sounds all wrong*) 'on the Heath and I only brought it back this afternoon. I expect you'll think I'm awful, keeping it nearly a month like that, only it was in the pocket of a coat I hadn't worn since I got back to Lukeborough, and I only found it when we came back to London. I do hope it didn't put you out awfully, my keeping it so long, I mean,' and she stopped abruptly and laughed again.

She had not intended to ramble on so incoherently, but when once she began to talk she had found it impossible, from embarrassment, to bring her remarks to an end. He listened with a slight smile, but without much attention or interest.

'Oh, that's all right,' he said at last, sitting down and beginning to pull Emma backwards and forwards by her legs while she squealed with delight, 'I think Grantey saw to it, she does all that sort of thing for us. Don't worry about it, really,' he added, as Margaret once more started eagerly to say something, and she checked herself and stood looking down at him as he played with the children, while her cheeks burned with self-consciousness and annoyance. She hardly knew herself what she had expected him to say or how she had wanted him to behave, but his casualness irritated her in the same way that Mrs Niland's had done, and in his case she was not charmed by his appearance, and she was also angry with herself for having talked so much and so disconnectedly.

Yet, as she watched him holding the laughing Emma above his head, and swinging Barnabas round and round, she began to feel that charm which the sight of a man playing with little children always exercises over a woman, and her irritation gradually subsided. Once, when the children's shrieks grew very loud, he glanced across at her and laughed, and she thought how much more impressive his face became when it was animated and how like his large, slightly dim violet-grey eyes were to those of Barnabas, although the child's were so clear.

'That's enough, that's enough,' he said presently, standing up and letting Barnabas slide all the considerable way down from his chest to his feet. 'And you'd better calm down, too, Emma, or I shall have Grantey after me.'

'Is your wound hurting?' demanded Barnabas.

'It is rather,' said his father, smiling again at Margaret. She smiled in return and wondered what the child meant.

'Is it bad? Is that why you can't play with me and Emma any more?'

'It isn't very bad, but I want to go and read the evening paper.'

'Why do you?'

'Because I do.'

'It's an awful, silly, lousy old paper. Gosh, it is lousy,' said Barnabas.

'Yes, well, all right. Don't say lousy. Good-bye,' and he waved to them all and made for the door.

'Will you come and see me in the bath?'

'Yes.'

'Promise?'

'Yes.'

'And see Emma in her bath?'

'Yes.'

'Promise honour bright?'

'Perhaps. I'll see.'

He went out of the room, and Margaret heard him stop to speak to Grantey as he passed her on the stairs, Well, she thought, sighing, I've seen him and spoken to him, which is more than I thought I'd have the luck to do when I started out this afternoon, but I can't help it; I *am* disappointed. He's so ordinary.

67

'There we are, all clean and paid for,' said Grantey, bustling in. 'Now, how about that game before bedtime? Miss Steggles, do you know any nice games?'

Margaret recalled her wandering thoughts with difficulty. To tell the truth, she was beginning to be a little tired of the children's company, and to feel need of adult society. Young children are the most exhausting creatures in the world, even to those who find them interesting as well as lovable; and Margaret, although her youthful energies were well fitted to sustain the pressure of ceaseless noise and demands for attention, was not sufficiently happy or at ease in her own heart to be able to give that calm and undivided application of herself to the children's needs which the successful nurse or mother gives. She felt a sudden irritation. *How long before they'll be in bed?* she wondered, but the thought was immediately followed by the sobering one, *And then I shall have to go home.*

As she helped to draw up chairs to the table upon which Grantey had placed a large bright box filled with counters and games, she was thinking how strange it was that Mr Niland should want to read the evening paper, just like all the ordinary men who were not geniuses who travelled in the Tube every day. How could he paint beautiful pictures if he were not always thinking beautiful thoughts? And how could he think beautiful thoughts if he liked – as he presumably did – reading the tediousnesses and the horrors in the evening paper? She abandoned the problem, and gave her attention to the game.

A little later she was still more tired of the children's company, for Barnabas turned extremely naughty just before being put into the bath, and began to scream, and Emma joined in. Side by side they sat in the bath, with tears rolling down their crimson, distorted faces, while the flannel manipulated by Grantey travelled swiftly but thoroughly over every inch of them, and Grantey herself kept up a low sarcastic commentary upon their behaviour, rhetorically demanding of them at intervals what Miss Steggles would think of them. Margaret handed warm towels and was kept busy between the bathroom and the night nursery, where a rosy lamp was dimly burning and the stove was alight and the two white beds stood side by side. She was charmed by the room, which looked like a night nursery out of *Peter Pan* or *Now We Are Six*, but as she remembered Barnabas's contorted countenance and the shrieks of Emma, she felt that she understood those mothers who go out at night and leave their children locked alone in the house.

Grantey jerked the last button of Barnabas's dressing-gown into its buttonhole with such vigour that he stopped crying.

'There!' said his mother's voice and her head came round the bathroom door. 'Just cheered up in time for me.'

She did not ask what had been the matter; indeed, no one knew.

'Hullo, Mummy,' said Barnabas in a faint and heartbroken voice.

Emma stopped crying too, and began to push her arms into the nightgown which Margaret, upon whose lap she was sitting, had been manoeuvring over her head. She stared at her mother, while her sobs gradually died away.

'Hullo – still here?' said Mrs Niland, looking across at Margaret. 'Aren't you nearly dead? Come down when they're in bed and have some sherry.'

'I'd love to,' said Margaret eagerly.

'Miss Steggles and me are going to catch the bus from Jack Straw's,' said Grantey, in a warning and important voice. 'I've got to be back at seven, Miss Hebe.'

'I know, but it won't take her five minutes,' said Hebe soothingly. 'You come down,' she murmured to Margaret, and retreated. Margaret heard her voice as she went along the passage. 'Earl will bring their supper up, Grantey; he's getting it now.'

The curtains, which Margaret noticed as she went between bathroom and night nursery, were of rich red or green or yellow velvet, and every lamp was shaded in amber, and the glowing, jewel-like impression of the cottage which she had received in the afternoon was strengthened, now that the darkness had come, by the emerald-green or carnation-red carpets which covered all the floors and the staircase. She was enjoying every moment (apart from those spent in listening to the yells of Barnabas and his sister), but as she carried Emma into the nursery she was wondering nervously how she would get on downstairs while she was drinking the sherry; who would be there, and what she should say, and what they would think of her.

Emma was now calm, and felt warm and soft inside her miniature dressing-gown. Her feet were still bright pink from the bath and she wore slippers shaped like rabbits. Her sweet-smelling hair tickled Margaret's nose.

'There!' said Margaret, setting her down in the cot and covering her up, having first removed the slippers. Emma looked up at her but said nothing.

'Hullo, therr!' said a soft voice at the door, with a slur on the 'r,' and Margaret looked up. A fair young man of medium height, wearing the uniform of an American private, stood looking into the room through his glasses.

'Hullo,' she said pleasantly. She was not afraid of him, because he looked so young and probably was not a genius.

'I've brought their rations,' he said, coming forward with a tray. 'Hullo, Barnabas,' to the little boy, who had scrambled into his bed, kicking off his slippers as he went. The soldier put the tray down on the table.

'Hullo, Earl,' said Barnabas, and tried to stand on his head, suddenly overcome with self-consciousness.

'Barnabas, darling, I don't think Grantey would like you to do that,' said Margaret gently.

'Don't care.'

'Now that won't do,' said the soldier, taking him by the slack of his pyjamas. His touch was not expert but Barnabas allowed himself to be put right way up and given his bowl, and began to eat his supper.

'Mrs Grant'll feed Sister,' said Earl, going over to Emma's cot and putting her bowl on the table. 'You can't quite be trusted yet, can you, Sister?' and he stood gazing down at Emma with his hands on the rail of the cot, while she gazed steadily up at him.

He suddenly glanced across at Margaret.

'Aren't they swell?' he said simply. 'It's a great privilege – coming into an English home like this, and I can tell you it means a whole heap to me.' His grey eyes were youthful and clear behind his glasses.

Margaret was moved. The pretty room, the rosy children eating their supper in the peaceful hush, seemed suddenly to typify all that was still safe and happy in England, while the boy's words seemed to go out and away, across the dark dangerous Atlantic, to the home that he had left behind him when he came to fight for freedom. So touching were her thoughts that she was both astonished and indignant when another American voice said mockingly:

'The hell it does.'

A second soldier, tall and dark and flashy, stood at the door looking into the room. He took no notice of her. 'Will you come on down, Earl,' he said, and turned away.

Earl looked hurt, but made no comment. He turned to Margaret, 'I'm Earl Swinger, late of Swordsville, Kansas, and now of the United States Army. I'm pleased to know you.'

He held out his hand and Margaret took it. He gave it a firm shake.

'I'm pleased to meet you, too,' she said, and feeling that more was demanded of her, she added, 'I'm Margaret Steggles, of Highgate, London.' She felt foolish as she said it, but then she wondered why. This was a sensible social custom which established a stranger's name and locality firmly in one's mind.

'*Mrs* Margaret Steggles?'

'Oh, no – *Miss* Margaret Steggles,' she laughed.

'And your profession? (Shall I lead the way downstairs?)' he went on, going ahead of her down the passage.

'I'm a schoolteacher.'

'Why, that's vurry interesting,' said Earl, turning to look at her. 'I was a professor myself at Swordsville Carllage before I volunteered. May I ask where you were educated? Excuse me, this way.' He preceded her down the stairs.

Margaret thought that he seemed very young to be a professor but had no time to say anything more, because he was leading the way into the sitting-room.

Hebe was on a couch with her feet up, and the room was dim in amber light and full of the scent of dying violets. The dark soldier and Alexander Niland were standing talking by a tray of drinks.

'Hullo,' said Hebe, smiling. 'Lev, bring some sherry over. *She's* got to fly off with Grantey.'

'Light or dark?' asked the soldier, turning to Margaret with a decanter in each hand. He had a big nose and dark bloodshot eyes and she disliked his expression.

'Oh – er – light, please.'

'This is Arnold Levinsky,' said Earl, as the soldier came over to her with the drink. 'Lev, meet Miss Margaret Steggles, of Highgate, London.'

Margaret muttered, 'Pleased to meet you,' which seemed to be the formula, and Lev made a vague flip of his unoccupied hand and looked down at her with a casual smile, but he did not speak and at once went back to Alexander Niland. Margaret sat on the edge of her chair, nervously sipping her sherry. No one took any notice of her and she tried to make the most of her last few minutes in Lamb Cottage, for very soon the enchanted afternoon would be over. She longed to say something that would startle and impress them all and make them want to see her again, but it was of no use; she could not think of even the most ordinary remark, not even a comment upon the baby's jacket which Hebe was placidly knitting, and she sat there in silence, feeling a growing resentment against them which mingled uncomfortably with her fascinated interest.

She began to listen to what Alexander Niland and Lev were talking about, but was disappointed to find that it concerned the difficulty of obtaining matches. The painter was holding up a box to the light, which fell slantingly upon his slightly podgy cheeks, and saying:

'Well, I got these from that little man in Holly Square. He let me have them because he knows us, but he told me he has two or three hundred boxes in every Thursday, and they're gone in a couple of hours.'

'You're telling me,' said Lev.

'I once knew a man who collected match-boxes,' put in Hebe. 'Alex, would your stew be burning?'

'Oh, God, yes, excuse me,' he said and hurried out of the room. No one said anything. Hebe continued to knit, and Earl, who was standing near the head of the couch, watched her flying fingers, while Lev had picked up the evening paper and was glancing over it. How rude they are, thought Margaret; the Wilsons have much nicer manners. Not that these people say anything worth listening to when they do talk. I wouldn't have believed a genius, and anyone so fascinating as Mrs Niland, could have been so dull.

'Is your home far from here, Miss Steggles?' suddenly inquired Earl earnestly, crossing the room and sitting down at her side.

73

She turned to him gratefully, thinking how kind and perceptive he was, and that he at least had nice manners.

'About three miles. I live on the other side of Highgate Hill,' she answered.

'Highgate Hill? Then I expect you know the beautiful home of Mrs Niland's parents,' said Earl. 'Lev and I hope to have the pleasure of visiting therr soon.'

'No, she doesn't,' put in Hebe, 'but she does live quite near my mamma and papa.' Margaret was surprised, but then reflected that Grantey must have been talking to Mrs Niland.

'Oh, it's a swell place,' went on Earl, 'the sort of house we think of at home as typically English.'

'There are some typically English ones in the back streets round Euston depot, too – what's left of them,' put in Lev.

Hebe, who had been knitting with her amused eyes fixed on Earl's solemn young face, now laughed outright, and Earl looked pained.

The door opened and Alexander came back, and behind him the face – most unwelcome to Margaret – of Grantey.

'It's all right. Tastes superb,' said Alexander. 'It's nearly ready, and Mary's in.' (Mary was the maid, obtained with much difficulty and filling up of forms, from Eire.)

'Thank heaven; I'm ravenous,' said Hebe, putting away her work.

'Miss Steggles, we ought to be going; we've just got nice time if we go at once,' put in Grantey, beckoning. Margaret put down her glass and stood up. Earl stood up too, but Lev stayed where he was.

'Good-bye, Mrs Niland. Thank you very much. I *have* enjoyed it so,' said Margaret; instinct told her not to put out her hand.

'I'm so glad. You've been an angel with the brats,' smiled Hebe. 'Good-bye.'

Earl was holding the door open for her. Lev and Alexander

Niland glanced up from the conversation which they had resumed, and Lev nodded, while Alexander gave her his radiant smile. Earl held out his hand, which she took.

'Good-bye, Miss Steggles,' he said warmly. 'I am glad to have had the pleasurr of meeting you and I certainly hope we shall meet again.'

'Oh . . . thank you; so do I. Good-bye, Mr Swinger.'

She was relieved that she had been able to remember his name. In another moment she was alone with Grantey in the blackout, turning up her collar against the cold wind and noticing the searchlights wandering over the dark cloudy sky. It was ridiculous to have tears in her eyes over the casualness of those people, she knew, but the afternoon had meant so much to her, and nothing to them, and she had never said good-bye to the children!

Grantey was saying importantly: 'Better let me hold your arm; I know my way down here better than you do, I expect. Now there's no need to rush; we've plenty of time. That sitting-room clock's ten minutes fast.'

This information rendered Margaret silent for some time.

'Who *is* that?' demanded Alexander of his wife, as soon as Margaret had gone. 'She was in the nursery when I got home this afternoon.'

'Her name is Stubbles or something. She brought back my ration book. She's been nursing it for weeks.'

'Oh yes, she did say something about it, but you know I never hear what anyone says,' said Alexander. 'She has a rather striking head.'

Hebe made a face.

'Do you want to paint her? I should think she'd faint with joy. She never took her eyes off you.'

'Not while I'm still doing raids. Do you think there'll be one to-night?'

'I wouldn't know,' laughed Hebe, and she glanced at Lev, who was also laughing. Earl looked argumentative.

'Would you say,' he began, 'that while you are making your mental colour-notes (if you will permit a layman to use the expression) in an air-raid, the danger and the loss of lives mean nothing to you?'

Alexander shook his head.

'I'm so interested in what I'm looking at that I forget to be afraid, and I don't think about the poor devils who're being killed.'

'That shows a vurry high degree of artistic detachment,' said Earl. 'I am afraid that I should never be capable of that.'

'You never know,' said Lev.

Alexander looked a little bewildered and offered Earl another drink, which was accepted, and in a few moments they went in to supper in the studio.

Alexander had recently become interested in the colours of winter, and had taken to spending hours on the roof of his studio wrapped in airman's kit which belonged to a friend who would fly no more, and studying the light and size of the winter stars, and the varying shades of black and brown and blue that make up the winter night sky. On one of these occasions a raid had occurred, and the effect was so awesome and fine that he had been excited by it, and had afterwards made some sketches which he now thought of expanding into a picture. The noise was unpleasant and he did not like it when large pieces of shrapnel fell on the roof, but it was not possible to make satisfactory sketches of the night sky during an air-raid without such events. Hebe, who had never been afraid of anything in her life, found his new experiment as amusing as it was natural.

'I have often wondered about something in connection with your arrt, Alexander,' pursued Earl as they sat at supper, 'and if it will not give offence I should be glad to state my difficulty and get the matter cleared up.'

'Oh, yes,' said Alexander. 'Isn't this salad good?'

'Yes, vurry; thank you, I will take a little more. My difficulty is this,' went on Earl, steadily dealing with the salad as he talked, 'why do you not consider it your dooty to paint contemporary subjects? How do you reconcile your natooral urge towards escapism with your obligations as a citizen and a member of the United Nations?'

Alexander thought for a moment or two, while he ate celery, but from his expression it did not appear that he was thinking very deeply. At last he said, 'How do you mean?'

'Well,' said Earl, taking another roll and turning his glasses upon Alexander, 'you have, if you will permit me speaking frankly, a definite Pollyana complex. You look on the bright side. All around us we see death, danger, despair and the collapse of civilizations (more than one civilization), and this world-sitooation is reflected in the work of such of your contemporaries as Henry Moore and Salvador Dali –'

'*Can't* he draw!' exclaimed Alexander, looking up quickly with a smile of pleasure.

'To name only two,' continued Earl, 'among the sculptors and painters, while among the black-and-white artists it is possible to detect the same sense of insecoority and the disintegration of the capitalist system. Of course,' he added more tolerantly, 'we all have our private worlds, but surely there was never such a difficult time for the artist as to-day, when he must choose between retreating into his private world and thereby losing touch with reality and hence his prospects of healthy artistic growth, or else paint the chaos and horror he sees about him and do violence to his own vision; in your case, Alexander, what our Dr William James would have called a *once-born*, or optimistic, outlook on life,' ended Earl, not without a note of triumph at having coiled up his sentence at last.

There was a silence. Hebe was serving a cold sweet while Lev wheeled a trolley packed with plates over to the door, where Mary silently received it into the kitchen. Alexander appeared to be thinking over what had been said, while gazing at a bowl filled with red and dark-blue anemones. Some of the fringed green sepals were already hidden beneath open curved petals, dusted with black pollen and flushed at their base with deeper colour, while others were buds, still bloomy and closed on thick stems. Earl waited patiently.

'I don't think Alex *does* only paint cheerful things,' said Hebe suddenly, putting a plate of something pink down in front of Earl so quickly that she made him start. 'Look at that one called *Old Man Asleep*. My mamma can't look at it without dissolving. Of course I know she belongs to a weepy generation; she actually is an Edwardian, you know; she was born in 1901, but it even gets me and Beefy and Auberon down, and we aren't Edwardians.'

This was a long speech for Hebe. She took up her fork and began to eat pink stuff in silence. Earl looked slightly dazed.

Alexander suddenly looked up. 'I've never thought much about what you've been saying, Earl; and I'm not quite sure that I see what you mean. But look here. Renoir was painting all through the Franco-Prussian War of 1870. People still looked paintable and enjoyed things, and Renoir enjoyed painting them. It's like that with me. That's really all there is to it.'

'Don't you mind him, ducky,' said Hebe, and Lev suddenly laughed.

'It all sounds too simple to be convincing,' said Earl, shaking his head. '*When I am faced by a simple Aesthetic statement, I suspect it.* That was what my Professor of Modern Aesthetic Trends used to say to us at Swordsville Carllage. You quote the example of the Franco-Prussian War of 1870. But surely that cannot be compared with the struggle which confronts us to-day. You must have some theory behind your work.'

Alexander shook his head, and congratulated his wife on having obtained some brown sugar, which he preferred in coffee; he did not seem to want to talk any more.

'*You,*' said Hebe, suddenly turning her beautiful eyes upon Earl, 'ought to have a long talk with my papa.'

'I should greatly appreciate the honourr,' he said, paling slightly under her look.

Hebe made a face, and began to talk about the film which she and the Americans had seen that afternoon.

6

The next day was Sunday. Margaret had been so strongly impressed by all she had seen at Lamb Cottage that she would have been very willing to spend the day thinking over the events of the afternoon and the further facts concerning the Nilands and the Challises which she had gathered from Grantey on their way back to Highgate. She now knew that Alexander had been so seriously wounded at Dunkirk that he had been invalided out of the Army, and the disappointment she had felt in his unhealthy appearance and his uninteresting conversation was modified by respect for him as a man. He must have looked more ordinary than ever in uniform, she thought, especially as he wasn't even an officer, only a lance-corporal. She had been recalling those of his pictures that she had seen, with a feeling of surprise at the residue of beauty which they had left in her memory.

But on Sunday there was no opportunity for even that day-dreaming which can be indulged in while one is doing housework, for Mrs Steggles insisted upon preparing an unusually elaborate lunch for some relatives who were passing through London, and who were going to look in upon the Steggleses about twelve o'clock. Margaret had to spend the morning chopping, peeling, straining, rolling, basting and spreading, and listening to her mother's irritable conversation in the hot little kitchen. The afternoon could not be looked to for much relief, as the relatives would be there at least for the earlier part, and afterwards she would have to make sure that her clothes and books were in order for her first day at the new school.

Her reveries on Lamb Cottage were not entirely bright; disappointment and disapproval were both mingled with them. However, the fascination exercised by the Cottage and its inhabitants over her imagination was stronger than her memories of Alexander's baldness, Hebe's casualness, Lev's disagreeable expression and Barnabas's rudeness, and against the disadvantages she could set the courtesy of Earl and the friendliness of Grantey.

But the thought which returned to her again and again during the morning was that there had been no hint of further intercourse with the Nilands, much less with the Challises. *That* could not be got over. The afternoon was ended; as Hilda's boys would say, 'You've had it,' and there was nothing she could do, except perhaps to send Grantey a merry card at Christmas with '*How's the ration book?*' on it. She thought, however, that that would look forced and pert, and could only make Grantey disapprove of her.

It was true that as they had parted outside the iron gates of Westwood, the big house itself being invisible in the darkness, Grantey had said something about 'come and have a cup of tea with me one of these days,' but Margaret had known that she had not meant it as an invitation. Grantey must know that most people – even nowadays, when everyone was so busy and had so little time for social life – would have been pleased with an opportunity to get to know the Nilands of Lamb Cottage and the Challises of Westwood, and Grantey was the typical old servant who would be jealous of the privacy and exclusiveness of the family she served; she would not easily issue an invitation, even to tea in the kitchen.

But Margaret's dissatisfaction was increased by the feeling that she herself *had* had an excellent opportunity to make the families' acquaintance, based upon a solid excuse, and that she had not made the best of it. She felt that she had nothing to offer Mrs Niland and her husband and the soldier they called

Lev; she could not talk lightly and amusingly (not that they had done so, for that matter); she had no poise; she cared too much about Art, about Love, about the World and the War, and *everything*. Earl was the only one of them all with whom she felt she had anything in common (and she suspected him of being attracted to Mrs Niland, who probably encouraged him). Even Grantey had a managing, sensible way with her which, although comforting, was also damping, and made Margaret feel that she herself was making a fuss about nothing.

As she dished up the lunch she was thinking how absurd it was of her to suppose that she might be asked again to the house by Mrs Niland, for she must now be looked upon as Grantey's friend. Grantey had asked her to stay to tea, Grantey had accompanied her home, and of course she would be relegated to Grantey's social standing. All the same, she thought, pushing a lock of hair off her hot forehead as she wheeled the dumb-waiter into the dining-room, Mrs Niland did ask me to have that sherry with them and if I'd been interesting I don't believe they would have cared a hoot if I *was* Grantey's friend. Whatever else they may be, they aren't snobs.

Her mother had of course wanted to know why she was so late home, and she had had to admit that she had been returning a lost ration book which she had forgotten for nearly a month. She made the household at Lamb Cottage sound much less interesting than it had appeared to her, and as soon as Mrs Steggles heard that Mr Niland was an artist, it became a point of honour with her to dismiss the incident with a few jokes about Margaret's tastes.

Margaret had suppressed the fact that two young men had been present, as this might have roused an unwelcome train of thought in her mother's mind, and in half an hour, in the bustle of preparing supper, Mrs Steggles had forgotten the matter.

The remainder of Sunday passed uneventfully but busily, and

Margaret's obsession with the Nilands became less as she grew absorbed in her preparations for the next day. An item which she happened to see in the Sunday paper turned the current of her thoughts towards her own good fortune in being a teacher, with some control over her own life, and some leisure in which to indulge her own tastes. Had she been in one of the unreserved professions for women, she would have been called up and directed into an aircraft factory or a Government office, as Hilda had been (not that Hilda minded being in the Food Office, for her fear of 'being shoved into the A.T.S., and bossed around by a lot of old trouts,' was the only one that ever darkened her existence, and to her the Food Office was pleasant by contrast with the A.T.S.). But Margaret went to bed that night with gratitude in her heart that she was still comparatively a free woman, and even felt a little shame that she was discontented.

One afternoon some weeks later, Hilda was seated at her desk in the Food Office dealing with a timid little woman who suggested, rather than proposed, that she should go away for a week to Cheam, and had come to get emergency ration cards for herself and her little boy.

'Yes, well, that's two of you, then,' said Hilda, bestowing upon the little woman her dazzlingly cheerful smile. 'Now how long are you going for?'

'A week, we thought,' said the little woman, nervously fixing Hilda with her large pale eyes. 'I wouldn't be going at all, see, only my Derek he's got this bad cold and it does pull them down so, and the food isn't what it used to be, say what you like (not that I'm blaming you, my dear) and my sister says she can have us just for a week.'

'And when do you think of going?' inquired Hilda patiently, leaning an arm, rounded as a vase in the tight sleeve of her pale-blue jumper, upon the desk, and gazing at the little woman with her head on one side. A stifled giggle came from Miss Potts, busy over the Extra Milk applicants; it was near the end of the day and the temporary servants of H.M. Government felt that they might relax.

'Next Thursday,' said the little woman, brightening and nodding as if she had just made up her mind.

'The 21st,' said Hilda encouragingly. 'And when did you think of coming home?'

'On Thursday week,' smiled the little woman, nodding again.

'Then I'll make you out cards for the 21st to the 28th,' said Hilda. 'Got your books?'

The little woman reluctantly handed them over. 'I'm afraid they're rather grubby,' she said.

'Oh, that's nothing,' said Hilda cheerfully, busily scribbling and stamping. 'You ought to see some we get.'

The little woman watched for a moment or two, then suddenly said, 'I s'pose I oughtn't to be going at all, really – they do ask you is your journey really necessary.'

'Oh, I wouldn't worry; a break does you good,' said Hilda soothingly, handing back the books. 'It's your duty to keep your strength up, you know. Bye-bye.'

'Bye-bye, dear, and thanks ever so,' said the little woman, and hurried out. She was the last of a queue, and for the moment there were no more.

'Lady Woolton, that's me,' said Hilda, leaning back with a yawn. 'What's the time? Oh, goody.'

The Food Department was accommodated in the large Assembly Room of the Town Hall. The spacious windows were permanently blacked-out and the officials worked by electric light, while the central heating made the place very warm. Behind the girls and women seated at the counters was the spectacle (reassuring or depressing according to the beholder's views on bureaucracy) of tier upon tier of files mounting the walls in ridges; files stuffed with applications and information, and correspondence extending over the war years; records of changed addresses, and pints of milk consumed by then-expectant mothers whose children were now four years old; details about orange juice, and Short Leave emergency cards, and balancer meal for backyard poultry-keepers, and all the paper framework of that vast, cumbersome, yet astonishingly successful organization called Rationing.

Twenty minutes later Hilda was standing in a tightly packed Underground carriage on her way home. There was no question of any gentleman getting up to offer his seat to a lady; the gentlemen were too tightly wedged to move, and the ladies could not have accepted the offer if it had been made because they were wedged too. Everyone looked good-tempered, though tired, and when the train stopped at a station and people struggled off but more people struggled on, everyone laughed. Was it because the air was stiflingly warm and the lights brilliant that people bore the discomfort cheerfully? Overhead in the raw foggy December night the people on the buses were abusing each other and occasionally even scuffling.

Hilda stood squeezed between an American soldier and an old man who smelled of beer. Fortunately both for Hilda and the soldier, they were standing face to face, and every time the train lurched, up swept Hilda's eyelashes and her blue eyes met the soldier's, and they both smiled. All the old man saw was the back view of slim shoulders in a grey coat, and an orderly arrangement of fair curls which smelled of shampoo, but the old man smelled so strongly of beer himself that this delicate scent was wasted upon him, and he was not interested in fair curls, anyway, only desiring to get home and take his boots off.

All this smelling and squeezing was peculiarly distasteful to one member of the homeward-bound crowd. An unusually tall man wearing a black diplomatic hat was standing just behind Hilda's soldier, with a resigned expression of suffering upon his handsome pale face. This gentleman disliked the human race, and was only travelling home by Underground from Whitehall because his Daimler was temporarily out of order, and he had been unable to persuade a taxi-driver to drive him out to Highgate in the increasing fog.

But suddenly he saw a face at which he could bear to look; nay, could even look at with pleasure. It was a face of delicate aquiline beauty, with brilliant eyes of sea-blue. The pale curls and grey coat made a sober setting for its liveliness, and there was also – for the gentleman was fastidious in these matters – a neatness in the well-fitting gloves and the large handbag which attracted him.

He had long been hoping against hope to have an affair with someone which did not become irritating and hot and untidy as soon as the poor human affections unfolded and had their way. He was always hoping to find a woman (or a girl; he was not particular) who would conduct an affair with him gracefully, as if they were dancing a minuet or playing in a string quartette together; a girl who should appreciate *diminuendo* and *largo*, so to speak, as well as *presto* and *appassionata*. So far his search had been in vain, and of course only a boy of twenty would romance about a girl seen in the Underground. But what nymph-like eyes! What joy to wake their coolness to warmth (but not too much warmth or else everything would get complicated and annoying).

Here the old man who smelled of beer tramped heavily upon the gentleman's toes in the act of forcing his way through the packed passengers to the door, and the gentleman made a pained face. Opening his eyes, which he had closed in the access of agony, he met the eyes of Hilda, who was laughing, and he smiled back.

It was a well-bred smile, simple, human and friendly (he saw to that), and there was no eagerness in it. He found it delightful to smile at this nymph, hatless as nearly all of them were nowadays, and radiantly young, and he wondered if the next station were hers as well as his, and hoped very much that it was. He almost decided to speak to her.

Up the moving staircase they went together; the gentleman overcoming his inclination to stand still and be borne restfully along because Hilda was walking briskly ahead of him. They passed the ticket-collector almost together and hurried up the slope which led to the exit. When they reached it, Hilda paused, and searched in her handbag. Outside the dimly lit entrance there was impenetrable darkness, and the air was full of fog, floating in visible wreaths in front of the subdued lights. The gentleman paused also, and produced from his brief-case a large and handsome torch which he tested and found in order. People were crowding about the entrance exclaiming in dismay at the thickness of the fog, which had come down over London in all the muffling, deadening density of 'a regular old-fashioned pea-souper' during the time they had spent in the train coming from the City.

He heard Hilda give an exclamation of annoyance. Her torch refused to work. He waited, lurking in the background and congratulating himself upon his luck. He was excited and full of hope. The truly romantic heart is ever young, and goes on being a nuisance to all its friends long after its owner has reached what in most people are years of discretion.

At last Hilda shrugged her shoulders crossly and stepped out from the entrance into the blackout. The gentleman followed. People were flashing their torches in the blackness on all sides, but they only shone on the greasy pavement, for the fog was so thick that no light could penetrate it further than a foot or so. Hilda moved confidently forward, trying to make her way by the light from other people's torches, but suddenly she gave a cry and stumbled as she missed the edge of the curb.

The gentleman was at her side in an instant.

'Are you all right?' he exclaimed in a frank hearty tone, grasping her arm and switching on his torch.

'Yes, thanks, I didn't see the curb,' she answered, rubbing her ankle. 'My torch has given out. It would.'

'I have been sent by Providence especially to escort you,' he answered, relapsing into the whimsical, mocking tone which he always used with common little girls. '*My* torch, as you see, is in excellent order,' and he flashed it over her feet, observing with satisfaction that they were pretty.

'Yes. It's a young searchlight,' retorted Hilda, still rubbing. He thought it best to relax his hold upon her arm. 'Aren't you lucky!'

'Very,' he answered gravely, but putting a smile into his voice. 'You see, this hasn't happened by chance. We were fated to meet.'

'You sound like Lyndoe,' sighed Hilda, standing upright. 'Well, since you *have* got a torch and you want to escort me – do you live near here? I don't want to take you out of your way.'

He laughed. 'I don't live anywhere. When I have seen you home I shall vanish into the fog, and you will never see me again.'

'I can't see you now, so it's all the same to me, but as you've got a torch and I haven't, and I've got to get home somehow, I shall just have to take a chance.'

'I assure you I am respectable,' he said playfully.

'Well, you would say that, wouldn't you? Here, do you know where we're going? I want to get to Alderney Gardens; it's at the bottom of Simpson's Lane.'

'I haven't the pleasure of knowing Alderney Gardens, but I know Simpson's Lane well, and I will take you there and doubtless we can find our way after that.'

'I hope so,' said Hilda doubtfully. 'I say, isn't this awful. My mother will be having fits.'

'Oh, you have a mother?'

'Of course I've got a mother! Well, I had when I left home this morning and I s'pose they'd have let me know. What on earth do you mean?'

'I mean your eyes. They look as if your mother might have been Thetis.'

'Who's she when she's at home. Oh, gosh, there I go again!' and she stumbled once more and clutched at him.

'Would you care to take my arm?'

'I wouldn't *care* to, but I suppose I shall *have* to,' and she put her own firm young one through his. His heart beat faster. There was silence for a little while. Now and then he flashed his torch upon a house to make sure that they were on the right road. Occasionally they passed a street-lamp, but its tiny glimmer was hidden in the fog that floated high above their heads. At last he coughed and said, 'Don't you want to know who Thetis was?'

'I can't wait.'

'She was a sea-goddess,' he said, frowning slightly.

'Aren't we nearly there?' said Hilda, coughing.

'We are about half-way down Simpson's Lane,' and he flashed the torch upon some wrought-iron gates set in an ancient brick wall which they were at that moment passing. The light shone on the name of the house, Westwood.

'Thank heaven for that,' sighed Hilda. 'We shan't be long now. I say, I do hope I haven't taken you much out of your way?'

'I don't know yet.'

'Isn't it a bit early in the evening to be feeling like that?'

'I don't know how far you may have taken me out of my way. You may have set my feet upon a strange and enchanted path.'

Hilda was beginning to feel annoyed. She was not used to this sort of talk, and for Thetis and enchanted paths she could not have cared less. She said suddenly:

'Are you on the B.B.C?'

'Good heavens, no!' he replied, shuddering. 'You odd child, why do you ask?'

'You talk like one of the announcers; Robert Robinson, I think his name is. And you sound like one, too,' she added darkly.

'No,' he said, after a pause, 'no, I have nothing to do with that institution for perverting the taste and moulding the opinion of the masses. If I told you my name I doubt if you would know it.'

'No, I don't expect I should. Be funny if I did, wouldn't it? Shall I have three guesses?'

She knew that they were nearly at the end of Simpson's Lane and that in a few moments she would be home, and this made her feel better-tempered.

'As you please, Primavera.'

I'm getting some names to-night, thought Hilda. Aloud she said, 'Archibald Screwy?'

He was not sufficiently acquainted with contemporary slang to realize how pert this was, but he shook his head. 'Nowhere near it.'

'Freddie Grisewood?'

'*No.*'

'Dr Goebbels? – No, you don't limp. I give up.'

There was a pause while they made their way across the road. He flashed the light upon a wall and saw the words, 'Alderney Gardens.'

'I suppose you wouldn't be Frank Phillips?' said Hilda. 'I live at number fourteen.'

He said suddenly, 'I would like you to think of me as Marcus.'

'Anything you say. I say, I *am* sorry, I'm sure I've brought you simply miles out of your way. It's very kind of you. Marcus what?'

'It has been the purest of pleasures.'

'Marcus what?' repeated Hilda.

'Just Marcus. Or Marcus Antonius, if you prefer it.'

Hilda shook her head. 'Life's too short. Well, Marcus, here we are, and thanks for the buggy-ride. If it hadn't been for you I should still be at Highgate Station.'

He stood looking down at her, hat in hand.

'May I see you again one day?' he asked simply. 'Say "yes" . . . please.'

Hilda paused with one hand on the gate and spoke impressively:

'Marcus, if I saw every boy again who asked me to, I should never go to business or have time for a perm, or get any meals, and if you're looking for a girl friend it's just too bad you should have picked on me, because I've got so many boys now I don't know which way to turn. But it was nice of you to suggest it. Aren't you married?' she ended suddenly.

He shook his head.

'Oh. I thought you might be. You look as if you were.'

He winced.

'Well, at least may I know your name?' he asked.

'With pleasure. It's Hilda Wilson.'

He shook his head. 'I would sooner think of you as Daphne.'

'Yes, so would I, but I was called Hilda after Mother's only sister. It's an awful name, I quite agree with you, but I manage somehow. Now you run along home, Marcus. Good night, and thanks again,' and she waved gaily and went in at the gate. He raised his hat and turned away. Suddenly the front door was flung open, regardless of the blackout, and a woman stood peering out anxiously into the fog.

'Hilda? Is that you? My goodness, we have been worried

about you. Dad's just changing his shoes to come out after you with a torch. We thought yours might have given out. Isn't it awful?'

'I'm all right, Mother. Who do you think saw me home?' Then, raising her voice so that the gentleman, who was not yet out of earshot, might hear, she carolled joyously, 'Freddie GRISE-WOOD!' and ran in and shut the door.

'Hilda, don't be so absurd!' said Mrs Wilson delightedly, beginning to help her off with her coat. 'It's all right, Dad, here she is,' she called. 'Are you very cold, dear? There's a lovely fire in the dining-room, and I've got an extra-nice supper waiting.'

Hilda hugged her. 'I'm all right, ducky. No, I don't suppose it was Freddie Grisewood, really; it was an old guy I clicked with in the Tube; quite bats, but rather sweet; he came all the way home with me.'

'That was unselfish of him,' said Mr Wilson dryly, coming into the hall and surveying his daughter's glowing face and brilliant eyes. 'A real sacrifice that must have been, poor chap.' He put out his cheek and Hilda dropped a kiss on it. 'Ted Russell just rang you up, Hildie. He's got forty-eight hours' leave and he'll be round after supper.'

'Oh, goody! No,' said Hilda, following her father into the dining-room and laughing, 'I don't think he was trying to get fresh. I think he was just lonely, poor old thing.'

7

The gentleman calling himself Marcus walked briskly homewards, the unpleasantness of his journey and the acrid fumes of the fog alike forgotten. The little adventure had awakened all the romance in his nature, without which he found life savourless and dreary. He had not seen so attractive a face and form for many months, and her cool manner only added to her charm for him. He had known one or two with that manner, and it had been a pleasant task to break it down into shyness and then into warmth, and to reach at last the sensitiveness of the youthful soul and heart within. He had every intention of seeing Daphne (he really could not endure to think of her as Hilda) again, and soon, but he would have to think out the safest plan for their meeting; meanwhile it was delightful that she lived near, for he would never go out now without the hope of encountering her by accident. Later on, of course, when the affair was over, it might be awkward, but that moment was not yet.

Here it is time to explain to the more suspicious among our readers that all that this gentleman required from the pretty young girls whom he picked up was romantic and spiritual sustenance; manna, so to speak, from the heaven of their youth which should feed the yearnings of his soul. It was true that they often became tiresomely importunate, and that he had to end the relationship abruptly (with pain to himself, for his was a nature that disliked giving pain to others), but that was never his fault.

There had been Peter, who lived in one room in Hampstead and earned three pounds a week as bookkeeper to a small firm which made meat paste in Islington. Peter's dark eyes had shone at the music of Bach and John Ireland, and he had met her in a crowd, coming out of the Queen's Hall. Music had been the bond between them, until Peter grew clamorous and wanted him to leave the wife she was sure that he must have, and he had been forced to end the affair. Iris had been fair and shy, with a job as receptionist in a photographer's in Baker Street, and had adored modern poetry, but she had gone the same way as Peter, in tears where Peter had stormed. And these were only two of many affairs; so romantic when we read of their like in the pages of Proust (that other admirer of girls seen in the street) and so pathetic and sordid and such a waste of time and energy when viewed in terms of human happiness.

He would have said that as he did not finally possess their persons, no harm was finally done, which was an odd conclusion for such a connoisseur in spiritual values to have reached.

As he walked home he wondered if Hilda were musical or stage-struck or poetry-mad? He assumed that she must have some aesthetic taste, for he could never have been attracted to a girl who possessed none, and a girl could not look like a nymph and have the soul of a typist. (That was how he put it to himself.)

Yet as he opened the gates of his home he recalled certain words, certain phrases of hers, which jarred upon him in a way to which he was not accustomed, and a doubt passed over his mind. It could not be possible that for the first time in his life he had been attracted by merely a pretty face? No; there is spiritual passion there, he thought, shutting the iron gates behind him and looking up at the long, dim shape of the mansion. That manner is merely defensive. I will see her again, and soon.

'Darling, would that be you?' inquired Mrs Gerard Challis, seated that same evening before her mirror. She referred to sounds proceeding from behind the door of the bathroom into which her bedroom opened.

'Of course,' answered Mr Challis, after a pause. He was sitting on the bathroom floor with nothing on, doing his yoga exercises. He sat cross-legged, only it was more complicated than that, and he looked beautiful; he was more than fifty years old, but his tall person retained the slenderness and much of the supple-ness of youth, and his serious deep-blue eyes had the tranquillity belonging to people who have always done what they wanted to without arguing with their consciences.

'Whom did you think it was?' he asked a moment later, almost good-humouredly. The exercises induced calm and well-being.

'I thought it was probably you. It's ages since I've really seen you. How are you?'

'My cold has gone, thank you.'

'So glad, sweetie,' murmured Mrs Challis. She slipped off her house-coat and stood looking at herself in the glass. She was large and lovely, with the high bosom and long slender waist of a goddess. Twenty years ago such amplitude had been unfashionable and had forced her to adopt a rigid diet, and now her loveliness was a little old, and her neck and hands were beginning to go, but she still had the childlike look that had enslaved people in the Gay Twenties. She had been one of the legendary Bright Young People, and as Seraphina Braddon had appeared upon the front page of the London evening papers more frequently than any of her set. And now in her conversation, in her attitude to life, she was as faintly and charmingly and inexorably dated as a novel by Michael Arlen.

'Hebe's got her ration book back,' she said, beginning to get into a dark-blue dinner-dress with gold sequins encrusted upon the bosom.

'I did not know that she had lost it,' said Mr Challis, appearing at the bathroom door in a dressing-gown of yellow and purple Persian silk, and brushing his thick silver hair.

'Darling, I told you. Weeks ago. We decided Alex must have dropped it when you and he were charging over the Heath that afternoon.'

'I seem to remember now.'

'Grantey was *hopping*. She said it was your fault – just when Hebe needs all her extra milk and stuff.'

'Absurd. How could it be my fault when Alex dropped it?'

'I expect you were talking.'

'I dare say. How unpleasant this hair-tonic smells.'

'I know; too lousy. It's the war as usual.'

'I wish you would not use that expression, Seraphina. If only you had imagination –'

'Too sorry, darling.'

There was silence for a moment, then he said, 'How did she get it back?'

'Someone picked it up. A schoolmistress, Grantey said. She took it back to the cottage.'

Mr Challis yawned and stepped into his trousers.

'Nice of her.'

'She spent the afternoon there, looking after the children. The schoolmarm, I mean.'

Mr Challis was silent. The subject of his grandchildren was distasteful to him.

'Blast, there goes my stocking,' murmured Seraphina.

'Haven't you any more of those things, points, whatever they're called?'

'No, my angel, I have not. Hebe has had most of mine. I shall have to pinch some more of Barnabas's.'

'Who are these Americans who are coming to-night?' demanded Mr Challis, reclining on his wife's bed and opening a typed manuscript with corrections in a dashing female hand.

'Earl and Lev, darling.'

'That tells me nothing. They do not sound like the names of human beings.'

'You remember. Alex picked them up in a milk bar. He's painting Lev.'

'Do you mean that portrait of a Jew?'

'Alex says he's amusing. I hope he'll make me laugh,' said Mrs Challis, who enjoyed laughing.

Mr Challis, who had been married for twenty-five years, was again silent. He was fond of his wife, though he had long ago decided that her nymph's face had led him up a garden path where the flowers were not spiritual enough for his taste, and he deplored her frivolity. Her grandfather had made a large fortune out of beer, and something of the delicate yet sturdy open-air grace of the hops seemed to cling about Seraphina: she was not a complex woman.

'How's the new play going, sweetie?' she asked, beginning to brush her hair.

Mr Challis frowned. Her tone was even lighter than usual.

'There are certain difficulties which refuse to resolve themselves,' he answered reservedly, turning over the pages of the typescript. Mrs Challis felt the disapproval in his voice and, being a woman who liked life to run easily, she tried to put matters right.

'You did tell me about it, didn't you, darling? Isn't it about an Austrian tart?'

'I suppose it might be described in those words,' said Mr Challis, with a smile like an east wind. 'It does concern a Viennese woman who is compelled by her conscience to become a whore.'

'Gerard, darling, you know I *never* butt in, but honestly – *no one* calls them that nowadays; it's *too* tatty.'

'I do not clothe my conceptions in the language of the cocktail bar.'

'I know, sweetie, but everybody will –'

She stopped, just in time. Everybody *had* laughed at one scene in Mr Challis's last play. Hermione and Marriott are alone in the laboratory of the tsetse-fly research station in the middle of the Uganda jungle, and he has rolled up her sleeve in order to inject her with the serum, when he stops and says (harshly), '*There is a shadow in the crook of your elbow.*' The feeling of the audience had expressed itself in an amiable and audible mutter from the stalls, where sat a man in the Tank Corps. 'Oh, for God's sake get on with it,' he had remarked, and then the scene had been held up while the house laughed.

This incident had wounded Mr Challis more deeply than he cared to admit even to himself. He was proud of the pontifical influence which his beautiful, careful, serious plays exercised over the taste of educated England and America. He had wrought for himself a strikingly distinguished style. It was difficult to describe, but he himself had not demurred when one admirer had coined for it the phrase 'a style of iron and shadows.' He was still puzzling as to why the tension had failed at that particular moment in his play. There was nothing in the dialogue to explain the failure. He always wrote obliquely of people's personal charms, making a man say to a woman, '*Your throat is a taut chord,*' or '*Your ankle bone is softly modelled.*' Why should Marriott's remark, which was indicative of the struggle between duty and passion within him, have caused boredom in the stalls and then inane laughter? The only explanation, to which he returned again and again, was that it was the Mean Sensual Man who had laughed; the eater and drinker of husks amid the swine, who saw only the coarse side of sex. Well, there should be even fewer concessions made to *him* in the new play, Mr Challis promised.

'But I expect you know best,' ended his wife amiably.

'I think we may take it that I do,' he said courteously.

Unfortunately, Seraphina was not in a prudent mood that evening. She returned to the subject, against her wiser judgment, because she was curious.

'Darling,' she began carefully, smoothing her waves of hair back into the shingle which she had worn since she was seventeen and which was now a little too youthful for her, 'you said her *conscience* forced her into being a you-know-what. It sounds awfully funny-peculiar.'

Mr Challis affected not to hear, but his wife, feeling the silent thunderbolt poised, drew back in time.

'Oh well, I shall see it all on the first night, shan't I?' she said smilingly, and murmuring, 'I'm going to see if everything's all right,' she made her escape.

Outside the door she gave a little giggle and thought that she would tell Hebe Dadda's latest. Oh, what a comfort was a daughter! Husbands took up with dreary hags, and sons were angels, only girls took them away from you (as of course was natural, but hard). But a daughter, and two angelic grandchildren, and a third coming! When you had those, you could take *anything* on the chin.

Left alone with the typescript, Mr Challis's expression gradually became softer. It was not the pages of the very bad novel before him which caused this thawing, for he had come across several would-be humorous scenes in it and Mr Challis had no use for humour; he had more than once publicly and severely put it in its place (where, with Shakespeare and Jane Austen, it stayed) and it was not to be found in his own works. No, it was the memory of the writer, who had hurried up to him as he was leaving the Ministry on the previous evening and thrust her manuscript at him, saying with a break in her ardent voice, 'I don't care *what* you think of me, you've *got* to read it!' Then she had darted away, leaving him with an impression of a young pink face and brown eyes. Pleasing, distinctly pleasing, and touching too. Her name and address was on more than one part of the manuscript.

Here was this gifted and fortunate man, the writer of plays admired by the cultured few and yet financially successful, married to a delightful woman, father of three satisfactory children, living in an ancient and beautiful mansion, handsome in his person, and possessing ample means derived from his personal salary in the higher ranks of the Civil Service and his private income. And was he happy? He thought that he was not.

Spiritual hunger was what he suffered from; yearnings, lookings before and after, and pinings for what was not. He thought of it as a divine thirst which no religion could satisfy, and no woman (as he flung one after another impatiently aside like used matches) could assuage.

Mr Challis must be given credit for a virtue: he did work hard at his plays. Sustained by a sense of their excellence and importance and of his own unusual gifts, he laboured over their plots and their characters and their dialogue (which was full of references to mathematics and Saint Augustine) and succeeded in creating an atmosphere upon the stage as if no one had a stitch on, though nothing ever happened which justified this effect.

Yet there was a doubt in his heart. He knew that his plays were good; each one better than its predecessor. *Mountain Air*, the one about six women botanists and a male guide isolated in a snowstorm in a hut on the Andes, had been surer in its approach and handling than his first one, *The Hidden Well*, which concerned the seven men and one female nurse on the tsetse-fly research station, already referred to; while *Kattë*, the one upon which he was now engaged, dealt with an Austrian woman who was bandied about by the officers of a crack regiment in Vienna, and was, he felt convinced, his masterpiece.

He was for ever thinking up new permutations and combinations.

But would the public appreciate his *Kattë*? Ah! That was the doubt.

He was always in love with his heroines; those women of fire and dew who represented the Eternal Mistress of Man, and each time one of them went out into the world in a play he trembled for her as if she were a breathing, suffering, living woman, and it hurt him if all women did not envy her and all men long to possess her. (None of his heroines ever had any children, for he did not consider that a woman with children was also fitted to be a fiery, dewy mistress.) Each time he met a woman who seriously attracted him, he put her on her mettle by indicating that he had never met his Ideal Woman outside his own plays, and then she would try to be fiery and dewy, until the inevitable moment arrived when she had had it.

Mr Challis put the manuscript away in a drawer and gave a final glance at his reflection before going downstairs. The fact that its young author worked in the Ministry automatically ruled out any meeting for tea at some discreet café and a discussion of her manuscript, but he would certainly write the pretty little fool a kind letter; it would delight her, and give him but little trouble, and kindness never harmed one's reputation.

He went downstairs feeling elated. Mr Challis never rubbed his hands or hummed to express his satisfaction; he left such manifestations to lesser men; but when his spiritual gloom was temporarily lifted, a watery humour broke through the cloud of his reserve like the sun coming out on a wet day, and his acquaintances and family were regaled with sly digs in Greek and cracks in medieval French.

As he crossed the hall he was surprised to observe a fire burning in the grate. A back, neatly dressed in grey with a white apron, was at that moment bending stiffly to place a log upon the blaze.

'Grantey,' began Mr Challis authoritatively, going towards her, 'it was quite unnecessary to light a fire. The central heating –'

Grantey slowly straightened herself and dusted her hands. 'It's a nasty raw night, and they'll be cold, coming over that Heath,' she said, as if to herself. 'Good evening, sir,' she added, apparently seeing Mr Challis for the first time, and disappeared through the door at the end of the hall which led to the servants' quarters.

Mr Challis looked disapprovingly at the fire, which, in a grate that size, was necessarily upon a lavish scale. He kept a sharp eye upon the household expenses, for he was fond of money and had a strong sense of its value, and it pained him to see a fire alight when the central heating was working. It was true that it was not working well, and that Westwood was a very large and awkward house to warm; still, to light a fire at all had been an act of disobedience, a defiance of his express orders. Grantey frequently made such sallies. If she had not been such an old servant (she had been with Seraphina's family for forty years) and if domestic help had not been so difficult to obtain nowadays, he would have taken a firmer stand with her; much firmer. And Mr Challis took up the evening paper and stood by the fire, studying its pages and warming his legs.

Seraphina did not go down into the kitchen, because Grantey was in charge there and everything would be in order, but she glanced into the morning-room, which the family had used as a dining-room since the war. A tiny dark woman in a black overall was moving about, setting the table.

'Good evening, Zita,' smiled Seraphina, and immediately prepared to depart.

'Goot efening, Mrs Challis,' said the little creature eagerly, and her eyes brightened and grew moist, and over her incredibly sensitive and mobile face, whose expression changed several times a minute, there passed a look of shy and mournful pleasure.

'Everything all right?' inquired Seraphina.

'Everythink. Except dot I am so sad. But you do not want that I tell you about it,' and her face became extinguished, as if someone had blown it out.

'Not now,' said Seraphina firmly, 'but I'm sorry to hear you're sad again.'

'I am always sad, but it is nodding, and I do not wish to worry you, Mrs Challis. It is somesing Mrs Grant say to me.'

'I'm sure she didn't mean it.'

'Dot is what make it so hurtful, Mrs Challis. I am not like you English. I feel it in my heart,' and she spread a surprisingly youthful little hand upon her bosom, 'I *feel* and I *feel*.'

'Never mind, Zita. There's a lovely concert on the wireless to-night at eight o'clock. Drop everything else, and be sure you don't miss it.'

'Oh *sank* you, Mrs Challis! Dot is goot! I shall enjoy much to hear it. It will make my heart cry, and I shall then be better. Ach! – no – I forget – I haf to go out and make a speech.'

'Oh – too bad. We –' and Seraphina smiled radiantly and went away, thinking: poor little beast, but really she is a trial.

The staff of Westwood, like that of every other big house in Great Britain, had been much reduced by four years of war, and at present most of the rooms were shut up, while the family lived in two or three of them and were waited upon by Grantey, her brother Cortway, who drove the car, and Zita Mandelbaum, one of a series of refugee mother's helps. Grantey had a reserve of daily women in the neighbourhood who still came in to scrub and polish, but their ranks were thinning steadily as the British Restaurants and part-time work in local factories lured them away, and it was a source of constant – though silent – anxiety to her lest one day she should be left entirely without help for 'the rough.'

Before the war Grantey had been cook-housekeeper, and had

kept a parlourmaid, housemaid and kitchen-maid contented and in order, while Cortway looked after Mr Challis's clothes as well as carrying up coals and cleaning the car. But slowly the orderly hierarchy had crumbled; the kitchen-maid, who was the humble but necessary keystone of domestic efficiency, was tempted by an offer to do bookbinding in the firm which employed her uncle, and left; the parlourmaid and housemaid refused to prepare vegetables or to undertake any of the rough kitchen duties, and while they were still working under protest, they were both called up. Grantey understood their reluctance to depart from the duties for which they had been trained, but deplored their unadaptability; she herself had begun as a maid in the Braddon nurseries, but was so devoted to her Miss Seraphina that in the course of years she had become more than willing to perform any duties that the perilous and changing times might make necessary. She was a natural servant, performing all her tasks with conscientiousness and perfection; and knowing her keenest pains and pleasures through the fortunes of the family which she served.

Neither household realized that if anything serious happened to Grantey their comfort would collapse.

8

Zita went on laying the table, arranging the wine-glasses and thin, ancient silver spoons and forks with the pleasure which beautiful objects always gave to her beauty-loving nature. Although she looked much older, she was only twenty-three, and although her nose was long and she had a moustache, she was never without a lover; a large and spotty, or small and sallow, young man with whom she would hold interminable conversations in the Old Vienna Café at Lyons Corner House on her afternoons off. She never had any difficulty in acquiring or changing her admirers, and she was always in a state of indecision, indignation, apprehension and general ferment about them. She was easily hurt and easily moved, but she was far from always coming off worst in the scenes with her followers; indeed, as they were also easily hurt and easily moved, she often came off best; and fat letters would arrive for her on the day after one of these scenes, beginning, 'Zita –' and covering twelve pages with spiky handwriting and recriminations, or a stiff masculine voice would demand on the telephone to speak to 'Miss Mandelbaum, pliss, if iss conwenient,' and when she came, it would melt into abject apologies.

A nature which puts such zest into all its activities cannot truthfully be described as unhappy, and although Zita (if anyone should be rash enough to question her and thus open the floodgates) always said that she was unhappy, she was not always so. When she was happy she was very happy; she both melted and shone, like a boiled sweet left in the sun. Music made her happy, and sitting up very late at night talking about herself, and the casual notice of the Niland children. The beauty of Westwood was always new and delightful to her, and so were the beauty and the kindness of Mrs Challis, for whom she had an adoration. She considered Mr Challis, to whom she had not spoken more than a dozen times, to be the wisest, noblest and most gifted of men, and Alexander's pictures moved her to loud exclamations of pleasure.

She belonged to a Free German Club with headquarters in Swiss Cottage, and there she would go on most evenings after dinner, heedless of the blackout and the difficulty of the cross-country journey, often having to walk home because she had missed the last bus.

Grantey crossly dismissed her as mad, but admitted that she worked hard and could make a few branches and some leaves look ever so nice in a vase, and lay a table nicely, too. In Grantey's eyes she was such a bird of passage in Westwood, so like all the other refugees who had worked there for a little while and then departed, that she was hardly a person at all.

But there was one point upon which Grantey treated Zita with respect and pity. Her family had lived in Hamburg, and when she spoke of them, and of what had happened to them, Grantey would press her lips together and work faster and faster at whatever she was doing, until at last she would burst out with, 'Never mind, Zita my girl, the mills of God grind slowly but they grind exceeding small, and as sure as my name's Alice Grant, that wicked man will have to pay for what he's done,' and then she would give Zita a quick pat on her thin shoulder and in a moment tell her to make herself a cup of coffee.

But what Zita missed most at Westwood was a confidante. She came from a large, affectionate, talkative family with many girl cousins and relations to whom she had been able to pour out her joys and troubles, and at Westwood there was no one who wanted to listen to her. No one liked sitting up over a dying fire until one in the morning, making fresh coffee and talking and talking and talking; people were always saying that it was time they turned in, had their beauty sleep, went off to Bedfordshire, and they tended to keep their joys and sorrows to themselves and expected Zita to do likewise. She found this hard to do, and although she met plenty of Tonis and Trudas at the Free German Club in whom she could confide, it was not like having someone close at hand.

In the kitchen, Grantey and her brother, Douglas Cortway, were preparing dinner. Here Science was harnessed in the service of Gastronomy, and amid the elaborate and expensive machines Grantey and Cortway moved about like two obstinate secretive gnomes whom there was no pleasing. Both were small, and both were thin and elderly, and their grey hair was brushed back in the same way, and their lips were pressed together in the same disapproving line.

Grantey was stirring a sauce at the stove, while Cortway polished a little silver shell designed for holding salt.

'I saw that Miss Steggles to-day,' said Grantey presently.

'You did? Where was that?'

'Getting off the bus this evening. She didn't see me, and I was over the other side of the road or I'd have gone up and spoken to her. She's a nice young person. Not like some of them. I liked her way with the children, too. I wonder how she's getting on with that teaching in her new school.'

'You ought to ask her in for a cup of tea some time.'

'Oh well, I don't know about that,' answered Grantey with reserve. 'We'll see when the better weather comes. I've got plenty to do just now, with all this knitting and making things for the new one. Miss Seraphina said she wanted the Spanish dish for the mussels; I'll go and get it. Here, you can be getting on taking the beards off these here creatures,' and she untied a small sack smelling pungently of the sea, and poured a stream of muddy dark-blue mussels into some fresh water.

'Wonder if you'll ever be sending up oysters again,' said Cortway, beginning to wash the shellfish.

'These are a quarter the price and just as nice – if you like them. They were Mr Alexander's idea, they were. The water's just on boiling,' and Grantey went out to a cupboard in a stone passage beyond the kitchen, where the light was faintly reflected on rows of glittering shallow champagne glasses and big bulbous brandy glasses, odd cups encrusted with gilt mouldings and pink roses or banded with plain gold, and all manner of quaint French and German and Italian pottery which were spoils of the Challises' travels.

'Here you are,' she said, bringing in a large round shallow dish whose copper lustre glowed over a dark-blue pattern.

'These won't take long,' said her brother, putting the mussels into the boiling water.

'Well, this time the day after to-morrow I'll be at Harpenden,' he went on, for he was fond of talking, and one of his grievances against Zita was that when she was present he did not get a word in edgeways. 'Wonder if I'll have as easy a journey as I did last time.'

'Going on the Thursday I expect you will. They ask you to go on a Thursday.'

He nodded. 'I'll get that letter off to Mother this evening. I expect she'll be all on about not giving her longer notice. I can't help it; there's always such a lot to do.'

The brother and sister took it in turn to pay a monthly visit to their aged mother, who lived in a tiny cottage on the outskirts of Harpenden in Hertfordshire on the allowance which they sent her from their wages and her old-age pension. She was nearly ninety, and of a lively and adventurous turn of mind and body, and never hesitated to rebuke them sharply if they failed to pay the strictest attention to her instructions and comfort. She liked to know at least a week in advance when to expect her son or daughter, in spite of the fact that the visits had been an unvarying custom for fifteen years. Seraphina and her children and the little Nilands all took a feudal interest in old Mrs Cortway, and every Christmas she sent the children hideous pen-wipers made of black and purple wool.

'Well, I'm sure I hope there won't be a raid while you're gone, for *I* can't work that old stirrup-pump,' said Grantey (Cortway was Number 1 on a party which included Mr Challis and Zita; they were responsible for the defence of the helpless, ancient, beautiful mansion should incendiary bombs set it on fire).

'They won't come while I'm away; I've asked them not to. There you are, that's the lot,' and he began expertly on the bearding of the mussels.

Upstairs, Alexander and his friends had arrived, and were warming themselves at the fire in the hall, a necessary proceeding after their walk across the dark, cold Heath. Alexander, apart from his liking for good food, never noticed if he were uncomfortable or not, and it never occurred to him to alter his plans with a view to his greater ease; it was quickest to walk across the Heath to Highgate, and so he walked; the reluctant Americans accompanying him, with Earl trying to figure out the exact psychological motive for this disagreeable excursion and Lev sardonically resigned to whatever might happen. But when they reached the house, their journey seemed more than worth while to them both. Earl, as he stood warming himself and gazing about the hall, was already planning a letter to his mother and sisters describing this stately home of England, while the half-Jewish Lev's sensuous love of beauty was instantly charmed.

'You certainly have a beautiful home here, Mr Challis,' said Earl. 'It is a privilege to see it.'

'Charming of you to say so,' retorted Mr Challis drearily. 'Sherry?'

Earl would have preferred a whisky-and-soda, but did not like to say so. Lev, however, said easily, 'I'd rather have a highball, if that's O.K. by you.'

'Of course,' said Mr Challis, thinking what an unpleasant language American was; at once low, confusing and illogical. As he poured out the drink he was wondering why on earth Alex had brought these two dull young men here, and also making a mental note to tell Seraphina to tell Hebe to tell Alex not to do it again. It would be an exhausting evening, wasted in trying to entertain them, and he would otherwise have spent it in working on *Kattë*. Their obvious admiration for his home did not disarm or touch him, for he was used to such demonstrations, and as it seemed natural to him that a man of genius should live in a house worthy of him, he took Westwood's graces for granted.

However, he was a gentleman by birth and education and this evening he was a host, so he exerted himself, and asked Earl how long he had been in England, and whether he did not find the climate trying, and soon there was a general conversation between the Challises and Alexander and Earl, but Lev did not take much part in it.

As he sat in a great chair, made from oak so ancient that it was black, with back and seat padded by a tapestry of large red roses and green leaves worn threadbare in the passing of three hundred years, he was thinking about the room in New York in which he had grown up; with the smell of the chemicals which his father used in the photographic business permeating the close air of the apartment, and the clang of the elevated railway sounding always in his ears, and its lights gliding at night across the dark, hot room in which he slept.

It's queer, he thought (as he leant back in the chair which a cousin of the infamous Duke of Buckingham had given to an ancestor of Mr Challis), how different places can be. If anyone'd asked me when I was a kid if I thought I'd ever hit the high spots I'd have said, sure I will, and meant it too, but I never figured on being in a place like this. I didn't know there were such places outside of the movies. And yet it isn't like on the movies, either. It's smaller.

And he sat there, with his small melancholy dark eyes hardly moving except to turn from one lovely and ancient object to the next, with his long legs in their pale drill trousers extended on a rug from Persia whose faint reds and greens blended with the English roses on the great chair, and the Duke of Buckingham's cousin himself could not have kept more still or seemed more reserved.

Cortway came in and announced dinner and then retired, for nowadays they waited on themselves.

Mr Challis conversed with everybody in his musical voice as if from an immense height on the top of a mountain on a very cold day, though what he said was not noticeably dictatorial or condescending, and Seraphina laughed and talked and was like the sun in the valley. Lev could not take his eyes from her, although he kept in self-defence a sarcastic half-smile on his lips. Earl led the conversation round to books, for he was sure that so cultured a man as his host must like to talk about books.

'In the intervals of my military dooties,' said Earl, smiling round upon the company with a display of superb teeth, 'I have been reading, I might almost say studying, a book by a famous modern Chinese philosopher, Lin-Yutang. Have you come across *The Art of Living*, Mr Challis?'

'A bold title,' said Mr Challis. 'Yes, I have glanced at it.'

'Isn't he the man who says we all ought to be old rogues?' inquired Seraphina. 'I think it's a divine idea myself; I'm *too* ready to be an old rogue.'

'It is essentially a masculine philosophy,' said Earl, turning to her and looking shyly into her laughing face for some likeness to Hebe. 'I cannot imagine it applying to – to – ladies.' (He had not liked to say 'your sex, Mrs Challis.')

'Oh, do you mean you can't imagine women sitting around being old rogues while other people do all the work? I think you're *too* right, myself, most women are *never* happy unless they're being martyrs, don't you think? But I'm sure I'm a *natural* old rogue.'

'So is Hebe, I think,' observed Mr Challis, with a smile suggesting a gleam of sunlight upon a glacier.

'Oh – I can't admit that!' said Earl, laughing and going red, and flashing his spectacles from one to another. 'Alex, can you admit that?'

'Hebe? I should think so. I haven't read it, but I think it describes her very well,' said Alexander absently. 'Seraphina, aren't these *real* pea-nuts?'

Seraphina made a graceful gesture towards Lev. 'Yes. *Aren't* they divine? I'd forgotten how good they were. Lev brought them.' And her large eyes danced kindly upon him.

'Would you like some chocolate?' he asked. 'I can get some if you would.' His deep musical voice was not congruous with his unprepossessing face.

'*I* daren't eat it, though it's *too* sweet of you, but my grand-children would adore it,' said Seraphina, who had no false shame about Barnabas and Emma. (Mr Challis refrained from outward wincing, but inwardly he winced hard.)

'I bombed them up this evening with candies,' said Lev.

'It's too angelic of you,' said Seraphina. 'They always eat all their ration in one go, and then poor Alex's too. Hebe won't let them have hers.'

'I don't mind,' said Alexander seriously.

At this moment Zita came in with coffee. She made better

coffee than anyone in the house; far better than Mr Challis, who went to the most terrific pother with special earthenware saucepans from Paris and a very difficult sort of chicory that no one else had ever heard of, and exact calculations as to when to add the coffee to the water, and goodness knows what, and then produced a correct but unexciting beverage hardly worthy of all the fuss. Zita boiled water in a little black saucepan, and then threw in handfuls of coffee, saying carelessly, 'It is easy – you chust make it strong enough,' and out came a blazing-hot, fragrant black liquid worthy of Brillat-Savarin at his best. This annoyed Mr Challis, and Grantey said it was a waste of coffee.

'Thank you, Zita,' smiled Seraphina, and went on, as she began to pour out the coffee into Japanese eggshell cups decorated with gilt flowers and grey birds, 'no one makes such good coffee as Zita. These Americans have come all the way from New York and Swordsville, Ohio, just to taste your coffee, Zita. Aren't you flattered?'

'Oh, Mrs Challis! You are choking!' exclaimed Zita, her eyes moist with delight and her face changing with emotion as she glanced eagerly from the smiling Earl to the unsmiling Lev.

'Not a bit of it. Isn't that so?' to Lev.

'Sure,' he nodded, taking his cup from Zita and smiling unwillingly down at her. He was not attracted. How well he knew that quivering responsiveness of the German Jewess! But she'd bawl you out if she got mad, he thought, sipping the coffee. Now this Challis dame, she's got class, and she'd never bawl you out. She'd laugh all the time, even – I like a dame that laughs.

'Zita?' said Seraphina, with the coffee-pot poised over a cup. 'You'll stay and have some?'

'Oh, no thank you, Mrs Challis. I haf to go to my club, dey expect me. I am to make a speech this efening.'

'Is that so?' said Earl respectfully. 'May I ask what is the naturr of your club?'

'It is the Free German Club in Swiss Cottage. I go dere two three times in a week. We read papers and haf discussion. Dis efening I open a discussion on Stresemann.'

'Should be vurry interesting,' said Earl. 'Maybe I'll have the pleasure of hearing you some time.'

'Dot iss very kind of you, but I am not good speech-maker. Still, I do my best. Now I must go. Good night, Mrs Challis, sank you. Mr Challis. Mr Niland. American soldiers. Good night.' At each name she put out her hand and each person had to give it a little shake, and when she came to the 'American soldiers' she smiled at her small joke, and they smiled too, while Earl wrung her hand almost painfully. Then she hurried away, leaving a pleasant impression.

'She's a good little soul,' murmured Seraphina, lighting a cigarette at the flame Lev held out for her, 'and rather wonderful, too. Her people are Jewish. They lived in Hamburg, and – oh well, it's a beastly story.'

They were all silent for a moment, watching the smoke from their cigarettes or staring at the floor.

'Well, that's what *we're* here for,' Earl said brightly at last.

'You may be. I'm here because I got caught in the draft,' said Lev, very dryly. 'Mrs Challis, I hate to break up the party, but Earl and me haven't got a late pass to-night. Thank you for a vurry pleasant evening, but we'll have to be going: is there any chance of a taxi around here?'

'Just stand in the middle of the road and shine a torch on your uniform,' said Seraphina.

Mr Challis, who often had trouble with war-time taxi-drivers because of his remote and haughty manner, looked annoyed, but everyone else laughed and Lev thought again how lovely – in the American sense of the word – his hostess was.

'Well,' observed Earl as he and his friend were riding homewards, 'in my opinion we have passed a most instructive evening, as well as a mighty pleasant one. It is a privilege not many G.I.s get, to be received as guests in a real histawrical English home.'

Lev said, in the slow voice that meant he was thinking something out, 'Oh, sure. They were swell. But that joint – when I think about what most places are like, most places you and I've been in all our lives, well, maybe not you so much, but me – I get mad thinking about it. It's got class, anyone can see that, but it's dead on its feet, too.' He was silent again for a moment. Then he said suddenly, 'But it has got class. It's beautiful.'

9

As Margaret travelled home in the bus every evening, she was conscious of the enormous labyrinth of dark streets stretching away on all sides until it ebbed out in the little houses and unmade roads under the Downs in the south and the Chiltern Hills in the north, and it seemed to her that danger, the danger that had always lurked in the alleys and old houses of London but which had been banished into a few dark, poor neighbourhoods by the modern street-lighting and the modern police-force, had returned to the whole city with the coming of the blackout. The stealthy footfalls and muffled figures that haunted the pages of old novels were reappearing in this battered London of the nineteen-forties: again murders were done in the dark, and people waited until there was moonlight before going to dine at one another's houses, just as they used to do two hundred years ago. Those words of Winston Churchill's, *a darkness made more sinister by the lights of a perverted science*, returned to her again and again as she watched the searchlights sweeping and probing the dull night skies; and although there was a fearful fascination in her mood and her thoughts, she was relieved to open the front door every night and step into the ordinary, brightly lit hall of her home, and to shut away the silent, darkened city with its endless maze of houses. It is an underground life that we live, and I have escaped out of the maze by going to ground in it, she would think, as she stood, letting her hat fall from her hand while she gazed unseeingly into space, and she longed for the spring to come with long blue twilights and the almond blossom budding along the leafless branches.

Then she would go slowly upstairs, thinking of the feast of pleasures and sightseeing that would unfold before her when those light evenings came; the music that she would hear and the theatres she would go to, and the bright rough surfaces of the pictures in the art galleries that she would visit on Saturday afternoons.

The school was situated in a peculiarly depressing neighbourhood which had once been a handsome, stately residential quarter but was now rapidly deteriorating into a slum. The houses were large and solid, with fifty stairs from their front gardens to their attics, and their grey or cream façades were now discoloured and peeling. They no longer had railings or gates to protect their privacy, and their large windows were either boarded up because they had been blown in by blast, or covered with strips of paper. Cats and dogs and children darted in and out of the defenceless gardens, and trod down what little grass survived, and fragments of newspaper blew into the dusty hedges of privet or laurel, and lodged there until they became yellow with age. Behind the dark windows glimpses of objects in the rooms, as if in an aquarium, could occasionally be obtained; a large bronze statuette of three girls in peasant dress, or an elaborately carved overmantel laden with vases filled with artificial flowers; or, more rarely, a shelf of books that looked as if they were loved and read, and hyacinths growing in a glass.

Margaret tried not to let her thoughts dwell upon the number of ugly and useless objects that must be collected together in the square half-mile of Curtis Park, Highbury, for the picture depressed her and actually made her feel physically confused. She hurried every day through those long, graciously curved avenues and crescents, for the ghost of the leisurely, spacious, orderly Victorian life that haunted them had no power over her imagination.

The numbers of the Anna Bonner School for Girls had

increased considerably since its return to London from Worthing, where it had established itself in two large houses belonging to an elderly relation of its founder. Many of the secondary schools were still evacuated, and pupils who would have gone to them went to the Anna Bonner instead; as a result, it now had nearly two hundred girls, and still they came. The houses on either side of the school building (which suggested a chapel, with its rusticated stones and heavy gables) had been taken over to accommodate the new pupils, and the classes had grown so large as seriously to reduce the amount of individual attention that could be given to each girl. As individual attention was one of the traditions of the school, Miss Lathom, the headmistress, had set herself to deal with the problem by making two extra forms, consisting of the overflow from other classes, and putting two new mistresses in charge of them. One of these mistresses was Margaret.

The type of child which attended the Anna Bonner had changed in the twenty-six years that had elapsed since the First World War. The school had begun as a private venture in the 'eighties, modelled upon the famous Frances Mary Buss Schools in Camden Town, and its first pupils had been the daughters of prosperous shop-owners, dentists, business men, or Civil Servants, with a few doctors and parsons; but as the years passed, and Highbury and Curtis Park steadily deteriorated and the big handsome houses were turned into flats and then into tenement houses and the doctors and dentists made money and moved away to newer and more fashionable suburbs, the differences between the Anna Bonner and the secondary schools became less marked.

The Anna Bonner, faced with prospective pupils growing up in a neighbourhood that was still attractive to new, if poorer residents, because of its big gardens and wide roads, was forced to open its doors to anyone who could pay its fees and struggle through its entrance examination. Its name as a private school (though it now had a board of governors and was grateful for some help from the Board of Education) gave it the slight extra prestige sought by ambitious parents and it had traditions and customs that made it a little different from the secondary schools.

But the girls were not the ladylike little creatures of 1918, who never took off their hats in the street or talked loudly in the trams because Anna Bonner girls did not do those things. They were sturdy young amazons who played in shorts on games days, and cheeked the Air Cadets at the street corners on their way home from school; they went to the cinema regularly two or three times a week as a habit, and knew the number of husbands owned by every film star. Their fathers were shop assistants, linotype operators or wireless engineers, with a sprinkling of skilled factory workers.

Miss Lathom, the headmistress, thought that the new type of Anna Bonner girl had some excellent qualities. She was less sentimental and quarrelsome than her mother, attending the school at the same age, had been. She had more sense of humour, and she took (perhaps because the school compelled her to take) more interest in public affairs. It was the fault of her home, rather than of herself, that the Anna Bonner found it more difficult each year to impose upon her the qualities of *Conscientiousness, Concentration and Courtesy* upon which the founder had based the school tradition.

Margaret found these quick, casual, bright-faced Londoners noticeably different from the children of Lukeborough, but she was not so nervous of them as might have been expected. She was neither timid nor self-conscious except when in the company of people like Hebe Niland, who possessed all that she most wanted and were all that she most desired to be, and in the presence of these Cockneys, perhaps the least impressionable class in the world, she was efficient, firm and successful. They were more impressed by personality than by any other human quality, because it was the quality they looked for and admired in the cinema stars; and she had enough personality to impress them. She deliberately acted a part with them; did not speak unless it was necessary, was witty when the opportunity arose, and used surprise, gravity or sarcasm to control them.

She was surprised at her own success. At the end of the first fortnight, as she sat on the dais surveying the rows of heads bending peacefully over their work, she experienced a stimulating sense of faith in her own capacities which was new to her. She despised these giggling fresh-faced children who still all looked alike to her, even when she had learned to distinguish Shirley Bates from Grace Plender, and she was scornful of the attempts at decoration in the classrooms, whilst the elderly staff seemed to her over-talkative and old-fashioned. Nevertheless, this was an old-established and prosperous London school with a reputation, and she, Margaret Steggles, at the age of twenty-three was a form mistress in it, and a successful one. It was a small triumph, she told herself; nevertheless, it was pleasant.

She would have been more pleased with her achievement if she had known how satisfied Miss Lathom was with her. Miss Lomax, of Sunnybrae Preparatory and Kindergarten School, Lukeborough, had written to her old friend and former staff-mate of the Leather-Workers' School, Croydon, and told her about this interesting young woman who was teaching at Sunnybrae, and who was (according to Miss Lomax) wasted there. Miss Lomax thought that Margaret had a future in the scholastic world; she might one day make a notable headmistress. She had a gift for teaching, Miss Lomax considered, and considerable force of character.

Miss Lathom herself was not attracted to Margaret. Like most people, the headmistress was more susceptible to charm than to force in a character, and it was an additional handicap to Margaret that she had none of that immediate friendly interest in other people which sometimes serves to make a naturally charmless person likeable. Miss Lathom (who prided herself upon being a natural reader of female character with powers developed by twenty-five years as a headmistress) knew well that beneath her too-eager manner and self-absorbed expression there were strong feelings and much warmth of heart; but she also knew that nothing had yet happened to the girl to draw these qualities out and make them stronger than her self-centredness. There is a nature, mused Miss Lathom, which will have to be crushed by tragedy before it will blossom and give forth its perfume.

But if Miss Lathom was not drawn personally towards her new form mistress, she was pleased with her work. Margaret had been entrusted with a form which included one or two unpleasantly lively spirits, and if she had been incapable of managing them the fact would have been apparent within a few days. There had been no signs of failure. Miss Lathom had happened to go past Form IV's classroom more than once during Margaret's first two days in the school, at times when she might reasonably have been supposed to be in her own room, and had been reassured by the sound of a clear, composed voice dictating in the midst of an attentive silence. She was relieved, too, that Margaret's appearance was conventional and neat, and that her artistic tastes (emphasized by Miss Lomax) did not express themselves in purple capes or very large black hats. The only unusual note in her style was the little black velvet bow, and although Miss Lathom had at first had her doubts about that and feared that worse might follow, she finally decided that it was harmless.

Margaret would have been dismayed had she known that the fate of the little bow had hung in the balance, for it was dear to her since Hebe Niland's comment upon it, and every time she put it on she thought of Mozart and music, and the Past, and Hebe, and all the people at Lamb Cottage.

She had not seen Grantey since the afternoon at the Cottage, nearly a month ago, and she had not walked over to Hampstead since. Although she frequently passed Westwood on her way to shop in Highgate Village, and always looked in through its gates, she never once caught a glimpse of its inhabitants. The windows were screened by curtains of net through which it was impossible to see, and had it not been for the well-kept appearance of the mansion, it might have been shut up. She would loiter wistfully past, trying to find fresh food for her imagination and yet not appear to be rudely staring in, wishing that the front door would open and Gerard Challis himself come out.

The thought of Gerard Challis attracted her even as did the house's exterior, and every day she found her imagination playing about him and about the inside of the house – which she believed that she would never see.

How she longed to see the inside of Westwood! Every time she passed by and gazed at it, the same thought struck her: in spite of the changes that had overtaken social life in England in the course of the past four years, and the crumbling of so many conventional barriers, and the invasion of private life by public control, an unofficial person like herself was still unable to obtain the entrance to the home of a celebrity; less able, indeed, than she would have been eighty years ago, when social barriers were higher, indeed, but the educated and the unedu-cated were separated by a wider gulf than they are to-day, and she, as a well-read and educated young woman, would have been on the same side of the barrier as Gerard Challis. She might even have been invited to a summer garden-party or winter evening *conversazione* given by Mrs Challis to the educated portion of the community in the little, isolated Highgate Village of those days. And so far as the peculiar social advantages of to-day were concerned, she was also out of luck. She was on the fire-watching rota for Stanley Gardens, but she watched with the fat efficient man who owned the greengrocery in Archway Road and a girl cashier from a local bank, while Mr Challis, presumably, watched with others in Simpson's Lane, and although less than a quarter of a mile separated their homes, they never met. It's like *The rich man in his castle, the poor man at his gate*, thought Margaret despondently. We all live in a sort of organized chaos nowadays when you might expect to meet anyone, but in fact you don't. And it is so maddening that I *do* know someone who lives in that house; I know Grantey, but I simply can't do anything about that. I don't know why; I just can't.

In fact, she was too sensitive to force her society where there had been no sign of its being welcome, even when the person concerned was an elderly servant.

She spoke to no one of her obsession with Westwood and its master, for she was afraid of seeming *escapist*. While there was agony and misery all over Europe, it seemed to her despicable that the chief interest of her secret life could be a beautiful playwright living in a beautiful house! She was ashamed of herself.

Had she been old enough to suspect how many other people were sustained by their secret lives *because* of all that was going on in Europe, she would have ceased to feel ashamed.

She had indeed hinted once or twice at her feelings to Hilda, but had received so little encouragement that she had withdrawn into her reserve again. There was no trace of romance in Hilda's early morning nature; it was all sparkling dew and cool sunlight and its few slight shadows were speedily dispersed. Delightful as such a companion might be to a deeper nature for a few hours, there was sometimes a sense of something wanting, and as the weeks passed, Margaret became aware that her friendship with Hilda was not turning out to be the unalloyed pleasure to which she had looked forward.

It was not that Hilda was so absorbed by the claims of her boys that she had no time to spare for Margaret, for she was always pleased to see her or to hear her voice on the telephone, and they usually managed to go to the pictures together once a week and often, if the weather was not too severe, for a walk on the Heath on Sundays; and these occasions were very pleasant, for Hilda was at her most entertaining when walking swiftly through the cold air and chattering away like a much-courted blackbird, or seated beside Margaret in the cinema and excitedly pinching her arm, but she could not, or would not, be serious. She would immediately change the subject if Margaret began to speak of the many topics, including her own dissatisfactions, that interested her. Hilda had made up her mind, after hearing the story of Frank Kennett, that Margaret ought to snap out of it, and she discouraged the discussion of reconstruction or religion, because it always ended in Margaret's getting browned-off. It was done in all kindness, for she was fond of her friend, and had, she thought, her best interests at heart; but Margaret was beginning to find it irritating and to wish for a companion who would some-times permit her to talk about the dreams which thronged her mind. She still loved her friend; Hilda would always have that place in her affections which is reserved for the oldest friend; the friend with whom there is often no link surviving save the twenty-five or so years which have elapsed since a mutual youth; but she sometimes felt, not without guilt, that she had outgrown her.

10

The short winter afternoon was drawing to a close as Margaret walked quickly through Highgate Village. It was a Saturday, and she was anxious to find a plumber to attend to a dripping tap in the kitchen which had suddenly increased its flow to such an extent that Mrs Steggles had become alarmed. The air was clear and intensely cold; the sun had almost disappeared behind a bloom of opal clouds, but the windows still flashed back its scarlet light and the houses, the pavements, the spire of the church, were pale and clean in the radiance. Margaret's finger-tips ached with cold as she hurried absentmindedly on. She had come up another turning than the one leading past Westwood, but (as always when she came to the village) her thoughts were busy with the house as she pushed open the door of the ironmonger's.

An elderly lady was at that moment being courteously attended to by the proprietor. She was explaining about the particular type of knob which she required to be fitted on the door of her coal-cellar.

'We'll do our best, madam,' said Mr Hudson, smiling and nodding and taking it all in. 'I can't promise to have a man there until Tuesday but we'll do our best to get it done before.'

'And remember I want a *china* knob,' said the elderly lady impressively for the fourth time; 'not one of those metal things, they bang against the wall when my maid opens the door to get the coal, and get dented, and that loosens them, of course, and then . . .'

Margaret's attention wandered and she began to look

dreamily round the shop, but she was still far from the peace of middle age, which has learned to enjoy gardening more than people, and people were what interested her, not wheelbarrows and secateurs. There was only one other person in the shop besides herself and Mr Hudson and the elderly lady; a small dark woman wearing a bright red beret. Her face was so alive with impatience that it did not occur to Margaret whether she was plain or pretty, and she was actually standing on tiptoe with eagerness; swaying slightly in her desire to attract Mr Hudson's attention away from the elderly lady, and soundlessly opening and shutting her lips as if rehearsing the sentences which would burst forth the instant the elderly lady should cease to speak.

Margaret watched her with interest which quickly changed to indignation when, the elderly lady having concluded her remarks and turned away to leave the shop, the little woman darted forward in front of Margaret before the latter could take her turn and immediately burst into a flood of speech about an electric-fuse.

Mr Hudson listened smilingly, apparently unaware that Margaret had been supplanted, and even glancing at her once or twice to confirm his own amusement as the little woman's foreign accent became more pronounced, but Margaret listened with a graver face than usual, for she was annoyed.

'I'll do my best, Miss Mandelbaum,' said Mr Hudson at last, interrupting the flood of broken English, 'but I can't promise. I've got —'

'But it iss for der party! Mrs Challis iss gifing a party dis efening!'

'I know — very awkward, and I'm sorry. But it's the week-end, you know, Saturday afternoon. My man's out on a job.'

'Dere will be no lights in der hall und der drawingroom! Cortway hass gone to see his mother, and so he cannot mend it.

Dere iss no one at home now but me and Mrs Grant, und we do not know how.'

A thrill ran through Margaret, whose attention had already been caught by the name 'Challis,' and she gazed eagerly at the little woman. She must be from Westwood!

'Well, if my man comes back before half-past five, I'll send him along, but I can't promise, Miss Mandelbaum.'

'I suppose,' put in Margaret, in her deep voice to which the last weeks had given a new authority, 'that that goes for a tap that wants a new washer, too?'

'I'm afraid so,' smiled Mr Hudson. 'It's the week-end, you see. These things always seem to happen at the week-end, don't they?'

The little woman flashed a despairing smile at Margaret and flung out her hands.

'Dere iss a party to-night, it iss at der big house in Simpson's Lane, Westwood, under der fuse he has blown out. Dis afternoon he blow out. It iss a party for Mrs Niland who hass had her baby –'

'Oh, indeed! I'm glad to hear that. Is it a little boy or a little girl?' interrupted Mr Hudson pleasantly.

'It iss a little boy. But Mr Hudson, if you do not mend dis fuse, dere will be no light in der hall and der drawing-room!'

'Well, I'll do my very best,' promised Mr Hudson, 'and for you, too, madam,' to Margaret. 'If my man comes back to the shop before he goes home I'll try and get him down to – what was it, did you say?'

Margaret told him about the tap and gave her address, but she found difficulty in concentrating upon what she was saying because she had suddenly thought of a plan which would provide her with the perfect excuse for getting inside Westwood, and she was afraid that the little foreigner might hurry away before she could put it into execution.

Miss Mandelbaum was gazing tragically at the unruffled Mr Hudson with half a dozen expressions a minute passing over her face. She opened her mouth to begin again.

'I'm so glad Mrs Niland has got her baby,' said Margaret boldly, smiling at her. 'I had the pleasure of meeting her at Lamb Cottage a few weeks ago when I took back her ration book; I found it on the Heath. She's a charming person, isn't she?'

There! The sentence was out, and she congratulated herself upon having a foreigner to say it to. She was not nervous of foreigners, and besides, she could see at a glance that this one was emotional, friendly and easily impressed.

Miss Mandelbaum nodded vigorously. 'Oh yes, she iss charming. Zo!' – smiling archly – 'it iss you who find der ration book! Oh yess, I hear all about it from Mrs Grant. You are Miss – no. It iss a difficult name and I do not remember.'

'Steggles. Margaret Steggles.'

'Miss Steggles.' She stumbled over the pronunciation. 'And I am Zita Mandelbaum.' She held out her hand, which Margaret took, and they exchanged a firm shake, smiling at one another. 'How do you do,' said Zita, laughing, and Margaret too laughed excitedly. She felt herself already within the walls of Westwood.

Some other customers entered the shop at this moment and she took advantage of Mr Hudson's preoccupation with them to say in a lowered tone to Zita:

'Look here, I can mend a fuse. Would you like me to come and have a look at yours?'

Zita's face brightened so quickly that Margaret was afraid Mr Hudson might notice it.

'You can mend a fuse!' she cried. (Margaret was all the time moving towards the door and Zita was following her.) 'But how wonderful! (I cannot do dose sings; I am der artist-type, I do not know machinery.) But of course you must come! We go now, dis minute! I take you dere,' and she opened the door and almost pushed Margaret out of it.

Ah, you needn't 'take me there,' I know the way; I'd know it blindfold; I've been there in dreams, thought Margaret ecstatically, as they hurried through the village, Zita chattering all the way. A red glow lingered in the west and below it, visible between the houses, there were woods of a dim, cold blue. A host of seagulls flew overhead on their way to the water in the north where they roosted each night, slowly moving their long wings which the rays of the sun, still shining in that upper air, touched with gold. Margaret's head was filled with thoughts of the past, and strains of music, and dreams of London's history. The vast city lying in the valley was blue; amethyst, sapphire, turquoise and a strange grey-blue that lay between spires and terraces and made them spectral. White smoke from the trains puffed and rolled up into the still, icy air. In a moment I shall be inside Westwood, she thought.

Simpson's Lane was a narrow ancient thoroughfare between the village and Archway Road, steep and unfrequented, with the wall which surrounded the spacious gardens of Westwood running its entire length on one side, and some old cottages and lofty trees on the other.

Westwood, though partly hidden behind its wall, dominated the landscape because it stood upon the lane's highest point.

There was no one in sight as the two girls approached. The light was still clear, because there were no clouds in the sky, and the house appeared dark yet distinct against the glow; among the leafless trees and in the recesses of evergreen foliage lingered gem-like colours born of the winter mists and light.

'Here we are –' cried Zita, and pushed open the delicate iron gate of Westwood.

The proportions of the house and the drive were so planned that, on the instant of stepping through the gate into the garden, the visitor experienced a sensation of privacy and solitude as if he stood before some mansion set deep in a park, though in fact the garden in front of the house was not large. Margaret was so conscious of this feeling of retirement that for the moment she could think of nothing else, and followed Zita, who was hastening along the path encircling the oval lawn of grass so ancient and close that it resembled moss, without looking at the house – whose outward appearance, indeed, she knew by heart.

But as they approached the door, which was set in a porch supported by four Ionic columns and approached by three hollowed shallow stone steps, she glanced upwards at the bust of the goddess or amazon which stood above the portico, with lovely weather-worn countenance turned a little sideways as if she were listening, and a delicate happiness filled her heart. It was so different to look at Westwood from outside its gate, and to stand here, upon its steps, surrounded by lines and curves of lawn and wall and window which were all perfect, and all beautiful, no matter whence they were viewed! She was surprised, too, by the comparative smallness of the house: although it consisted of a tall building in the centre flanked on either side by two smaller wings and had eight long windows in the central façade, the impression produced upon the eye was neither overpowering nor stately; the prevailing impression was one of elegance; that quality which the contemporary world is forgetting as rapidly as it is losing the power to create it.

'Ach! Here he is!' exclaimed Zita, turning to smile and hold up the key, and she fitted it into the lock, turned it, and opened the door.

Square, low-ceiled and lovely was the hall, and again (thought Margaret, hesitating for a moment upon the threshold) unexpectedly small compared with the impression given by the exterior of the house. As her eyes wandered thirstily from detail to detail she became unable to attend to Zita's chatter, and only wished that she would be quiet, so that the beauty of the white marble mantelpiece adorned with plumed scrolls and swags of fruit and flower supported by cupids might make its full effect upon her. Doors opened off from the hall, and there was a carpet in dim hues of rose and red and green: she saw chairs of fragile design adorned with harps, or bows, or loops of shining wood; mirrors reflecting their own gilt candle-holders; and many large brown branches and exotic striped leaves in white vases – and there, in the farthest corner, was something – oh, why was Zita hurrying her away, across the hall with its faint odour of cold marble and wood smoke, before she could gaze at *the staircase*?

'It iss in here,' said Zita anxiously, flinging open a door covered with green baize and revealing a narrow dark passage that smelled of cooking. 'I go first, you come after. Be careful, Miss Steggles, pliss, there iss bump in the floor,' and she turned on the light.

There is a point at which age, in a house that is still occupied, ceases to exert a spell and becomes faintly disgusting. This phenomenon is usually accompanied by dirt, which may serve to explain it, but sometimes it occurs when an ancient house is clean, and then there is no rational explanation. Margaret experienced a revulsion of feeling as violent as her first delight as she hurried after Zita through the corridor, and although the walls were white-washed and there was drugget upon the floor, the unevenness of the latter and certain cells and caverns which they passed upon their way, with the concavities of worm-eaten wooden staircases above them, made her long for the open air.

'Here are der fuses,' said Zita, stopping in front of a row of boxes along the wall and switching on another light.

Margaret opened the nearest box and cautiously took out the first fuse container, hoping to find that the trouble would not be anything more complicated than a burnt-out wire, which she knew how to replace.

'Have you any fuse wire, five amp?' she demanded in a brisk professional voice.

'I haf no idea,' said Zita gaily, 'I do not know what dot is, but I will go and look.'

At this moment, as if attracted by the sound of their voices, a figure appeared at an open door at the end of the passage. Margaret glanced up and perceived with some dismay that it was Grantey.

'Zita? Is that you down there?' she called, peering at them. The light from a hidden window shone coldly upon her white apron and some shelves of green and gold plates. 'What are you doing?'

'We mend der fuse!' Zita called back. 'It iss Miss Steggles. You remember her? (Podden me that I say *her*, Miss Steggles, I wish to improve always my colloquial English.) She says she knows you and Mrs Niland.'

Grantey, to Margaret's increasing dismay, said nothing to this but at once advanced briskly down the passage. Margaret took out a third container and carefully examined it.

'So it's you,' exclaimed Grantey, halting beside them and grimly surveying Margaret. 'Where did Zita pick *you* up?'

Her tone was so suspicious as to be insulting, but Margaret refused to be flustered, for it struck her that here was an opportunity to put a slight but necessary barrier between herself and the old servant. Zita, Margaret was sure, could now provide the entrée to Westwood.

'Good afternoon, Mrs Grant,' she said pleasantly, glancing up and smiling, but going on with her work. 'Yes, I met Miss Mandelbaum in Hudson's, and as I know how to mend a fuse she asked me to come along and look at the trouble here. I hope I can put it right for you; Mr Hudson seems very doubtful whether he can get a man down here this evening, and I understand you have a party to-night.'

There was just enough easy authority in her voice to irritate Grantey, and yet to 'put her in her place'; that place which had been chosen for her by her own nature. She answered more tartly than ever, 'Very kind of you, I'm sure. My brother would have done it in no time if he'd been at home, but he isn't.'

'Then I'm glad I happened to come along,' said Margaret cheerfully, taking out the fifth container and examining it. 'Ah!' She held it towards them and tapped the broken wire.

'Here we are. This is where the trouble is. Have you a screwdriver, Mrs Grant? – a small one?'

'You haf der mind for machinery,' said Zita solemnly, peering at the wire. 'It iss a gift. Me, I haf it not. But I do not care. I haf der artist-soul; it iss better.'

'I don't understand electricity, and don't want to,' said Grantey. Margaret could see that she was reluctantly impressed. 'You don't mean to say you can *mend* that, Miss Steggles?'

'Certainly I can – if you can let me have a piece of wire. Have you any fuse wire, five amp? If you haven't, any thin little bit of wire will do, but the proper wire is better.'

'My brother may have a bit in his tool-box; I'll go and see,' and Grantey hurried off, her suspicions lost in relief that Miss Hebe's party was to go forward without mishap.

Zita winked at Margaret, who smiled brilliantly. She was elated with triumph.

'Zo! Zat is better, when you smile. Your face go alight,' said Zita approvingly. 'She is an old –' She jerked her head after Grantey and giggled; then her face suddenly became funereal with remorse. 'No, I do not say so. She iss kind. But she iss old too and she does not like der new peoples. I like *you*, Miss Steggles.'

'Thank you. I like you too,' said Margaret, who in her present mood would have liked anyone.

'Good. Den we are friends,' announced Zita, putting out her

hand while her eyes overflowed. Margaret took it and they exchanged a solemn clasp. 'Oh, Miss Steggles – what iss your name?' she demanded, interrupting herself.

'Margaret.'

'Zo. I shall call you Margaret. You will call me Zita?'

'I'd love to, Zita.'

'Margaret, I haf a many sadness. I tell you about it.'

Margaret was so inexperienced as a confidante that no feeling of dismay overcame her on hearing this threat; indeed she hardly heard what Zita said, so overjoyed was she at the prospect of frequent visits to Westwood as Zita's friend.

'Oh, yes, I'd love to help,' she answered.

'Und you shall tell me your sadnesses too,' said Zita, gazing at her with a sentimental expression, 'und sometimes we shall be happy und laugh much, no?'

'Oh – yes – rather.'

'Here's the wire, Miss Steggles, and the screwdriver; I'm sure I don't know if it's what you want, but it's all I can find,' said Grantey, bustling up with her ill-humour apparently forgotten; and she and Zita watched curiously while Margaret loosened the screws and deftly inserted the wire (which fortunately was the correct sort), then re-tightened the screws and replaced the container.

'There!' she said, dusting her hands. 'Pray heaven it'll be all right. Zita, would you like to go and test it?'

'How do you mean, Margaret?'

'Switch the lights on in the hall and the drawing-room to see if they work.'

'I am afraid,' said Zita, violently shaking her head.

'Whatever for?'

'Sometimes zere is a blue light und he go *bang*!'

'Oh, that's when it blows out. I hope it won't do that this time, but I'll come with you if you like. Mrs Grant, will you stay here and watch to see if anything happens?'

'How do you mean, Miss Steggles – happens?'

'Blows out or makes a blue spark or anything. Come along, Zita,' and she hurried down the passage with Zita after her.

'Nice thing if I'm blown up, I must say, I've got cooking to do to-night,' called Grantey after them.

'She iss not cross any more,' said Zita confidently.

When they came out of the passage into the hall, twilight had fallen, and the rose and green carpet had almost lost its colour in the dimness; the long windows were dark blue, and at the further end of the hall glimmered the staircase, a broad weir of white marble with a balustrade of scrolled iron whose delicacy contrasted with the solid richness of the stone. Margaret stared at it, entranced, while Zita hurried to the electric switch.

'Ah! Goot!' she exclaimed, as the hall was suddenly filled with the subdued glow of concealed lighting, and all its colours were deep again and the windows became black.

'Der drawing-room – der drawing-room!' she cried, hurrying through an open door. Suddenly a huge chandelier sprang out of the dimness; all its myriad crystal pendants glittering with bluish rainbow fires.

'Oh – beautiful!' cried Margaret.

'You sink so? Ach, zo do I! It is goot to see him shine again. We like der same sings, Margaret; we shall surely be friends.'

The front door slammed, and both girls started as a tall figure strode forward into the hall.

'Zita? What on earth are you doing? The blackout!' exclaimed the gentleman who had entered, in annoyed authoritative tones, flinging his hat and brief-case on a chair and striding to the window. 'I could see the light as I came down the hill,' and he jerked the curtains across.

Margaret had followed Zita to the other window and was ineffectually pulling at the draperies. Her heart was beating fast, for here was Gerard Challis himself!

'I am zo sorry, Mr Challis,' said Zita abjectly, turning away from the window, 'we haf been mending der fuses, Cortway iss from home to-night and dey could not send a man from Hudson's, und so Miss Steggles came und mended dem, und we were chust trying dem to zee if dey would work,' and she drew Margaret forward.

Mr Challis's manner when he met a new young woman was of course different from his manner when he met a new young man. Now, despite his irritation, he drew himself up and turned upon Margaret, from his imposing height, his full grave regard. She looked up at him in awe, and as her gaze wandered for the first time over the faint lines and worn contours of that beautiful face, there came into her memory a phrase from some half-forgotten old novel – *'the deep blue meditative eyes that were like the eyes of the Roman Augustus.'*

'Mr Challis, may I introduce to you Miss Margaret Steggles; she iss my friendt,' said Zita.

'How do you do?' said Gerard Challis, and slowly, slightly bowed, while his eyes never left Margaret's face.

'How do you do?' she murmured.

'And so you have been mending fuses together?' said Mr Challis, his interest a little aroused by her voice and the expression in her eyes as she looked at him. 'Are you an electrician by profession, Miss Steggles?' He allowed amusement to creep into his voice.

Margaret could only smile and shake her head, but Zita laughed delightedly.

'Mr Challis iss choking! No, no, but it iss Miss Steggles who bring back Mrs Niland's ration book.'

'Indeed. Then we have double cause to be grateful to her' – and for the first time he smiled – 'although I do not quite see the connection.'

'We meet in der ironmonger.'

Mr Challis nodded sympathetically, but Margaret was colouring, for she could see, which Zita could not, that he was amused.

'It wasn't anything; it was easy, really,' she muttered.

'You found it easy, no doubt. There are few things that your sex cannot achieve nowadays. I admire you but – shall I confess it? – I am also a little afraid of you. I know that *I* could not mend a fuse.'

'You –' Margaret began, then had not the courage to continue. She had been going to say that he could do so much more!

At this moment a door opened, and Grantey appeared at the end of the hall. Zita turned at the sound and Grantey beckoned imperiously.

'I must go, she want me,' said Zita, and sighed. 'Margaret, I ring you up on der telephone. What your number iss?'

'Cranway 9696.'

'Goot. Perhaps I ring you up to-night after der party?'

'Oh, do!' murmured Margaret, and Zita smilingly pressed her hand. Mr Challis was refastening his coat, which he had loosened, and turned away to take his hat from the chair where he had cast it down, while Margaret watched him in incredulous hope.

'I will see Miss Steggles to the gate,' he said, dismissing Zita with a smile. 'It is not easy to avoid walking into the shrubbery in the darkness, especially if this is your first visit,' to Margaret.

'Sank you, sank you; it iss so kindt of you, Mr Challis; goot-bye, Margaret,' and Zita hurried away.

Margaret's nervousness was as keen as her delight as they walked together across the great faded carpet to the door. As he opened it, he turned to her once more with his grave searching look, and she experienced a delicious tremor. He paused, and glanced leisurely back over the silent hall, where purple and red hyacinths were grouped upon a white metal stand and the sprays of yellow and bronze leaves displayed their symmetry against white marble.

'There is a helpless quality, don't you agree, about a room that is prepared for a party,' he observed. 'The silence and flowers are like victims, awaiting the noise of conversation and the cigarette-smoke and dissonant jar of conflicting personalities that shall presently destroy them.'

Margaret had been thinking that the hall looked perfectly lovely and wishing with all her heart that she were going to the party too, but she hastily readjusted her point of view, and answered solemnly, 'Yes, I know just what you mean.'

He said no more, but pushed the door open and put his hand lightly beneath her elbow as he guided her down the steps. It was not yet completely dark, and the air was scented with the cold bitter odour of laurels and other evergreen shrubs; Margaret could hear the rising wind rushing through their heavy leaves. The stars were shining. Mr Challis turned to the right, along the path which curved past the lawn and under a wall with an arched door of wrought-iron. Margaret could just discern a dusky garden beyond this door, sloping down to dark trees. She wished that she could think of something to say, and suddenly, yielding to the impulse in her heart, she exclaimed, 'Please forgive me for saying it, but I do want you to know that this is the greatest moment of my life.'

'Thank you, my child,' replied Mr Challis, promptly and with grace, 'I am really happy to know it, and you need not ask forgiveness for expressing any pleasure that my work may have given you.'

'Oh, you *have*,' she assured him incoherently as they reached the gate, standing still and looking up at him. 'Ever since I was at school, I mean, I've always adored your plays; I think they're absolutely wonderful, I mean. They've *helped* me such a lot, too, if you know what I mean –'

'I hope I do. I think that I do,' he answered. 'Allow me –' and he reached past her to open the gate; then stood still, with one slender gloved hand resting upon the wrought-iron, looking down with a faint smile into the eager face, just visible in the dusk, uplifted to his own.

'Tributes such as yours, you know, are very sweet to an artist, especially when he recalls them in moments of discouragement or doubt,' he added.

She was silent. She could have stood there gazing up at him all night; but Mr Challis closed the interview by bowing to her, and adding:

'And now, good night. To descend to a lower plane, thank you for mending the fuse –'

'Oh, it was nothing, really!'

'And I hope that we may meet again,' he concluded, casting this final dazzling hope at her as he smiled and raised his hat and gently shut the gate and turned away. She could not help herself; she stood watching him until his tall form had disappeared into the dusk; then she began to walk quickly, dreamily homewards, with her mind in exquisite confusion.

Half-way down Simpson's Lane she heard a taxi approaching, and it stopped just as she passed it, and two people alighted. A torch shone on a Fleet Air Arm flash while its wearer paid the fare and Margaret had a glimpse of sables and caught a breath of perfume.

'That's all right – thanks – good night,' and the young man put his arm through that of the lady and they went on up the hill. 'Bit of luck, this, isn't it, Mummy,' Margaret heard him say as their footsteps died away in the blackout.

I expect they're going to the party – lucky, lucky people, she thought – though I expect it will be very hot and noisy with lots of people there who won't fit in well together, she amended hastily.

11

She went early to her room and sat there correcting exercise books, having had to listen to her mother's accusations of being unpatriotic because she lit the gas-fire. All the evening she was hoping that the telephone-bell would ring, but as eleven o'clock drew near she put her work away and reluctantly began to prepare for bed, deciding that Zita had been too busy to keep her promise and feeling deeply disappointed.

At a quarter past eleven she crept down in her dressing-gown and sat on the bottom stair, determined to intercept the call before her mother could come downstairs, and to explain afterwards; her father was at present doing night work for another newspaper and seldom returned home before midnight.

At exactly half-past, the telephone-bell rang.

'Hullo?' she gasped, snatching off the receiver.

'Ach, hullo, hullo, Margaret! It iss Zita here, at last! How are you, my dear friendt? I do not disturb you at your work?'

'Oh no, rather not,' said Margaret; it evidently did not occur to Zita that her dear friend might have been in bed and asleep.

'How did the party go?' Margaret went on.

'Go? It iss not gone; it is still going. Mr Beefy is home here on some leave und he hass bring some of his friendts. There is much noise and laughing, but I come away to dis liddle room vere dere iss a telephone und all is quiet to speak to you, Margaret.'

There was a pause that breathed sentiment. Margaret felt that she was expected to make some appropriate response, but all she could think of was:

'It's awfully sweet of you, Zita. Er – who is Mr Beefy?'

'He is der eldest child – son, I mean – of Mr and Mrs Challis. Oh, so charming a young man!'

'Oh,' said Margaret, trying hard to think of something to say next, 'er – I hope you haven't been having a very tiring time.'

'I am always tired,' answered Zita, with a touch of indignation which sounded disagreeably upon Margaret's ear. 'I work for my liffing and it is hardt.'

'Oh – that's too bad. I'm awfully sorry, Zita.' Margaret tried to sound warmly sympathetic. 'You must get to bed as soon as you can and have a good rest.'

'Dere will be all der washing-up.' The voice was now despairing.

'Can't you leave that until the morning? To-morrow's Sunday.'

'Oh no, Margaret. Der washing-up iss der best part. Ve do her – it – all together und afterwards we make tea und Mr Beefy helps us and we laugh much.' Towards the end of this sentence the clouds began to lift and by the final words Zita's voice positively carolled.

'It does sound fun,' said Margaret wistfully.

'It iss fun, Margaret. But now I wish to speak to you about a concert ve vill go together, no?'

'Oh *yes*, I'd *love* it!'

To her annoyance the line became indistinct at this promising moment, and when she could again hear clearly, Zita was saying:

'– und next Sunday she haf been singing for forty years. I haf buy two tickets und ve vill together go. (Go together, I mean to say.) I buy von for my friendt but now he iss my friendt no more!'

A dramatic pause.

'Oh dear, I am so sorry,' said Margaret feebly.

'Oh no, no, Margaret, it iss a goot thing I find him out. He iss a rubbish!'

Margaret managed in spite of stifled laughter to convey that she was sure Zita was well rid of him.

'You laugh, Margaret,' said Zita, sounding pleased. 'It iss goot. Too sad iss your face.'

'Is it? I didn't know that.'

'Yes. Ven I see you first I think you are a widow or some poor girl who hass been betrayed.'

'I say, how *awful*! I really didn't know —'

'Yes. So you must laugh und your face will get better.'

'All right. I will.'

'Und to-morrow we meet outside der Apollonian Hall at a quarter to three o'clock. It will be a wonderful lieder concert of Schubert und Brahms und Hugo Wolf. You love der songs of Hugo Wolf?'

'I'm afraid I don't know them. Is it very awful of me?'

'Ach, you miss a much pleasure. Nefer mind. Tomorrow we hear dem und you shall come to love them.'

Zita seemed willing to continue their conversation indefinitely but Margaret, though she found it so fascinating that she would willingly have prolonged it, feared that her mother might be awakened and rang off as soon as was politely possible.

The great artist of whom Zita had spoken was now sixty years old. As she stood on the platform of the concert hall on the following afternoon, surveying the crowded room with calm eyes, her appearance suggested that of some cultured *hausfrau* dressed to entertain friends in her own drawing-room, rather than that of a singer who had delighted discriminating listeners and Royalty all over the world. Her majestic form was covered by a dress of soft pale-green material with ample sleeves, and her only jewel was a necklace of small pearls, while her hair was drawn straight back from her beautiful profile in that uncompromising style which is always thought of as typically German.

When she smiled her severe expression changed to a sweet warmth that suggested the taste of fresh bread and other homely delights; and two portraits, which appeared on the programme Margaret was earnestly studying, emphasized the singer's charm by their suggestion that her development had been continuously harmonious. One showed her as a round-faced girl of twenty with a tiny sweet mouth and the elaborate puffs and curls of a German beauty of 1903, while the other showed the mature and still beautiful artist of to-day.

It was a friendly as well as an admiring audience, for there was a murmur of affection as Madame came out from the artists' room on to the platform; and already at the back of the hall attendants were assembling the baskets of orchids and violets and chrysanthemums upon which that unmusical race, the English, had lavished large sums of money, in the heart of winter and in the middle of the worst war in their country's history, in order that the singer might know how grateful they were to her and how much they admired and loved her.

Zita had explained to Margaret that this was a Jubilee concert, commemorating the fortieth year of Madame's career, and Margaret listened with deep interest, reading through the stilted prose translations of the songs and trying to memorize their meaning so that she need not glance at the programme during the music, but it was difficult to fix her attention, which was attracted by the many interesting faces in the audience. She was also tempted at first to ask Zita about the previous night's party at Westwood, but Zita was in a rarely silent mood, and Margaret, who did not know that this was always her mood when music was to be heard, felt slightly snubbed.

Presently there rang out upon the silent, listening air the first notes of Schubert's *Suleika*. Margaret listened with such close, such almost painful, attention that any pleasure she might have felt was lost in the effort of concentration, and it was not until the first applause had died away, and the singer had bowed, and the hush had again fallen over the room, and the first chords of *Die Stadt* sounded, that suddenly all effort and concentration was swept away in a rush of delight, and she sat motionless, with her hands lying on her lap, listening to the slow melody that wound out into the stillness like mist over the silent twilight water in the song, while gradually the towers and castle of the ancient city loomed up in her mind's eye, entranced in heart-broken grief. The sadness of it chilled her heart; night was coming down over the rippleless water without a star to shine through its blackness, and in the heart of the singer there was an even darker night. When the last chords had died away, and the applause began, she joined in it until the palms of her hands were stinging.

'You like it?' demanded Zita in an absent tone, her eyes fixed upon the bowing singer.

'Oh, yes! It's wonderful!'

'She will sing better later on, when the voice has become, as you say, warm.'

Margaret was not prepared for the variety of range and expression in the singer's voice, which had been deep and solemn in *Die Stadt*, and now was soft and tender in *Auch Kleine Dinge*, and rang robustly in the impatient masculine joyousness of *Abschied*. As she listened and watched, the stout elderly figure before her seemed to become that of a white witch who could produce any feeling or picture from the instrument of her voice, and whereas at first she had been disappointed with Madame's apparently unromantic appearance, she now began to appreciate how truly romantic that appearance was, because it harmonized with, and helped to express, the German beauty of the songs.

For what began to grow in Margaret's imagination, as the afternoon drew towards its close, was a picture of a Germany which she did not realize was lost for ever; gone with its serious innocence of roses and doves and linden trees into the past, its very memory only returning for brief moments in the minds of the few thousand people in the world who love these German songs. As the enchantment of her senses grew, she did not think about the Germany of to-day at all; her fancy was busy with a country of fresh northern loveliness where the song of the Lorelei in her river sounded above the hammer-strokes of the trolls in their mountain mines, while over the vine-terraced hills and through the deep fragrant pine forests roamed bands of young men and women, the *Wandervogel*, whose singing mingled with the song of the broad grey rushing Rhine as they carried on the tradition of the wandering musician who had so often, in the medieval world, been German.

How beautiful it all was! She felt as if a treasure-house had been opened to her, and she sat in a dream when the interval came and the baskets of flowers were brought in procession down the hall and handed up, amidst prolonged and delighted applause, to the singer.

Madame received them with a slight chiding frown and compressed lips which did not immediately smile; there was even a slight shake of the head as if to imply, 'T't! Wasting all these on me, and flowers the price they are!' Nevertheless, it was clear that she was touched, for when at last she ceased bowing and looked out across the clapping, laughing audience, itself moved in many cases to tears, she brought out a little handkerchief and did not attempt to thank all her friends, but only smiled and put it to her eyes, and stood there gazing at the excited crowd.

'Nefer have I heard her better sing,' said Zita, who was also weeping. Margaret's own eyes were dry, but the tumult in her imagination more than atoned for it. 'You are enjoying it?' Zita went on rather sharply.

'Oh, Zita! So much. I can't thank you enough.'

'Ve haf der goot seats,' said Zita, glancing complacently at the crowded rows around them. 'Der iss not one left, I think. Three weeks ago I book dese seats. Dey cost eight shillings und sixpence each.' Margaret felt sure that the last sentence was said with meaning, and a blush began to come up into her face.

'If my friendt had come with me he of course would haf paid the money again to me,' said Zita, as Margaret was silent. 'He wass a rubbish, but he pay for himself – most often.'

'And of course you must let me do the same,' said Margaret quietly, for the incident jarred more seriously upon her than anything that had so far happened between herself and her new friend.

'I hope so, I hope so!' exclaimed Zita with a shrill, disagreeable laugh, 'for I am not rich, Margaret.'

Margaret began to suspect that the entrée to Westwood might not be so easily purchased as she had at first supposed, for Zita's was clearly a moody, touchy character and her greater sensitiveness might not prove so attractive in the long run as Hilda's unfailing gaiety and common sense. But would Hilda have spent eight shillings and sixpence on a seat for a concert of German songs? Margaret could imagine Hilda's comments upon the mere suggestion, and even if she had been treated to one by Margaret she would only have been bored by what delighted Zita. Margaret resolved not to let the incident spoil the afternoon.

The songs in the second half of the programme were if possible even lovelier than the earlier ones, but gradually she became aware that their profound sadness was oppressing her spirits, and that there was a quality in these nightingales and lakes and ancient cities about which the songs were woven that chilled her blood. Beneath the calmness she detected the note of insane despair; the images of graveyards and death and pining sadness haunted the exquisite airs, and even in those which sang of peace there was only a heartbroken gentleness; the past, the quiet dead, the days when the poet was still the beloved, appeared over and over again in a luxury of beauty and grief that she found oddly disturbing; and when the singer left the platform for the last time after a series of encores whose titles she had announced in her pretty accent, Margaret made no move to get up and go towards the exit with the rest of the audience but sat still, lost in thought; while Zita briskly put on her scarf and gloves, and glanced at her long nose in a little mirror; and when they were at last out in the dark streets and hurrying towards the Underground, Margaret was still silent.

'Yes!' said Zita suddenly, 'it is all so peautiful! But dere is somesing frightening dere too.'

'What do you mean?' asked Margaret, startled.

'Der songs. In dem dere is a madness. Dere is a madman in der German cottage and sometimes he look out of der window.'

'Don't!' said Margaret; the image was unpleasantly vivid.

'Yes, he look out. I haf seen him!' She was silent for a moment and the hand which was clasping Margaret's arm began to tremble. 'Und my fader und mudder haf seen him also, und all my people. Since a very, very long time ago he haf live there, und when he look out he see only darkness und sad cruel things. Efen the sunlight to him it is sad.'

'The song called *Auch Kleine Dinge* wasn't a bit sad, or that one called *Theresa*,' protested Margaret.

'No; there are other peoples live in the cottage too, and they are not mad. But der madman, he is always there, you may be sure of dot.'

There was silence for a moment. A slight rain was falling and making the dark pavements slippery.

'Sometimes he come out of der cottage too,' said Zita with a long shuddering sigh. 'Gott help us all when he come. Now' – she gave the arm a sudden pressure – 'we speak no more of these sad things. You think I am unkind to ask for the money-ticket, oh yes,' shaking her head as Margaret tried to protest. 'I know. I see in your face. And I am sorry I ask. If I was still in Hamburg und you were staying with me und my parents, I have you for my guest and I nefer, nefer think to ask. But now I am so poor! And I am not use to it, Margaret. I do not know how to be poor, and I hate it.'

'I am so sorry,' said Margaret, pressing the thin arm linked through her own and feeling for the first time a genuine warmth towards Zita, 'I should never have let you ask; I ought to have offered to pay for myself when you first suggested our going. Let's always go halves in future, shall we? Hilda and I always do.'

'As you say, Margaret,' said Zita dejectedly. 'It will be better. Hilde? She is anoder of your friend?'

'Oh yes! My oldest friend, really.'

'You like her better than me.' It was a statement, made over Zita's shoulder while she took two tickets from the machine.

'No, I don't, Zita, truly. I like you both in different ways.'

'It iss the same thing,' said Zita, standing on the moving staircase and gazing up at her with miserable dark eyes. Margaret could only helplessly shake her head, and presently Zita's smart appearance attracted the attention of a foreign soldier who gazed at her with such marked admiration that she began to giggle.

'You know vere ve are going?' she suddenly interrupted herself to ask as the train drew near to Highgate station, 'I take you to tea at home.'

'At Westwood?' exclaimed Margaret. 'Oh, thank you, Zita, but won't you come back to tea with me? Mother does half-expect us.'

Zita made what used to be described as a *moue*, and tilted her tiny hands from side to side.

'Thank you, I come some other day, perhaps,' she answered rather dryly, and Margaret gathered that the idea of a hostess who only half-expected her guest was not attractive. Poor and plain and a refugee Zita might be, but there was no doubt that she could take care of herself.

Westwood was shut up and chilly and dark, and everyone appeared to be out. Zita hurried her in by a back entrance and upstairs and along dim corridors, and up and down dark little crooked flights of stairs, until she was bewildered. At last, however, Zita opened a door, exclaiming, 'We are here! Go in, Margaret,' at the same time turning on a light.

'Grantey has blacked-out,' she went on, going over to the window and rearranging the folds of the curtains. 'Now we will make ourselfs comfort.'

Presently they were seated on a Victorian couch before the fire, eating cakes and sipping scalding tea. The change from cold and darkness to warmth and light was so pleasant that for a little while Margaret did not take much notice of her surroundings, while Zita sat upright with a cake held in one hand and her cup in the other, looking like a marmoset and gazing pensively into the fire.

'You like dese?' she asked suddenly, holding up a cake. 'I make them. It iss a German way.'

'Very much,' nodded Margaret. 'You have a nice room,' she added shyly, glancing about her.

Zita shrugged her shoulders. 'Mrs Challis let me bring a lot of things from other rooms because ven first I come it iss so empty.'

Margaret could believe this, for there were many draperies and cushioned chairs, and it was obvious that Zita's oriental taste for luxury had overlain the austere, shabby elegance of the room's original furnishings. Portraits of lively Jewish faces were on the mantelpiece; groups of smiling girls in white dresses and gentlemen in long coats and top-hats, and ripe little dark-eyed boys; and in spite of the fact that the room could have

149

existed nowhere but in the house of well-bred English people, there was no incongruity between it and the photographs of a vivacious alien race, for there were a gilt dancing Buddha and Burmese swords and a Chinese cabinet already at home there, and they all looked like loot gathered in by English Empire-builders and set down carelessly yet harmoniously with the grey and white chintz and the worn red carpet and the red and gold Moorish curtains at the windows.

'Is it at the back?' asked Margaret. 'I'm hopelessly lost.'

'It look out at the garden' said Zita, and just then the door opened and a voice said:

'Zita? Are you having tea? May I join you? Oh no – I'm so sorry –'

And the smiling lady who had opened the door was already withdrawing when Zita hurried across to her, exclaiming:

'Oh, please do come, Mrs Challis! It iss my friendt Margaret, Miss Steggles; we haf been to a concert, and we should be so please if you haf tea with us.'

'If you're sure I'm not butting in,' said Mrs Challis, and came over to the fire and knelt down and stretched her hands to the warmth.

'Isn't it a revolting evening?' she said, turning her large amused eyes upon Margaret. 'And now there's a fog coming up, of all things.'

Margaret murmured something. The mixture of admiration, envy and despair which she was experiencing made her forget her manners.

'Don't we have to thank you for finding our ration books and mending our fuses and all sorts of things?' Mrs Challis went on, putting down her cup and slipping out of her coat. Margaret recognized the perfume of the previous evening, and to her extreme annoyance found herself tongue-tied at the moment when she most desired to make a favourable impression. Mrs Challis chatted on:

'What heavenly tea! I was nearly dead with the cold. Is everybody out? There's nobody in the kitchen.'

'I think Mr Challis write in his study,' said Zita solemnly. 'Mrs Grant haf taken the children home und Cortway iss not yet come back.'

'Not yet?' said Mrs Challis, pausing with a cake half-way to her lips and staring. 'Oh dear. Old Mrs Cortway must be ill.'

'Or perhaps deadt,' said Zita, dropping her voice.

'Oh, come, we hope not,' said Mrs Challis with one irrepressible glance at Margaret. 'I expect he'll be here by dinner-time. Well, was it a good concert? Was she in good voice – dear old thing. Are you a great concert-goer, Miss Steggles?' she added, turning her sweet flushed face upon Margaret with such a kind interest that the latter received an impression of actual warmth like sunlight.

'Not really, but Miss Mandelbaum – Zita – was kind enough to take me and I've *never* enjoyed anything so much in all my life,' she answered; with too much vehemence, she felt.

'What fun,' said Mrs Challis. 'Isn't Madame an angel? I adore her bun; she never varies it, and it suits her *too* marvellously. Oh well, there are lots of lovely things to go to this month, and when you can't get into town you must come in and listen with Zita in the Little Room; it's quiet in there and you can imagine you're having the concert all to yourselves.'

She stood up and brushed crumbs from her dark wool dress, which was fitted closely to her figure by means of intricate seaming and had no ornaments except its own folds and cut. Margaret had seen photographs of such dresses in *Vogue*, but never before on a living woman.

'Thank you very much, Mrs Challis; it's awfully kind of you and I should love to,' she murmured, overjoyed but conscious that Zita's dark eyes were glancing suspiciously, jealously from Mrs Challis to herself.

'There's Grantey now,' said Mrs Challis. 'I can hear her riddling the Esse. Thank you for my lovely tea. Good night, children,' and she nodded radiantly at them both and went away, with her fur coat hanging over one shoulder.

Margaret glanced inquiringly at Zita.

'Riddling –?'

'The Esse. It iss the cooking stove and ven you rake him out it is called riddling! I know not why,' said Zita crossly, beginning to pack up the teacups.

'Let me help,' said Margaret, getting up.

'No, no. I do it. I haf to begin work again soon, so why not now?' cried Zita, whose mood seemed to be going rapidly downhill. But Margaret took the cups which she was ill-temperedly clashing about and neatly stacked them on the tray, whilst she, defeated, stood watching with her arms folded.

'Now,' said Margaret with determined brightness, 'where do we wash them up?'

Zita shook her head. 'I shall not tell.'

'Then I'll take them down to Mrs Grant,' and Margaret moved towards the door.

'Do not – do not!' hissed Zita, darting in front of her. 'She does not like me to haf friends to tea!'

'You should take no notice of that, if Mrs Challis doesn't object. Mrs Grant is only the cook.'

'It iss eassy to talk,' retorted Zita gloomily, and Margaret (in spite of a triumph when the enemy suddenly rushed across the landing and showed her a housemaid's cupboard and sink) had a fleeting suspicion that it was.

'I am bad to you!' announced Zita, when they had washed and dried two saucers and a knife.

'Oh, no,' soothingly.

'Yes, yes, I am. You will want me no more.'

'Don't be so –' (She was going to say silly, but substituted 'sensitive, Zita,' instead.) 'I like you very much indeed and I hope we shall be real friends and have lots of good times together.'

'You are so kindt!' said Zita, weeping, and mopped her eyes with the teacloth; then exclaimed in disgust and flung it on the floor. 'You forgive me when I am bad,' she added, taking out a handkerchief.

'Well, *do* be happy again,' and Margaret rescued the teacloth. ('Cheer up' hardly seemed a phrase which Zita would comprehend, for 'cheer' was such an English word in all its implications.)

'I will try,' sniffed Zita, resuming the drying-up, and in five minutes was laughing over an arrangement to meet Margaret at the Old Vienna Café in Lyons Corner House one day next week.

It was nearly seven o'clock when Margaret came out of the side entrance to Westwood. This was one of the rare occasions of her life when she felt extremely tired, but it was not bodily tiredness; it was the temporary exhaustion produced in the nervous system by dealing with a strong, capricious and moody human personality. In return, she had had two hours of a new and exquisite pleasure – a pleasure so rare that it could truthfully be called happiness – and she had secured, as easily as picking a flower, an invitation from Westwood's mistress to drop in frequently to Westwood. But the continuance of such advantages depended upon her remaining friends with Zita, and she really was not sure if (as Hilda would say) she could take it. How very, very tiring Zita was!

As she turned into her own road, a disturbing idea struck her. 'I wonder if I ever tire people like that?' she thought.

12

The Wilsons had lately had an addition to their household; an Alsatian dog named Bobby. As was usual with the Wilsons' pets, he had been given to Hilda by a young pilot – as a parting gift when the latter had been posted abroad – and on the afternoon that Zita and Margaret went to the concert, Hilda, wearing a scarlet Juliet cap and scarlet jacket, was exercising Bobby on the Heath. That wide path which runs along the edge of Kenwood and looks down upon London was one of Hilda's and Margaret's favourite walks, and Hilda (who had that pleasure in walking even on a dull day which has increased noticeably among Londoners during the last twenty years) was enjoying the keen wind, the slow sighing of the beech trees above her head, and the glimpses of Saint Paul's dome through the mists in the valley, and whistling as she went.

Another and very different procession was wending its dismal way through the wood itself while she was walking on the outskirts. This was none other than Grantey, Barnabas, Emma, their new brother Jeremy, and, of all things, their grandfather. A number of circumstances had conspired to produce this surprising (and so far as Mr Challis was concerned, undesirable) circumstance. The Nilands were staying the week-end at Westwood for the christening party, and after lunch Hebe and Seraphina had gone off with Beefy to spend the last hours of his leave at a film, leaving the children with Grantey. Mr Challis, encountering them as he crossed the hall on the way to his study and a quiet, fruitful afternoon of creative labour, had stopped to speak to them and, never knowing what to say to children, had commented upon the weak sunlight struggling through the grey clouds, falsely saying that he wished he could accompany them on their nice walk home to Hampstead.

'Oh, do come, Grandpa; oh, do come!' shouted Barnabas, seized with one of those illogical and maddening desires which frequently overtake children, and Emma also began to squeak and implore. The baby slept, small and warm in the deep shell of his pram.

'Well, that would be very nice, I'm sure, if Grandpa would come with us,' said Grantey, fixing Mr Challis with a severe, respectful eye.

'Oh do – oh – do – oh – do!' shrilled Barnabas and Emma in chorus, hopping up and down and clawing at the luckless man.

'Hush, Barnabas and Emma, you'll wake Jeremy,' said Grantey. 'It's a nice day, sir,' she added. It was plain that she would think badly of him if he did not come.

If only Mr Challis had given a short incredulous laugh and bounded away up the stairs, patting his grandchildren upon the head as he fled, and saying firmly, 'No, no, poor Grandpapa has work to do,' all would have been well, but he did not. He hesitated, looking down at the two little figures in their bright coats. Emma had a hood edged with fur and looked like a child from some painting of the Whig Age; so well-bred, so confident and happy. They really are beautiful children, he thought, momentarily proud that they were of his blood.

'Oh yes, Grandpa, oh yes!' implored Barnabas, dragging at one hand, while Emma caught at the other.

'Well, only a little way then,' said Mr Challis weakly, but they instantly burst into a chorus of gratified squeaks:

'Grandpa's coming, Grandpa's coming! Oh goody, oh goody, goody, goody!'

'There, isn't that nice,' smiled Grantey approvingly, and Mr

Challis, still adding warnings about his only coming a little way to which no one paid the faintest attention, went to put on his coat and hat. He felt a little flattered, not realizing that his grandchildren would have been just as delighted had Cortway proposed to accompany them: novelty was all.

'The sun's going, we'd better go straight down Hampstead Lane and into Kenwood for a little while, then along the Spaniards and home to our tea,' said Grantey decidedly, as they began to mount the hill leading to the village.

'Legs a'' said Emma as if to herself.

'Rubbish,' said Grantey, 'we haven't been out five minutes; they can't ache. Grandpa will hold your hand if you ask him nicely, I expect.'

Emma mutely lifted her eyes to Mr Challis, at the same time stretching up a hand in a tiny fur glove.

'There, is that better?' he said awkwardly, taking the little hand in his own. Emma did not reply.

'Don't go in the road, Barnabas, a motor will come along and cut you in half,' said Grantey. 'You take Grandpa's other hand, there's a good boy now.'

It was a cold afternoon, but they made such a good pace up the hill that they were all warm when they reached the village.

'Perhaps you'd better carry her across, sir, she sometimes lets go,' said Grantey. Mr Challis lifted Emma with one hand and steered Barnabas across with the other. It was surprising that such a fairy could weigh so heavy and the fur of her hood tickled his nose. Barnabas tried to pull his hand away.

'Don't do that, Barnabas, you'll make Grandpa drop Emma,' observed Grantey in a detached, slightly melancholy tone. 'Oh, dear, was that a drop of rain?'

'I don't think so,' said Mr Challis, pausing on the pavement and endeavouring to set down Emma, who resisted. One or two ladies walking to half-past three evensong glanced with approving smiles at the tall, handsome gentleman carrying the quaint little girl.

'I expect you'll have a job making her get down now; she'll want to be carried all the way,' said Grantey in a low voice, gliding onwards with the pram and speaking over her shoulder: 'Get down now, Emma, there's a good girl, you'll tire poor Grandpa out.'

'Cawwy,' said Emma, snuggling closer.

'Come along, now, you're quite big enough to walk,' said Mr Challis, trying to speak playfully and only sounding irritable.

'Yes, Emma, poor Grandpapa,' warned Grantey, now some distance ahead with the pram. 'Get down at once, now.'

'You'll have to carry her,' remarked Barnabas. 'If you don't, she'll scream.'

Half an hour later the party had decided to walk through Kenwood to escape the keen wind, and as Grantey feared that she would disturb Jeremy if she were put into the pram, Mr Challis was still carrying Emma.

Stalking along the dull paths between the rhododendron thickets where the melancholy odour of autumn lingered, chilled by the shade of the giant beeches and oaks, his arms aching and his nerves jangled and disturbed by shrill little voices and Grantey's flat tones, Mr Challis had almost decided to take a high hand and declare that he had remembered important business and must return home *at once*, when between a gap in the trees he saw Hilda. He recognized her immediately, and his discomfort and irritation was complete. What! to be seen by Daphne, the sea-goddess's daughter, while he was carrying one grandchild and accompanied by two others, one an infant in the least interesting stage of infancy, and their nurse? In his annoyance he halted rather suddenly, but even as he determinedly set Emma down upon the path, Grantey said:

'I think we'd better go out at that entrance now, sir, and

straight home. It isn't far and there's a good path for the pram.'

"Ank 'oo, Grandpa,' said Emma cheerfully, running away to shuffle through the leaves. Whether her thanks were for the ride or her release, her grandfather was too irritated to decide.

'Oh – very well,' said Mr Challis. 'I shall leave you here. Good afternoon. Good-bye, children,' and he was turning thankfully away, raising his hat, when Grantey said:

'Say good-bye to Grandpa nicely, Emma, Barnabas,' and up they came, and Barnabas was encouraged to put out a limp hand. He kept his face turned away in a bored manner while saying his piece, and was reproved by Grantey and made to say it over again.

'That's right. Now Emma. A nice kiss for Grandpa. There's a good girl.'

The impatience with which Mr Challis touched Emma's cold pink cheek with his lips was only just perceptible.

'Good-bye, Grandpa,' said Emma.

'Good-bye, Grandpa,' said Barnabas.

'*I* like to be called "Gerard," not "Grandpa,"' exclaimed Mr Challis with a fleeting smile; his ears seemed to have heard nothing but that name, with its low comic associations, all the afternoon, and he resolved to put a stop to the children's using it. 'You may call me that if you like.'

Barnabas and Emma stared up at him, and it was evident that they did not understand.

'Gerard, not Grandpa; you may call me by my name,' he repeated irritably.

'But your name *is* Grandpa!' shouted Barnabas, as though making a discovery.

'Oh well, never mind now,' he said, giving it up. 'Mrs Grant, you might see that they learn to use my Christian name.' He raised his hat again and hurried away.

'What did Grandpa mean about?' asked Barnabas, presently. 'Doesn't he like us to call him Grandpa?'

'Of course he does; don't be silly,' said Grantey. 'Hurry up now, I want my tea, and so do you.'

'G'an'pa,' said Emma softly to herself as she rustled through the leaves.

Mr Challis's search was unsuccessful for what seemed to him a long time. He began to fear that Hilda must have gone home, for the afternoon was now drawing in and a few drops of rain were beginning to fall. He was just sparing a thought for the party which he had left, and hoping that they would not get wet, when he turned round a large hollybush and there was Hilda, walking quickly just ahead of him. She was accompanied by a dog and an exclamation of annoyance actually escaped Mr Challis, who liked dogs no more than he liked children. He increased his pace almost to a run and dodged right round her and stood in her path.

'Daphne!' he said, taking off his hat.

Hilda, not at all startled, looked at him.

'The name is not Daphne,' she said pleasantly after a pause, 'and don't say you've met me before somewhere because I was just going to say it to you. No – don't tell me – I want to guess.'

The peculiar charm which she had had for him was immediately reimposed by her sharp, sweet young voice.

'I know!' she said. 'That awful fog a week or two ago. You lent me your torch.'

'I had the delight of seeing you home,' he said, falling into step with her.

'Bobby!' called Hilda, turning away from him and peering keenly into the rhododendrons. 'He thinks there are rabbits in there, poor mutt,' she explained.

'He is not mistaken,' said Mr Challis. 'I myself have seen rabbits in Kenwood.'

'Bobby, Bobby, come here!' shouted Hilda, and as Bobby shot obediently out of a thicket she grasped his collar and put on his lead. 'All the more reason he shouldn't hunt for them if there are any,' she said. 'Well, I'm going home. It's cold and I want my tea,' and she nodded kindly at Mr Challis and was evidently preparing to leave him.

'I will walk with you,' he said. 'You look like a painting by Signorelli in that cap.'

'There we go again,' said Hilda, aside.

Mr Challis did not speak for a moment, for the scene was beautiful. The grey sky had a few streaks of red breaking its monotony low in the west, and the boughs of the beeches knotted against it in a darker grey had an ethereal look, despite their massiveness, where they silverly reflected the fading day. On every side avenues of glossy rhododendrons wound away into a premature twilight, with here and there a hollybush gleaming out in scarlet berries, and far off, between thickets and trees, were glimpses of cold green hills and the misty city in the valley. A bell was tolling faintly in the distance. Hilda's beauty, keen and bright as the winter air and the holly-berries, glowed in its scarlet trappings, and the gossamer sheen of youth and health was upon her hair.

Most of Mr Challis's troubles could have been traced to his thirst for perfection; he was no maker-do with what God provides; he must have perfection and here, for once (he told himself with beating heart), perfection was.

Still he did not speak, but continued to look at Hilda so intently that he stayed her from moving on; she returned his gaze inquiringly, holding back the dog which was eager to be off.

'Something wrong?' she asked at last.

He started, and a smile, youthful in its ingenuousness and warmth and almost shy, passed over his face. So he had sometimes used to look twenty-five years ago, before he had become famous.

'Everything is right,' he answered impetuously, 'and you are so beautiful!' He timidly put out his hand towards her. 'May I take your arm?'

'If you like,' said Hilda, looking at him curiously.

'Are you quite sure you feel all right?' she added.

'Quite,' he said, drawing her arm within his own, and walking on. 'It is only ("only," great heaven!) that I think I have found something I have been looking for all my life.'

Hilda was not unused to this sort of talk, though she usually heard it in a simpler form, and she did not feel so bewildered as might have been expected. Masculine admiration was of course acceptable to her, and provided that boys behaved them-selves (and they usually did) she accepted it with pleasure and gave in return her friendship, a kind sympathy and interest, and occasional sweet fresh kisses, that made her the secret dream in many a young man's heart in many parts of the world.

Mr Challis was not a boy, but he was saying the same sort of things that her boys usually implied, and she felt agreeably flattered, and thought that she and Margaret would have a good laugh over this later on.

'Let's see, your name's Marcus, isn't it?' she said as they walked along.

'How wonderful of you to remember!'

'How could I forget?' said Hilda in a tone which Mr Challis was too bemused to identify. 'And you live quite near me.'

'Yes – er – yes, I do.' Mr Challis did hear this sentence clearly, and its implications disconcerted him. He did not want Daphne to know who he was and where he lived. Something precious and new was beginning for him to-day, he thought; something which was to give him back the fresh intensity of his youth; but even the beginnings of this lovely and rare experience were slightly influenced by the secrecy and caution that he had used in his former affairs. He could not help it; he had acquired technique and finesse and tactics in twenty years of amorous-spiritual intrigue, and even Love itself was not strong enough to stifle these disagreeable qualities immediately.

'Don't worry, I'm not curious,' said Hilda, laughing. 'I shall call you Marcus the Mystery Man.'

'All men are mysterious,' he said absently, and thought – *I shall be able to work to-night. Is she going to stimulate my imagination, as none of the others ever did, so that I can create more vividly than ever before?*

'My dad isn't,' said Hilda promptly, 'and by the way, we're having a party this evening. Like to come?'

Mr Challis ventured on a fine, withdrawn smile as he pictured the crowd of dull young people assembled in the ugly little suburban house, playing noisy games and drinking beer.

'It is very kind of you, Daphne,' he said gently, 'but this evening I have to work.'

'What a shame, on a Sunday,' said Hilda. 'But perhaps you want to?' she added, surprising him. 'I bet your work's something intellectual, isn't it?' and she went on, without waiting for a reply, 'It isn't really a party; my mother sort of keeps open house every Sunday night for any of my friends that like to come in. But we don't just have pot-luck. Mum hates pot-luck. She says it's lazy. She makes smashing sandwiches out of recipes in the papers and Dad knows a man who can get sherry and things, and Mum makes a sort of punch. And we have all the best mats and china out. The Service boys like it. Everything's so rough for them, you see, and they do like to see things nice for a change.'

Mr Challis realized that his picture of her party had been unlike the reality, but this did not make him realize that his imagination belonged to a common-place type, for he was used to thinking of it as belonging to a rare one. Her next remark, however, did surprise him very much.

'And sometimes we have concerts,' said Hilda. 'A lot of my boys are ever so musical and they bring their records along, and play them on my Dad's gramophone. There's one – Arthur – he's a Yorkshire boy, he plays the piano beautifully.

'Indeed! What does he play?'

'Bark,' said Hilda.

Mr Challis could only stare at her.

'Too much like scales, Dad says it is,' said Hilda. 'Of course, we aren't always highbrow. Sometimes Mum rolls the carpet up in the drawing-room and we dance. It's smashing, really,' she ended.

Perhaps Mr Challis's voice, and something in his manner, and that slight smile which had yet been pronounced enough for her to notice it, had prompted her to give these details. She knew that he was a gentleman, and she suspected that he was wealthy, but that did not excuse his smiling like that at her parties, which were famous among her friends and of which she and her mother were justifiably proud.

She did not organize her friendships, and it had not occurred to her that benefits might accrue to her from Mr Challis's apparent wealth and superior social position. Unlike the working-girl of fifty years ago, whose desire for luxury and comfort was often the cause of her downfall, Hilda was not tempted by luxury. She had as part of her everyday life the cosmetics, clothes and amusements which fifty years ago had been reserved for ladies or unfortunates, and to which poor chaste girls could never hope to aspire, and there were so many modest and easily obtained pleasures between herself and the mink and diamonds possessed by film stars that her simple desires never mounted thereto. Therefore, wanting nothing material, social or spiritual from Mr Challis, she was able to treat him as a man and a fellow-being, and it was no wonder that he found her attitude unusual and therefore attractive.

I'm sorry for the poor old thing, thought Hilda, as they walked through the wood arm-in-arm, and she chatted to him about her work, interrupting herself every now and then to address a remark to Bobby. I'm sure he's lonely, and though he's a bit sniffy there's not a bit of harm in him, you can see that. He's so open about it.

As they came out into the long quiet lane, bordering the edge of Kenwood, where Coleridge is supposed to have met Keats and conversed with him about mermaids, Mr Challis began to feel increasing uneasiness lest he should be seen and recognized by some of his acquaintances, though it was true that he had not many in the Village and those he did have were not given to walking upon the Heath on dull December afternoons.

'I cannot persuade you to come into town and have tea with me?' he said as they walked (at his suggestion) up a lonely road running parallel with the hilly western approach to the Village. Here they might indeed have been miles from London, for the distant city was no longer visible, and the long tree-covered ridge of Kenwood dominated the scene, while the yet-wild meadows of a large private estate lay on one side of the lane and on the other there were the grounds, shaded by ancient beeches, oaks and elms, of large old-fashioned houses which had formerly been country mansions.

'Sorry, Marcus, but it just can't be done,' she answered, glancing at her watch. 'Nice of you to ask me, but it's half-past four now and I've got to get back and help Mum get things ready. Sure you won't come back and have a cup with us? It'll be in the kitchen, so You Have Been Warned.'

'You adorable child!' muttered Mr Challis, and stooped quickly towards her cheek. Hilda dodged expertly, with no change of expression, and whistled to Bobby.

'I – no, thank you, I too must be getting home,' Mr Challis said, discomfited.

'How about a cup in that bachelor flat of yours?' she said in a mischievous voice which he did not like at all. 'I'm sure you've got a marvellous flat in High View, haven't you?'

High View was a block of modern flats upon the summit of the hill, where an immense cedar tree conspired with the architect's carytids to bestow, for once, the dignity and beauty lacked by most contemporary blocks of flats.

Mr Challis only smiled in answer; if she thought he lived in High View, so much the better.

'Then will you come out with me one evening next week?' he went on, his tall head bent over her fair one in its scarlet cap. 'Will you dine with me on Tuesday and we will go to the theatre – or perhaps you would prefer a film – afterwards?'

He himself would prefer a film; he was too well-known as a theatre-goer, and none of his acquaintances were likely to go to any film that Hilda would want to see.

'Well, that's very nice of you,' she said in a more formal tone than she had yet used with him, and looking up honestly into his eyes. 'I'd like to, thanks ever so. You *are* like somebody out of a book,' she added.

Mr Challis, who rarely laughed, did so now.

'Am I? Whose book?' he said, expecting her to say Marie Corelli or Ethel M. Dell.

'Well, I don't read much, but there's a girl in my office she's mad on a writer called Ann Duffield; she nearly always writes about foreign places; they're love stories, really, only not too bad, I've read one or two. You're like one of the men she writes about.'

'Well, what sort of men does she write about?' he asked. He had never heard of Ann Duffield.

165

'Oh, rather *interesting* men. You know, a bit different,' and she gave him a glance in which flattery and mockery were mingled.

Mr Challis accepted it with the delight of a man falling deeper in love every moment, but he did spare a thought for the fact that apparently there existed novelists of whom he had never heard, whose works were read and enjoyed by common little girls. All his other little girls had had smatterings of literary taste and had yearned for him to improve their minds; they had admired the novels of Charles Morgan or quoted by heart the poems of T. S. Eliot, but he was sure that Hilda had never heard of T. S. Eliot. Well, he admitted handsomely, I had never heard of Ann Duffield.

They had by now reached the village. It was nearly dark and a fine rain was falling, and the High Street was almost deserted.

'You *will* dine with me on Tuesday?' he asked, pausing at the top of that little flight of steps between two houses which leads from the Square into the village itself.

'Yes,' said Hilda. 'Where'll I meet you? Tottenham Court Road Tube Station outside the bookstall at six o'clock?'

'I will have a taxi waiting outside the main entrance to your place of business at six o'clock,' said Mr Challis repressively, after a pause: she must learn that it was he who would make the arrangements for their excursions.

'That suits me,' she said cheerfully. 'O.K., good-bye till then, Marcus.'

'Will you kiss me?' asked Mr Challis a little diffidently.

Hilda shook her head. 'We'll have to see later on,' she said brightly. 'Bye-bye,' and hurried off into the dusk, followed by Bobby.

No sooner was she alone than she regretted the arrangement. Her evenings were precious, and even on rare occasions when she was not going out with a boy or entertaining one at home, she always had stockings to mend or letters to write or old Mutt (otherwise Margaret) to see, and she feared that Marcus's company for some hours on end might prove dull, and not worth the sacrifice of an evening. If she had not felt sorry for him she would not have said yes; he was sufficiently unlike her usual admirers to make her faintly interested in him, but only faintly, and suppose he got fresh?

Well, I can always slap him down, she thought, and opened the front door, singing:

> *'Congratulate me, Ma –*
> *Congratulate me, Pa –*
> *I'm going out to dinner with a Duke!'*

'Go on, you mad thing,' grumbled her mother proudly, coming out of the kitchen. 'What's all that about?'

'The old boy I picked up in the tube – I met him on the rustic bridge at midnight again this afternoon (sounds a bit mixed), and he's asked me out to dinner next Tuesday. *Dinner*, mark you. Anybody 'phone?'

'Jack and Arthur. They're coming, and Pat.'

'Oh, good. I'll change and be right down to give you a hand.'

'Hilda, who is this old boy? What's he like?'

'Oh, he isn't really old – about fifty, I should think.'

'A man is in his prime at fifty,' said her father, passing through the hall carrying a festive bottle in each hand. 'I shall be fifty next birthday.'

Neither of his womenfolk took any notice.

'And rather cultured and all that sort of thing. He's always telling me I look like old Italian pictures.'

'I don't like the sound of it,' Mrs Wilson called up the stairs as she went into the dining-room to set out the embroidered mats.

Hilda, from the bathroom, gave a shriek of laughter.

'Mum! If you could *see* him! Nothing is further from his thoughts!'

'Hilda, I don't like you to talk like that.'

'Sorry, ducks. But he's all right, really he is.'

'What's his name?' called Mr Wilson from the kitchen. 'Where does he live?'

'Marcus. High View, I think.'

'Marcus what?'

'I don't know. Mr Marcus. Mum, is there a cup of tea?'

'Yes, a lovely hot one left. Hurry on down and have it before you start on the sandwiches.

'Did Mutt 'phone up?'

'No. Why?'

'Oh, nothing. She said she might, that's all. She is an old misery lately; I never see anything of her. I wanted to tell her about Marcus. Doesn't matter.'

13

Margaret and Hilda were so busy in the week before Christmas, which was the one following upon the incidents just described, that they had no opportunity to meet, and although they exchanged cards and presents and a telephone conversation, they did not see one another until New Year's Eve, when the Wilsons gave a party to which the Steggleses were invited.

Margaret's family had spent a quiet Christmas, for her brother had been unable to get leave and they had as yet no friends in London except Mrs Piper, who was busy with her own family's Christmas plans, while Mr Steggles's journalist friend, Dick Fletcher, was working over most of the holiday.

Margaret had lunched with Zita at the Corner House as arranged, but Zita was in a hurry to meet her latest boy friend, with whom she was to spend her afternoon off, and amid the noise of chattering foreign voices in the Old Vienna Café they had almost to shout to make one another hear, and Margaret for her part said nothing but commonplaces, listening to Zita's shrieked account of her latest conquest with a fixed smile and a frequently repeated nod which did not, she felt, much advance their friendship.

She had made for Zita a little purse of bright felt, and was rather satisfied with her work, but late on Christmas Eve there arrived for herself an enormous handbag of black, green and yellow tie-silk, made with professional exaggeration and finish by Zita, and this made her dissatisfied with her own small offering.

'Oo!' exclaimed Hilda, fixing her eyes upon the bag as she

greeted Margaret in the hall of the Wilsons' house on New Year's Eve. 'I say! Who did you knock down for that?'

'That refugee at Westwood made it for me, for Christmas. You know, Zita Mandelbaum. I told you about her on the 'phone.'

'It didn't register, I was so rushed that night. Isn't it swell, though?' examining the yellow lining.

'Mother says it'll show every mark.'

'She would. Oh – excuse me –' and she ran to the door to greet some new arrivals. 'Go on up and leave your things on my bed, will you, Mutt?' she said over her shoulder, 'Hullo, Shirley, hullo, Pat!'

Margaret went upstairs; her mother had already left her fur coat and her scarf on Mr and Mrs Wilson's bed and was standing uncertainly on the landing, peering inquisitively about her.

'Do hurry up,' she whispered. 'I don't like to go down alone.'

The little house was decorated with scarlet, green, yellow and pink paper chains, saved by Mr Wilson from several Christmases ago, and mistletoe hung above the lights in the hall, while holly was arranged above the heavy golden picture-frames and sprays of polished laurel were grouped above the mirrors. The air was warm and smelt wholesomely of hot soup and coffee and cigarette smoke, and from downstairs came the cheerful murmur of voices and bursts of laughter, causing Mrs Steggles to frown.

'Do I look all right?' she whispered to Margaret, smoothing her dress and patting her hair.

'Very nice, Mother.'

'I wish you'd put on something a bit lighter,' with a discontented glance at her daughter's dark dress, unrelieved except for a gilt necklace and the brilliant handbag slung from her shoulder. 'It looks so funny our both being in dark things.'

Margaret did not reply and they went downstairs. She had

become discontented with her bright clothes since seeing Mrs Challis's dark ones, and her attire this evening was the nearest she could get to an imitation of Mrs Challis's style.

Indeed, as they crossed the hall she felt discontented with her presence at the party, the prospect of the evening's noisy fun, and all the people whom she would meet there. There had been a time, three months ago, when a party at Hilda's home had provided material for anxious consideration; she used to dream of meeting interesting people there, and brood afterwards over the uninteresting ones whom she did meet, feeling the impact of their personalities too strongly upon her own, as socially inexperienced people often do. But since her meeting with the Nilands and the Challises she felt nothing but impatience and boredom with Hilda's parties and her friends; it was all so insipid, so hopelessly inelegant, compared with what went on and who was entertained at Westwood!

She opened the door into a small, brightly lit, crowded room in which the heat was too great to be pleasant, where two groups of people, seated at either end, were excitedly racing to beat each other at a game of 'Subject and Object.'

'Margaret! We want you!' shouted the young soldier who was in charge of one group. 'We need the best brains; you have them!'

A groan went up from the other party as Margaret went across and joined the circle. Mrs Steggles stood by the door, glancing about her with a smile which she tried to make pleasant, and in a moment Mrs Wilson came in and took her arm and drew her away, laughingly explaining that Margaret had brought her into the wrong department and that there was whist going on for the quieter guests in another room (*as though I didn't know it's the dining-room*, thought Mrs Steggles, *such nonsense*). Mrs Wilson said 'quieter,' but she meant 'older,' and although she referred to her daughter's friends as Noisy Monkeys, it was clear where her own tastes and sympathy lay.

'Will Mr Steggles be able to come?' asked Mrs Wilson, as she settled Mrs Steggles at a table with three elderly pleasant people. 'Mr Wilson is so looking forward to a little chat with him about the war; there's nothing he likes better than getting hold of a newspaperman; down at The Woodcutter, you know –'

'Oh yes, he hopes to, but it may not be till about ten,' interrupted Mrs Steggles, who did not want to hear what went on at The Woodcutter, 'and he said he hoped you wouldn't mind, he might bring a friend. I did tell him it was only one more mouth to feed, but you know what men are!'

Mrs Wilson assured her the more the merrier, and having seen her settled and comparatively content, went away to make sure there was still plenty of beer.

The evening rolled on – 'but oh! how heavily it rolls for some!' as Mrs Hungerford points out so truly in her novel *Doris*; and Margaret found it increasingly tiring to laugh, to glance with smiling interest from one face to another, to make suggestions and jokes and to laugh at other people's suggestions and jokes, while the heat grew steadily greater, and the beer in the thick glasses grew lukewarm, and the cigarette smoke made her eyes smart; while all the time, beneath the noise and heat and laughter, her thoughts dwelt upon the mansion standing on the hill less than a quarter of a mile away; its windows gleaming darkly in the winter starlight, and within it the elegance, the peace, the flower-filled silence, and above all the blue eyes that were like the eyes of the Roman Augustus. Perhaps he was writing in his study, his beautiful profile outlined against the radiance of the lamp on his desk, while his long hand moved steadily across the paper, and behind him in shadow was the gleam of gold lettering upon brown, ancient books, the noble sightless eyes of some marble bust, the play of firelight over the rich folds of velvet curtains (velvet curtains she *knew* there were, because Zita had told her which was his study, and she had caught a gleam of crimson at the long windows). How warmly, how deeply from her heart, did she wish him a Happy New Year! – but perhaps he did not want one; his plays were all so sad.

While she was huddled up against Hilda in the warm darkness of the linen cupboard waiting to be joined by the other Sardines, her feelings found expression in a long, deep sigh.

'What on earth's the matter?' asked Hilda, who was so exhausted with heat, laughter and beer that she was quite glad to be silent for a little while. 'You'll blow the door open if you sigh like that.'

'I was thinking about a poem by Mrs Norton.'

'Never heard of her.'

'You wouldn't have. Never mind.

> *'I do not love thee! no! I do not love thee!*
> *And yet when thou art absent I am sad;*
> *And envy even the bright blue sky above thee,*
> *Whose quiet stars may see thee and be glad.'*

– and I can't remember the next two verses, but it goes on:

> *'I do not love thee! yet thy speaking eyes,*
> *With their deep, bright and most expressive blue,*
> *Between me and the midnight heaven arise,*
> *Oftener than any eyes I ever knew.'*

'It's rather nice,' said Hilda sleepily. 'Go on.'

> *'I know I do not love thee! yet alas!*
> *Others will scarcely trust my candid heart;*
> *And oft I catch them smiling as they pass,*
> *Because they see me gazing where thou art.'*

'I don't see why that should make you sigh like a grampus – whatever a grampus may be.'

Margaret did not reply, and Hilda was too sleepy to be very curious; she leant her faintly scented head against Margaret's shoulder and said drowsily:

'What have you been up to?'

'Nothing much.' A pause. 'Oh, Hilda, Westwood is such a wonderful place!'

'Wherever *is* everybody?' demanded Hilda sleepily. 'Have we got to sit here all night? I'm slowly roasting. Why is it so wonderful?'

'Because it's beautiful and the people who live in it are exciting and different. And Gerard Challis, the dramatist, you know, oh, he's *marvellous!*'

'So that's it. I thought you were very wrapped-up in Finkelsfink or whatever her name is.'

'Zita Mandelbaum. She's nice, truly, Hilda.'

'She'd better be, with a name like that. Well, I've got a new boy friend.'

'You always have.'

'Ah, but this one isn't a boy, he's rather old really, and ever so rich. I *dined* with him last week and my dear, where do you think we went? I'd never heard of it, but it's called Jones's Hotel and it's miles away at the back of nowhere near Hyde Park, and the bill came to five pounds; I couldn't help seeing – I *ask* you.'

'That's a new departure for you, isn't it – rich old men.' Margaret spoke dreamily, gazing out at the darkened landing, where the only illumination came up dimly from the hall.

'He isn't really old and he's quite harmless and rather boring.'

'Why go out with him, then?' asked Margaret.

Hilda did not like to admit that she was sorry for her admirer, so she said vaguely:

'Oh, I'll try anything once.'

'Was the food marvellous?'

'Not particularly. It was all bits of things.'

'And I suppose you had champagne?'

'No, we had some Italian stuff. Muck, I thought it was, but he fairly lapped it up.'

'Did he kiss you?'

'Not yet.'

Margaret smiled at the picture of a gross elderly stockbroker being kept at arm's-length by Hilda, but she was also a little repelled, and her sense of estrangement from her friend increased. She said, no more than civilly and pretending to an interest she certainly did not feel:

'What's his name, Hilda?'

'Marcus.'

Margaret was about to say, 'Oh, a Jew,' when a man's figure came quickly and stealthily up the stairs, glanced round the dim landing, and darted over to the linen cupboard and opened the door.

'Ah-ha!' he exclaimed, and sat down next to Hilda.

'Hey-hey!' she protested. 'Who are you? I don't seem to know your face.'

'Dick Fletcher – friend of Jack Steggles,' he said, still in a whisper. 'It's all right, lady, I'm not gate-crashing.'

'Pleased to meet you, I'm Hilda Wilson,' whispered Hilda, 'and this thing here,' nudging Margaret, 'is Mr Steggles's only daughter, Margaret Mabel.'

'How do you do, Margaret Mabel,' he whispered, and put a hand out in the darkness which Margaret (who disliked characterless handshakes) firmly pressed, whispering, 'How do you do.' She had never met him, in spite of her father's friendship with him, and now glanced curiously towards him. She could make out a high forehead faintly reflecting the light, and the dim outlines of a clean-shaven face, and he seemed to be of slight build and medium height. His presence was accompanied by an odour of tobacco and beer which she found offensive.

'I'm going to stand up,' announced Hilda, 'or there won't be room in here for any more. What ages they're taking to come up.'

'They're still eating,' said Dick Fletcher, but even as he spoke another form came noiselessly up the stairs and was soon pressed up against the group in the cupboard, and after this the numbers increased rapidly until the final moment when they were discovered, and the hot, giggling, closely compressed mass burst into a simultaneous shout of laughter and someone turned on the lights, revealing flushed faces and laughing eyes bewildered by the sudden brilliance.

'Thank heaven, another minute and I should have melted,' sighed Hilda, pushing back her hair. 'Now, who's for more beer? Come on, folks,' and she led the way downstairs.

Margaret stood a little to one side to let the others precede, and glanced up to find that Dick Fletcher was regarding her with friendly curiosity. He smiled.

'This seems rather a good party, don't you think?' he said.

Her nerves were irritated by the boredom which she had endured throughout the evening, and she had found her recent close bodily contact with strangers very distasteful. His question proved too much for her self-control, and it was with a full curl of her lip that she answered:

'Do you think so?'

His pleasant expression changed to one of impatient gloom, but he only said:

'I'm enjoying it, anyway. Shall we go down?' and stood aside to let her pass.

He made no further attempt to talk to her, and moved away among the crowd where she soon saw him laughing with two girls. She found a seat in an alcove and sat down with a drink and a sandwich, realizing thankfully that the time was now nearly ten minutes to twelve and that in a short while the ordeal would be over.

For lack of more interesting occupation she studied Dick Fletcher as he stood laughing and talking with the two young women. She disliked him because she had betrayed her ill-temper to him, but she admitted that her dislike was unreasonable; all that she actually had against him was his appearance, which suggested the typical journalist of an earlier day, with shiny, shabby clothes exhaling an odour of beer and tobacco, and the touch of his hand, which was disagreeably moist. The fine skin of his face was deeply lined; more, she thought, by worry than by time, for he appeared to be only in the late thirties and the remnant of a brilliant youthful colouring lingered in his cheeks and hair, the latter being of a peculiarly bright brown and growing thickly at the sides of his head, but tending to baldness above the forehead. His large grey eyes were liquidly bright, his mouth long and thin and his nose pointed, with wide nostrils. She found his air of eagerness and ill-health unattractive, and turned away.

Shortly afterwards the company linked hands to sing 'Auld Lang Syne,' and after the darkest young man present had been made to step over the threshold to bring in the New Year's luck, the party broke up.

Margaret and her mother came down into the hall in their outdoor clothes to find Mr Steggles and Dick Fletcher standing with their hosts.

'I shall be all right,' Dick Fletcher was assuring them, turning up the collar of his overcoat. He had no hat and his forehead looked damp. 'No, really, old man, I don't want to put you out.' Mrs Steggles glanced sharply from her husband to his friend; what had Jack been suggesting?

'Mabel, Dick must come back with us, mustn't he?' demanded Mr Steggles. 'He's lost the last bus and it's a beastly night, we can't let him – nonsense,' putting his hand on Fletcher's arm, 'of course you're coming.'

'I can get a taxi, Jack. You know me; taxis run when I whistle,' said Fletcher.

The Wilsons laughed, and then Mrs Steggles said, 'If Mr Fletcher doesn't mind waiting while the sheets for the spare room are aired – and there's no blackout, I'm afraid – but if you're sure you don't mind –'

Her husband gave her one glance of fury, then immediately looked down at the floor and was silent. It was as if he could not trust himself to speak lest he should break into abuse. Margaret keenly felt her mother's lack of hospitality, and suddenly moved forward and broke the awkward silence: 'Do come, please, Mr Fletcher. You must have some of my special after-midnight coffee. It's good, isn't it, Dad?' She put all the warmth of which she was capable into the words, and her voice rang richly with it.

'It's grand,' said her father heartily, giving her a grateful glance. 'Now come on, Dick, that's settled,' and he took his friend by the arm and moved towards the door, followed by the Wilsons, to whom everybody began to express their thanks for a delightful evening.

Dick Fletcher, who now looked both tired and ill, said to Mrs Steggles: 'It's awfully nice of you; I'm afraid I'm giving you a lot of trouble,' and she answered:

'Oh, that's nothing, we'll soon fix you up, Mr Fletcher, if you're sure you don't mind about the blackout,' in a tone which she managed to make sufficiently pleasant; and the party, having waved good-bye to the Wilsons as they stood in the lighted hall with Hilda leaning smiling upon her mother's arm, set off down the damp, silent road. They were all tired, and Mrs Steggles's thoughts were running upon pillow-slips.

'That's a pretty girl,' said Dick Fletcher suddenly.

'Isn't she!' said Margaret eagerly, pleased with the praise of her friend, and turning to him as they walked side by side. She hoped that he would continue to talk of Hilda, but he said no more, and the conversation was carried on by Mr Steggles, who asked Margaret what were the names and pre-war occupations of all the young men who had been at the party, while Mrs Steggles commented upon the attire of the young women.

'Since you were so ready to ask him here, you can make his bed,' whispered Mrs Steggles in a low angry tone, as soon as she and Margaret were upstairs, the men having gone into the dining-room. 'Shouting out like that – I never heard anything like it. Whose house is it, I should like to know?' She jerked open a cupboard and began to collect bed linen.

'Well, Mother, we *do* owe him Dad's job,' said Margaret in the same tone, taking the sheets. 'If it wasn't for him we shouldn't be here at all.'

'Well, yes, I suppose so,' said Mrs Steggles grudgingly. 'As a matter of fact, I'd forgotten that. But what I'm complaining about is *you* taking it on *yourself* to ask him here.'

Margaret suddenly put an arm round her shoulders and gave her a quick kiss.

'You know you don't really mind!' she said.

'That's all very well,' grumbled Mrs Steggles. 'There, you've upset my hair.' But her tone was softer, and when Margaret fixed an improvised blackout at the spare-room window she expressed approval. (I believe if I kissed Mother more often we should get on better, thought Margaret, as she made the bed, but the trouble is that I *cannot* kiss people unless I really feel like it. Poor Mother, she doesn't get many kisses.)

'You surely won't make coffee at this hour?' said Mrs Steggles as they went downstairs.

'Depends if they want it,' said Margaret, almost as blithely as Hilda would have done, and went into the dining-room. Both men looked up as she entered.

'Now how about that coffee?' she asked, smiling.

'That's a very good idea,' said her father cheerfully, stirring the fire. 'Dick, you'll have some?'

'Thank you, I'd like some very much.'

'It doesn't keep you awake?' she asked.

'Keep him awake? You should see him in the Reporters' Room, swilling it down in bucketfuls, black as your hat and no sugar,' laughed her father.

She smiled and went into the kitchen to begin her preparations.

'Oh dear, I *am* so tired,' said her mother, leaning against the dresser and yawning. 'Do you think I need stay up?'

'Of course not, you go up to bed, I'll look after them,' said Margaret. 'We needn't be up very early tomorrow.' (This was one of the privileges of the Christmas holidays which she much appreciated.)

'Poor Mr Fletcher, it's so sad for him, that awful woman,' said Mrs Steggles, beginning to go up to bed but lingering, as some people do.

'What awful woman? Oh yes, of course, he's divorced, isn't he? He divorced her, I mean.' Margaret was putting the milk on to heat.

'Yes. Oh well . . . I'm going up. Good night, dear. Don't be too late coming up.'

Margaret sat before the fire and poured the coffee for her father and their guest. The house was hushed, and outside there was the dead quiet of the first black, damp, starless night of the New Year. She was silent, listening to the talk of the men, which, while not profound, was sufficiently different to the feminine conversations to which she most frequently listened to hold half of her attention: the other half was still turned dreamily towards the mansion on the hill.

14

At this hour its owner was still sitting by the fire in his study, with a drink and a cigar, at the end of an evening's work on his play. Seraphina was seeing in the New Year with a gay party somewhere.

He looked much as Margaret had imagined him. His profile *was* outlined against the radiance from the lamp, and in the shadows there *were* volumes bound in gilded calf-skin, and the velvet curtains, of the rich hue of a redcurrant, *did* hang down in sumptuous folds; there was even the bust of a Roman emperor of the Silver Age, with sensual lips and ox-like curls.

The firelight played over the plaster mouldings on the ceiling and deepened the colour of the carpet, which was that worn red drugget, once of excellent quality, only to be found in old-fashioned hotels and the homes of the English upper classes. Tall green candles in massy silver sconces stood upon the marble mantelpiece, which was carved with the heads of pouting cupids, and coils of vine and sprays of curling feathers. At one side of the fireplace were stacked some large logs of solid beech, their silvery surface covered with a thin green lichen where for a hundred years the west wind had blown upon them with its burden of rain. A third rested upon the fire, with green and bluish flames just beginning to lick over its round dark sides. The time was nearly one o'clock in the morning.

Mr Challis was thinking about the evening which he had spent with Hilda and trying to analyse what was her charm for him, but he could get no further than that she reminded him of the sharp fresh taste of a young apple, while her colouring had the apple-blossom's pink and white, and her eyes the blue of the sky between the apple-blossom leaves; she even had the apple-blossom's cool fragrance. He had enjoyed their evening together, but not as much as he had anticipated, for he had by now reached a stage in vanity and loneliness when another human being only served him as an audience, a mirror, or a thurifer, and Hilda was not fitted for any of these offices. True, she had been friendly and polite and cheerful, but this was not at all what Mr Challis wanted; he was a subtle, dissatisfied adult being (he told himself) and demanded a response for these qualities in the women he entertained. She had also, towards the close of the evening, displayed a puzzling interest in his welfare; asking him in the taxi if he felt a draught, making him promise to go straight to bed when he got home, and so on; and much as he would have liked to he could not attribute this solicitude to a passion for himself. He could not make up his mind quite *what* it was due to; unless she was intensely motherly and liked, so to speak, to tuck her admirers up? He hoped not. It was many years since he had been tucked up and he had never felt the want of it.

The evening had not been a complete success, though she seemed to have enjoyed it all; even the dreadful film about two excitable young people, Judy somebody and a dwarfish boy-man all over freckles, who kept singing and dancing. Mr Challis had suffered considerably, but had passed the time by reflecting how far gone in degeneracy was Western culture. He would have preferred to take her to see a revival of *Carnet de Bal*, but feared that he might see someone he knew there, and so had deferred to her choice.

And as that evening, in which sweetness and weariness were so strangely mingled, drew towards its end, he had begun to experience a division of personality which was disturbing; he had put it down to the noise and the excessive tedium of the film. It was as if he were at once two people; his own cultured, detached, fastidious self, and another man; a much simpler man who did not care where he was so long as he was with Hilda, and could drink in the sharp sweetness of her voice and laugh and catch the blue flash of her eyes as she glanced sideways. By the end of the evening this simple man had been completely in the ascendant, and Mr Challis, after one practised attempt in a taxi which Hilda had dealt with by forthright impatience, had pleaded as abjectly as any boy of eighteen for a good-night kiss.

It made him hot to remember how he had pleaded, and he would not let himself think about what Hilda had said, and yet he could not forget it; it returned again and again to his thoughts, making him move restlessly as if under a stab of pain.

At last he got up, and stood with his arms leaning upon the marble of the mantelpiece, staring down into the fire while the light played over his beautiful discontented face.

It's no use, Marcus, I don't like you enough yet. I don't mean to be rude, but I just can't.

It was the first time that his kisses had ever been refused, and his vanity writhed and writhed again. He had the usual theories about amorous experts, and when Hilda had admitted with a laugh that she often kissed her boys good night ('and good morning and good afternoon too, if they're good'), the thought of her exchanging hearty hugs with amateurs in the Services was to him as inexplicable as it was humiliating.

He would have salved his vanity by thinking that she suffered from all sorts of peculiar complexes, but his intelligence rejected the solution: apple-blossom and complexes do not go together.

No, thought Mr Challis, standing upright with a sigh, I confess it; I cannot understand her, and as he sighed, the clock silverily struck one.

* * *

184

At breakfast at the Steggleses the next morning there was only the usual conversation about how the members of the party had slept and comment upon the war news, and Dick Fletcher did not join in it much, but he looked rested. As was usual when she had dispensed hospitality and found the experience less disagreeable than she had anticipated, Mrs Steggles was in a gracious mood and addressed most of her remarks to him, telling him among other things that now he had found the way there he must come out and see them again.

'Yes, you can give me a hand in the garden, Dick,' said Mr Steggles, winking at Margaret.

'Oh, Dad's no gardener,' said Mrs Steggles instantly, laughing, 'and Margaret's busy at school all day and I've got my hands full, queueing and cooking and cleaning, I'm sure I'm ashamed of that wilderness out there.'

'Are you a keen gardener, Mr Fletcher?' asked Margaret.

He shook his head. 'I haven't even got a window-box.'

'Hasn't your flat got a garden?' asked Mrs Steggles.

'Only about two square feet, and that belongs to the people downstairs.'

'Oh, a garden's a great joy, I always think, but it does bring the dirt into the house. I used to say to Mr Steggles when we were in Lukeborough – garden as much as you please, I'm sure no one likes to see flowers about the place better than I do, but you leave your boots outside the scullery door before you come into the house, I said, *if* you please,' and she laughed.

'Yes, it does tread the dirt in,' said Dick Fletcher, after a pause. Margaret had the impression that he would rather not have spoken and only did so because she and her father kept silent, and for an instant his face wore the impatient, gloomy look which she had brought to it by her own sneering remark on the previous evening. That thin face showed all changes of expression very plainly.

'You ought to come up one Sunday and help Dad dig up our wilderness; stay to lunch and go for a walk on the Heath in the afternoon,' said Mrs Steggles, while Margaret listened in surprise. Had her mother taken one of her sudden likings to Mr Fletcher? 'Get some of our Highgate air into your lungs.'

'It's awfully kind of you, but I'm afraid my Sundays are always booked up,' he smiled.

'*Every* Sunday?' cried Mrs Steggles archly.

He nodded, still smiling.

'Well, Dick, I suppose we ought to be moving,' said Mr Steggles, getting up from the table, and shortly afterwards they went off, and Margaret and her mother began upon their morning's work.

'Poor man!' exclaimed Mrs Steggles, after a silence, running more hot water into the basin, 'I expect it's a change for him to come into a real home.'

'Why? Is his flat so uncomfortable?'

'Oh, I expect so. He does everything for himself.'

'Can't he afford a housekeeper?'

'I don't know, Margaret,' said her mother mysteriously, 'that's just what puzzles me. He gets the same as your dad, I believe, yet he looks – doesn't he?'

Margaret nodded, bored.

'Shabby,' said Mrs Steggles. 'Did you notice?'

This was the type of conversation which Margaret disliked more than any other, and she was silent. Mrs Steggles went on: 'Poor fellow! No wife to look after him – no wonder he's let himself go. I'd whip such women, that's what I'd do – have them publicly whipped.' She scrubbed a saucepan vigorously.

'Who was his wife?' asked Margaret, at last, knowing that her mother would become irritable if she did not make some comment.

'Oh, some girl up in Birmingham. She was mixed up with

186

the Repertory Company there somehow. I don't know the rights of it; I don't think she was exactly an actress. She was *very pretty*, by all accounts.'

'Didn't they get on?' said Margaret, hanging up the damp tea-towel.

'He spoilt her,' said Mrs Steggles. 'Gave her anything she wanted and then she wasn't satisfied. She went off with some rich chap, so the story goes. I don't know. It was Mrs Miller told me. She knew some people who knew them in Birmingham.'

'Were there any children?' asked Margaret.

'Oh, no, I don't think so; Dad's never mentioned any.'

'Mother, shall I shop, or will you?' said Margaret, pausing at the door.

'I hope he *will* come here often, if he wants to,' burst out Mrs Steggles, giving a last polish to the gleaming sink. Her face was flushed and her eyes wet. 'Poor fellow! I can sympathize.'

Margaret hesitated. She had never before taken any outward notice of her parents' unhappy relationship, feeling that to do so would only have increased her mother's sufferings. But her mother had never before indulged in such an outburst, and Margaret felt that it must be because she felt a need, which had become unbearable, for comfort. Perhaps it was the renewal of old torments in a new place, where she had hoped to find respite, that had broken down her control.

Father must have got hold of some new creature, thought Margaret in disgust, and just as I thought things were getting better. It was now clear that her mother's championship of Mr Fletcher was due to her feeling that both he and she were victims of Bad Women.

At least Margaret's sympathy could flow from her heart. She *did* feel her mother's sorrow; she *did* feel anger at the way her father behaved, and she went over to her and put an arm about her shoulders.

'Mother, I'm so sorry,' she murmured, kissing her. 'It's such a shame –'

'Why, my dear – that's all right,' said Mrs Steggles, looking up in surprise but returning the kiss. 'It's all all right, really, Margaret,' she added in some embarrassment.

'You mean – there isn't anything new to upset you?'

'Something did happen last week to upset me, but it wasn't anything new and there's no need for you to worry about it, anyway. Your turn will come soon enough,' said her mother, with some return of her usual manner. 'Now, let's hurry up and get the beds done and you can get out early, or all the best greens'll be gone – what there is of them.'

How sordid it all is! thought Margaret. If it weren't for Westwood, and thinking how happy he and she are together, I'd have nothing beautiful in my life – nothing.

She was still thinking of Mr and Mrs Challis when she went out an hour later. Her nature was jealous, as was to be expected when a capacity for romantic passion is allied to strong feelings and both are denied expression, and her feeling for Gerard Challis was not so spiritual as to exclude jealousy. That first sight of Seraphina had filled her with a painful mingling of admiration and despair; it was not that she had hoped to attract his affection towards herself; she not only felt him too far above her, but also had a distaste for marital infidelity and intrigue which amounted to horror, but the knowledge that so lovely a creature shared his life, and was woven throughout his intimate being, emphasized the gulf between him and herself: Margaret Steggles, unlovely and heavy in manner, and craving for beauty both earthly and divine that could never be hers.

But even in the short time that Mrs Challis had spent with the two girls, Margaret's heart had been won and her jealousy lost in admiration, and now she could think of their mutual happiness almost without pain. One doesn't envy the angels in Heaven, she thought, as she went into the greengrocer's.

She was at once wished a Happy New Year by Zita, who was out buying potatoes, and in the next breath was invited to go to Westwood that evening to listen to a broadcast concert of Chopin's music, arranged under the auspices of the Free French and the Polish Governments in London. She accepted with delight, and the winter day instantly seemed to glow with colour and the anticipation of pleasure. She arranged with Zita to go in by the back entrance to Westwood at ten minutes to eight that night.

Mrs Steggles vaguely realized that her daughter had some new foreign friend who had a job in the big house up on the hill, but she was not particularly interested and made little comment when Margaret said that she would get supper early for herself as she was going out for the evening to Westwood.

She went; she opened a narrow door in a wall and saw, high above her head, in the faint moonlight, the bust of the goddess gazing towards the little garden beyond the iron gate. Frost on the grass, every laurel leaf masked with frost! Oh, beautiful, she thought, and went down the pathway leading to the house.

15

It was the first of many journeys along that path, for throughout January and February she was invited by Zita to attend their 'private concerts' in the Little Room, two or three times a week. Her work at school began to suffer, and so did her health, for after she returned home, bemused by the splendid sounds still ringing in her ears, perhaps exalted and stirred by a distant glimpse of Gerard Challis, she would sit until one or two in the morning correcting the exercise-books which she should have dealt with earlier in the evening, and in the morning she never awoke in time to take her dressing and breakfast in comfort, but had to be aroused by her mother, who scolded her while she was hastily swallowing the meal. In time, however, she grew used to being slightly poisoned by lack of sleep and even found that her senses responded more acutely to sounds and colours, and that her brain was stimulated by the privation.

She decided that if she chose to do without sleep it was no one's business but her own.

She found Zita's company less trying on these evenings than at any other time, for she never talked, or even moved, while music was in progress, and when it was ended she appeared at her best, soothed and calm and almost like a rational being. Sometimes when the concert was over they would have a modest supper together on a tray in front of the fire; some sandwiches and coffee coaxed from Grantey, or sausage-rolls brought by Margaret and washed down with little bottles of beer provided by Zita, but usually Margaret went straight home through the cold dark night with themes from some Beethoven sonata or Brahms symphony singing in her head, relieved that the echo of the lovely sounds had not been dispelled by an hour of gossip.

The Little Room was reached by three downward steps at the end of the corridor, and had for generations (so Zita told Margaret) been used as a sewing-room. It had a faded but still gay wallpaper of bright little leaves and berries on a white ground, which had been designed and made by William Morris, and was sunny and quiet. It was pleasant to think of women sewing here in the sunlight throughout the last two hundred years; the shadow which the seated, peaceful figure threw upon the wall changing in the course of time from a profile crowned with a mobcap to a profile with short hair crowned by a ribbon bow; the needles and cotton gradually becoming finer, the material upon which the seated figure worked changing from the lustrous stiff satin, the cotton printed with tiny sprigs of flowers, of the eighteenth century, to the thin rayons and brilliant patterns of the twentieth. In the world outside the Little Room great events occurred, and continents were conquered, and empires were built or destroyed, and the backwash of these happenings came into the sewing-room in the shape of materials, stuffs from America or Bradford or Japan; and women sat tranquilly sewing at them, while the sunlight shone into the Little Room and the shadows of young trees, that gradually grew massive and tall, danced upon its walls.

Margaret had been disappointed to learn that the Challises had been living at Westwood for only ten years, for she had hoped that the family had lived there for generations. However, Mrs Challis did carry on the tradition of this room, for there were two sewing-machines standing on a large firm table in a corner, and in one cupboard there was an Ellen Maria, or dummy, upon which dresses could be modelled, with the slender waist, rounded hips and full bosom which were evidently the measurements of some Victorian lady, and Margaret wondered very much how Ellen Maria came to be there, for she was sure that the dresses worn by Mrs Challis were never planned upon such a creature. Another sign of the room's traditional use was a little work-table made of polished mahogany, with a 'well' covered in striped yellow and blue silk for holding heavier materials, and when Margaret once ventured to open its drawer she found a nest of boxes and containers covered in faded cherry-red moiré, for sewing implements, and many reels of brilliant cotton and silk. This was the room where Grantey came to 'run-up' little frocks and undergarments for Emma, and Zita came to mend the linen, and she confessed to Margaret that it was here that she had found the materials for Margaret's Christmas present, having asked Mrs Challis if she might take something pretty from the rag-bag.

The rag-bag was as large as a sack and hung in the cupboard with Ellen Maria for company, and once when Zita was delving into it, on an evening when there was no music to which they wanted to listen, Margaret delved too, and was impressed by the variety and quantity and attractiveness of its contents; pieces of turquoise velvet, strips of black gauze starred with silver, scraps of lilac silk, fragments of lawn of a fairy fineness, and most striking of all – a ragged old Doctor of Laws gown, made of thin red cloth resembling felt.

'If I had time I make slippers for *all* at my Club,' said Zita, covetously handling the beautiful old material, 'but time I haf none.'

Grantey and Cortway did not like the kind of music which Zita liked, so Mrs Challis had had to buy another wireless cabinet and install it in the Little Room. It was a good one, for Mr Challis's meanness vanished when confronted by The Arts, and he would not permit great music to be heard in his house in a distorted form through an inferior instrument.

Grantey and Cortway therefore sat in comfort in the servants' parlour listening to their type of music while Zita and Margaret sat up in the Little Room in equal comfort listening to the late Beethoven quarters.

Music from the Little Room did not penetrate to the rest of the house, and Margaret soon abandoned her hope that Mr Challis would be attracted by the sounds and frequently drop in; indeed, after her second visit she ceased to expect to see him and only delighted in the music; with the knowledge that he was somewhere in the great house adding to her happiness.

She had from the first decided that she must take the greatest, most subtle care to keep her secret from Zita. She knew that it would be difficult, for Zita had the devilish capacity for stumbling upon secrets often possessed by excessively feminine women, and Margaret knew that if she once discovered that her friend cherished a romantic adoration for Mr Challis she would either tease or become sympathetic, which would be worse. Therefore Margaret was careful only to ask such questions about the house and its master as were natural where two such interesting objects were concerned, and cultivated precisely the most convincing mixture of respect and interest when Mr Challis's tastes and activities were under discussion.

Her desire to become an accepted visitor at Westwood was favoured by the fact that when Hebe and Alexander had been living there for the first months after their marriage while looking for a house, they had both taken up with anybody who was odd or amusing or what Alexander called 'nice' (a word upon which he put his own interpretation) and filled the house with people who might, with a host and hostess of less elegance, have created a squalid milieu.

After the young people had moved to Hampstead, life at Westwood had become more conventional, but the tradition created by Hebe and Alexander lingered. Mr and Mrs Challis were used to meeting intense young women in the corridors and talkative old men in the shrubberies, and to hearing that the strangers were friends of the Nilands, and so it seemed as natural to them that Margaret should drop in whenever Zita wanted her to come as that Zita's young men should brew coffee and jabber Czech in the kitchen. Margaret was indeed an improvement upon some of their former visitors, and Seraphina liked her quiet clothes and her courtesy (though she was a little inclined to smile at the seriousness of the latter), while Mr Challis had received from his wife the impression that Zita's new friend was musical, and he knew that she admired his works, while her eyes had betrayed that she admired him, so he felt benevolent towards her, if no more.

In the darkest months of the winter he thought about little besides his work at the Ministry and *Kattë*, which he now knew was to be his masterpiece. Kattë herself had changed since he first conceived her six months ago. She had then been a dark girl with burning eyes. She was now a fair girl with laughing eyes, and whereas the tragedy as he had originally visualized it lay in Kattë's determination to degrade herself because her lover falsely imagined her to be degraded, and she felt that an inner degradation must already exist in her because of his mistrust, the tragedy now lay in Kattë's fatal attraction for men, which she could not help and which bewildered and distressed her by the pain which it inflicted. Mr Challis fairly spread himself over this theme, and he felt that he had created in Kattë that spirit of joy and light love, which could so swiftly turn to tragedy, dwelling in the Vienna of the years before the First World War.

If he knew that *Kattë* was his best work so far, he concealed from himself the increasing pain which accompanied its creation, and explained his persistent longing for Hilda by the fact that she was − not his model, but his spring, his inspiration, for the character of the new Kattë. Experienced dramatists, he told himself, do not convey mannerisms and traits of character direct to paper and thence to the boards, but mannerisms and traits pass through the furnace of the creative artist's imagination and thence emerge transformed to gold. Of course he had not 'written a play about' Hilda; but Hilda had taught him more about Kattë, and by stimulating his imagination, Hilda had enabled him to create.

He began by thinking her delightful; as the winter wore on, the frankness which at first he had smiled at and hardly believed in gradually grew to have for him a strong attraction. But of course he could not accept it as mere frankness; he thought up all sorts of explanations to account for it, and studied Hilda's every word and action in order to fathom her true character, which he was certain would one day pop out and give her away. As the weeks passed, and they continued to dine together or to meet sometimes on Sunday afternoons in Kenwood to exercise Hilda's dog, and Hilda remained unchanged and no dramatic popping-out occurred, he was at last forced to accept the surprising conclusion that, as he saw her, so she was – and also the painful conclusion that she had no intention of giving him any more than a brief touch of her fresh mouth when they said good night. But when the spring came, he planned to take her one afternoon to Kew Gardens (which was a favourite haunt of his because its landscapes contained both the exotic and the formal) and there, amidst the flowering magnolia and azalea bushes, he would dazzle her by revealing his fame and ask for her love. He looked forward to the day with longing, imagining the scene; with the white and cream and pale magenta cups of the flowers making a stain of colour above themselves in the clear spring air, and in the distance the fresh ripple of the river, and near at hand the pear trees smothered in blossom rising into the blue sky, and breathing over all the scene – the conservatories, the sloping lawns, the expanses of water covered in lily leaves – the fragrance of April.

Yes, in April he would take her there, and tell her of his love; or perhaps in late March, for April was so far away!

Meanwhile, Hilda had had a talk with her mother about Mr Marcus, and they had decided that as he really seemed to admire Hilda in a nice way and to mean no harm, she should continue to go out with him. Mrs Wilson, who sometimes had plans which Hilda did not suspect, pointed out that Hilda only found Mr Marcus dull because she had never had an elderly admirer, and reminded her of Auntie Freda's Mr Rodney, a widower in the building trade who had been very much in love with Auntie Freda when she was Hilda's age, and had taken her out to quiet, really good places for lunch and to poultry shows at the Crystal Palace, and *that* had ended in a proposal. Of course Auntie Freda hadn't had him, because there were thirty years between them, but that was what it had all led up to. Hilda said that Marcus had better not try taking *her* to poultry shows, and if he was leading up to a proposal, he had a hope, and Mrs Wilson suggested once more that he should be asked round to tea one Sunday, and on Hilda's saying, 'It's no use, Mum, he won't come,' the subject was dropped.

Hilda was mildly interested in the aroma of an unfamiliar way of living and feeling that clung about Mr Challis; she liked his gentleness and courtesy, and she mildly pitied his state, which was perfectly plain to her. But one day I'll get browned-off with him altogether, she thought. He's a bit of a bind.

Every few days he telephoned to her at the Town Hall, his light, beautiful speaking voice causing something of a flutter amongst her fellow workers.

'Hild, it's your B.B.C boy!' someone would whisper with popping eyes, handing over the receiver. 'Oo, he does sound lovely! Aren't you lucky!'

'He *sounds* all right,' Hilda would say cryptically, not wishing to encourage the suspicion that she was flirting above her station. 'Do not judge the contents by the picture on the sound-box.'

As the evenings of February lengthened and the snowdrops bloomed, Margaret and Hilda saw even less of one another. Margaret's time was fully occupied with school work and visits to Westwood or to theatres and concerts with Zita, and Hilda, quite aware that she was being supplanted, concealed her natural feelings and even made excuses for her friend, reminding herself that Mutt had always been highbrow and now had found someone to share her tastes. Hilda had that impenetrable reserve which frequently accompanies a sunny temperament; her dislike of displaying her deeper feelings was almost neurotic, and when one of the young men with whom she went about was killed, she would fly into a rage, weep furious tears for a quarter of an hour, and then never mention his name again; hardly ever think of him; thrust the pain and anger deep, deep into the recesses of her mind and forget it.

On the rare occasions when Margaret telephoned to her or dropped in at the Wilsons', Hilda's manner was unchanged, but she herself never went to Margaret's home unless she were invited, and when she and Margaret met they only exchanged their usual affectionate banter and Margaret found it increasingly difficult to speak to her friend of the change that had taken place in her nature since Zita had opened to her the world of music and the doors of Westwood. I am so much happier, she would think, but she was compelled to admit that the ecstasy with which she listened to music and the thrill she experienced at a distant glimpse of Gerard Challis were too intense to be happiness.

During February she was annoyed by her mother's efforts to drag Mr Fletcher into the family circle. He had been given a standing invitation to Highgate for every Saturday afternoon and most irritatingly accepted it, and might be seen in the garden in his shirtsleeves, digging in company with Mr Steggles.

If Mrs Steggles had hoped to reform Mr Steggles by getting him to take an interest in the garden she was disappointed. Mr Steggles was bored with the garden and did not like real flowers, preferring velvet ones smelling of Californian Poppy, and he only put in an appearance in the garden out of affection for poor old Dick, who genuinely seemed to like gardening. How thankfully did Mr Steggles hear the summons to tea at five o'clock! and with what even deeper gratitude did he push aside his empty cup after listening to the six o'clock news, and suggest to old Dick that they should go out and have one at The Woodcutter! Usually they went on to a game of poker with mutual friends in London which lasted until Mr Steggles caught the last train home.

When Saturday afternoon was fine, and sometimes when it was not but stopped short of actual rain, Margaret was told by her mother that she must go out and entertain Mr Fletcher and help Dad. Usually she firmly refused on the excuse of exercise-books to correct, but on one occasion she did step out into the little square of earth, damp and desolate under the cloudy February sky, and picked up the smaller spade and turned up a spit or so while she addressed remarks to Dick Fletcher, who was digging away steadily with a red face and his sleeves rolled up. The wet clay clung to her shoes and the handle of the spade blistered her palms and she was bored by gardening and wanted to get back to a quiet room and an open book lying on a table. Dick Fletcher, too, was paying so little attention to what she said that she had the added annoyance of feeling she was wasting her time, but she kept on:

'Can you understand people getting utterly absorbed in gardening the way they do, Mr Fletcher?'

He made some inarticulate reply.

'It seems to me it's a whole-time job, not a hobby. You can't just say, "I'll go out and do half an hour's gardening," and then go back into the house and get on with something else; you find yourself having to spend half a day –'

He suddenly stopped digging and turned on her a heated face:

'If you're going to dig, *dig*, and don't talk. I can't do both!' he snapped, and drove the spade into the earth again.

Margaret was very surprised, and also experienced that shock which we feel from a gross and uncalled-for rudeness. She was about to retire in offended dignity when he glanced up again, this time with a smile.

'Go on, jump to it!' he said. 'Bet you a shilling you haven't finished that bed by tea-time!'

'You've won,' she said, leaning the spade against a tree and dusting her smarting hands. 'It's too much like work.'

He did not answer, and she stayed for a moment to look up at the tree under which they were standing. It was a tall young willow with a full shapely head now covered in swelling buds of silvery green flushed with pink, and the lingering spring light seemed caught in its airy mesh. Not another bud was to be seen in the garden, but the freshly dug earth smelled sweet and the mildness of the air was entirely different from that of autumn.

'You don't often see that pink kind,' he said, resting on his spade and also looking up at the tree.

'No – isn't it lovely.'

He nodded and smiled, but without any look of pleasure, and took up the spade and began to dig again. Margaret changed her mind about returning to the house, and began to pull up armfuls of fluffy grey golden-rod.

'Hullo, Margaret, given up already?' called her father from the far end of the garden.

'I'm doing this.' She held up the golden-rod. 'It ought to have come up last autumn. We'll never get this place looking decent for the summer.'

'I'm not trying to,' muttered Mr Steggles, straightening his back.

'I'd like to see it looking nice,' said Margaret suddenly, standing with her arms full of the eldrich seeding plant, her dark head lifted eagerly against the sky, 'only I wish we needn't have a lawn with flowers round it. Everybody has that. I'd like something more unusual.'

'You would, eh?' Dick Fletcher glanced up and laughed. 'Why not have the grass round the edges and the flowers in the middle?'

'Well, why not?' she cried, 'Tudor gardens were like that.'

'Were they?' he said wearily, resting again and wiping his forehead. He looked at his watch.

'Yes, that's just exactly what I was thinking,' said Mr Steggles, throwing down his spade without reluctance. 'And here's Mabel, just at the right moment.'

Mrs Steggles was standing at the French windows of the drawing-room and indicating that tea was ready.

At tea they all agreed that the garden did begin to look better, and Mr Steggles heard with dismay that now they had made a start on it they would have to keep on; a full programme for the coming months was unfolded by Mrs Steggles which included spraying the greenfly and applying lawn sand.

'Oh, there's always something to do in a garden,' she ended cheerfully. 'It's like a house in that way. More cake, Dick? You look better for the fresh air.'

'I feel it,' he said, and Margaret thought that he meant what he said. 'I look forward to coming up here every week,' he added, but whether he meant that or not, she could not be sure.

'It's a pity you can't come for a whole week-end, and really get the benefit,' said Mrs Steggles.

'It's very kind of you, but I'm afraid I can't; my Sundays are always engaged.'

'Oh, Sunday! Yes, we mustn't ask you to give up Sundays! I quite forgot!'

Mr Fletcher looked both ill-at-ease and annoyed, and Margaret wondered that a man of his age and experience should show so much embarrassment over a commonplace situation.

After the men had gone, she went out into the dusk and finished pulling up the golden-rod. The grass scattered cold dew on her ankles, and her wrists were scratched by the long stiff stems. The air was deliciously fresh, and over her head the young willow tree held a crescent moon among its branches. While she worked, not thinking of anything except the scents and pleasures by which she was surrounded, there came a far-off faint piping high overhead, and across the sky swept five ducks with necks outstretched, that were outlined for an instant against the clouded moon and the budding tree and then were gone. She followed their flight until they vanished in the direction of Kenwood, then let her gaze linger on Westwood, high on its hill.

'What do you suppose Mr Fletcher does on Sundays?' said Mrs Steggles, when they were seated at supper.

'It's rather obvious, isn't it,' replied Margaret, not pleased at the reopening of the subject.

'Oh, there's a lady in the case, of course. But why should he want to keep it so dark?'

Margaret was silent, thinking that her mother's mind was more ingenuous than her own.

'There's no reason why he shouldn't marry again if he wants to,' pursued Mrs Steggles. 'He wasn't the guilty party.'

'Perhaps the "lady" isn't free,' said Margaret, trying to put her suspicions as delicately as possible.

'Married, you mean? Oh, I hope not. I don't like to think of him carrying on with somebody like that.'

Margaret thought that the conversation was straying towards

a dangerous area, and tried to change it by saying that she had enjoyed her gardening.

'Yes, it will do you good, you don't get enough fresh air, stuck in school all day and sitting up half the night. I like Dick, and I'd like to see him settled with some nice girl. Don't you?'

'Like him? Yes, more than I did. I don't think he's easy to get on with.'

'Well, neither are you, Margaret. He thinks *you're* standoffish.'

'How on earth do you know, Mother? Did he say so?'

'Of course not. He's always most polite. But I can see, I'm not blind. He'd be friendly enough if you'd let him.'

'Do you mean he likes me?' Margaret was irritated to feel herself colour, but it was only at the memory of her mother's interference in her first love affair.

'Not in that way, Margaret. I'm afraid you aren't the type that attracts men, so we'd better face it. But he'd find it easier to be pleasant if *you'd* talk more and not be so stiff.'

'Well, I must try,' said Margaret amiably, with no intention of doing so, but anxious to end the conversation. She herself thought that Dick Fletcher was too far gone in disappointment for any friendliness of hers, or of anyone's, to make much difference to him. She pitied him, because that lingering youthfulness of colouring and occasionally of manner suggested that he had once been an ardent and a happy man. But some spring had dried up in him, and she had neither the inclination – nor the power (she felt) – to set it flowing again.

16

Margaret's feelings were still a girl's feelings, but they were stronger than those of most girls, and she was not satisfied by the glimpses which she had of Gerard Challis. She longed to talk to him and (although she knew that the longing was most unlikely ever to be satisfied) to become his friend. Such a friendship as Alice Meynell had with George Meredith seemed to her a beautiful relationship and one not lacking in spiritual excitements; if she could have had such a friendship with Gerard Challis, she told herself, she would have had nothing more to wish for.

She had bought all his plays and knew many passages in them by heart, and had been three times to see *The Hidden Well*, which had been revived in London; once with Zita and twice by herself. That rare mind! What a joy it was, to see it revealing itself through the words and gestures of the actors! How spiritual yet passionate was his approach to *Love*! When his men and women spoke of their love for one another she felt as if they were expressing her deepest feelings; and she felt none of the faint embarrassment and distaste which had affected her when she looked at Alexander Niland's picture of the lovers lying in the summer grass.

But daydreaming, and reading his plays and going to see them performed, were not satisfying; and sometimes she experienced a slight revulsion of feeling as if she had been eating sickly sweets. She was disturbed by the disloyalty of such feelings but admitted their existence, and even began to realize that they were due to the scanty diet upon which her emotions were compelled to feed.

Therefore, when she opened the door of the Little Room one Saturday afternoon in March and saw him seated by the open window, her astonishment and joy were so great that she coloured deeply.

He took that as inevitable and no more than his due, and rose slowly and gracefully and stood by the window, his tall slight form dark against the brilliance of the spring day, with one hand resting on the back of the little Victorian couch upon which he had been seated. He smiled at her and she tremulously returned the smile, and then he said:

'I shall not disturb you if I remain here for a little while?'

'Oh no! I – are you sure – I shan't disturb you? Zita and I are making – doing some sewing – and I thought – she is out, but I have the afternoon free – I might be getting on with it.'

How truly thankful she was that 'it' was of a nature which permitted it to be worked upon under his eyes without embarrassment! – and how far gone she was in romantic love that the thought did not incline her to smile.

He bent his head and stood courteously while she took from a drawer the blouse of white net which Zita was helping her to make and sat down at the far end of the room, and then he reseated himself upon the little couch, and, extending his arm along the curve of its back, gazed into vacancy in silence. Margaret, bending over her sewing, found her hands shaking and barely capable of their task. Suddenly it occurred to her, increasing her agitation, that he was studying the Little Room, absorbing its atmosphere to use it in the new play which she knew him to be working upon. And she was here with him, alone! a witness (but that she dared not look up) of his creative ardour! It was almost too much. Suddenly he spoke, and to save her life she could not have repressed her convulsive start.

'Women have been imprisoned in this room for two hundred years,' he said abruptly.

In spite of her happiness and agitation, this remark did surprise Margaret very much. The Little Room was such a quiet, pleasant, sunny place, she herself was fond of sewing, which soothed her restlessness and satisfied her own creative instinct, and she had so liked to think of other women sewing here as long as the house had stood, that it required a distinct effort to think of the Little Room as a prison. However, she made the effort (in spite of some difficulty in knowing just what to reply) and looked up, murmuring intensely, 'Yes . . . I know.'

'Women, with their half-formed desires timidly pressing forward into the unknown world outside these walls. Here they sat . . . sewing.'

Impossible to convey in print the chill irony he put into the last word; any self-respecting needle would have melted before it, and Margaret only made a soft affirmative sound in response, for his tone was contemplative, musing, as if he were talking to himself.

'I want,' he went on, leaning forward and clasping his hands over his knee, 'to convey in one sentence of dialogue that feeling of half-conscious imprisonment, the restlessness that was sewn into the er – the – er – the –'

Margaret waited, while he hesitated. Was he seeking for the right word, the perfect phrase of which he was a master? Or was it – she hardly liked to think that he did not know *what* it was that women sewed?

'– the hemming of handkerchiefs,' concluded Mr Challis, with delicate contempt.

'Oh, but surely it wasn't only –' began Margaret eagerly, then stopped, horrified at herself. What had she been about to say?

For the first time he turned his head slowly and looked at her. His face was in shadow by contrast with the brilliant day outside, and his eyes seemed bluer than usual and were shining with a strange reflected radiance. He looked like a seer.

'I used "handkerchiefs" as a symbol,' he said gently, as if he knew what she had been about to say and understood her difficulty and was compelling himself to be patient, 'a symbol of the necessary, the commonplace, even the sordid.'

Margaret, in spite of her alarm at her recent narrow escape from having corrected him, was deeply interested in this discussion and longed to help; what tiny details dramatists had to contend with! And he had said that by the use of such details he wanted to convey, in one sentence, the vast emotions of all imprisoned womanhood! How she burned to have the courage to suggest dish-cloths instead of handkerchiefs! But it was useless; the courage would not come. And did one hem dish-cloths? No; surely one knitted them or used a bit of rag. Tea-cloths? No; that suggested something quite different. But it's fascinating, working it out, she thought, and then became aware that he was speaking again.

'You understand what I'm doing here, don't you?'

'Oh, yes!' she breathed. 'Absorbing the atmosphere.'

'Rather, letting it absorb me,' he corrected, 'and thus I shall become, for an hour, a part of it, and reproduce it, when the moment is ripe, in art.'

She sat with her hands folded upon her work, and her eyes fixed fervently upon his face. There was another long pause.

'The woman I have in mind died thirty years ago,' he said abruptly, 'but you – you are alive to-day. The sunlight is warm upon your cheek and your hands experience the fine texture of the chiffon which you are sewing. And you think that you are free; free as that woman who died in Vienna thirty years ago never was. But *are* you?'

She was so confused by this sudden introduction of a personal note into the conversation, and so overjoyed at being taken into his confidence, that she could not assemble her thoughts in time to give a suitably subtle reply and made the mistake of giving a literal one.

'Oh well, I am much freer than most girls of my age,' she said with a nervous laugh. 'I teach, and so I'm in a reserved occupation.' (I wonder if I ought to tell him it's not chiffon, she thought. Perhaps he said chiffon on purpose. He wouldn't know, of course, about having to give coupons for chiffon and net being unrationed.)

'I meant free in spirit,' he said sharply, frowning. 'Freedom of body is nothing.'

Now Margaret had a strong vein of common sense and sense of duty to her fellow beings which was inherited from her commonplace ancestors; and, in spite of the delightful confusion of her feelings, her immediate response to that authoritative *Freedom of body is nothing* was a vehement *Rubbish!* which, unuttered, caused the blood to rise to her face and thoughts of the prisoners in camps all over the world to rush into her mind with a sensation almost of audibility, as if she heard millions of voices imploring for liberty.

'The mind is all, the body all too, but in a way so different that the comparison only provides an ever-expanding paradox,' he went on. 'In the case of freedom, the final victory is always with the mind.'

She murmured something about that being proved by the peoples of Occupied Europe, but Mr Challis, who never thought about the war except when at the Ministry, paid no attention to this and only repeated his question:

'And you — are you free?'

It required considerable courage for Margaret to reply:

'No, because I am not happy.'

'The food of fools,' said Mr Challis promptly, dashing her hope that he would ask her why, and that this would lead on to a long and wonderful talk which would change her whole life, 'No fully adult being wants to be happy.' He stood up and began to pace the room with his hands behind his back, which was a habit of his, while she wistfully watched him; wistfully, but also with a faint feeling of incredulous disappointment, for she did not agree with some of the things he had said!

'Don't you think that that's what most people want?' she said timidly.

'Most people are fools,' he answered with his faint, frosty smile. 'No, it is not happiness that should be the aim of our minds and bodies; it is intensity and integrity. And the shaping power – which forges and tempers the human spirit and renders it fit to serve integrity with intensity – is not happiness but suffering; privation, abnegation.'

At this moment the door was opened quickly, and round it came a face under a madly silly spring hat while two eyes, softly grey as pewter, glanced ironically from Mr Challis's inspired countenance to Margaret's solemnly attentive one.

'Hullo, Pops!' said Hebe. 'I heard you holding forth all down the corridor. Have you seen my brats anywhere? Hullo –' and she raised a finger to Margaret, who was far from pleased to see her and found her greeting of her father highly inappropriate.

Mr Challis looked disconcerted, and seemed to recall his thoughts to the visible world. 'Oh – er – no – hullo, my dear, I think your mother is with the children somewhere.'

Hebe nodded, and looked round the room. 'This place still smells of old rags,' she said. 'What are *you* making?' and she bent quite closely over Margaret with her mocking smile and a waft of flowery scent. 'How chaste. Well –' and she nodded and withdrew.

The glamour was dispersed and he seemed to feel it, for he looked uncertainly about him, then muttered something about an appointment and with a courteous inclination of his head in her direction, as if he were saluting a stranger, left the room. Margaret was not familiar with those parties in which an absorbing tête-à-tête is broken up by an expert hostess bent on circulating her guests, but her feelings were exactly those of a guest thus interrupted, and in addition she felt the pain inflicted by his abrupt change of manner and the bewilderment caused by her disagreement with his views. But she bent over her work again and tried to concentrate upon it, and as her feelings became calmer she was able to reflect that the greater part of their talk had provided not pain but pleasure; true, a pleasure of that too intense kind to which she was accustomed to associate with him, but certainly pleasure, and she began to recall his changes of expression, his every word, and above all his confidences about his work, and by degrees her discomfiture subsided; all was glowing recollection, except for the increasing conviction that Hebe found her amusing and that she disliked Hebe.

Mr Challis was a man not happy in his relatives: as well as the burden of three grandchildren and the prospect of more when his sons should marry, he was also plagued, as we shall see, at the other end of the family scale where a man might reasonably expect his relatives to be dead. On his way to his study – for his talk of an appointment was of course untrue – he encountered a procession (why did his grandchildren so often present themselves as a procession, accompanied by nurses and grandmothers and mothers carrying and supporting them as their slaves support and augment the triumphal marches of Eastern monarchs?), consisting of Hebe, Jeremy – who was now a fair baby, very large for his months, with his mother's sleepy grey eyes – Seraphina holding Emma by the hand, and Barnabas and Zita bringing up the rear and engaged in argument.

'Hullo, darling,' said Seraphina, as the convoy swept past him, compelling him to stand aside at the head of the staircase, 'we're just going to spend our sweet ration. Great-granny rang up about ten minutes ago; she wants you to ring her up before four.'

'It is ten minutes to now,' said Mr Challis irritably, glancing at the clock with delicately painted flowers upon its sky-blue face which stood on a boule table at the head of the staircase. 'Did she want anything particularly?'

'To arrange about our going down I should imagine, darling,' said Seraphina, and Hebe made a face.

Mr Challis, looking impatient, followed them downstairs, necessarily at a slow pace because of the uncertain steps of Emma, who was still at the stage when each marble precipice had to be a matter for separate management. Just in front of Mr Challis were Barnabas and Zita, still arguing.

'Well, well, do as you wish, Barnabas. I do not care. But when at der end of der month you cry for sweets and no sweets there are, remember what I haf said.'

'Why can't I buy some more?'

'Stupid boy! Because Mr Churchill will not let you buy dem. You haf so many a month and no more. If you buy all to-day, there will no more be for three week.'

'Why not? Why does Mr Churchill say I mustn't?'

'Because if some liddle boys and girls buy all der sweets there no more are for der others. You all do haf a share each.'

'Well, does he mind if I buy all *mine* this afternoon?'

'Of course he does not mind, but I *say* to you dot *if* you buy dem all *now*, there no more will be *until three week*.'

Mr Challis, conscious that the time was drawing nearer to four o'clock, attempted gently to make his way past Emma, who, interrupted in the act of cautiously placing one foot into the void below the stair on which she stood, glanced up at him in dignified amazement.

'Let me pass, please, I must telephone to Greatgranny,' he appealed to the party at large.

Immediately they all burst into cries of 'Poor Grandpa! Let Grandpa go by, then, Barnabas, get out of the way Emma, come to Granny and let poor Grandpa –' in the midst of which uproar Mr Challis waved hastily to them and hurried away towards the sanctuary of his study. It was just five minutes to four.

He gave a number near a village in Bedfordshire and soon there was a click at the other end of the line and he heard a number of confused sounds which suggested that much activity was going on in the room where the telephone was; he could hear a piano going, and people were singing shrilly, and there was also a sustained whirring noise. Mr Challis winced.

''Ullo?' said a young voice suddenly. 'Sorry – Martlefield 3 here. Who's that?'

'I want to speak to Lady Challis.'

'All right, I'll go and get her. She's in the garden.'

Mr Challis sighed. When was his mother not in the garden?'

'Who's speaking, please?'

'Mr Gerard Challis.'

''Old on, please.'

The voice then went away, and Mr Challis held on patiently and presently footsteps were heard approaching, accompanied by the barking of more than one dog, and then a clear old voice said cheerfully: 'Gerry? Is that you, dear? Good. We're all going to the Red Cross Concert to-night and just going to have high tea. Now about your all coming down in May. The fourteenth would suit me. The hawthorn's sure to be out by then.'

'That will suit us, I expect. I will get Seraphina to telephone you to-morrow and confirm it. How are you, Mother?'

'Very well, thank you. There are a hundred and fifty daffodils out in the orchard.'

Mr Challis made a congratulatory sound.

'And my parrot tulips are going to be a *spectacle*.'

Mr Challis repeated the sound in a higher key.

'And those wild pansies we picked in Patt's Wood last year have taken, and they're coming up in an absolute carpet.'

Mr Challis, who had an engagement in town, glanced at his watch.

'How are you all?' went on Lady Challis.

'We are all well, I think. The child had a slight cold some days ago, but seems to be better now.'

'Which child?'

'The baby.'

'Good. And how is my dear Grantey?'

'Oh – she hasn't been well, I believe; I seem to remember Seraphina saying something about it.'

'What's the matter with her?'

'I really don't know. She was complaining of breathlessness, I believe.'

'Make her see a doctor at once,' said Lady Challis firmly. 'I don't like the sound of it.'

'Really, my dear Mother –'

'You none of you realize what a treasure she is.'

'I will suggest to Seraphina that she should see a doctor. You must forgive me if I go now, Mother, I have an appointment –'

'And you'd all be in no end of a hole if anything happened to her.'

'I am sure there is no need to worry. I really must go now, Mother. Good-bye – I will ask Seraphina to telephone to you to-morrow.'

'Not before lunch, then; I'm going to distemper the scullery.'

Mr Challis was late for his appointment.

*   *   *

Zita and Margaret spent a pleasant hour before dinner in sewing and talking, and then Zita went downstairs to lay the table while Margaret prepared to go home.

While she was putting away her work she heard voices outside in the corridor. Evidently someone had paused at the large cupboard opposite the Little Room door.

'He was holding forth to Struggles,' said Hebe's unmistakable voice.

There was a laugh.

'Darling, *need* you call her that?' said Seraphina's voice. 'It's *too* perfect, but is it *kind*?'

This time it was Hebe who laughed.

'I wish you could have seen her. She looked like a dog waiting for "Paid for!"'

'Sweetie, she has *very* nice manners, much prettier than yours,' said her mother. '*Here* it is, I knew it must be *somewhere*,' and voices and footsteps receded.

Margaret was very angry and her admiration for Hebe was now definitely replaced by dislike. But how sweet Mrs Challis had been! how kind! And what a comfort it was to hear that her manners were approved! All the same, her cheeks were burning as she walked home.

I needn't let it make any difference to me, she thought. Hebe doesn't live at Westwood and I hardly ever see her and she wouldn't take the trouble to set her father and mother against me; she wouldn't think it worth while. But how cruel she is! She has everything and I have nothing, and she only thinks I'm funny. She doesn't appreciate what she's got, and she encourages men to be in love with her, and she neglects her children. I hate her.

17

In the walled garden at Westwood a tulip tree was in bud. The olive leaves and the petals flushed with purple looked over the wall, and every evening Margaret strolled up to gaze at it and give herself refreshment before she slept. The grass of the oval lawn was growing so rapidly that it had to be clipped every two or three days by Cortway. He was frequently there when she walked past about eight o'clock, moving the mower to and fro over the lawn in long hurrying sweeps, keeping his head down and never looking up.

The gardens were as old as the house, and in course of time their shrubs had thickened and spread and become sturdy tufted tyrants, casting a dense shade and discouraging the growth of flowers; there were Portugal laurel, myrtle, rhododendron and bay. The common laurels were kept closely cut, but their leaves looked as strong as veined green marble, and there was more than one pine and monkey-puzzler to add to the garden's darkness. Scattered among these sombre, scanty-flowered bushes were beds shaped like diamonds or hearts or ovals filled in season with yellow and scarlet and blue flowers; but during the winter, when all the flowers were absent, the garden seemed most truly itself; as if its dark, grave spirit were released. The picture which it made was park-like and curiously lacking in the refreshing power of most gardens; the combination of darkness and brilliance was hard. When Margaret walked out one still, sunny evening with Zita and saw hundreds of large daffodils standing in yellow sunlight below the thick dark shrubs, she found the contrast almost unpleasant. But then she caught a waft of budding box from the tiny clipped hedges bordering the paths, and for a moment a feeling came to her as if she had encountered something very old; and of course she had; it was the idea of a garden that had belonged to an older England; the clipped bushes, the herbs and shrubs, and a few flowers of stiff and cultivated beauty. The garden's darkness was increased by its lying in a hollow, and as only the low sparkling rays of evening or dawn sunlight pierced directly through the branches, it was most often illuminated by those strange transforming lights, its thick shrubberies protecting it from the glare of noon. It was an unusual garden, oppressive and quiet, but as the months passed and there were crimson roses under the glossy bushes of bay, she came to love it.

The front gardens were less formal. The small one on the left of the gates, where the tulip tree grew, had honeysuckle climbing over its walls, and Cortway kept the beds filled with pheasant's eye narcissus, tulips, wallflowers, nasturtiums and all the familiar glories. But beside the path that led to the side entrance of the house grew the feathery fern of the wild carrot, and all up one wall ran a tangle of the little pink convolvulus that has the scent of vanilla. Cortway never bothered himself with this part of the garden, for visitors were not supposed to see it and if it liked to grow weeds he did not care, but Margaret looked forward to going down the pebbled, narrow, mossy path in the lengthening twilight two or three times a week, and noticing what new tendrils and mats of flower and green were coming up as the tide of spring rolled forward over Europe.

Meanwhile, the Steggles's own garden had been transformed by hard work, and now had a lawn which, though still patchy, was green and healthy, and neat beds which would look less bare when the late summer flowers came, while there was a large bush of white lilac in full blossom under which Mrs Steggles sometimes sat. Dick Fletcher still came up on most Saturday afternoons, and on the last occasion had been rewarded with a large bunch of lilac, the first-fruits (Mrs Steggles told him) of his labours; later on there would be radishes and lettuces and runner-beans. He wrapped the lilac carefully in brown paper, showing none of the embarrassment men usually display at carrying flowers, and Margaret wondered if he would take it to his own flat or to the girl he went to see on Sundays.

The slight awkwardness there had been between them at first had disappeared by now, and she took him for granted as he seemed to take her, never thinking about him when he was not there. He fitted in well with the household's ways, seldom discussing any subject save those of general domestic interest and never arguing or holding forth. Sometimes he was silent or touchy, but the Steggleses were used to moods, and accepted them without comment. He seemed to like coming to the house, and Mrs Steggles kept to her decision to make him welcome whenever he did.

Margaret was so used to taking him for granted that she was surprised to see a new side of him one afternoon when Hilda came to tea. He began by being unusually silent and watching Hilda sulkily as she sparkled away, but soon he was laughing, and said one or two charming things to her, flattering and absurd.

'I like your dad's friend,' said Hilda, while she and Margaret were upstairs.

'He isn't usually silly like that,' answered Margaret, feeling ashamed for him.

'Who said he was silly? He's a dear.'

Margaret said no more, but she continued to think that compliments coming from Dick Fletcher were slightly undignified. She had yet to learn the plain woman's lesson; that a pretty woman will always make men lose their dignity willingly and with pleasure.

The weeks sped on pleasantly, for the long dull days of teaching were replaced by the holidays, with music, lingering light and flowers, and chance encounters with the delightful inhabitants of Westwood. She and Zita were now close, if not firm, friends; and they had made mutual plans that extended far into the summer and included a week's holiday to be spent together in learning the beauties of Salisbury Cathedral and listening to its music. This was to be in August, and Margaret longed for August to come.

It was at the beginning of the May term that she first realized that she was unconsciously looking forward to a time when she would no longer have to teach. For weeks during the winter term she had been preparing her work mechanically, and hurrying through the corrections of exercises in order that she might keep an evening appointment with Zita, and the end of the Easter holidays, during which she had been free to haunt Westwood as much as she liked and to make her own arrangements for pleasure during the day, came to her with a shock. The return to school was really hateful to her; the children seemed plain, uninteresting and stupid, and her colleagues prejudiced, uncultured and narrow, while her senses, fed richly on the beauty of Westwood, recoiled from the ugliness of the school buildings.

She began to be afraid of the long years ahead in which she would have to go on earning her living by work which was growing increasingly distasteful. She had made one or two attempts to convey to her classes the more easily understood of her enthusiasms, but she had been irritated by the slowness of the girls' understanding and had given up the idea; she had also suspected that some of the older pupils found her raptures ridiculous, and as she felt too deeply about them to adopt a cooler tone, she preferred to abandon the attempt altogether. She was still conscientious enough to attempt to pass on the joys which she had discovered to her pupils, who were less intelligent and fortunate than herself, but what could you do (she asked herself) with girls who remembered the tiniest detail about any film star, and could not be persuaded to show genuine interest in any other subject? She thought of their young minds as surfeited with a glutinous, oversweet fare and yet eager for more; fed on foam; growing up without a single quality making for solid contentment or one pleasure that would last them throughout their lives. She did not realize that theirs were still the imaginations of children, which do not see the real thing or the thing that adults see, but something beglamoured by that imagination, dazzling, dreamy and more satisfying than any solid mental food.

Her classes continued to be orderly but they did not do well in the examinations at the end of the Easter term, and she was made to feel this by Miss Lathom's manner. Miss Lathom was indeed surprised, for Margaret had begun well, very well, and her headmistress had not expected these poor results. Something must have happened in her promising new form-mistress's private life to upset her work, and Miss Lathom had to make an effort not to be irritated by the obvious fact. She had little sympathy with people who took up teaching without a vocation, and she now suspected that Margaret, though possessing many of the qualities that make a first-class teacher, had been guilty of just this fault, and was now being attracted by other interests. Miss Lathom was intelligent enough to hope that at least they might be connected with a young man, but feared (thinking of Margaret's looks) that they were not.

One afternoon towards the end of the Easter term Margaret was told by another member of the staff that Miss Lathom would like to see her at once, and hurried to the headmistress's room. Her heart was beating unpleasantly hard, for she feared that her class's disappointing results in the examinations were about to be discussed.

But when she opened the door in response to Miss Lathom's

'Come in,' she saw two figures sitting by the open window among the bowls of spring flowers, and one was Miss Lomax, her former headmistress at Lukeborough. Miss Lathom benevolently watched the greeting between them, and after a little general conversation there was a pause. Margaret was in a dilemma; she knew that she ought to ask her former headmistress home to tea or at least suggest that they should spend some time together that evening, but she and Zita had planned a walk to Hampstead to look at the beautiful old parish church, and she had been looking forward to this all day. While she hesitated, Miss Lathom glanced at her watch and observed:

'Well, Monica, I'm expecting a parent in three minutes, so I shall have to send you two good people away. That's settled, then; you'll have tea with me on Thursday. I expect Miss Steggles has a great deal to tell you,' and she dismissed them both with a smile, having previously told her old friend of her recent dissatisfaction with Margaret, and asked her to try to discover where the trouble lay. She would hear Miss Lomax's report on Thursday.

Margaret and Miss Lomax walked down the long bare corridors, chatting about Lukeborough friends and life in London, with Margaret feeling more and more bitterly the sacrifice of her evening. Her feelings towards Miss Lomax had always been affectionate, but tinged with awe for Miss Lomax's superior culture and strength of character. Now, as she looked down on the top of Miss Lomax's good plain felt hat from her greater height, she still felt affectionate, but the awe had quite vanished: Miss Lomax's manner seemed unnecessarily peremptory, rather than commanding, and her charmless clothes offended eyes used to those worn by Mrs Challis and Hebe Niland. The prospect of spending an evening with this emphatic little person was dismal indeed.

'You will come home and have tea with me, won't you, Miss

Lomax?' she asked at last, the very form of the invitation being different from what it would have been six months ago, and with sinking heart heard the reply.

'I should like to very much, Margaret,' answered Miss Lomax graciously; it did not occur to her that a junior mistress might have pleasanter occupations than the entertaining of herself. 'I shall enjoy seeing your mother again, and I want a good long talk with *you*.'

Nothing more of a personal nature was said on the bus-ride to Highgate, and during tea the conversation was general, though far from comfortable or entertaining, for Mrs Steggles, warned by telephone of the distinguished guest's approach, had got out the finest lawn tablecloth and rushed up some little cakes, the baking of which had left her flushed and irritable. She kept referring to Miss Lomax's kindness to Margaret and Margaret's good fortune in having such interesting work with such pleasant colleagues, and succeeded in creating such an atmosphere of insincerity and strain that Margaret was heartily relieved to find herself at last walking up the hill with Miss Lomax in the late sunshine, the headmistress having expressed the wish to see Highgate Village and then take the bus along the top of the Spaniard's Walk to Hampstead, where she was dining with friends.

But when they reached the village she suggested that they should walk along the Spaniards and enjoy the freshness of the spring air. On either side of the road steep banks sloped down into tangles of white-flowered bushes, full of the sweet evening calling of blackbirds and thrushes, and the cool blue sky was reflected in pools of rainwater gleaming in the hollows. The broad, lifted highway ran straight between the two commons lying in their valleys and over it, smelling of new leaves and rain, pounced the gusts of April.

'Why is it called the Spaniards?' demanded Miss Lomax, marching along and sniffing the air.

'It's the Spaniard's Walk, really: I don't know why,' confessed Margaret, recalling her attention with difficulty. She had telephoned Zita to cancel their appointment just before leaving the house, and Zita had sounded annoyed and hurt, and there would be all the tiresome business of soothing her.

'You should make it your business to find out,' laughed Miss Lomax pleasantly. 'There must be a rich field for the amateur antiquarian in these two villages, Margaret, and I am surprised to find you know so little about them. Have you been indulging your weakness for romancing over what's far away and out of reach, and neglecting the romance under your nose, I wonder?' she ended, with a keen glance and a twirl of her umbrella. She liked tackling people about their shortcomings and backslidings.

Margaret coloured so deeply that she was compelled to turn her face away in a glance over the valley, but it was not at what Miss Lomax said. Suddenly there had come into her disturbed, disappointed, weary mind a line of Alice Meynell's:

I run, I run, I am gathered to thy heart,

and for the moment she could not answer. She felt herself in Gerard Challis's arms, her face hidden on his shoulder, and all sorrow calmed and soothed away. She so seldom allowed herself to indulge in such daydreams that the power with which this one enveloped her was all the stronger.

'Have you?'

Margaret shook her head. 'I don't know, Miss Lomax.'

'Because that's always been your danger, you know, my dear. You have no idea of what real life is like, in its ugliness and harshness. You have always been very sheltered, Margaret.'

'Have I? I don't feel I have.'

'I don't expect you do. All the same, it's a fact. You have great

221

powers for good, as I have always told you, but they aren't yet directed upon anything *real*. Think of your blessings, your mercies. A good home, kind parents (I am prepared to admit that perhaps they don't completely understand you, but they *are* kind) and congenial work under a *wonderful* Head. And yet —'

'I haven't said I was discontented, Miss Lomax,' said Margaret, recovering herself and speaking with more force than she would have been capable of in her Lukeborough days. 'I am perfectly conscious of my advantages, I assure you, and very grateful to you for all your kindness.'

Miss Lomax said nothing for a moment. Margaret's new tone slightly disconcerted her. She thought her protégée much changed, and not for the better, though it was hard to say exactly where the change lay. She decided to alter her own tone.

'Well, there is something wrong, I am sure,' she said, almost playfully. 'What is all this I hear about poor examination results? After such a good beginning, too!'

Margaret met her inquisitive glance gravely.

'Yes, my class did do badly,' she answered with composure. 'It's because my heart isn't in teaching any more.'

'Well!' exclaimed Miss Lomax, after a rather appalling pause, 'that's candid, at least! Do you realize what you've just said?'

Margaret nodded. 'It must sound very bad to you, I know, and especially after you've been so kind to me. I'm sorry to seem ungrateful.'

'It isn't that, my dear,' said Miss Lomax seriously. 'I have always thought that you had a real gift for teaching, as you know, and I have been glad to put you in the way of developing it. But I am really worried, and alarmed too, to hear you say so calmly that your heart isn't in teaching. Where is it, then?' she ended, on the playful note, bearing in mind Miss Lathom's hint that there might be a young man in the case.

'It's not easy to say,' answered Margaret after a pause. 'Part of it is in Wolf's and Schubert's songs, and I've made some new friends – and –'

'Ah! So that's it!' said Miss Lomax keenly, her eyes positively darting with triumph and the umbrella twirling like mad. 'Now, who are these *new friends*?'

'I don't think you would find them interesting,' Margaret replied, in such a tone that Miss Lomax was completely silenced, and for what seemed a long time they walked along without speaking, while the varied colours of the April sky above them drifted towards a delicate sunset of grey and turquoise and orange-pink.

At last Margaret glanced down at the little figure marching at her side and felt penitent, for she had been both ungrateful and unkind.

'I am sorry I was rude,' she said, putting warmth into her voice, as she knew how. 'Please forgive me.'

'Ah, that is the Margaret I used to know!' said Miss Lomax, turning towards her a somewhat shaken face under the good felt hat. 'You sounded so hard, so bitter! I hardly knew you!'

'I'm not hard at all, really.'

'Well, I hope not, my dear, for your sake. But you are certainly changed. I have always thought, you know, that what you need to make a really fine human being of *you* is a great shock; suffering; self-sacrifice –'

'Someone else said that,' said Margaret, turning her face again towards the valley, 'though not about me specially.'

'– just as the camomile gives out a stronger scent when it is bruised,' ended Miss Lomax.

'And what about happiness? Can't that make a fine human being, too?'

'Happy people are always selfish, or nearly always. *Suffering is the anvil upon which the crystal sword of integrity is hammered*. I found that in a volume of plays I was reading the other day – I forget the author's name –'

'Gerard Challis. It comes in a play of his called *Mountain Air*,' said Margaret, still studying the valley.

'Well, it is true. Until you have *really* suffered, Margaret, you won't be the fine person you could be. And now, enough of lecturing! In spite of your heart not being in teaching, tell me how you are getting on at school.'

This conversation was duly reported to Miss Lathom on Thursday, and both teachers came to the disturbing conclusion that it was no temporary dissatisfaction with her profession Margaret was suffering from, but a corruption of her sense of duty by bad company, namely, the new friends of whom she had spoken. Miss Lathom could do no more than think of some phrases for that lecture for which she felt the moment was not yet ripe, but Miss Lomax could write a long, severe and vigorously worded letter, and did; hinting to Margaret that she did not realize how serious her neglect of her duties might be, and ending with these words:

'If we believe with Keats that this world is "a vale of soul-making" (and I, for one, do) we cannot ignore any opportunity for strengthening and sweetening and beautifying our own souls, or leave any other soul to flounder into the Slough of Despond without a word of friendly warning. This is what I am giving you, Margaret!'

It sometimes happens that an ordinary pleasant person whom we have known all our lives comes out with a remark which we never forget, just as it happens that a comparative stranger may let fall some comment or piece of wisdom that we treasure as a lifelong influence. Miss Lomax's quotation from Keats's letter was unfamiliar to Margaret, and it struck full on her imagination with a shadowy beauty, like that of a huge cloud at midday which stealthily obscures the sunshine but lends a new kind of light to the landscape. She did not take much notice of the rest of the letter, as it was exactly what Miss Lomax might be expected to think and feel; but the words of Keats haunted her and sank into her heart.

She did, however, take a *little* notice of what Miss Lomax so earnestly said, and as a result her class's work began to improve. She no longer gave all her ardent, conscientious powers to teaching her girls, but she no longer completely scamped the work, and she was cynically amused to see how well she could do by exerting only half her capabilities. Miss Lathom was relieved and her manner grew more cordial.

Meanwhile, Mr Challis's new play was completed and about to burst upon London. Margaret had heard scraps of gossip from Zita about its progress from time to time and had treasured them: a big parcel of memoirs by Austrian diplomats and Viennese society women had arrived from the London Library for Mr Challis; he was working every night until the small hours; he was reading Arthur Schnitzler; he was lunching with the notorious and ill-tempered woman who was considered to be the only actress with enough temperament to play Kattë. The play was in rehearsal; Edward Early was to play the hero, only Mr Challis says that there is no hero; the first night would be on the fourth of May.

Margaret, with the advantage of being primed by Zita, had a letter waiting for the box-office at the theatre on the morning that the date was announced by the Press – for she had insisted that Zita must not ask the family for a ticket, and had offered to pay for them both, realizing that she would have to go with Zita; all would be revealed to Zita's keen eye if she insisted upon going alone, and she would have to be content with going by herself later on. It would be a real trial to sit through three hours in Zita's company and conceal her feelings, but it must be done, and there was the prospect of seeing his play, and of hearing his beautiful work praised, to console her for the ordeal. As the fourth of May drew near she could think of little else.

One evening towards the end of April Mr Challis and Hilda, having dined early, were sitting in Hyde Park. Mr Challis did not like Hyde Park at any time, and now, full as it was of American soldiers and A.A. sites and tarnished pewter barrage balloons and scraps of paper and dust, it affronted his soul, but Hilda had suggested that they should go there and get a breath of fresh air before they went home, and he had agreed.

He was in a dreamy but exultant mood. In a few nights *Kattë*, in all her warm, pathetic, helpless loveliness would glow before the dazzled and desirous (that was how Mr Challis put it to himself) eyes of men, and when *Kattë's* fate had been decided, he would take Hilda to Kew and tell her of his fame and how she had inspired the masterpiece that was moving all London even to tears, and that he loved her. Meanwhile, he felt a sudden longing for her to see the play.

He turned towards her. She was observing the couples strolling past and commenting upon the girls' stockings.

'Pardon!' she smiled, turning her head.

'I asked if you were free next Wednesday evening.'

'Why?' inquired Hilda cautiously.

'If you are not free, it is of no importance,' and he turned to watch a passing car.

'Now don't be haughty. What's it all about? Tell Mum.'

Many of Hilda's expressions simply passed over Mr Challis's head as if she were speaking a foreign language, because he was so enslaved by his imaginative conception of her character that he did not try to interpret what she said, but only received a general impression of its meaning, which was given charm by the freshness of her voice.

'It is of no consequence. A friend of mine has written a play

226

and I wanted you to see it, and tell me what you thought of it, that was all!'

That was all. Only his masterpiece, built about the character of the girl at his side and ready to be laid at her feet! He felt that the situation called for a faint smile.

'Fancy,' said Hilda, patting away a yawn. 'Excuse me. How clever of him, but I suppose someone has to write them. Is it a thriller?'

'Not in the accepted contemporary sense of that word, but I hope that it may give the true *frisson* of pity and terror that purges an audience.'

Many of Mr Challis's remarks passed over Hilda's head on the foreign language principle, too, and she only received the impression that he was ever so highbrow.

'What's it about, then? (Just give me an idea and then we ought to be buzzing; it's getting late.)'

'It is about — a girl.'

'Oh, one of those musicals.'

'There is music in it, I hope, but not of the sort that is played upon instruments. This girl is a victim of her own power to charm.'

At that moment there were no couples strolling past, and Hilda was able to give her full attention to what Mr Challis was saying. She slowly turned her head as he finished speaking, and looked at him. Her suit was as blue as her eyes and her blouse of fragile white frills gave an impression of delicious freshness, but the look on her face was so *utterly* non-comprehending that a faint tremor assailed Mr Challis. He had expected *some* glimmer of understanding, however slight; he had felt that as she had suggested so many of the traits in *Kattë's* character, she *must* instinctively feel a little of *Kattë's* tragedy, for she herself would one day be the victim of her own power to charm, even as *Kattë* had been. (It may here be said that Mr Challis anticipated a sticky end of some sort for Hilda, based on his theory that nothing delightful lasted for long.)

'What on earth do you mean?' asked Hilda.

'I mean,' said Mr Challis, suppressing slight impatience, 'that she cannot help men falling in love with her, and when it – er – this fact causes pain, suffering, she finally comes to loathe her own power.'

'Whatever for?' said Hilda, turning to study a passing pair of stockings.

'Because she makes men suffer,' said Mr Challis sombrely, gazing at her, 'even as you do.'

'I don't do anything of the sort!' she exclaimed indignantly, turning round. 'My boys are always ever so cheery.'

'Perhaps they suffer without your knowledge.'

'Well, I can't help that, can I?'

Mr Challis shook his head. 'No, you cannot help it. Neither could she. That was her tragedy.'

'What happened to her in the end? (Look here, we must be getting a move on, it's after eight and I'm cold.)'

'She killed herself,' announced Mr Challis with dreary relish.

'Well, it does sound a nice cheerful play, I must say. What a *mind* your friend must have!' She stood up and smoothed her jacket. He stood up too, his disappointment written on his face. Hilda, with one of her rare friendly gestures, slipped her arm in his.

'Come on,' she said. 'Let's walk fast and get warm. The matter with you is, Marcus, you think too much. You ought to be on the Brains Trust. Come on!'

The pressure of her firm young arm was so comforting and kind that for an instant he had a glimpse of another world than his own; a world where feelings were simpler and life was accepted rather than dissected; it was one of those tantalizing momentary releases from the prison of personality which excessively self-conscious people sometimes experience; and it had gone in an instant.

'I should have known better than to tell you,' he said at last. 'I should have known that you would not understand. And I am content that you should not. It gives the situation an ironical symmetry.'

'That's all right, then,' said Hilda, looking from left to right as they crossed the road. 'But I shan't be able to see your boy friend's play. I've just remembered. I've got to go out on Wednesday.'

'That does not matter. Any other evening —'

'Oh, I suppose he can always get you seats because he wrote it. Well, I may as well get it off my chest, Marcus. I'd rather not see it, so that's that!'

Mr Challis actually stood still and gazed incredulously at her.

'You mean — you won't come at all? Never?' he said at last.

'That's right,' she said cheerfully, walking on. He followed, unable to believe what he had heard.

'My friend will be very disappointed,' he said at last in a low voice.

'Too bad about him, but there's enough misery in the world, 'specially nowadays, without writing stuff like that.'

Mr Challis had recovered sufficiently to laugh.

'My dear child, how little you understand! The world needs the purging power of great drama as never before.'

'Well, I don't, so your friend's got another guess coming. This our taxi? Aren't we lucky!'

She was completely unruffled during their journey homewards, for by now she took old Marcus for granted, continuing to go out with him every three weeks or so because he seemed to like it and she did not find it too bad; she was also amused by the slight oddness of their relationship, her not knowing his other name or the number of his flat at High View, and so on; and she was also more flattered by his attentions and her mother's remarks about prosperous and elderly admirers who Meant Business than she realized.

Mr Challis concealed his bitter disappointment and annoyance beneath his usual dignity. He was trying to listen to the voice of hurt vanity, which told him that Hilda was a common little girl without imagination, and silence the voice of love, which told him that she was a darling and forced him to admit that he would give up all his dignity and all his fame to have her kindness and her kisses.

18

There was not an empty seat in the house. Margaret leant her arms upon the green velvet of the balustrade and gazed down through the brilliant air into the stalls, where the party that had a warm personal interest for her was just settling into its seats. There was Mrs Challis, laughing and looking over her shoulder at the dark American soldier whom Margaret had met at Hampstead, and next to her sat Hebe in a pink and white dress that suited her pale dairymaid's looks, and next to Hebe was the other American, Earl, and Hebe was letting him have too many of her dimples, thought Margaret; and why was she not sitting next to her husband, whose figure (so different from his father-in-law's) was betrayed by tails and a white tie? He was the last of the row and sat gazing good-naturedly about him like a self-sufficient small boy at a party.

I don't mean a thing to any of them, thought Margaret. They're all very kind to me (except Hebe) but they wouldn't notice if they never saw Struggles again. Still, if anyone had told me a year ago that I should go in and out of Gerard Challis's house as I pleased, I simply wouldn't have believed it, and I mustn't expect too much. What a pretty theatre this is.

The jade-green, cherry-red and silver in which the theatre was decorated had nothing in common with that confused dark gold which glows forth from theatre interiors on the canvases of Sickert; indeed, one of the older dramatic critics had already observed that this place always made him think of a ladies' hairdressing saloon; nevertheless, the colours and light made a silvery background for dresses which the many lovely

231

women present had evidently put on in honour of Gerard Challis. The scene had not, of course, the brilliance of a pre-war first night at which the Smarty and the Arty were both represented, but there was a feeling of anticipation in the air, an excitement that expressed itself through the collective voice of the audience in a thrilling hum, while piercing through this steady background of sound came the gay sweetness of Viennese waltzes played by a small and perfect string orchestra.

'Der music iss goot,' said Zita, who had been listening intently. 'Und you hear how they play as if dey are a machine. Thot is clever. I think thot is *his* idea – Mr Challis.'

'How?' breathed Margaret, half turning.

'Yes. I think he mean the music to say – this woman *Kattë* is like a Viennese waltz; she iss so gay and lovely, but she is a nothing.'

Margaret nodded, looking at her and thinking how the vividness of her own outlook upon life had increased since she had known Zita, and how impossible it would be for herself, for any Englishwoman, to pare away all softness in her personal appearance until she had achieved the stinging smartness of Zita in her grey and orange striped dress, with her hair sleeked down like a wet black shell and an orange messenger-boy cap over one eye. An Englishwoman dressed like that would only look ugly or eccentric, Margaret thought, and it's no use saying that men dislike that sort of smartness because there are four of them with their eyes glued on her at this moment.

Nevertheless, she herself preferred a softer type of attractiveness, and she turned again to the stalls, where there were many lovely or striking faces and where her own long-standing interest in 'interesting people' enabled her to recognize some of them from photographs in magazines and the press. But her eyes always returned to the little group which she knew, lingering with reluctant admiration upon Hebe's childishly dressed brown curls and voluptuous form in the soft dress that suggested the sashed, high-waisted robes of Sir Joshua Reynolds's day; she had a style which, while never looking eccentric or tiresomely artistic, was all her own.

What a bad wife and mother she was! Flirting over their shared programme with that boy and leaving her children at home in charge of the ailing Grantey, while she ran around the West End in the blackout with American soldiers!

Her rather heated thoughts were interrupted by a soft 'Ach!' from Zita. The lights were growing dim.

A moment later the immense green velvet curtains parted with an entrancing rustle, and the audience looked in upon the bedroom of a Viennese girl of thirty years ago; the lace, the ribbons, the roses of an unashamed and victorious femininity struck upon their eyes and senses like a perfume, and there was a murmur of admiration (mingled with the slight sound of programmes being turned as some of the less devout tried to see who might be responsible for this ravishing *décor* and found that it was Gower Parks) as Miss Schatter, wearing a white lawn nightgown and with her dark hair unbound, sat slowly up in bed, linked her arms round her knees, and burst into peals of laughter. Margaret, scarcely breathing, settled herself to watch and listen.

The story unfolded while the audience sat as if under a spell. Not a cough nor a murmur broke the reverent hush. The long sentences of dialogue were perfectly shaped and written in Mr Challis's finest style, and there were many witty lines which brought that appreciative murmuring laughter which is sometimes the reward of subtlety in the theatre. The characters were firmly drawn yet complex; there was the piquancy of ironical contrast, as in the scene where Kattë and her friend, Trudi, compared the shape of their chests to win a bet for Trudi's impecunious lover, who shot himself off-stage as soon as the bet was won, because he was in love with Kattë. The curtain fell on Kattë, sitting up in bed once more and wondering if her life were as happy as she had always supposed it to be, while her latest adorer broke into a bitter laugh. The audience relaxed with sighs and little movements. The lights went up, people began to make their way to the bar, and the orchestra started to play French military marches of the period.

'Well, it iss beautiful. So true and fine,' said Zita, with a long sigh, turning to Margaret. 'Do you not think so?'

Margaret was leaning forward with her chin resting in her hands and gazing absently down into the stalls, where friends were crowding about the Challises and congratulating Seraphina upon what was obviously going to be her husband's finest play.

'I don't know,' she answered at last in a tone that sounded puzzled at herself rather than at the play. 'It is beautiful, of course, but –'

She broke off, wondering whether her present lack of excitement was caused by having looked forward to this occasion with such high hopes that no play ever written could have come up to them.

'I see no fault in it,' said Zita solemnly. 'It iss perfect. But we wait und we see. Perhaps something happen to spoil it all. But I think no.'

They said no more, both being rather tired, and were content to watch the audience and listen to the fierce, gay, cocky little French marches.

In the bar the critics were talking.

'It's the oldest dramatic recipe in the history of the modern theatre,' obstinately said the one who had been reminded of a ladies' hairdressing saloon. 'Frou-Frou and Camille done up with *confort moderne*.'

'But it always fetches 'em.'

'Of course it always fetches 'em and it always will, although this version is a bit dehydrated.'

'Yes,' murmured another, 'it's all there, but God just didn't blow.'

For another two hours the tragedy of Kattë unfolded, marching towards its inevitable end over the souls and bodies of her friends and relations. Her father shot her mother, for having borne him such a daughter, then jumped into the Danube. Her crippled brother's character was corrupted by the young officers who bribed him to carry notes to his sister for them and plead their cause, and he became a pimp. Her younger sister went insane with jealousy when she believed that her own lover had deserted her for Kattë, and the final blow was struck when the old nurse, with whom Kattë had lived since the break-up of her own home, was forced to sell the pet goldfinch to buy a little goulash for their supper and burst into sobs during the meal, blaming Kattë for the loss of the bird.

Many eyes in the audience were wet as the play drew towards its end, with the last rays of sunset streaming into the poor room in the nurse's apartment where Kattë sat alone. The lights were going up in the city of Vienna, whose roofs and palaces could be seen through the open window against a darkening summer sky, and from the street below came shouts and laughter as the happy lovers danced to a fiddler playing The Beautiful Blue Danube. The heavy, sensuously sweet melody seemed to be filling the room like water and rippling all about the motion-less form of Kattë as she sat by the window, staring out at the city, and nursing the revolver in her white hands.

A moment later and it was over; she lay dead, with her arms outstretched, and the music was still ringing joyously through the empty room as the curtain came slowly down.

Another moment, and what a storm of applause burst forth! and the curtains swung apart once more to reveal Miss Schatter, hand-in-hand with Edward Early, smiling and bowing to the enraptured audience and looking more lovely than ever with her hair about her shoulders and her face pale with exhaustion. How they clapped and cheered! Again and again the company had to come forward and be frantically acclaimed, and soon the shout of, 'Author! Author,' began to be heard.

Margaret, clapping as hard as the rest and delighting in her hero's success, felt her heart beat faster. In another moment she would see him! and the thought banished other and perverse thoughts which had insisted upon obtruding themselves during Kattë's closing moments.

'It will become a Classic,' said Zita solemnly, 'with *Hamlet* and *The Master Builder* and *Saint Joan* it will be.'

'Oh, I do hope so! Author! Author!'

She clapped the harder and called the louder because she was guiltily aware that during the last act she had wanted to shake Kattë, rather than weep over her, and tell her to have a straight talk with her friends and relations instead of looking at them in woeful silence or skipping away tra-la-la-ing. If only she had *explained* to her sister, Margaret thought, clapping away, that need never have happened. They were all so highly emotional. ('Author! Author!') Well, the Viennese are, of course. But are they quite as emotional as all that? Going mad and jumping into the Danube and shooting themselves for very little reason, really, except that everyone fell in love with Kattë. And it could all have been put right so easily!

The fact is, I don't believe a w —

But here her thoughts (perhaps fortunately) were distracted by the renewed applause as Gerard Challis walked slowly out from the wings on to the stage.

How distinguished he looked; how tired! and how sad was the fine faint smile that played about his lips. It means nothing to him, she thought. All this clapping and cheering is just dust and ashes; all he cares about is *The Work*, and that it should be good. He shrinks from the vulgarity of it all.

'Mr Challis certainly doesn't look very pleased,' observed Earl to Hebe, as they stood side by side clapping and gazing up at the stage. 'Do you think maybe he didn't like Miss Schatter's interpretation of the part?'

'Oh, Pops always puts on that face on a first night; he's as pleased as two niggers, really; he adores being clapped and having silly witches hanging on his every word; if you ask me, I think Kattë was the silliest witch of the lot,' retorted Hebe loudly above the din, and closed her flowerlike mouth again: it was the first long speech she had made that evening and her first and last comment, beyond significant glances at her mother, on the play.

Dear old Gerry, thought his wife, it's the dreariest one yet, but *isn't* he loving it all! This ought to keep him a good boy for weeks.

Alexander (who always enjoyed an evening out in his best clothes, though he enjoyed an evening at home in his old ones equally well) was also clapping, and enjoying the spectacle of the bowing company in their picturesque clothes with the brilliance of the footlights shining upon them. He thought the play was all right; but then, he did not ever care much for plays or poems or novels; he liked real objects best, and next to them, painting real objects.

Mr Challis stood there, still smiling faintly and bowing first to the line of smiling players on either side of him and then to the audience. He caught his wife's eye and gave her a slightly, but very slightly, wider smile.

'What do you know, Lev?' said Hebe out of the side of her mouth to the other American.

'It's a swell piece of dramma,' he answered briefly in the same way, 'but what's all the grief about anyway? A dame like that, there's only one thing to do with her –'

'You tell me presently,' said Hebe, and at that moment Mr Challis, registering reluctance, stepped forward and held up his hand. A hush instantly fell upon the excited house, and Margaret leant breathlessly forward, but even as he parted his lips to speak there arose, muffled yet unmistakable, the howl of the air-raid warning. A half-comical groan went up, and as Mr Challis hesitated a few people began to move unobtrusively towards the exits. Most of the audience, however, remained where it was and there were renewed calls of 'Speech! Speech!'

It would never have occurred to Margaret to do anything but stay where she was. But Zita had her by the arm; Zita was dragging her away, past the surprised faces of the people in the same row; Zita's thin cold hand was trembling and her face was white. Margaret tried to hang back and began to protest, but one glance showed her how things were, and, angry and contemptuous yet pitying, she allowed herself to be pulled down the deserted, softly lit corridors and down the stairs until they came out into the foyer, where a few people were gathered.

'Quick – quick!' muttered Zita, darting across to the door leading to the street. 'Dere is a tube across der road und we go down dere.'

'It probably won't be much,' said Margaret, as they came out into the street, where black buildings loomed against the soft, starry May sky. It was not quite dark and there was a ghostly reflected glow everywhere from the searchlights.

'Quick, quick!' said Zita, shivering, and gripped Margaret's arm and hurried out across the broad, pale, shadowy road, dodging in and out between the red and green lights of cars and street-signs and the gliding dark shapes of taxis.

'Here we are,' she muttered, darting into the entrance of the Underground and scurrying down the steps.

Margaret was still so annoyed that she could not trust herself to speak. She was also very tired from the intense excitement of the evening, and bitterly disappointed that she had not heard Gerard Challis's speech. It had been arranged that she and Zita should return to Westwood for supper, and she assumed that they were on their way there – unless Zita proposed to stay in the tube all night. What a little coward she was!

'Ach!' said Zita, with a great sigh of relief as they came out on to the crowded, stuffy platform. 'Now we are safe!'

Margaret, looking like a thundercloud, said nothing.

'Oh yess, oh yess, I know you are angry!' said Zita bitterly, tossing her head, 'but I am not staying up dere in der noise und der bits falling und der bombs – to please you or anyone.'

Margaret still said nothing.

'You think I am a coward!'

'No, I don't,' lied Margaret, stirred to response by the sudden thought that if Zita marched off in a huff there would be no visit to Westwood that evening, 'but I do think that you make too much fuss. These little raids aren't dangerous.'

'*So!* But for some dey will mean death, und why not for me? No, no,' laughing angrily, 'I take no chance und I come away quick down here.'

Margaret said no more, and just then their train came in and Zita was soon talking away amiably enough about the play, and Margaret, though half of her seemed to be still in the theatre waiting for him to speak, was diplomatically ready to fall in with her changed mood.

After a slower and much more crowded journey than usual, they got out at Highgate station and found that the warning was still on, but that there had been no gunfire for some time. People standing at the entrance were staring at a red glow in the sky over Hampstead Heath, and saying that a hospital had been hit by incendiaries.

'Shall we go?' said Margaret, breathing with relief the delicious freshness of the air.

'No, we wait for the All Clear. Perhaps dey come back.'

So for another quarter of an hour they hung about, while one person after another decided to risk it, and set off smartly for home, until they were the only ones left. All was quiet and the glow over Hampstead was dying down.

'Do let's go, Zita,' said Margaret impatiently at last.

Zita was just shaking her head obstinately when − suggesting as it always did to Margaret the sound of the Last Trump − the All Clear began.

'Ach! Goot!' she said. 'Now we go safely. So!' (looking upwards), 'You run away like the cowards which you are!' and she shook her fist at the peaceful night sky. 'It iss all over for this time and I alive still am! Come, now we go home and haf some supper.'

Margaret knew that Mr Challis was giving a party for the company and his family at the Savoy after the play, and therefore would normally not have been home until late, but she hoped that the raid might have upset their plans and caused the family to return earlier; this had been her chief reason for wishing to get to Westwood as soon as possible.

However, when Zita opened the front door everything else was driven out of their heads by the sight which confronted them.

A newly lit fire smoked in the grate, and every light in the hall was burning. Shawls and coats and shoes were scattered everywhere, slipping out of two large cases filled with children's clothes and toys, and in front of the fire in a low chair sat Grantey, leaning back and looking white and exhausted, with her eyes shut. In another chair Emma was half-lying, wrapped in a fur coat and crying noisily, and close to the fire was a big basket with Jeremy in it, also crying. Cortway was kneeling beside his sister, trying to force a drink between her lips, and on the hearthrug, surveying the scene with enormous scared eyes in a very pale face and wearing a coat over his pyjamas, sat Barnabas.

Cortway turned round as the two girls hurried forward.

'So someone's turned up at last!' he exclaimed. 'About time, too. 'Ere, you, Zita, give Mrs Grant a hand, will you, and you, Miss, see to the fire, it's going out with any luck. Alice, old girl' – he slipped his arm under his sister's shoulders – 'hold up a minute, here's Zita, she'll give you a hand up to bed. Oh, hold your noise, do!' turning to the baby.

Margaret was already on her knees attending to the fire, and Zita, loudly uttering ejaculations and questions, was helping Cortway to raise Grantey to a sitting position. Suddenly she opened her eyes. 'The children? Are the children all right?' she gasped painfully.

'Quite all right. All safe. All here,' said Cortway, bending forward and shouting into her ear.

'What the matter iss? What hass happened? Ach, mein Gott!' said Zita. 'Emma, you notty girl, quiet be!' and she turned distractedly to the chair and its weeping occupant.

Emma roared louder than ever, so Margaret, as the fire was now blazing promisingly, went over to her and picked her up. Emma's cries ceased as soon as she felt herself raised, and she allowed Margaret to wipe her eyes and tenderly rearrange her nightgown, over which a little frock had been hastily pulled. Her tiny feet were naked and blue with cold.

'Well, I couldn't find her blinking socks,' Cortway said defensively, seeing Margaret's frown. 'Half the side of the house blown out and the hospital across the road blazing – I thought me heart would have stopped when I came round the corner and saw it.'

'But what happened? Was the cottage hit?' said Margaret, raising her voice to make herself heard above Zita's noisy exclamations.

'Near enough,' said Cortway grimly, reaching across to Jeremy and beginning to pat him mechanically. 'I was just turning on to hear the news –'

'Oh, it was dreadful!' interrupted Grantey faintly. 'I was just getting Emma settled in the shelter and Barnabas was being such a good boy and helping me (Jerry was asleep, thank goodness; bless his little heart, he never stirred) and suddenly there was that awful whistling noise – you know –'

'I went under the table the tooter the sweeter I can tell you,' said her brother. 'Like old times, that was.'

'– and the most awful crash and then a sort of sighing sound and the Anderson kind of heaved up and down and then I heard the bricks come tumbling down. Oh, I was frightened! There, there, there's a good boy,' and she feebly turned towards the baby, whose cries were becoming less as Cortway steadily patted him.

'They copped it just across the road at the Black Bear and the front of Lamb Cottage was blown out,' said Cortway. 'The wardens got me on the 'phone and I went over and fetched Alice and the kids in the car. Nice state of affairs for Mr and Mrs Niland to come home to, I don't think,' he ended. 'Half your house gone and your kids frightened into fits. "*Oh, ain't it a lovely war!*"'

'I'm not frightened,' said Barnabas suddenly.

'Of course you aren't,' said Cortway, giving his white face a glance of approval. 'And you was a great help to Grantey too, and took care of your little brother and sister, didn't you? And now I'm going downstairs to make us all a nice hot cup of cocoa. How'll that be, eh?'

'I shall like that,' said Barnabas. He glanced across at Margaret. 'How is Emma now?' he demanded.

'Better, thank you, Barnabas. Look, she's nearly asleep,' and she gently moved aside a fold of the fur coat and showed the peaceful little face, with eyes dreamily watching the flicker of the fire, the lids slowly falling and then opening wide again.

'I'm glad,' said Barnabas. 'When will Mummy and Daddy come home?'

'Very soon now, sonny,' said Cortway, and went off to make the cocoa.

'Oh dear, I do feel so bad,' said Grantey fretfully, 'and it's not at all like me to give way. It's this *heart*, I suppose. The doctor said shock would make it worse.'

Margaret glanced inquiringly at Zita, not having heard of Grantey's heart before, and Zita made an ominous face. In fact, Grantey had kept her trouble to herself, merely letting it be known that she was not well and must take it easy – the latter prescription being a cause of much ironical laughter on her part.

'Douglas, Douglas – can't you make it tea, not that nasty heavy cocoa?' she now called imploringly after her brother. 'Make cocoa for Barnabas and the rest of us'll have tea.'

'A goot strong cup of coffee,' said Zita longingly.

'Tea for me,' whispered Margaret, looking up from the child with a warning grimace. But it was too late; Emma sat upright, cast off her coverings and looked about her.

'Co-co?' she said inquiringly.

'There!' said Cortway. 'Now we've done it. She loves cocoa.'

'I will come und coffee make,' said Zita, hurrying away. Grantey sank back again, but she looked slightly less exhausted and her gaze rested with languid satisfaction upon the children.

'Poor Miss Hebe, what she must be going through,' she murmured, as if to herself.

Poor Miss Hebe, indeed, thought Margaret scornfully. Why couldn't she ring up here? At that moment the telephone-bell did begin to ring, startlingly loud in the dreamy hush.

'Oh dear – that'll be Miss Hebe,' exclaimed Grantey, struggling up.

'I'll go – here, you take her,' said Margaret, quickly but gently putting Emma down on her lap, and she hurried across the hall.

'Hullo?'

'Is that Highgate 00078? Hold on, please; Martlefield wants you.'

A pause, and then a voice said:

'Is that Highgate 00078? Mr Challis's house? This is Lady Challis speaking. Are you all right?'

'All the children are safe but Lamb Cottage is damaged,' answered Margaret loudly and calmly.

'Oh dear! Badly damaged?'

'I don't know, I'm afraid.'

'Are Hebe and Alex all right?'

'I don't know, Lady Challis,' answered Margaret with heart beating fast, 'they aren't back from the theatre yet.'

'Oh yes – I'd forgotten. How did the children get over to Highgate? (Who are you, by the way?)'

'(I'm Margaret Steggles, a – a friend of Zita's.) Mrs Grant was with the children in the shelter when a bomb came down opposite, and Cortway went over in the car and fetched them.'

'Are they very upset, poor little things?'

'No, they don't seem to be.' A smile came into Margaret's voice as she glanced over her shoulder at the group by the fire. 'Barnabas has been so good, and Emma is asking for cocoa. Jeremy's asleep.

'Co – co!' repeated Emma cooingly from Grantey's lap.

'Thank God,' said Lady Challis cheerfully. 'And how's my poor Grantey?'

'She – she seems rather tired but –' said Margaret hesitatingly, glancing round again and receiving a series of violent shakes of the head from Grantey, 'but there's nothing really wrong with her, I think.'

'You mean that her heart's bad and I don't wonder,' retorted Lady Challis. 'Well, that's all I wanted to know, so I shall ring off now, but give them all my love, and if Hebe and Alex are all right don't ring me up; only ring up if there's anything wrong. Good-bye,' and she rang off.

Margaret returned to the fire and took Emma on her lap again.

'I hope you didn't give her ladyship the idea there was anything the matter with me,' said Grantey, with a touch of her old sharpness. 'There's enough to worry about without me. When I think of all Miss Hebe's things blown to pieces –'

'Piccy –' suddenly cried Barnabas, and burst into tears. 'Oh, poor Piccy – I left him behind!'

'It's his monkey,' explained Grantey, looking anxiously at him. 'Now cheer up, there's a good boy; I'm sure Piccy's all right, and to-morrow Grantey'll go over and find him and bring him back.'

'Piccy! Piccy! I want Piccy!'

Margaret went quickly over to the fire with Emma and sat down on the hearthrug.

'Look, Barnabas,' she was beginning persuasively, when there was a confused sound of the front door hastily opening and of voices, and the next moment she almost lost her balance as Hebe snatched Emma up and smothered her with kisses, while her eyes, looking black in the extreme pallor of her face, darted from Jeremy to Barnabas as if to make certain of their safety.

'Mummy! Mummy!' screamed Barnabas, stumbling over to her, and Jeremy stirred, awoke, and began to cry. Alexander, who had come in behind Hebe, looked tired and dirty, and had no hat, and his coat hung open, showing his evening clothes. He stared at the children as if he were bewildered.

'We thought we'd *never* get here,' said Hebe with a long sigh, sinking on to the hearthrug and putting the laughing Emma down on the outspread skirt of her dress while she gathered Jeremy into her arms. 'We tried to 'phone the cottage from the theatre, and of course we couldn't get through and we couldn't get a taxi for *any* money and so we had to go by tube; jam-full and everybody smelling like mad. Well,' turning abruptly to Margaret, 'let's have it. The cottage is flat, I suppose?'

Margaret started violently; she had retreated into a dark corner and was hoping to slip away unobserved.

'No, I don't think so,' she replied hesitatingly, 'I think the bomb fell on the Black Bear. It's the front of the cottage that's damaged, Cortway said.'

'*The Shrapnel Hunters* is what I'm thinking about,' muttered Alexander, who had seated himself on the hearthrug beside Hebe.

'Front blown clean out, sir,' said Cortway with gusto, approaching with a laden tray. Behind came Zita, carrying another tray. 'I couldn't see much because of the dust and those silly bleeders (begging your pardon, Miss Hebe) of wardens getting under your feet and telling you off, but it looked like the drawing-room's a gorner, and the nursery too. Nice goings-on!' he ended deeply, and put the tray down rather hard.

'If they're gone, *The Shrapnel Hunters* will be gone as well.'

'I couldn't say, sir. All the windows are gorn, for certain.'

'Und all the glass into the canvas has been driven,' said Zita funereally. 'It will be ruined – your masterpiece, Mr Niland.'

Alexander stared miserably at her.

'Sit down, sit down, for goodness' sake,' said Hebe impatiently, waving a sandwich at her husband. 'It's probably quite all right; I put it in the cupboard before we came out. I always do.'

Alexander knelt down and put his arms about her and Jeremy, whom she was supporting with one hand.

'You darling girl, thank you very, very much,' he said, taking her sandwich.

'Yes, well, don't get in such a flap,' said Hebe, returning his kiss and taking another sandwich. 'And now have something to eat, do. Here –' and she pushed the plate across to Margaret with her satin-sandalled foot. Margaret gave a nervous laugh and remarked that she really ought to be going, but as no one took any notice and she very much wanted to stay, she accepted a sandwich and ate it in her shadowy corner, glancing from time to time at Hebe surrounded by her children and deciding that she might be rude and a flirt, but that she undoubtedly did love them.

'I pour out?' inquired Zita, kneeling among trays and children in front of the fire.

Hebe nodded, working off her shoes by rubbing one against the other. Barnabas was sitting between his father's knees eating a piece of Spam which he had picked out of a sandwich.

'This is the latest I've ever sat up,' he said proudly. 'What's the time, Grantey?'

'Nearly ten. You'll all be dead in the morning,' she said resignedly, but she looked less exhausted and her colour had returned.

'Co-co,' implored Emma sweetly, holding out her arms.

'In a moment you shall haf,' said Zita, smiling down at her and giving her a biscuit. A peaceful silence followed, filled with sippings and munchings. Nobody seemed inclined to talk about the play, and Margaret, who had looked forward to discussing it with Zita, suddenly found herself so tired that she only wanted to go home and get to bed, but she did wonder how the Challis's party at the Savoy was going, and presently observed in a low tone to Zita:

'I do hope Mr and Mrs Challis are all right?'

'Oh, no bomb would dare fall on Pops,' said Hebe, making signs to Alexander to carry Emma, who had fallen asleep, back to the chair where she had first been lying, 'especially on a first night. Look, Jeremy's asleep too, isn't he a lovekin.'

'I go und put up the beds,' said Zita, standing up.

'Put Alex in the Peach Room and all the brats in with him,' called Hebe after her. 'I'm dead, and I want some sleep to-night. You don't mind, do you?' to her husband, who shook his head.

'I'll take Jeremy in with me, Miss Hebe,' said Grantey, beginning to bestir herself. 'The cot's in the first attic; Douglas, get it down into my room, will you? I'll be there in a minute.'

'Can I help?' asked Margaret, also getting up.

'So I should hope!' said Zita, with the laugh that meant she was cross. 'Dere is much to do und we all are tired.'

As she followed Zita across the hall Margaret heard Hebe mutter, 'I suppose this means camping here for the next week or so. What a bore.'

It was nearly two hours later that Margaret at last left Westwood, having seen all the beds made up and the children asleep in them. The only exciting event in the latter part of the evening had been a telephone-call from the Savoy to know if everything were all right, and she had gathered that Mrs Challis, not Mr Challis, had made it after many failures to get through which had naturally alarmed her, and that she would come home at once. (Margaret herself had telephoned to her mother while she and Zita were waiting at the Tube station, and told her not to wait up as she might be late.)

The waning moon was rising as she walked quickly down the hill. In the air there was the beginning of that beautiful sensation, which reaches its height in full summer, of night being not a separate condition but a deepening of the day in which hidden beauties become visible. There was no sound save the ring of her footsteps along the empty street, and although she had intended to think about *Kattë* and make up her mind about it, the stars and the strangely shaped setting moon and the bright veils of cloud drifting swiftly across the sky were all so beautiful that she ended by thinking of nothing but how delightful it was to be walking alone at night.

19

The next morning she was aroused out of a deep sleep by someone shaking her and her mother's voice saying crossly:

'Margaret! Margaret! Wake up – Mr Fletcher wants you on the telephone!'

Margaret sat up, pushing the hair from her face and repeating stupidly:

'Telephone! What's the matter?'

'It's Mr Fletcher, I tell you. He wants to speak to you on the 'phone; he's holding the line.'

'What on earth does he want me –' Margaret muttered, getting unsteadily out of bed and putting on her dressing-gown. She was not fully awake.

'I don't know what he wants you for. He sounds very upset. Hurry up, do. I'll go and tell him you're coming,' and she hurried away.

'Hullo? Mr Fletcher?' said Margaret, struggling with a great yawn as she took up the receiver.

'Margaret? Is that you? I'm sorry to get you out of bed, but I'm in a hole and I want your help. Can you meet me outside Brockdale Station in half an hour?'

Margaret answered at once: 'Yes.'

His voice was so urgent and unhappy that the thought of refusing never entered her head.

'Thanks. It's awfully good of you. I'll explain when we meet,' he said gruffly, and rang off.

Mrs Steggles was hovering in the background, her face alight with curiosity.

'Whatever's the matter?' she demanded.

'I don't know, Mother. He just said he's in a hole and wants me to help, and will I meet him in half an hour outside Brockdale Station. I'll have to hurry. Will you be an angel and make me some tea?'

'It's ready – I'll bring you up a cup while you're dressing,' said Mrs Steggles, going into the dining-room. 'But what an idea, dragging anybody off at eight in the morning! Has his wife turned up again, do you think?'

Margaret was hurrying into her clothes and did not answer. Her thoughts had flown at once to Westwood. She had planned to telephone Zita after breakfast, and ask if she could be of any help during the day (which was fortunately a Saturday) by looking after the children or fetching things from the ruins of Lamb Cottage. Now this plan must be postponed. It was annoying, and she wondered crossly and without much interest what could be the matter with Dick Fletcher? Nothing interesting, that was certain!

Ten minutes later she was hurrying down the long staircase leading into Archway Tube station and feeling as if a strong force were drawing her back to Westwood while she was compelled to go in the other direction. It was a lovely summer morning, and in other circumstances she would have enjoyed the journey, but she was wondering whether Alexander's picture had been saved from Lamb Cottage and if she would get away from Dick Fletcher in time to telephone Zita before lunch, and scarcely noticed the sunlight and the cloudless sky.

He was waiting for her outside the station, and started eagerly forward as she came towards him. He was very pale and looked as if he had not slept.

'Hullo, Margaret, this *is* good of you,' he exclaimed. 'I'm sorry to have got you up so early. I did wait until eight o'clock.'

251

'That's quite all right, it doesn't matter a bit. Er – I hope it isn't very bad news?'

'Oh –' He hesitated a moment, looking at her and biting his lips and she was just thinking that her mother's guess must be right and that his wife must have turned up again, when he said impatiently:

'Oh, it's nothing serious, it's only that I'm in a hole, and you're the only woman I know; well, the only *nice* woman' – laughing awkwardly – 'and I want you to help me. Let's go this way.' He took her arm and began to walk rapidly away from the station towards the High Street. 'It's all right, there's nothing to worry about. I'll tell you in a minute.'

He was suddenly silent. Margaret felt that he was trying to decide the best way to tell her, so she kept silent too, and they hurried along through the sunshine, both frowning and quiet.

She was very conscious of his arm thrust carelessly through her own, like that of an old friend or another girl. Women who are not often touched by men naturally respond strongly when they are touched, however casually, and Margaret was no exception to the rule. She did, however, like his arm thrust through hers. She at once felt closer to him and more friendly and willing to help. A number of miss-ish prejudices seemed to drift away and she glanced at his face and thought, I do like him, really.

'My housekeeper was hurt in the raid last night,' he said suddenly, as if her glance had made him decide to speak, 'and she's in hospital and likely to be there for at least three weeks. The trouble is, there's no one to look after my daughter.'

'Your daughter? I didn't know –'

'Didn't know I had a daughter?' turning to look at her with a troubled smile. 'Oh yes, Linda's nearly twelve.' His voice was tender as he spoke the name. 'That's where I go on Sundays, to see Linda.'

'Do you?' said Margaret, in a low tone, much ashamed of her past suspicions.

'Yes. I've got a little house out here where she lives with Mrs Coates, my housekeeper. You see, the trouble is' – he hesitated, then went on quickly – 'Linda isn't quite like other children; not quite up to the standard for her age, and so she doesn't go to school or anything of that sort or see many people. I wondered if you could spend the day here, just until I can get a nurse or somebody – she'll be all right when once she's used to the new person – she's very loving, bless her, and gets on with anybody, but I've got to find somebody *absolutely* reliable.'

'Where is she now?' asked Margaret, feeling revulsion, though her tone expressed only sympathy.

'At home. Oh, she can be left quite safely for half an hour,' glancing at her suspiciously, as if trying to detect signs of shrinking. 'But she doesn't like being alone for long. She – she's so gentle. You'll love her,' he ended confidently.

'I'm sure I shall. She sounds –' Margaret left the sentence unfinished, in a vague murmur. Like most people who worship physical beauty, she had a horror of deformity and her imagination at once began to paint a monster.

'Could you stay for a bit?' he said eagerly, as they crossed the noisy High Street and approached a quieter road. 'I should be so grateful, and it would be such a weight off my mind.'

'Of course I will,' she answered at once, and was rewarded by his look of relief and a smile that made him seem years younger. She put out of her head all thoughts of going to Westwood that day and reluctantly decided that if she refused him or made excuses, she would never forgive herself. Heart and duty both told her clearly what she ought to do. All the same, she was so dreading the first sight of Linda Fletcher that she was afraid he might notice her agitation, and exclaimed,

'What unusual houses!' in order to distract his attention from herself.

'Yes, no two of them are alike. I wanted somewhere really nice for her to live, quiet, you know, and pretty, and we were lucky enough to find one to let here.'

'Have you been here long?'

'Ever since I came to London.'

Margaret could not make up her mind if it was a relief that no two of the houses were alike, for they were so ugly that it was as well they should not be duplicated, and yet uniformity must have imposed some of the restfulness of monotony. Each house looked as if it had been designed by a border-line gnome. Towers, gables, rustications, lanterns, dormers and leaded panes abounded, and so did angles, bright tiles and horizontal windows, the gnomes having combined Pseudo-Tudo with Lutyens-Functional. At the end of the avenue there were two houses built of small bricks in a plain Georgian style that looked good enough to eat.

'Those aren't so pretty,' said Dick Fletcher, indicating them as he went down a side turning.

Here the houses were smaller, and so madly fanciful, with their gardens full of fuchsias and pink hollyhocks, that they had lost all contact with reality. The scene made Margaret think of the Lollypop house in the opera, *Hansel and Gretel,* for beyond the gnome-houses the sky was blue as a forget-me-not, and butterflies were fluttering over brilliant flowers still dewy with morning. In the quietness, broken only by the ordinary sounds of a suburban road at nine o'clock in the day, she heard a faint silvery tinkling like water-fairies singing.

Dick Fletcher was smiling. 'Can you hear Linda's windbells? She's got them all over the house. I thought they might get on people's nerves but no one seems to mind.'

'It's a lovely sound,' said Margaret, nervously biting her lips.

'Linda loves them. She's very fond of music, too. Here we are,' and he pushed open a little blue gate of fanciful design.

The icily sweet noise of the wind-bells was loud here, and Margaret could see the long strings of painted glass dangling at every window. She followed him up a stone path, between two miniature lawns of grass that really were smooth and green as velvet; in the middle of one was a little pool with two golden fish poised between the dark stems of a budding water-lily, and on the other a bird-bath where some sparrows were drinking and splashing. All was bright, doll-like, delicate, as if nothing ugly or disorderly were ever allowed to intrude here. The name of the house hung above the front door in gold letters. It was Westwood.

Margaret was still recovering from this when Dick Fletcher opened the front door and went into the hall, and she received an impression of sunlight and soft bright colours and flowers.

'Linda,' he called, a little anxiously. 'Darling, where are you? It's Daddy.'

The noise of the wind-bells died away to the softest tinkling as the wind slowly dropped into stillness. There was a moment's silence. Then a young voice, not quite distinct and sounding as if speaking to itself, repeated,

'It's Daddy,' and a child came down the hall against the sunlight from the garden.

Margaret caught her breath, but it was with relief. The little face, lifted to her father's with a smile, was dark and calm, like that of a Japanese. Her dark hair was plaited with red ribbons, and she wore a flowered summer dress. She fixed her eyes upon Margaret, the smile lingering as she gazed at her, but without surprise.

'Daddy,' she repeated, and put a soft little paw into his hand, still looking at Margaret.

'This is Margaret. She's very kind. She's come to look after you while Mrs Coates is away, Linda. Say "How do you do, Margaret!"' he said.

The child came forward and obediently held out her hand. He watched, smiling anxiously, and glancing from one to the other.

'How do you do, Margaret.' Her speech was not exactly broken by a lisp but it was not completely clear. Margaret took her hand, and pity and revulsion were so mingled as she touched its cool skin that she had to make an effort to say, 'How do you do, Linda,' but she suddenly felt that she *must* make some gesture towards the child that would reassure the father, and she knelt down and put both her hands on Linda's waist.

'Where have you been?' she coaxed. 'In the garden? What were you doing? Tell me.'

'In the sun,' answered Linda, her smile widening, as her small, gentle dark eyes dwelt on Margaret's smiling face. 'It's warm. I was so cold.'

'We'll have some tea,' exclaimed her father, rubbing his hands and hurrying through to the kitchen. 'Linda and I have had breakfast but you'd like some, wouldn't you, Margaret?'

'I'd love some,' she answered, following him in and shutting the door. She glanced about the hall, which was scented by branches of lilac grouped in a large jar. The few pieces of modern mass-produced furniture and the parquet floor were well-kept and gleaming.

'Will you show me where the cups are, Linda?' suggested Margaret, and soon Linda was opening and shutting cupboards and clumsily but carefully putting plates on the table, chattering the while about poor Mrs Coates, who was ill and had to go to bed and be away from home. There was no trace of sorrow on her face and every now and again she gave a little laugh, empty and sweet as the sound of the wind-bells.

'And the tea you put in *there*, Margaret. Put the *water* on it and make it hot. And then the lid. You put on the *lid*,' she said, her voice sounding like the copy of an older voice that had said these things to her. 'Bread and butter. It's warm to-day, Margaret.'

'Yes, Linda, it's lovely. Presently you'll show me the garden, won't you?'

'Yes. It's nice in the garden. It's warm.'

The kitchen was painted blue and white, and all the tins and saucepans matched it. A white geranium growing in a blue pot stood on the window-sill, breathing out the faint aromatic scent of its leaves to the hot sunlight. A kitten wandered in from the garden half-way through breakfast, and Linda went off to play with it. Her father watched her go, then turned to Margaret.

'Do you think she seems happy?' he demanded.

'Completely happy,' she answered. 'I can imagine one would get to love her,' she added – not quite truthfully, for the vacancy in Linda's eyes and her vague, unfinished movements made her flesh faintly creep. The child was completely unlike the monster of her fancy, but she was very different from a normal child, and the fairy prettiness of this house that was both her world and her prison did not make Margaret feel any less uncomfortable. It had none of the ordinary worn apperance of a London home in war-time, and she knew now why Dick Fletcher's clothes were shabby and his flat in Moorgate comfortless; every penny of his handsome salary, except what he needed for his bare necessities, went on Westwood for Linda.

She was still marvelling over that coincidence about the name. Opposite the house there was a clump of fine old trees still standing, part of the woods on the large estate where the houses had been built, which obviously gave it its name. Nevertheless, the coincidence struck her as uncanny.

'She is lovable, isn't she?' he said eagerly. 'Mrs Coates is devoted to her. As soon as she came round after the raid she asked for Linda.'

'However did it happen?' asked Margaret. 'Surely she hadn't gone out and left the child alone in the house at night?'

'Oh no, I was here. She'd gone over to see some friends at Finchley, and she was in their house when it was hit. They got her out almost at once, but she was hurt and didn't come round until about three o'clock this morning. They 'phoned me to let me know that she was safe but would be in there for quite three weeks, and then I thought of you. I've got to go into the office this morning and on my way down I'll look in at the Women's Voluntary Services and see if they can send someone along later. The trouble is, you see, it isn't quite an ordinary situation.'

'No,' answered Margaret thoughtfully. She was wondering just what she had let herself in for. It was clear that he did not want a stranger from the W.V.S., however kind and competent she might be, to look after Linda. It was also clear that she herself could not be here indefinitely. Yet he had thrown himself upon her mercy, and she felt that she must do all that she could, and even more. And meanwhile what was happening at Westwood-at-Highgate? Was *The Shrapnel Hunters* safe? And had Barnabas found his monkey? And what had the critics said about *Kattë*? Reluctantly she brought her thoughts back to the problem of Linda.

'I was just wondering what's the best thing to do,' she began. 'I can stay here to-night –'

'Oh, that's awfully good of you,' he interrupted, 'but I can be here to-night. If you could just stay here to-day, and then come over on Sunday; I've got to go down to Newmarket on a story this week-end but I needn't leave until mid-day Sunday. The trouble is that I don't know quite what time I'll be back.'

'I'll come,' said Margaret, smiling. 'Don't worry.

'You are a brick,' he said gratefully, and lit a cigarette, giving a long sigh. 'Oh – I'm sorry.' He offered her the case.

Margaret's week-end schemes for helping at Westwood-at-Highgate went up with the first puff of smoke, but (as so often happens when a cherished plan has been sacrificed to duty) she felt curiously happy. The warmth and peacefulness were soothing, and they sat over the pleasant litter of the teacups in silence.

The little garden, visible through the open windows, was crowded with pink roses climbing over a miniature arcaded walk; the candid, gold and cherry-pink rose named Dorothy Perkins. Linda was singing a low, rhythmic song to herself as she played.

'Roses are my favourite flowers,' said Dick Fletcher suddenly, following Margaret's glance.

'Are they? Yes, they are lovely. You've got a fine show there. Who does the garden? You?'

'Mrs Coates, mostly. She's very keen.'

Mrs Coates is a treasure, indeed, reflected Margaret. A marvellous housewife, fond of Linda, *and* green-fingered. I could have bet his favourite flower would be roses, he's so absolutely ordinary. I wonder what *his* favourite flower is? – if he has one.

(Mr Challis, should the reader care to know, favoured orchids. They are difficult to obtain, sophisticated, and expensive, all qualities which he liked. They also – if a flower can – look perverse, and he liked that, too. He was always failing to notice exquisite ordinary objects under his nose, and so he never noticed the tiny wild flowers which are perhaps the loveliest things in the world; at once sturdy and delicate, with their pure scents that seem half wildness itself; the very breath and spirit of meadows distilled in a cup a quarter of an inch wide. But had the corncockle measured six inches across and cost half a guinea a spray, no one would have admired the corncockle more than Mr Challis.)

259

'Do you mind if I telephone my mother and tell her what's happened?' asked Margaret.

'No, of course not. I ought to have told you both before about Linda, but somehow – your father knows, of course.'

'Does he?' she exclaimed, very surprised. What extraordinary creatures men were, keeping secrets and never even hinting!

'Oh, yes, he's known for a long time,' and he gave her a quick, ironical smile, as if he knew just what she was thinking. 'I must go now, I'm afraid, but I'll be back by five. If I were you I'd sit in the garden. It's going to be blazing hot.'

It was already very hot. Before he went, he pulled a striped curtain over the front door and let out an awning over a little balcony at the back of the house.

Margaret and Linda stood at the door to wave him down the road, then turned slowly back into the house. It was ten o'clock. A heat haze shimmered over the pavement and the wind-bells hung motionless and silent.

'Hot,' said Linda, blinking and smiling up at her.

'Very hot, Linda. Would you like to take off your shoes and stockings? Does Mrs Coates let you?'

'Take my shoes and stockings off? Yes. When it's hot, Linda, you may take your shoes and stockings off.'

'And shall I pin your hair round your head? That will make it cooler for you.'

'Yes, that will make it cooler. Isn't it a *lovely* day?'

She stood docilely in her pink and white bedroom while Margaret performed these little services for her and found her a pair of cool sandals. The braided hair increased her Japanese look and Margaret shuddered inwardly, though the effect was quaint and even attractive. She did not like touching Linda, and each time she did so it was a conquest of herself. When the child had gone to a shady part of the garden to play with sand, she went to telephone to her mother.

It was a long conversation, for Mrs Steggles was full of amazement, indignation at what she regarded as Dick Fletcher's slyness, and curiosity about Mrs Coates, the house, and Linda – in that order. She made Margaret (who quickly became impatient with her questions) describe the road, the rooms, Linda's clothes and the extent of Mrs Coates's injuries, and ended up by saying that there was not the slightest doubt that she was trying to marry Dick Fletcher.

'Mother, what nonsense! I really must go now, I've got to wash up and dust.'

'Well, you mark my words, she is, and she won't like your getting a foot in there.'

'Oh, Mother, it isn't like that at all! I shan't be coming here again after Sunday.'

'Ah, you don't know what you've let yourself in for; you mark my words.'

'Mother, I simply *must* go now. Good-bye. I'll be home about six.'

After she had finished the housework, she decided she might allow herself to ring up Zita. It was only a quarter to eleven, but already she felt as if she had been at this other Westwood for days.

Having offered Linda some milk and biscuits which the child placidly accepted, she went again to the telephone, but twice in a quarter of an hour she found the line to Westwood-at-Highgate engaged, and decided that she would telephone again later in the evening; evidently the telephone would be busy all day.

Feeling more cut off from the outside world than ever, she wandered through the sunny rooms.

A clock chimed too sweetly every quarter of an hour, and sometimes the wind-bells tinkled faintly in the warm breeze and then the sound died away. The rooms were decorated in pale pink or blue, with pictures by Margaret Tarrant of angels and children and rabbits, and there was a nursery in pale yellow with white shelves full of children's books; the Beatrix Potters and the Arthur Ransomes and the M. E. Atkins, all new and all apparently unread. There were many large bright pictures of children picking primroses or playing with lambs, the type sold in the children's department at Heal's or Selfridge's; and in the nursery in a miniature cot was a china doll exquisitely dressed in white, with long eyelashes lying upon her peachy cheeks in sleep.

It's the sort of house a child film star would live in, thought Margaret, whose association with the little Nilands had robbed her of some illusions about children. It's got all the things grown-ups think that children like and none of the unexpected things – old dolls made out of stockings and grown-up books with gruesome pictures – that children really do.

But Linda seems perfectly happy; it's him I'm so sorry for.

Presently she found a basket with some of Linda's stockings to be darned and sat down with them in the drawing-room, where the French windows opened on the garden. The long, hot day wore on, and presently she found herself soothed by the quietness and peace. She prepared lunch for Linda and herself, having patiently extracted from the child information about what Mrs Coates usually gave her, and after the meal was cleared away and the washing-up done, the two wandered into the garden under a big varnished paper parasol which Margaret found, and Linda showed all her favourite places and treasures; not as an ordinary child would, by pointing and displaying, but by murmuring over them and sometimes glancing up at Margaret with her dim, smiling eyes. She was friendly and confiding and seemed to have no fear, and Margaret thought of the old belief that naturals were specially protected by God, and understood for the first time how the legend had arisen, for only a very cruel person would betray that happy and instinctive trust.

In idling in the garden and watching the goldfish and the kitten, the afternoon passed by, and at four o'clock she began preparations for tea. She felt as if she had been cut off from her own life for a very long time, and hoped that Dick Fletcher would not be late, for she was eager to get away and refresh herself with everyday life before she returned here to-morrow.

'Daddy will be here soon, Linda,' she said. 'Will you go and pick some flowers to make the table look pretty for him?'

'Daddy,' murmured the child. 'Linda pick roses,' and she ran awkwardly out into the garden.

'Roses,' she repeated, standing by the table in a little while with a bunch of pink carnations, and smiling up at Margaret.

'No, Linda, those are carnations. Come along, we'll get the roses together.'

While they were standing under the arcade pulling down the laden sprays, Dick Fletcher came out through the French windows and Linda ran to meet him. He lifted her off her feet with an effort, for she was not lightly built and he was a slight man, and called to Margaret:

'Hullo! Had a nice lazy day? (Well, my darling, and how's Linda?)'

'Lovely, thank you,' Margaret answered smiling, but she thought that he was taking her sacrifice of nine precious hours of leisure too lightly, and she made up her mind not to offer to come again after to-morrow.

'Margaret mend Linda's stockings,' said Linda in her indistinct voice, whose sweetness almost compensated for its impediment.

'Did she?' he answered, swinging her backwards and forwards. 'Isn't she a grand girl? I'll just go up and wash and then we'll have some tea,' he added to Margaret, who suddenly felt that she could not endure this atmosphere for another moment and

263

had been about to suggest that she should go home immediately. Instead, she found herself saying:

'Yes, it's all ready; I'll just make the tea,' and soon they were sitting round the low table in the drawing-room and she was doing what she had never done in her life before; controlling her own feelings in order to make the occasion pleasant for a tired man. She did not realize what she was doing; she only felt sorry for him, as he unobtrusively guided his daughter's clumsy hands and helped her with an occasional low tender word to eat and drink.

When they were smoking after tea, he told her that he had been to the offices of the Women's Voluntary Services, and that they had promised to send one of their members in on Monday and during the whole of the coming week to cook Linda's lunch and get her tea. He himself would live at the little house until Mrs Coates returned.

'But what will Linda do all day?' interrupted Margaret. 'You can't leave her alone.'

'The people next door have promised to keep an eye on her,' he said, frowning. 'They've been very kind; everybody has, considering I don't know any of the neighbours, really. But it's a risk, of course.'

'You can't leave her here alone,' said Margaret decidedly. 'Just suppose something happened! She must come and stay with us.'

He expressed relief and gratitude in his glance, but he said:

'But what about your mother? You're out all day, and –'

'Mother won't mind. When I get home this evening I'll say I've told you Linda's coming,' and she laughed, more cheerfully than she felt, for she had spoken in haste and was already repenting.

'Well, it's awfully good of you, and it would be a godsend, but there's another difficulty,' he said hesitatingly. 'Linda's never been anywhere but here. She isn't used to strange people or houses.'

'Doesn't she go shopping with Mrs Coates? She told me she did.'

'Yes, she does, but that isn't like staying with strangers.'

'I'm sure she'll be all right, really. She's such a friendly little girl, anyone would like her.'

His expression changed to a passionate tenderness. Margaret had used exactly the right words, and for one heavenly second his child had seemed normal. He glanced across the garden at the little figure playing in the sand, and said:

'Yes, I do think that most people would like her. But it's a big thing to ask your mother to do, all the same.'

'I'll telephone you later and tell you what we've arranged,' she promised.

Twenty minutes later she was flying, skimming like some released bird, down the road under the may bushes and breathing the delicious evening air. Oh! that house! That miniature fairy palace of eternal childhood that was no true childhood just because it was eternal! I *must* get Mother to say 'yes,' she thought. I don't think I can bear to go back to-morrow for another day of it, sorry as I am for him. Poor, poor Dick.

20

Mr Challis had paused on his way through the hall of Westwood-at-Highgate that evening and was standing by the window, apparently casually, but in fact completely, absorbed with the evening paper. As he read, he gradually began to frown and compress his lips, for the journal's Dramatic Critic did not think highly of *Kattë*; indeed, there was a peevish note in his remarks which suggested that he had not enjoyed his evening at all. Mr Challis did not mind that; he did not write plays for people to enjoy; he wrote out of the creative fire in his soul and hang everybody (and in this he was an artist and to be respected), but he did mind when dramatic critics hinted that he meant well but it hadn't quite come off, and that was what, with a dismaying unanimity, they one and all hinted about *Kattë*.

He made a pretence of never reading the notices; did not subscribe to any press-cutting agency, and affected indifference to the critics' opinions, but he could not resist reading them in secret, and in secret he cared very much what they said.

While he was standing there, his mind busily refuting the critic's accusations and his frown growing deeper, he became aware that someone close at hand was carrying on an irritable telephone conversation.

'Ach! it iss all excuses! All day I wait, und never one wort from you! Too much it iss!'

A pause, while the person at the other end of the line evidently tried to explain.

'Dick Vletcher, Dick Vletcher! And who iss he, I would like

you to say, that all day you go with him, when we here are in such great sorrow and trouble. Yes, yes, you haf let me down!'

Another pause. Mr Challis only half heard what was going on, for he was absorbed in what he was reading, but what he did hear jarred harshly upon his already strained nerves; the speaker (it is Zita, he decided distastefully) evidently thought herself alone and therefore under no obligation to control her voice or temper.

'No, I am angry, Margaret,' he heard her say next. 'You are not a goot friend. I haf said to Mrs Challis that perhaps you might here come and help us to-day, and when I ring up your home, you are gone out, where? Your mother she does not know!'

Pause.

'The line was not engaged all the day!' snapped Zita, after another listening silence.

Mr Challis thought that this noisy scolding had gone on long enough. It was apparently being carried on in the morning-room with the door open. Putting down the paper, he strode across the hall and looked in at the morning-room with an expression of grave inquiry. Zita, who was sitting at the table with a cup of coffee before her, smoking a cigarette and looking furious, gave a little gasp when she saw him and at once said into the receiver:

'Here iss Mr Challis wanting me and now I must go. Good-bye, Margaret,' and hung up.

'Yess, Mr Challis, you want to speak –' she was beginning eagerly, getting up and putting out the cigarette, but he merely gave her another grave look and withdrew. He had always found that look, and silence, very successful in dealing with women and inferiors.

He picked up the newspaper again and went across the hall to his study, avoiding on his way a little cart filled with bricks which stood forlornly in the middle of the vast expanse of carpet. Mr Challis frowned; already the house was showing signs that his grandchildren were in residence. One of them could be heard crying upstairs, and that morning there had been a rubber monster lying stranded in the bath when he went to take his own bath; and all day there had been nothing but talk about the damage to the cottage, and people coming in triumphantly or despairingly from visits to the ruins, and people running up and down stairs with bedding and cups of tea.

He glanced up and saw his wife coming down the staircase, looking as disturbed as her naturally gay expression permitted.

'Hullo, darling. Nice notice in the *Banner*?'

'I have not looked,' he answered coldly, and was going into his study when she went on:

'Gerry, I'm afraid Grantey's really bad. I've just been talking to Dr James, and he says we must have a nurse to live in, at least for a week or two.'

'Really?' he said, pausing, shaken out of his self-absorption by her tone. 'What is the matter?'

'Heart. He says she's worn it out with lifting things and carrying heavy babies up and down stairs for forty years. He told her weeks ago that she would have to be very careful, and she wouldn't, of course, and then there was that shock last night —' she ended, and went into the morning-room, whence Zita had fled, to try to arrange about the nurse.

Mr Challis went into his study and shut the door. The massive dog-grate was filled with little picotees from the garden which scented the air with cloves, and fuzzy crooks of young fern. Long rays of evening sunlight shone into the stately room with its grey-green walls — the colour of the picotee foliage — and red velvet curtains. He went to the window and stood looking out into the garden, where the flowers on the magnolia tree were dying, their widely expanded cups streaked with brown. The world seemed to him immeasurably old, as it sometimes does on summer evenings; a vast, ancient mass pitted with valleys and ocean-beds, and every forest, lake and plain covered with layers of human bones; deep, deep under the moss and the fresh rippling water and the rank wet tangles of black seaweed and the blue ice of crawling glaciers. There was no answer. He had been turning lately to the East for an answer, but there was none; none, at least, that satisfied him. A long time ago, so long ago that he could not clearly remember how he had felt when he had possessed it, he had known happiness. It had been when he was a very little boy, less than nine years old, and slowly, like an angel driven out by a fiend, it had gone away; and in its place reigned the fiend; the sad, ever-searching fiend who could find no satisfaction in all the world, and who was always yearning for the angel-happiness that it had driven away.

He sighed, and turned from the window. Was *Kattë* a success? Yes; the audience had proclaimed it one, even if the critics were doubtful. But this was the first time that the critics had been doubtful about a play of his, and he was chilled and depressed by their verdict. He wanted comforting, a sensation which was unfamiliar to him.

He glanced up as his wife came in.

'The nurse is coming to-night,' she said, looking distressed. 'Poor old Grantey; isn't it awful?'

'Do you mean he thinks she's going to die?'

Seraphina nodded, and sat down and opened the piece of gros-point work which she usually carried about with her and stared distractedly at it, and then she took out her handkerchief. 'He warned me that she may go any time. She's much worse than we knew.'

'It is strange to think of her dying,' said Mr Challis thoughtfully, after a pause. 'She is one of those figures I have always taken for granted; a background figure, so familiar that one never thinks of her. It is as if she were – er – one's toothbrush or something of that sort, such an unobtrusive part of life's pattern that . . .' His voice died away and he stared unseeingly into the sunset.

'She used to say my hair would never "come to much," ' Seraphina said at last, smiling and blowing her nose. 'I can smell that green soft-soap stuff she used on it now, and she used to curl it round her fingers, bless her, for hours.'

Mr Challis was silent, busy with thoughts of death. How would a narrow, ignorant old woman like Grantey meet that supreme experience?

'It will be like offering a cup of superb wine to a creature without a palate,' he said suddenly.

'What, darling?' Seraphina had now recovered herself a little, and was putting stitches in her work, but without much concentration.

'I was speculating on how she will face death.'

'Oh, well – she believes in Heaven, of course.'

'They do, I suppose, even nowadays – the older ones, at least.'

'Of course they do. And she prays for all of us every night, bless her; she let that slip when we were talking about the bomb.'

'Pathetic,' murmured Mr Challis.

'Isn't it sweet?' Seraphina had only caught an apparently sympathetic murmur. 'I must say it *comforts* me to think of Grantey praying for me. I'm sure God listens to her – dear, good, kind old thing,' and she fairly burst out crying, 'Oh, dear, it's so awful to think of her dying, and we've taken her so absolutely for granted for forty years – I simply can't *realize* it may happen.'

'Does Dr James give no hope at all?' he asked, after a pause in which he had gazed embarrassedly at her but made no attempt to console her; he was anxious to get on to the subject of the notices of *Kattë*, but did not wish to appear unfeeling.

'Well, he *did* say that he can't be *absolutely* sure, of course, but he's as certain as *anyone* can be that her heart can't last much longer. He said – he said – she – she was just worn out –' and Seraphina broke down again.

'Don't distress yourself, my dear,' he said, after a moment. 'She has enjoyed giving her life to us, you know. She is a slave by temperament and has passed her life in slavery; therefore she is fulfilled.'

'What a beastly thing to say!' said Seraphina, indistinctly from behind her handkerchief. 'Really, darling, you do say the most *swinish* things sometimes, anyone would think you were an absolute *brute.*'

Mr Challis shrugged his shoulders. Always, always, it was the same. Women could never face the truth about themselves or anything else. It did not detract from Mrs Grant's undoubted merits to call her a slave. In the Ancient World slaves had frequently been figures of nobility and fidelity. Because he looked at the situation with detachment, Seraphina thought him brutal. It was typical of the way she had always misunderstood him.

'And you're *really* very sweet,' said Seraphina, getting up and going over to a mirror to repair her face, 'only you won't *let* yourself be.'

'What do you mean?' demanded Mr Challis, shaken by this novel view of his character.

'I look like the Wrath of God,' murmured his wife.

'I asked you a question, Seraphina.'

'Darling, you sound like old Mr Barrett. All I meant was, you're naturally much nicer than you let yourself be. When I first knew you, you were an absolute *lamb.*'

Mr Challis for the moment had nothing to say.

'*Frightfully* solemn and funny. Oh dear, *how* I used to laugh at you, after you'd gone, you know. (There, that's better,' powdering her nose.) 'When we were engaged, sweetie – *you* remember.'

'I cannot say that I do.'

'You *were* such a pet, always wanting to improve my *mind*.'

'My desire seems to have remained unfulfilled,' said Mr Challis dryly.

'Well, you *must* remember me trying to read all those *alarming books* you unloaded on me . . . I did try . . . only somehow there was never any time for *anything*; there never has been, *has* there? – ever since we've been married. It's *years* since we really let our back hair down and had a good long talk like this, isn't it? Look here,' glancing at the clock, 'I'm *supposed* to be dining with the Massinghams to-night and it's after six now – do you think I can go, with Grantey in this state?'

'Zita is here, I suppose, and Hebe? Is Alexander going to be in?'

'I don't know – no – I think he said something about going *away* – in fact, I think he's *gone*.'

'Isn't that rather sudden?'

'Yes, I suppose it is, really – but the fact is' – she hesitated – 'I think he's been rather pining to get away and paint. Hebe says she and the children have been rather on top of him lately.'

'I sympathize,' said Mr Challis grimly.

'Don't be silly, sweetie. It isn't the same thing at all. The cottage was simply *minute*; no room for *anything*.'

'Have they quarrelled?' demanded Mr Challis, thinking impatiently that in family life there was always something happening to irritate and disturb the creative mind.

'I don't think so, darling. He just thought he would go off, and Hebe said it was a good idea.'

'But does she think it a good idea?'

'I wouldn't know, darling.' Seraphina had no intention of

exposing her daughter's matrimonial difficulties to her father's detached gaze.

'Doesn't she talk to you?'

'Not about Alex, darling,' lied Seraphina, though Hebe's laconic hints in any case could hardly be described as talking.

'I thought women always talked,' said Mr Challis, with a little sneer. Like most seekers for an ideal woman, he did not really like women, believing that they disappointed and failed him on purpose.

'Gerry dear,' said his wife gently, turning to him as she stood by the door with the sunlight on her face, looking like some Julia or Dianeme from a poem by Herrick, 'I don't mean to butt in or be rude, and of course I do know everyone *says* you're such a *marvellous* psychologist and I'm not highbrow or anything, but honestly you *don't* know much about women. The women in your plays are such *hags*, darling; absolute witches and hags, if you don't mind my saying so. I don't know *any* women like them and I've known *hordes* of women. Some of them were witches and some were hags, but they weren't witches and hags in *that* way – so highbrow and *pleased* with themselves and not having any *young*, or any fun, or anything natural. I don't know *why* I'm going on like this,' ended Seraphina, suddenly recollecting herself and giving him a dazzling smile, 'we *are* having a heart-to-heart to-night, aren't we? I expect it's all this worry about poor darling Grantey.'

Mr Challis said nothing for a moment. Much of what his wife had said he contemptuously ignored as the natural jealousy of an ordinary, attractive woman for the intense, gem-like goddesses of his creative imagination, but it did occur to him that, if she disliked his women, she might be able to suggest why the critics had turned in a body upon *Kattë*.

'Men and women never admire the same type of women or even see women in the same way,' he answered curtly. 'I am sorry that you do not find my heroines attractive, although I am not surprised, and I congratulate you upon having concealed your dislike of them so successfully and for so long. Er – do you think the critics agree with you?' he went on, with some embarrassment. 'Most of them seem to find fault with *Kattë*, though none of them agree on where the fault lies.'

'I expect it isn't cheerful enough, darling,' answered Seraphina at once. 'Everybody's so browned-off with the war just now, they don't want any *more* miseries – however well written they are,' she added hastily.

Mr Challis was so annoyed that he actually gave a bitter laugh, which is a thing people hardly ever do anywhere. This was exactly what Hilda had said to him in even cruder words. Oh, women, women! How narrow and earthbound had Nature created them! How infinitely better to design and create one's own!

'There was never a more urgent need for great tragic drama than now,' he said – almost snapped. 'Have *none* of you any conception of the meaning of that great phrase, *to purge with pity and terror*?'

'I know, darling, but we *are* purged, every time we open a newspaper or go to the pictures. We're being purged *all the time*; I mean, *I'm* not, because I don't mind the raids except when any of you are out in them, and when they show you those films of dead Japanese and General MacArthur walking on them I always shut my eyes, and *I* never read the papers but *everybody* can't do that, and when they go out for a spot of fun they don't *want* to be terrified and purged, unless it's a thriller or a nice juicy murder.'

'They flocked to see Gielgud's *Macbeth*.'

'Well –' said Seraphina delicately, and paused. 'Shakespeare's different,' she said at last, thinking – *Poor Gerry. He doesn't know, but he's had it*. 'And so they'll flock to see *Kattë*,' she went on gaily.

'*No one* takes any notice of the critics, you know, and the Camberhams and the Wynne-Fortescues thought it was *too* marvellous, the best yet. So *do* cheer up, sweetie,' coming over and dropping a kiss on his head. 'I must fly now, I'm *too* appallingly late.'

'The Camberhams! The Wynne-Fortescues!' muttered Mr Challis, uncomforted. As she went out of the room he said:

'Er – see that Mrs Grant has all she wants, Seraphina.'

'There, you see, darling, you *are* much nicer than you think you are!' said Seraphina as she shut the door.

Upstairs in her attic room, Grantey was lying in bed glancing at an evening paper which Hebe had just brought up to her. Hebe was sitting in the window-seat, between the faded curtains of ugly yellow cotton, and gazing out across the garden (which was even darker than usual in the shadow beneath the afterglow) at the glimpses of London, exquisitely distinct in the clear evening light. Every steeple and tower and white mass of buildings was visible, vivid and yet soft, as if seen in one of her husband's paintings. She herself looked paler than usual, and tired, and the sleeves of her grey cotton dress were still damp and rolled up from giving the children their bath, a task which Grantey usually performed for her. The baby was already asleep, being still at the stage when he could be pinned down and must stay down, but from the large apartment on the next floor, which Emma and Barnabas were to share with their mother that night, thumps and shrieks could be heard; not shrieks of anger or pain but the more ominous shrieks of a six-year-old who will not drop asleep until after nine o'clock.

'They'll wake Jeremy,' muttered Grantey, frowning slightly but not looking up from her paper. Though the seriousness of her illness dated only from yesterday, she already showed an alarming obedience to the doctor's orders and a lack of interest in matters which only a little while ago would have engaged all her attention; her responses to the children's naughtiness, the

275

damage to Lamb Cottage, and Mr Alex's going off so sudden-like were mechanical, as if her real interest were somewhere else. And indeed, it was; for the first time in her sixty-seven years it was concentrated, though without her knowledge, upon her own exhausted and failing body, and from now on her strength would be devoted to keeping that body alive. All that she had said was: 'I am tired, and that's a fact; a bit of a rest won't do me any harm,' but the meekness of this admission had sent a thrill of alarm through Hebe and Mrs Challis; when had Grantey ever confessed to being tired?

'Nothing wakes him when once he's gone off,' answered Hebe listlessly. Then, as if unwilling to admit by tone or pose that she was not her usual self, she sat upright, clasped her arms round her knees and said:

'Well, how's the b. war going?'

'Don't, Miss Hebe,' murmured Grantey, reaching for her spectacles in their worn blue case. 'I can't make out what they're doing in Burma.'

'We should worry what they're doing in Burma.'

'Poor boys,' said Grantey, arranging the spectacles on her nose. 'It does seem hard — all this destruction and wickedness.'

She so seldom referred to the war that Hebe was a little roused by surprise. She drew up her knees closer within the circle of her arms and said:

'Grantey, you know I don't care a hoot about the war except for Beefy coming out of it all right, but — you believe in a God, don't you?'

'Now, Miss Hebe, don't talk like that,' said Grantey, with some of the severity of Hebe's nursery days, and at last glancing up from the paper, 'it's not pretty or right.'

'Well, but you do, don't you, angel pet?'

'Of course I do, Miss Hebe, and so do you, or you were brought up to.'

'Oh – yes – but never mind that now. And you believe God is Love and all that, don't you?'

'*I* want to read my paper, Miss Hebe. I like to have you with me if you can be quiet, and we can both get a bit of a rest, but if you're going to talk in that way, you had better go downstairs,' and Grantey put down the paper and looked steadily for a moment at Hebe over her glasses.

'All right, but I'm twenty-two, not ten,' said Hebe, laughing but with another expression in her eyes, 'and if I want to stay here, I shall. If you believe God is Love, how can He let the war go on?' (*And Alex behave like a cruel stranger that I've never seen before, and go off and leave me and the children and not say when he's coming back?*)

'That's men, not God,' said Grantey briskly, but settling herself in the bed with a weary movement, 'and it's all part of God's plan for doing away with war for good and all.'

'How come?' asked Hebe, still laughing. 'You tell me.'

'All these dreadful explosions and atrocities and secret weapons they keep on talking about,' began Grantey, 'and not knowing when you go to bed at night if you'll be alive when you wake up in the morning – that's all part of God's plan. He's letting it get worse and worse so's it'll destroy itself, like; it'll get so bad not even wicked people'll want it, and then it'll stop. Not that *I* mind, for myself,' she went on in a lower, more thoughtful tone, turning her head slowly towards the window and looking out into the fading light, 'I never think about it much, I've got too much to do, but I do think about all those poor souls over there, in those concentration camps and all that, and that *does* upset me.'

Hebe said nothing. Her mouth was set in a hard line.

'And then I think it's all part of God's plan to end war, and if we have to worry about the sufferings of others that's our part in the plan – our share of the Cross.'

'I expect that's what it is, Grantey dear,' said Hebe more gently, after a long pause.

'When I was a little girl,' Grantey began again, in a still lower tone, as if she were talking to herself, 'Mother used to take Douglas and me away to the seaside for a week every summer to stay with her sister, our Auntie Belle. She and Uncle Frank lived in a little place on the east coast (Bracing Bay, it's called now, it was Clackwell in those days, I'm speaking of over fifty years ago) and the sea was at the end of their road; on quiet nights you could hear the waves breaking on the shore. Mother would put me to bed in a little room with very high walls (at least, they seemed high to me), with a shiny striped wallpaper all over little bunches of flowers, very pretty, I thought it was, and texts hanging up in gold frames – *God is Love*, with red and blue birds and wild roses painted on them. Oh, it was so quiet and peaceful!' She gave a long sigh, and lay still for a little while, remembering. Hebe remained silent. The room was filling with soft shadows.

'Mother would leave me a night-light, and there I'd lie in the big bed, half awake and half asleep, listening to the sound of the waves coming up from the beach and watching the night-light, and the shiny stripes on the wallpaper and the little birds on the texts. They used to look so far away! – the walls being so high and me being so little, but I was never a bit frightened, it was all so beautiful, with *God is Love* watching over it all. I've never forgotten it. And that's my idea of what Heaven'll be like; just peace and quiet and a nice sound coming from somewhere far off, and flowers and birds to look at, and *God is Love* over it all.'

'I'm sorry I was a pig, Grantey,' said Hebe, after another long silence. She moved from her cramped position, stretched and yawned.

'You'd better go and change your frock. Dinner'll be ready

in a few minutes,' said Grantey, glancing at the clock and receiving
the apology with a tiny, grim smile. 'Though, goodness knows
what Zita and Douglas'll have got for you to eat between them.
Is Mr Challis going to be in?'

'I expect so. Shall I do your blackout?'

'Douglas'll do that when he brings up my supper. What time
is this here *nurse* coming?'

'After dinner, Mum said. I'll bring her up to you, shall I?'

Grantey sniffed, and Hebe laughed and ran downstairs.

In the hall she found her mother, waiting for a taxi which
Cortway had been fortunate enough to secure. Hebe fell into
a chair and stuck her feet out in front of her with a long sigh.

'Tired, sweetie?' asked Seraphina.

'*Dead*. Mums, it is going to make a difference having Grantey
ill, isn't it?'

'Yes, I'm afraid it is. I don't think any of us realized how
much we all depended on her.'

'Won't Granny crow! She always says we don't appreciate
Grantey.'

'She won't crow, darling, but she'll be very sorry and upset.'

'Haven't you told her yet?'

'I couldn't *face* it,' sighed Seraphina, peering desolately at
herself in a tiny mirror, 'not that she *fusses* but –'

'I'll tell her, if you like.'

'Will you? That's very sweet of you,' with a surprised glance.
'Won't that be dreary for you?'

'I don't mind that sort of thing. I'm stinking with moral
courage,' said Hebe gloomily, staring at the stubby toes of her
little shoes.

This was true. She never minded what she said to anyone
and never had; when they were children, it was always she who
had told some unwelcome little guest that it was time he went
home now, as it had been she who had braved the grown-ups

when there was a row on; and now that she was grown-up herself, she would neither smooth out difficulties nor lie about them; the rough, loving nature that dwelt so unexpectedly within the shell of her placid beauty insisted upon complete honesty and a childish fair-dealing between herself and her husband and her friends, and although she made her tacit demand bearable because, unlike many women, she never discussed personal relationships and never analysed difficult situations, some people were incapable of fully meeting her demands. Apparently Alex was among them.

Her mother vaguely realized all this, but the relationship between herself and her daughter was tender and gay, rather than highly articulate.

Seraphina's early married life had been so full of interest and the delightful experiences of motherhood, without any of those anxieties due to lack of money or an over-anxious maternal nature, that she had little experience of unhappiness and not much wisdom to deal with it. She had been amused at Mr Challis's spiritual infidelities rather than wounded by them (although there was a growing, suppressed sense of injury now that both he and she were older, and he still showed the same romantic heart to everyone but herself) and she did not know what to make of Alex's departure, or what to advise Hebe to do about it. Men were always rather a nuisance, in Seraphina's opinion; one liked them around, of course, and they were lambs and it would be a dull world without them, but, really, they were always either trying to make love to you or upsetting you by making love to somebody else, and the best thing to do was just to be nice to them and not take them too seriously.

She took out the tiny mirror again, glanced into it and sighed, and at that moment Cortway came to announce the taxi.

'Good-bye, sweetie,' said Seraphina, relieved at being able to get out of it all for a few hours but glancing uncertainly at her daughter, who was still sitting staring at her shoes. 'Have a nice dinner, and *don't* sit up half the night listening to whosit on the gramophone.'

'Bartok.'

'Well, don't, anyway, will you? Cortway, have you got something really *nice* for dinner?'

'There's fish, madam,' answered Cortway disapprovingly. 'Haddock, Zita said, and she's done it in one of those German ways. With herbs and all that.'

'It sounds delicious,' said Seraphina, trying to catch her daughter's eye, but Hebe's face remained sullen and pale, like a child's who has been crying. 'Good-bye, darling, I must fly.'

'Good-bye, Mummy. Have a nice party.'

After she had gone, Hebe remained in the chair staring at the fading sunset. What had happened to her darling friend, Alex, with whom she had shared jokes and love and her quick angers with the children and her bear-like hugs for them when their sweetness overcame her? Alex had said that she and the children were a damned nuisance; all over him when he wanted to paint and getting on his nerves and in his way when he wanted to be quiet and read the paper. Hebe had set her soft mouth, after saying, 'Don't talk such –; it's as bad for me as it is for you,' and then said no more except: 'All right, then, you'd better go,' after he had said that he was going away for a while. She had neither cried nor made a scene, although this was their first serious quarrel.

Presently she went upstairs and washed her face and put on a fresh dress and came down to dinner, ignoring the sounds from the children's room which suggested that someone was dragging someone else by the legs across the old wooden floor. Blast him, he'll get splinters in her seat, thought their mother resignedly, going on downstairs.

There was not one shred of solacing romantic misery in her

STELLA GIBBONS

heart as she sat opposite to her father in the beautiful room full of rich shadows and peaceful evening light; such feelings only sustain the inexperienced or the eternally young in spirit, like Mr Challis, and are of no use to a woman who has had three children by a man. Her happiness is as real as her own body, and its loss is as uncomfortable as if she were suddenly to become a ghost. The only feeling which kept Hebe from being wretched was sulky, smouldering anger with her husband.

What with Alex and the dramatic critics, Mr Challis and his daughter dined in almost complete silence.

Far in the West of England there is a tract of country on the edge of the moors, soaked in frequent rains, its deep woods thick with hart's-tongue and lady-fern and the rich green lace of bracken, and seldom out of the murmuring sound of a mild, long arm of the inland sea. Its hills are covered in pink heather, and upon the farthest horizon, like the dark threat of a storm that never breaks, are the mountains of Wales. Here there is one hill, lower than the immense, rounded bare hills that are the beginning of the moors, but far lovelier.

Ancient and enormous pine trees grow upon its summit, with massive trunks and matted, spreading branches of darkest green, throwing their dense shade upon the heavy, pale, unripe cones and the grey and white feathers of birds that lie scattered among the red pine needles on the ground. Below this hill roll away miles of valley filled in summer with fern, waist high, curled and stiff and fresh with sap from the rich and ancient soil whence it springs; the walker must wade through it as if through a heavy, motionless sea or follow the narrow tracks that wind through it; opening now and again upon a space of turf where tiny flowers grow, the pale yellow lady's bedstraw and the deep yellow crowsfoot; where the stag leads his does to browse, leaping away into the bracken when the stranger approaches. Here are wider

valleys, where beech trees climb the hills, every valley ending in
the flat shore and pale purple or grey boulders of the inland sea;
and here, in the moist sweet air, among glossy ferns which might
be the houses of fairies, the legend of Arthur is rooted deep as
one of the ancient pines, and yet it is also like the scent of wet
fern and fox-lair on the wind; it is a spirit haunting the region;
the spirit of old, green, wild England, lingering on, lovely and
lonely and wreathed with mist, in the heart of the northern seas.

On this night in early summer Alex Niland was lying under
the pine trees in a sleeping-bag with his mouth full of bread
and cheese, watching the darkness come down, and not thinking
about anything, except that he was rather sorry he had been
angry with Hebe, and hoping that rain would not fall before
morning. Tomorrow he would go on down to Minehead, where
his father was a stonemason. The family had been in the trade,
and that of building, for many generations, and there was a
tradition that a Niland had been among the medieval workmen
who had carved the rood-screen of Dunster Church. Afterwards,
he planned to return to London and stay with a painter who
was very poor and lived in one of the squalid turnings off
Tottenham Court Road. He was not fettered by deep need of
anyone or anything except by the need to paint, and when he
felt that need he indulged it, not so much pushing obstacles
aside as never noticing that they were there.

Above him was clear grey air, going up millions of miles to
the trembling silver drops that were stars, and under his back,
hard yet comforting, was the earth. The dim purple sea was below
his line of vision; all that he could see was black foliage with
stars darting between, and all that he could hear was the occasional
long, soft sigh of the wind through the pines. The air smelled of
warm earth and young leaves, and coolly touched his forehead
and cheeks. Presently he shut his eyes, and soon he was asleep.

21

Margaret hurried home in a bad temper, disturbed by the fear that she might have lost Zita's friendship and with it the precious privilege of visiting Westwood-at-Highgate. She suspected that Zita was likely to throw away a friend as easily as she would an old newspaper or anything else that had ceased to be useful to her; her moodiness and her jealous fits all pointed in the same direction, and Margaret (who was determined *not* to be thrown away) arrived home in a state of exhaustion, irritation and worry, anxious to arrange Dick Fletcher's problem for him, and to be reconciled with Zita, and ready to quarrel with her mother on very slight provocation.

Within a few moments of her arrival they were quarrelling, for Mrs Steggles was so eager to hear all about Margaret's day that she followed her upstairs, questioning and exclaiming. At last Margaret interrupted, and bluntly asked her if she would have Linda in the house for a fortnight?

'What! Look after an idiot?' exclaimed Mrs Steggles. 'No, thank you, I've something better to do. I never heard of such a thing! I hope you didn't tell him I would!'

'I said I'd ask you. And she isn't an idiot; she's just backward,' snapped Margaret, who was pulling off her dress and putting on a house-coat.

'It's the same thing. Ugh! I can't bear anything like that. I've always thanked God that you and Reg were normal, bonny babies.'

'I can't bear it either, as a rule, but Linda isn't like that at all; there's nothing repulsive about her, and he does love her so, you can see it when he looks at her.'

Mrs Steggles shuddered. 'Can't he send her into a home, just for the time being?'

'Mother!'

'Well, I don't see why not. They make them wonderfully comfortable at these places, so I've heard.'

'I do think you might have her,' said Margaret, tying her girdle tightly round her waist. 'It's the first time I've ever asked you to do anything of the kind for me. We've got plenty of room, and Dad and I are out all day –'

'A nice thing, your dad coming home in the evening and finding an idiot slobbering round the place!'

'She does *not* slobber, Mother. I tell you she's almost perfectly normal.'

'Well, I like people who are *quite* normal round me, thank you. It's no use, Margaret, I won't have her, and you'll have to tell him I won't. It's like your cheek, anyway, taking it on yourself to say I would.'

'Mother, I *didn't* say so; I only said I'd *ask* you.'

'Well, now you have asked me, and I've said no, so there's no more to be said, is there?'

Margaret flung her head back so that the thick limp mass of her hair fell all about her flushed face. 'I suppose not,' she said bitterly at last. 'But it's going to make it very awkward for me.'

'You should have thought of that before you told him. You got yourself into this mess, now you can get yourself out of it,' said her mother, going out of the room.

'Mother!' (calling after her) 'what excuse can I make? He'll think it so *horribly* unkind!' she burst out, flinging the brush on the bed and thrusting her fingers into her hair. She was trembling.

'Say I don't want the responsibility of it. Who would? I ask you! He'll understand.'

But Margaret, struck by a sudden idea had darted out of her room and was already half-way down the stairs.

'Oh, Mother, do let me get past – I'm sorry –' she exclaimed, pushing by her mother to get to the telephone: 'I'm sorry I was rude – I've just thought of someone who might –' and she began agitatedly to dial a number. Mrs Steggles glanced contemptuously at her, still annoyed but also curious to know what she would get up to next.

'Oh, Mrs Wilson –' Margaret began. 'Is that you? This is Margaret. No, nothing's the matter, it's only that I wondered if you would look after a little girl, the daughter of a friend of mine, for a fortnight – let her come and stay with you, I mean. She's a backward child – you know – but very sweet, and the housekeeper has been injured in an air-raid last night, and her father hasn't anywhere to send her.'

'I would have, and glad to, Margaret,' replied the unruffled voice of Mrs Wilson from two streets away, serene in the possession of a genuine and cast-iron excuse, 'but my sister's staying with us for a fortnight and we've only got the one spare room. I'm ever so sorry. Whose little girl is she?'

'Mr Fletcher's – he came to your New Year's Party. The little girl's a sweet little thing, really, but of course she can't be left, and he's at the office all day –'

'Yes. It is awkward nowadays, isn't it, with everybody called up and working in factories, there's no one to do all the little odd jobs, like looking after kiddies and invalids,' said Mrs Wilson cheerfully. 'Have you tried the W.V.S. or the Citizens' Advice Bureau?'

Margaret explained the circumstances more fully, and as civilly as she could, but it was clear that there was going to be no help from Mrs Wilson.

'You see, Mother doesn't want the responsibility,' she ended in a lowered tone, and Mrs Wilson answered:

'Yes; well, it is a bit of a responsibility, isn't it, somebody else's child and a backward one at that; I expect he will find it difficult to get anyone.'

When Margaret replaced the receiver she had the disagreeable conviction that she had worked herself up into a state and quarrelled with her mother and flung herself upon the mercy of Mrs Wilson (for whom she had some contempt as an entirely commonplace woman) without having helped Dick Fletcher in the least.

Her mother was sitting by the open French windows of the drawing-room with the evening paper, enjoying the gentle sunset light and faint breeze coming in from the garden. She glanced up and said sarcastically:

'Well, of course she's going to have her?'

'Of course she isn't. I don't know what to do about it; I'm at my wits' end.'

'That'll be your permanent place, my dear, if you start taking on other people's troubles,' observed Mrs Steggles, glancing discontentedly at the clock. Mr Steggles was late, as usual.

Margaret sat down and swung one foot idly. Her mother returned to the paper.

'Aren't you hungry?' she asked at last, without looking up. 'We won't wait for Dad, if you are.'

'Not very,' said Margaret, indifferently. 'What have you been doing to-day?'

'The usual things. I went to the pictures with Elaine this afternoon.'

'Who on earth is Elaine?'

'Mrs Piper. Her name is Elaine Sybil,' retorted Mrs Steggles.

'Gosh!' and Margaret forgot her cares in a giggle. 'Er – was it a good film? What did you see?'

'*The Four Feathers*. Rather far-fetched, I thought. All about the desert.'

'I think I'll just ring up –' muttered Margaret, getting up and hurrying out of the room.

'Hullo?' said Dick Fletcher at the other end of the line. 'Oh, Margaret. I didn't recognize your voice at first.' He sounded tired and depressed.

'Dick, I'm *awfully* sorry,' began Margaret tragically, 'Mother says she can't have Linda; she thinks it would be too much responsibility. And I *did* ring up that neighbour of ours, Mrs Wilson, and she would have had her, but they've only got one spare room and she's got someone coming to stay. So I think the best thing –'

'It's awfully good of you to have taken so much trouble, but our next-door neighbour's come to the rescue,' he answered, sounding a little surprised. 'She's going to come in and spend most of the day with Linda, and someone from the W.V.S. is coming in every morning while she does her shopping.'

'And I'll come over every evening, in case you want to go out,' interrupted Margaret, rather resenting the intrusion of these other women into her new Westwood, and determined that they should not take her place.

'Will you? That's very sweet of you,' he answered, and the words did not sound conventional. 'But won't it be an awful drag for you?'

'No, I shall like it. What time shall I come over to-morrow?'

'Oh, about twelve, if you will. I'll have lunch nearly ready. I'm quite a good cook.'

She made a sympathetic sound but it did not express a quarter of the sympathy she felt for poor Dick, blundering about among the frying-pans. She was not one of those women who admire domesticated men, and she felt impatient when they invaded the kitchen, a place she herself was far from fond of.

'Good-bye till to-morrow, then,' he was saying. 'You are a brick. Good night.'

Margaret was strongly tempted to ring Zita up again. But pride prevented her; she felt that she really could not allow Zita to be so rude and unjust without showing some resentment, and accordingly she went to bed without knowing whether Barnabas had found his monkey or not.

This proved to be the right way of dealing with Zita, for the next morning before Margaret set out for Brockdale she rang up, laughingly dismissing her annoyance of yesterday and eager to take her friend for a walk on the Heath. There was some return of her irritation when Margaret said that she had to go out, but Zita had so much of interest to tell that she suggested coming round for half an hour and walking up with Margaret to the station.

Margaret carried deck-chairs and cigarettes into the garden, and soon Zita arrived, very smart in a linen dress with enormous sleeves, and they sat down in the sunshine to smoke and gossip.

Mrs Steggles watched them from her bedroom, where she was pottering about, with disapproving eyes. Talk – talk – talk! That little creature hadn't stopped waving her hands about and chattering since she came into the house. Mrs Steggles did not despise Zita, having been impressed against her will by Zita's manners (which were those of a wider world than Mrs Steggles's own) and her clothes when she first came to the house to tea, but she thought her odd, and an unsatisfactory friend for Margaret; one likely to put ideas into her head and increase her arty fads. We never see anything of Hilda nowadays, thought Mrs Steggles. I suppose she's too busy running after all her precious boys.

Margaret listened eagerly to all that Zita had to say; Grantey had taken to her bed, and Mr Niland's great picture was safe, after all; Piccy had been found covered in white dust, but otherwise undamaged among the rubble, and, most exciting of all (very sad, of course, dreadful, really), Mr Niland had *gone*;

left Mrs Niland and the children without saying when he was coming back!

'Perhaps nefer,' concluded Zita, looking bright as a button under a stiff little straw hat like those worn by mashers in the 'nineties.

'I'm sorry,' said Margaret thoughtfully, after a pause. Her first excitement was replaced by shame at her own appetite for sensation. She envied Hebe and disliked her, but no one who is *sérieuse* can hear of a broken marriage without regret, although she did not experience that personal shock which she would have felt if anything so unlikely as the breaking-up of the Challises' marriage had occurred.

'I am not, I am glad, it serves her right, she hass no soul for art, she iss only a *mutter*,' said Zita scornfully. 'It iss wrong that she should be married to a great painter und so he hass gone to a mistress.'

'Oh, Zita, do you really think so? How dreadful!'

'Of course I think so. Where else should he go? He hass some cultured woman, beautiful and with much sex, und to her he hass gone.'

'But Mrs Niland – Hebe – *is* beautiful!'

'She hass no sex appeal. All my boy friendts think so. I have ask them all, und they all say the same. Men know such things.'

Margaret had nothing to say to this, though it occurred to her that such unanimity of judgment was suspicious. She would have liked to discuss with Zita the difference between sex appeal and beauty, a point which had puzzled her as often as it puzzles most good women, but she was shy and did not wish to sound ingenuous, and it was getting on for the time when she must leave for Brockdale. She was just opening her mouth to say that she must go, when –

'Und Dick Vletcher – who iss he?' suddenly demanded Zita, leaning forward with a roguish look and smiting her lightly upon the knee. 'All day you were with him, alone. He iss your boy friendt!'

'Oh, no –' exclaimed Margaret. 'He's years older than I am, he's a friend of Dad's.'

'And a friend of Margaret's too!' said Zita archly. 'Why haf you not told me about him? You close your heart to me, Margaret,' and her marmoset face relapsed into extreme dejection. 'Can you not trust me with your secrets?'

'It isn't a secret. I only went over to his house to help look after his little girl because his housekeeper was hurt in the air-raid.'

'But you did not tell me!'

'Well . . .' said Margaret, not liking to remind her that every attempt to explain over the telephone had been angrily interrupted.

'You are in lof with him,' announced Zita, surveying her with narrowed eyes and looking more like a very smart monkey than ever.

'No – no –' laughed Margaret soothingly, content that if there must be suspicion it should alight upon Dick Fletcher rather than upon Gerard Challis.

'But you like him – and he attracts you – he iss a man attractive to women,' persisted Zita, following her into the house.

'No, he isn't, Zita, really. I suppose you don't know anyone who would have a little girl who is backward but a pet to stay in their house for a week or so?'

But Zita would not give her attention to the question; little girls who were backward did not interest her, except as subjects for sentimentally horrified comment, and she made some vague answer which was no help at all. They walked to the station still gossiping, and Margaret eagerly listened to all that Zita knew about the notices of *Kattë*; she herself had ordered copies of the *Observer* and the *Sunday Times* to see what the dramatic critics of those papers had to say about the play, and she had both concealed in her handbag; she would read them when she was alone in Westwood-at-Brockdale.

She had some difficulty in soothing Zita when the latter learned that all her evenings for the next three weeks were to be occupied, but she managed it somehow; and Zita parted from her at the station with frowns but not serious frowns.

Margaret sat down in the train with a sigh of relief, and gazed absently out of the window. Really, Zita was a great trial; her first pleasure in that lively society was gradually being replaced by exasperation at continually having to placate and soothe her; and yet, whenever she went to Westwood-at-Highgate, its charm was so strong that she felt any sacrifice was worth while to keep her right to visit the house. She went off into a day-dream about its age and beauty, reflecting that she did not yet know in what year it had been built, as Zita was not interested and Margaret had been too shy to ask Mrs Challis. However, under her arm she had Lloyd's *History of Highgate*, and she intended to make time to read it while she was with Linda.

Dick went out immediately after lunch. He took her presence there for granted, she thought, and seemed preoccupied and rather impatient; she did not like him as well as she had on the previous day and began to regret strongly that she had offered to come over every night for the next three weeks – *every* night, without any respite or refreshing visit to her own Westwood to break the strain. But Linda seemed really glad to see her, shambling forward with a sweet vacant smile and confidently slipping her cold hand into Margaret's, and standing happily by her side to wave good-bye when her father went away.

When she was settled with her sand-heap in the garden, Margaret turned eagerly to the notices of *Kattë*.

The *Sunday Times*, after referring to Sarah Bernhardt and Janet Achurch, arrived at the conclusion that Miss Schatter was so greatly aided by her physical affinity to the type portrayed in *Kattë* that she deserved less credit for her creation of the part than she might otherwise have done, and the word it used to describe the play was 'painstaking.'

The *Observer*, without referring to Janet Achurch or Sarah Bernhardt, said much the same thing.

Margaret put down the papers with a feeling of dismay.

Why was it? Why had the critics, who had devoted so much respectful attention to his work before the war and even during the first two years of the war, suddenly become almost impatient with it, finding nothing, or almost nothing, to say in praise of it, save that at least it dealt with passions and predicaments which will endure as long as the human race, and not with merely topical matters or with propaganda? Was it that the mood of England had changed, and that the people had seen and experienced such horrors at first-hand that they did not want to see tragedy at second-hand for which there was no particular reason and in which they did not believe?

It was true that the public for thrillers and shockers was larger than ever, and that people would pay any price to see tragedies by Shakespeare or Ibsen, but in the first case the horror was softened in its effect by the unreality of the story within its rigid conventional frame, and in the second case the tragedies were great works of art.

Then were Gerard Challis's plays not great works of art? She had always believed that they were. But if he could not make people believe that Kattë's tragedy was inevitable, then they only felt impatient instead of being moved; it was like the last straw on the camel's back to go to the theatre nowadays and be asked to grieve over something that need never have happened if the people had only pulled themselves together.

They didn't even try, she thought, getting up and walking

out into the garden. They simply sat down under everything, and went from bad to worse. You can't feel sorry for people like that, you want to shake them. The reason why you feel so sorry for poor Maggie Tulliver is that she *did* try; she tried so hard, in spite of being weak and passionate and loving, and she was betrayed by her own weakness, and you feel she *was* good, in spite of her faults, and so you're all the sorrier for her.

After all, she thought, standing in the French windows and looking at Linda without really seeing her, I need not like all his plays equally well, and *Mountain Air* and *The Hidden Well* are beautiful. Nothing can take them away from me.

But I do wish the critics liked *Kattë*.

Then she turned from the window and sat down at a rickety little table which had certainly never been designed for concentrated work, and opened her notebook and Lloyd's *History of Highgate*.

She had bought the *History* as she was hurrying home on a close thundery evening during the previous week, from a little shop which sold old clothes and firewood, as well as a few books whose covers were so filthy that she hesitated to touch them; but as she was gingerly opening the nineteenth-century sermons and biographies of worthy nonentities long dead, she had suddenly seen this large old volume, once handsomely bound in dark green and still having a picture of the Highgate Archway stamped in worn gold-leaf upon its cover. No price was marked inside the cover, but when an ill-tempered woman came out into the shop in response to Margaret's entrance, the price was given as one-and-sixpence, and she carried the dignified old wreck of a book away.

During the last few days, she had only had time to glance at its wood engravings and the portrait of Coleridge (looking very inspired and uncomfortable) which was its frontispiece, but now, with a whole long sunny day in front of her, she looked forward to finding out something about Westwood-at-Highgate.

Slowly she turned the thick cream pages with their large legible type, noticing here and there some quaint verse bearing upon the village's history, or some paragraph in smaller type quoting from the ancient records of Hornsey and Harringay; pausing to read a footnote or study the drawings of long-vanished mansions and churches since covered by brick and mortar; and dreaming over the pastoral loveliness which, in spite of their stylized appearance and their stiff conventional figures of gentlemen and peasants, the pictures one and all conveyed.

But she could find no reference to Westwood-at-Highgate, for part of the index was missing, and so were some fifteen pages from the middle of the book, and she was forced to conclude that the house had never played an important part in the life of the village; and had never been considered striking enough even to deserve a picture in the *History of Highgate*.

It was disappointing, but she read on, her mind darting into the past like a swallow drinking from a fathomless tarn. The quiet minutes crept by; the sunlight poured through the thin silk curtains in a glory, and every now and again the wind-bells tinkled faintly on a passing breeze, and the sound died away. She read eagerly, impatiently, taking the words like *messuage* and *hundred* in her stride, guessing at the meaning and using it to build up the picture that was slowly growing in her mind. The history was not easy to read, because it gave so many sociological and geological and historical facts in their own technical language and no attempt had been made to combine them into a general description conveyed in smoothly flowing phrases; the book had been written in the 'eighties, when readers possessed both leisure and attention to give to their serious reading and expected, when they bought a book, to give both; and so the picture which began to form itself in her mind had not the specious clearness of one drawn in a reader's mind by that modern hybrid, a novelist-historian-antiquarian, but had something of the validity and unexpectedness of truth; it reared itself upon a base of facts plainly recorded, and the more attractive to her because of that plainness. Nevertheless, her imagination began to work.

Solitude; a solitude of thick forests, occasionally broken by glades and small meadows where the swineherds had their huts; little hovels as close to the earth, and as defenceless, as roots or mossy stones and as much a part of the landscape; a solitude whose rustling stillness was unbroken for days at a time by any sound of human life save the distant note of a hunting-horn. The huts and the fields and churches and even the castles were small in this Haia-gat (or hamlet-at-the-entrance-of-the-enclosure) of nine hundred years ago, and the people themselves seemed to be rising in their armour and straight red and blue clothes that had once been bright but were now stained and dim with dirt and age, out of a darkness of rotten leaves and putrid straw and filth; the peasants wore tunics made from animals' hides, with the hair left on them. Nothing was clean, as we know cleanliness, except the flowers and leaves and, in the monasteries, the Altar of God. The Name of Jesus was familiar in men's mouths, and His Name and Spirit burned in this world of nine hundred years ago. Sweet Jesus, they prayed. If a child sickened, it usually died, and so did men and women. There were miles and miles and miles of that fresh, shadowy, awesome forest, *horrida sylvis*, as the Romans called it; the forest swept up to Hampstead and over Harringay (or Harringhaia, 'the-enclosure-of-the-field-of-hares'); the forest rolled in blue-green waves in the summer, in brown-purple leafless waves in the winter, over the hills to the north of London. And here, riding through the endless forest along narrow tracks marked by wolf-droppings, came the Bishop of London, who owned these lands, to hunt the wild boar; the purple-black shape rooting busily in the tangles of blackberry bushes, shaking down their white flowers in spring and their red leaves in autumn as he dug for roots to eat. The bristles of the boar's forelegs were matted stiffly with mud. Margaret thought of the Prince-Bishop's feet in leather hunting-boots, and the dagger in its chased silver sheath at his side. Every article of his dress had been made by hand and was precious in its rarity; every shoe, hat, glove, was precious in those days because there were so few of them and they took so long to make and so long to send to the few hundred shops in Europe. She remembered a pyx that she had once seen, made in 1520, that had been slightly irregular in shape, beautiful, and with the pathos of an object made by hand and displaying the hand's fallibility. In the towns – she thought – in the towns the streets were not paved and there were no lights at night. On the long summer evenings, in the streets of those wooden towns built round a small castle of wood and stone, the children must have played in the dust. Perhaps a bell rang from the stone church, tiny and dark, with one Latin book locked away in a wooden chest. They were Christians, those people.

The forest trees threw their long shadows out into the glade where the town stood, and the women carrying water in wooden buckets glanced into the forest, where it was already dark, and thought of the winter and wolves.

She looked down at the book again. *The killing of a deer or boar, or even a hare*, she read, *was punished with the loss of the delinquent's eyes.*

And then, with her imagination glowing like a window of rich stained-glass, she read of the tradition that Odo of Bayeux, brother of William the Conqueror, was the first Norman owner of the forests of Highgate; and how one of these hunting-crazy bishops (possibly Odo himself) had in the years between 1066 and 1080 caused a hunting lodge to be built on a hill in the forest, and formed the great park of Haringey (Hornsey) into a chase.

Entranced, she read on; the hunting lodge was *doubtless a square embattled building of shaped stones . . . surrounded by a moat, the entrance being by a drawbridge.*

The Bishops of London used to live there occasionally and hunt from there, but *because of its age* and state of decay the place had been destroyed in the fourteenth century, and all that remained of it were traces of the foundation walls and the moat; some of the stones of these walls had been used in the rebuilding of Hornsey Church. These traces remained so late as the year 1888. Mr John H. Lloyd, author of the *History*, had himself seen them . . .

'Margaret, I'm hungry. Linda wants dinner,' said a plaintive voice at her side. Dazed, still hearing the hunting-horns of nine hundred years ago, she looked slowly up and met Linda's mild eyes. For a moment she gazed at her without speaking. So strong was the potion in which her imagination had been steeping itself that she experienced no sense of shock at returning to the contemporary world. The glamour extended itself to the room in which she sat, to Linda, and to every object surrounding them both.

'Linda's hungry,' said the child again, gently putting a hand on her arm.

'And so is Margaret!' she answered cheerfully, shutting the book and standing up and taking the little hand. 'Come along, let's see about some lunch – why, Linda! It's nearly one o'clock. No wonder we're hungry!'

She finished reading the account of the Bishop's Lodge that day, and although the first wonderful glow of imaginative delight did not return, she was left with the determination to go herself to look for the site of the Lodge, and to stand, if possible, upon the very ground where it had stood. For it was within two miles of her own home! A peasant living where she now lived could have seen the tower of the Lodge upon its hill from the low doorway of his hut, while from that tower itself the glint of spears moving across the wooded plain would have been visible for miles. She derived so much pleasure from these reveries, while she worked about the house and played with Linda, that the time passed quickly and she experienced none of the oppression felt on her first visit.

There was no doubt that Linda's was a happy spirit; a shade more of helplessness, a greater abnormality in the speech and the shape of eyes and hands, would have produced such a disagreeable impression that only a strong love could have endured the child's presence; but as it was, her loving nature (even more affectionate than is usual among such children) shone through the limitations of her body and almost atoned for its deficiencies, and by the end of the first week of her nightly journeys to Westwood-at-Brockdale, Margaret had begun to care for her, not as a little lacking girl for whom she felt shrinking pity, but as *Linda*; a person, though not a fully developed one; as much a person as some beloved cat or dog (piteous comparison! but not so piteous, perhaps, as it sounds); with the personal tastes and habits that form a character and mark its differences from other characters. There was no doubt, either, that Linda liked Margaret to be in the house and to read to her and play with her and sing to her; Margaret even thought, after her visits had been going on for about ten days, that she detected a slight, a very slight, improvement in Linda's speech and a quickening of her intelligence, and she put this down to the stimulus of her own young, quick brain acting upon a brain naturally retarded but also artificially kept back by the kindly, unintelligent conversation of a Mrs Coates. She did not dare to mention this to Dick; it seemed so arrogant, so unkind to Mrs Coates, who had endured two years of unnatural existence with a mentally deficient child, but she herself felt increasingly sure that Linda had been living a lonely and abnormal life in her miniature fairy palace, and that some outside companionship, even some childish companionship, would be beneficial to her.

22

But she found the journey out to Brockdale very tiring after her long day's work in the hot, noisy school, and for the first two or three evenings she had felt that she really could not go on with the plan; she did not get home before eleven at night, and then there were exercise books to be corrected and lessons to be prepared for her classes, and the weather was so hot (it was now the first week in a rarely beautiful May) that she could not get to sleep when at last, nearer one o'clock than twelve, she did go to bed.

It was her first experience of suffering endured in an unromantic and unselfish cause. Hitherto her sufferings had been romantic, though she would have been the last person to realize it; for if love and beauty and solitude enter into one's sufferings, even if these qualities be present only in the mind of the sufferer, of course the pangs are romantic; and her passion for Frank Kennett, her yearnings for a wider life, her adoration for Gerard Challis, had all been romantic as the pains of Heine. But it was not romantic to travel in a crowded train through dull, neat suburbs out to a house where a helpless little girl and a tired, rather impatient man awaited her, one eager for her attention and the other for the supper which she must cook; it was not romantic to wash up in a kitchen full of cigarette smoke after Linda had been put to bed, and sit listening to the nine o'clock news while Dick glanced through the evening paper and made little attempt at conversation; and it was certainly not romantic to drag herself home at eleven at night, tired out and carrying a case full of exercise books.

And all this time the lovely evenings, with their deepening blue skies and their soft stars and flowery trees, were lengthening, lengthening towards the longest day; she could feel and hear, as if in a distant land which she could not reach, England slowly stretching out her flower-wreathed arms in that long, long, fairy yawn that ends on the endlessness of Midsummer Night. Most of *that* night, Margaret thought hopelessly, as she trudged up the hill leading from the station, I shall be correcting French exercises, and I haven't telephoned Zita for a week, and I wonder how Grantey is, and if Hebe and Mr Niland are going to have a divorce. Oh, how is *he*? Was he very upset about the notices of *Kattë*? How long it seems since I saw him!

Mr Challis was at his best in the summer. His thin blood warmed and his smile became less glacial. It was fortunate, therefore, that the offending notices of *Kattë* should have appeared at the beginning of this heat-wave; as the play continued to run and to please the public, he could turn with a sense of relaxation to the enjoyment of the fine weather. Had any chance acquaintance of Mr Challis's been asked to take a bet on the likelihood of his playing tennis, they would certainly have betted that he did not. However, he did, and played it well, and (like the young King Henry the Eighth) it was a pretty sight to see him darting about the court in his becoming white clothes. Hebe was heard to remark that Pops was getting slightly sunburnt.

Greatly to his annoyance, the warm weather stimulated Hilda to an even faster whirl of social engagements; she was playing tennis on almost every evening with her friends, in a flutter of short white skirts and pretty bare legs, or going to dances with such of her boys as were on leave, or sometimes spending an evening at the local cinema, which activities prevented her from seeing Marcus, and caused him to ring her up every few days and testily try to arrange their visit to Kew Gardens. Hilda blithely made excuses; Marcus in the summer would probably be as dull as Marcus in the winter, and she did not like him enough to consider spending this lovely weather in his company. However, he kept on so about going to his blessed old Kew that at last she half-promised to go with him in a fortnight's time.

'That is a long time to wait,' said Mr Challis deeply.

'Ever so sorry, and all that, but it can't be helped.'

'The blossoming trees will be all over.'

'All over what?'

Mr Challis maintained an offended silence.

'Marcus?' said Hilda sharply. 'Are you still there? I thought you'd gone. Listen, I'll try and make it on Saturday fortnight; 'phone me up the day before in case I forget, but I'll try and keep it free. Bye-bye,' and she rang off.

Mr Challis replaced the receiver, and sighed. A distant howl resounded through the house; Barnabas was being taken off to bed. His grandfather knew that the nurse who was looking after Mrs Grant would brightly reprove him as she glanced into the bathroom on her way upstairs with Mrs Grant's supper-tray. Seraphina was sitting in the hall laughing with some friends who had dropped in, and downstairs in the kitchen (though of course Mr Challis did not think about *them*, for there were limits) Zita and Cortway were snapping at each other as they prepared dinner.

Westwood had become noticeably and rapidly less comfortable since his daughter and the three children had come to live there and Mrs Grant had been ill, and Mr Challis was growing increasingly conscious of the fact. It irritated him that Seraphina seemed to enjoy the noise and bustle and the children's belongings scattered all over the house; and she encouraged Hebe to go out to parties and picture-shows and first-nights and concerts and leave the children to the careless charge of Zita, while she herself, if she did not accompany Hebe, went off to other festivities of the same sort. Why could not his wife and daughter

303

STELLA GIBBONS

lead poetic, solitary lives, reading in the library or wandering in the shady garden, and keeping out of his way? That was what his own heroines always did (not that anybody ever wanted them to keep out of the way, of course; people, especially men, were always looking for them). Why must they rush about and laugh and talk such a lot? It created an exhausting atmosphere and one unfavourable to the creative spirit.

Maternity, if present at all, should be a passion, but Hebe neglected the children. Had not Mr Challis himself been compelled to take part in a painful scene which had occurred on the previous evening? He had found Barnabas, assisted only too willingly by Emma, attempting to clean Jeremy's one tooth with his own toothbrush and a liberal allowance of toothpaste, and on being asked what on earth he was doing, he had replied that no one ever cleaned poor Jerry's tooth, and it would go all green and fall out. Mr Challis, wincing at such plain speaking, had removed the surplus toothpaste from the roaring Jeremy's mouth as best he could and distastefully replaced the light coverings out of which he had struggled in his sufferings and sternly dismissed Barnabas and Emma, who were standing side by side in their night attire and gazing up at him in silence, to their own room, where he subsequently heard them roaring in chorus, apparently overcome by remorse and fear. No one was looking after them; no one seemed to be in the house at all; everyone might have been dead for all the notice anyone took of the children's cries.

Meanwhile, it seemed a very long time to wait until Saturday fortnight, and the next week-end would be spent in an exhausting and tedious expedition to the home of his mother in Bedfordshire, accompanied by his wife, his daughter, his three grandchildren and Zita to help look after them.

There was that to be got through, and then, in the background, unmentionable but unforgettable, was the fact of Hebe

304

and Alexander's quarrel, and the even more disturbing fact that Hebe had been living in her father's house for nearly a month and had so far made no attempt to find a new home for herself and the children. Mr Challis supposed that if Alex had been there he would have made some attempt to find a house, but Alex was not there, and apparently Hebe had not heard from him since he went away; and no one had referred to the matter; Mr Challis disliked open discussion of these family problems, but he did feel that this gay blindness, this deliberate assumption that everything was going on as usual, was carrying things too far, especially when the direct result of it was rubber monsters left in the bath.

Mr Challis had always admired his daughter's looks, and had at one time hoped that she would develop into a strikingly beautiful, witty creature of whom he could be proud; but after the age of fifteen she did not seem to him to have developed at all; she had had the same complexion and curls and plump body and downright manner then that she had now; and when people extravagantly praised her looks and style, her father only thought them easily pleased, and quietly recorded another disappointment for himself, another score against life, another setback in that search for perfection that was his master-passion.

But sometimes he remembered how she used to go for walks with him when she was a stout little girl of six; patiently collecting acorn-cups which she stowed away in her pockets and nodding satisfiedly to herself when she found an unusually large and shapely one, and scornfully throwing aside the small ones with broken edges which her younger brother, Auberon, tenderly retrieved and cherished. In those days he had been so proud of her, so fond of her, and so full of hope that she would grow up to resemble himself, that a strong impulse of affection (strong, at least, for Mr Challis) towards her lingered in his heart. It irritated and worried him to see the sulky silence by which she expressed her unhappiness, and he even thought of trying to find Alexander and having a talk with him about the situation, but he shrank from acting the unattractive part of interfering father-in-law; and besides, he respected Alexander's right as an artist to go off and paint in solitude if he felt the compelling need; it was what he, Gerard Challis, would have done long ago if *he* had had Hebe and Barnabas and Emma and Jeremy all over *him* while he was trying to work. Hebe must suffer, he decided; her youthful egoism must be crushed and enslaved until a soul, a woman's subtle, secret soul, was painfully born within her yet-childish body, and then she would find, perhaps, that Alexander, in wounding her, had given her a true and undying strength.

Having thus got out of tackling Alexander and telling him he was making Hebe unhappy, Mr Challis put that problem rather successfully to the back of his mind. The problem of getting the four Nilands out of the house, however, remained as acute as ever.

If only he were in South America with Hilda! It had been hinted to him that there was a probability of his being sent there soon on an official mission, and he would take her with him as his secretary. She would be dazzled by the chance of getting away from the monotony and restrictions of life in England, and to him it would be one long delight to wander with her through the white streets and agate mountains of those sunlit lands. When they returned he would be refreshed and fortified to take up his struggle in the world once more, and she would have beautiful memories that would last her for the rest of her life.

Meanwhile, it seemed almost impossible to get her to Kew Gardens, let alone South America, and he did not care to write to her because he never put anything in writing to his little girls, and every time he telephoned her at the Food Office he had to wait longer before she came to speak to him, and then she was pert, and she had told him bluntly that her father and mother thought it ever so funny that he never dropped in for Sunday tea or supper. (Mr Challis, of course, only smiled his fine inward smile at the picture of Hilda's parents thinking anything *he* did peculiar; he took no interest in them; he only found it surprising that such dreary commonplace people should have produced Hilda. Still, such things did happen, and her flowering would be brief enough. How he pitied women!)

Sounds from the hall now indicated that the visitors were going. Mr Challis picked up *The Times*, certain that his privacy was shortly to be disturbed, and sure enough in a moment or two the door opened and in came Seraphina, her face still alight from conversation and laughter.

'Darling, it's *too* tragic,' she began at once, 'that nanny has fallen through.'

'Do you mean the nurse Mrs Compton was talking about?' he said, after a pause for recollection.

'That's the one. *Too* sickening. Margery Hallet's girl has got her for the twins. And I thought we'd practically got our *hands* on her. Now there's nobody to come down with us next week-end. Oh – are you working? I'm *frightfully* sorry, I'll simply fly –' and she was retreating with exaggerated caution when he said irritably:

'It's all right, I'm not working. Surely there will be enough of you to look after the children?'

'Darling, Zita can't come. She's got to stay here and look after Grantey.'

'Won't the nurse be here?'

'Only for an hour every day, darling. Grantey *is* better, you know.'

'Is there no one else?'

''Fraid not, sweetie.'

'Surely, you and Hebe can manage the children between you?'

'We *could*, darling, but it would be rather *dim* for us and we shouldn't see much of poor Great-granny.'

After a pause Mr Challis said: 'I'm afraid I can offer only one solution; we must postpone the visit.' Hope gleamed in his eye.

'Oh, that's *quite* impossible, Gerry; you know we *always* go, *every* year.'

Mr Challis was silent. The gleam vanished.

'Well, I don't want to worry you about it, sweetie,' said Seraphina, preparing to depart. He took up *The Times* again.

'Seraphina,' he exclaimed, as she reached the door, 'what about that friend of Zita's – Miss – I never can remember her name. She is often here – you must know whom I mean. She appears to have plenty of leisure. Would she accompany you?' (He did not say 'us'; he intended to travel down by a later train.)

'Who – Struggles? *Darling*, what a *wizard* scheme! I'll get Zita to call her up at once – she can tell her *you* suggested it; that'll make *all* the difference!' Mr Challis did not look displeased, and his wife hurried away to set the wizard scheme in motion.

So when Margaret got home about eleven o'clock that evening, hot and weary, her mother at once met her with the information that that Miss Mandel-whatever-she-calls herself had been telephoning her all the evening; it was *very urgent* and would Margaret telephone her the *minute* she got in.

'Oh, blow her!' exclaimed Margaret, yielding to a natural exasperation. 'I'll bet it's nothing important, it never is. Still, I s'pose I'd better,' and she dumped her heavy suitcase on the floor with a sigh.

'P'raps you'll get sick of running after other people's troubles one day; you look worn out,' said her mother, going upstairs to bed. 'There are some sandwiches in the dining-room for you and some lemon and barley in the kitchen; I've had it keeping cool.'

'Thank you, Mother, you are a dear,' called Margaret gratefully, as she dialled the number of Westwood-at-Highgate.

'Margaret! At last!' exclaimed Zita's voice. 'All this evening I haf been 'phoning you. Listen with care, now. Mr Challis asks you to go with them all away for the week-end! There! How do you think?'

'Mr Challis?' repeated Margaret, with a thrilling sensation in the diaphragm. 'Are you sure?'

'Of course I am sure. It iss to help with the children. I cannot go (I am sorry, for Lady Challis iss a woman of great *Kultur*, most interesting), but here I must stay und see after Grantey und the house, so they ask you to go instead.'

'It's marvellous,' breathed Margaret, with excitement, happiness, and a chilling doubt – oh, *could* she get out of looking after Linda just for two days? – struggling in her heart: 'When is it? Next week-end?'

'Yess. And all expenses they will pay, of course,' Zita added in a lowered voice.

'Oh' – Margaret's tone was impatient, 'that doesn't matter. Listen, Zita,' she went on carefully, knowing that now, if ever, she must avoid treading on the touchy one's toes, 'it's awfully kind of you to have suggested my going. I shall adore it; I'm just aching for a change. Will you please tell Mrs Challis I shall love to come and I'm awfully proud to be trusted with the children.'

'There will be much to do. They can be devils,' said Zita, again in the lowered voice.

'Oh, well, I shall just have to do my best. Can I 'phone you up towards the end of next week and find out all the details? Or had I better come in and see Mrs Challis?'

'I find it out from her, all of it, und tell you,' said Zita importantly. 'Oh well, think of me at home here alone while you all are enchoying yourself!'

'I know, Zita. It's awfully sweet of you. I do wish you were coming too.'

'Oh, do not be so sorry for me; perhaps I go out to some beautiful concert while you are bathing them all!'

'Yes – well – I hope you will,' answered Margaret, thinking not for the first time how maddening Zita was. 'I must ring off now, my dear, I've got forty exercises to correct before to-morrow. Good-bye, and thanks again, most awfully.'

He asked me to go! *He* did, not Mrs Challis, she was thinking as she ate her supper in the tidy, silent kitchen with only the tick of the clock for company. Why on earth should he? I suppose he thinks I look *reliable*! Not very flattering, but one might look worse than reliable – though I'm sure it isn't a thing he usually admires in women (she actually smiled to herself). If only I can get Dick to let me go!

When she arrived at Westwood-at-Brockdale the following evening, she found the kindly neighbour who kept an eye on Linda during the daytime had just left, and on the telephone-pad (proudly pointed out to her by Linda, hanging on her arm) she had written a message that had come about six o'clock. It was from Mrs Steggles; Margaret's brother would be home on forty-eight hours' leave next Saturday, and her mother 'was afraid it was embarkation.' Would Margaret 'phone up as soon as she got in.

Margaret's first feeling was one of impatient despair; as though it wasn't enough to have her promise to Dick standing between her and the week-end with the Challises, Reg must come home on leave, and there would be an outcry if she failed to spend perhaps his last week-end in England at home with him and the family. But I *will* go, she vowed to herself, banging about the kitchen as she prepared the evening meal. I don't see why I should be done out of something that I want so desperately.

'Margaret's cross,' whispered Linda, who had been glancing up at her now and again from the corner of the table, where she was playing with some pastry, with a timid, puzzled expression.

'No, my pet,' said Margaret, shocked and remorseful, checking her violent movements and putting an arm for a moment about her shoulders. 'Not a bit cross. I'm sorry I made such a noise,' and for the first time she kissed the child's cheek. She did so without thinking, only wanting to comfort her, and remembered to move more gently about the room, and not to frown; and presently Linda's expression was tranquil again.

'Dick,' Margaret said nervously, while they were washing up after supper, 'would you mind very much if I deserted you on Saturday and Sunday?'

He looked surprised, but not in the least annoyed.

'Of course not, we can manage. It's been awfully good of you coming over here night after night; don't think I don't appreciate it. As a matter of fact, I had a letter from Mrs Coates this morning' (he felt in his pocket, but evidently changed his mind about showing it to her, for he withdrew his hand empty and looked slightly embarrassed), 'and they think she'll be out of hospital sooner than she supposed. About another ten days, they said.'

'Oh, good,' said Margaret, not feeling that it was at all good. She had become fond of Linda and – why not face it? – rather fond of Dick too; she was so sorry for him, and she liked the sensation of being useful and wanted, and did not relish the prospect of Mrs Coates's returning to take charge again.

'I don't know what we should have done without you,' he went on, putting away the plates he had dried. 'We shall miss you this week-end. Where are you off to?' he added, fixing his large, bright, tired eyes with a teasing expression upon her conscious face. 'Pub-crawling?'

'It's Reg; he's got forty-eight hours and Mother thinks it's embarkation leave,' she answered, ashamed to admit that she was going off for a week-end with some elegant and socially superior acquaintances.

'Oh, is that it? Poor old Reg; so he's for it,' he murmured, hanging up the damp tea-towel. He had long, thin hands; sensitive and well-kept and matching his fine skin. 'I'm sorry for your mother and father. It's a filthy business.'

He went upstairs to say good night to Linda, who was being encouraged by Margaret to undress and wash herself at night, and Margaret went into the dining-room to put away the table-cloth, for they had been having supper in the kitchen. In her abstraction of mind over Reg and the Challises and Dick and Linda, she opened the wrong drawer, and was surprised to find a face gazing up at her. It was the photograph of a woman, and in one corner there was the sprawling signature, 'Yours ever, Elsie.' Margaret, with a glance over her shoulder, bent down and studied it more closely, for letters had arrived at Westwood-at-Brockdale addressed to Mrs Elsie Coates, and she knew that this must be she. It was half with the object of being able to give her mother (who was consumed with curiosity about Mrs Coates) a description of her personal appearance that she examined the photograph, but when she had finished doing so, and had shut the drawer again, her whole attitude towards Dick, and the house at Brockdale, and her own position there, and her mother's views on the probable ambitions of Mrs Coates, had undergone a complete and rather disconcerting change; for Mrs Coates was not the faded matronly creature of her supposing; Mrs Coates could not be a day over thirty-five and Mrs Coates was pretty.

23

At half-past four on Friday afternoon, Margaret, almost sick with nervousness, was standing outside the front door of Westwood-at-Highgate.

It had meant a rush to get away from school in time to meet the rest of the party at the house, and she had had high words with her mother about being away from home for her brother's last week-end in England, but she was here! Here with her suitcase packed and only her very bright eyes to betray her painful excitement, and surely nothing could happen to stop her going with them now!

'Oh, God, here you are,' announced Hebe, who opened the front door to her. The remark was not as discouraging as it might have been, for the tone implied, *we're all in this together and isn't it a rigid bind.* 'I suppose you realize you've got to carry Jeremy?'

'Of course,' answered Margaret, who hadn't.

'Oh, well, so long as my mamma made it clear. I'll take him if he gets too awful. Cortway's just bringing the car round. Mummy, give Margaret Jeremy, will you?'

Mrs Challis came forward smilingly, and put Jeremy, a large form in a linen suit who looked hopelessly wakeful and already inclined to dance up and down, into Margaret's arms. She sat down composedly with him on the nearest chair, and he gazed up portentously into her face until she had to laugh.

'I thought his Moses-basket would be even more of a sweat,' said Hebe, also sitting down. 'Thank God it isn't a long journey. Barnabas, don't *do* that to Emma.'

'Why not?'

'She hates it. How would you like it?'

Then there was silence for a little while. The front door stood open, and the brilliant sunlight of half-past two miscalling itself half-past four flooded into the hall, making the faded green and rose of the carpet seem dimmer, and the marble urns filled with blue delphiniums and white lupins look the cooler, by contrast. Everyone seemed slightly on edge with the heat and disinclined to talk. Mrs Challis, who was dressed in an exotically printed cotton suitable for wearing in the country and a fine straw hat, sat silently gazing first at her grandchildren and then at her daughter, whose clothes were also countrified and made of cotton; even her severe little hat was of the same stuff as her dress, stitched and starched to keep it in shape. Margaret's own clothes were merely cool and inconspicuous.

'Where's Grandpa?' demanded Barnabas, uttering aloud the silent question in Margaret's heart; though she, of course, did not think of Mr Challis as Grandpa, and it came as a distinct shock to hear him thus described.

'At the Ministry,' answered Hebe, adding in a mutter, 'he's seeing to that.'

'Isn't he coming to see Great-granny?'

'Gey-ganny,' murmured Emma, busily picking at a button on her dress.

'Yes, you're going to see her,' said Margaret, thinking it well to establish a link with Emma as soon as possible. 'Won't that be nice? Come over and tell Jeremy all about it.'

Emma obediently came over and stood by her knee, gazing frowningly up at her from under a white muslin sun-bonnet.

'Isn't he going to see Great-granny?' repeated Barnabas.

'Presently,' said Hebe, and stood up. 'Thank God, here's the car. Get in, will you,' to Margaret. 'I'll bring the others.'

It was such a disappointment to Margaret to hear that Mr Challis was not travelling with them that she went off into a day-dream as they all settled themselves in the big, slightly shabby car; which still seemed more impressive than any car she had ever been in because it had once cost a thousand pounds. She came out of her dream only when they were half-way down Highgate Hill, and Barnabas aroused her by kneeling up to look out of the window with his feet grinding into her lap. She glanced at Hebe and Mrs Challis, who were in animated discussion, and wondered if she were supposed to correct him when necessary. She had not quite enough courage. On the other side of her, Emma had now struggled up and was peering out of the back window, but she was so small and soft that her weight as she leant against Margaret's shoulder was rather pleasant than otherwise. Barnabas continued to grind absently with his bony knees and Margaret suffered in silence. Suddenly his mother's small capable hand reached across, and without looking round or interrupting her conversation, she pushed his feet aside.

'You *must* slap him down,' she commanded, giving Margaret a brief, cross smile, 'or he'll get away with murder.'

Margaret murmured something, and the rest of the journey was passed in a silent bodily struggle between herself and Barnabas, which ended in a draw, but with herself both heated and annoyed, while Jeremy already seemed to weigh three times as much as he had at first.

At the station, Cortway went to get the tickets while the Challis ladies strolled ahead of Margaret and the children towards the barrier, Mrs Challis occasionally glancing round with her vague, kind, brilliant smile to make sure that they had not all fallen between the train and the platform. Margaret was compelled to hold Jeremy with one aching arm, for she had to give the other hand to Emma, and Barnabas kept her heart in her mouth by skirmishing between the porters and the piles of luggage and other passengers. Like most children, he became ravenously hungry a quarter of an hour after leaving the house on any journey, and he now demanded tea.

'Oh, but you *had* tea, Barnabas, before you came out,' said Margaret, wondering if she dare let go of Emma's hand to move Jeremy on to her other arm; the one holding him ached intolerably.

'No, I didn't. Did we, Emma? (*Say we didn't*),' he added in a hoarse, hissing whisper, and blew in her ear.

'Don't!' shrieked Emma, coming to an abrupt halt and going scarlet in the face, and jerking away from Margaret's hand.

'I didn't do anything, did I? a lovey, *precious* Emma?' His voice was now sinister with false affection.

'E'!' said Emma, gazing indignantly up at Margaret. 'Barney *bo*!'

'Don't do that, Barnabas,' said Margaret firmly, taking advantage of the pause to move Jeremy (who was silently gazing down at the goings-on of his relations with every appearance of interest) on to her other arm.

'I want some tea,' repeated Barnabas. 'We didn't have any before we came out and if I don't have tea before I go on a train I'm sick. Always. You ask Mummy.'

'Great-granny will have a lovely tea for you, I expect,' said Margaret, relieved to see Cortway at the barrier with the tickets, and that their train was in.

'Cawwy,' demanded Emma, halting once more and flinging up her arms imploringly.

'No, Margaret can't carry Emma now, she must carry poor Jeremy because he can't walk yet.'

Emma received this with a look of complete non-comprehension and repeated her request with a quivering lip.

'I'll carry you,' offered Barnabas, flinging his arms round her and beginning to haul her upwards so that her garments slid up and displayed her stomach.

'No, oh no!' cried Emma, struggling. Margaret was looking

wildly round for somewhere to lay Jeremy down while she parted them, when Cortway's voice said authoritatively: 'Here, here, what's all this? You put her down at once; I never heard of such a thing,' and Barnabas abruptly set Emma upon her feet.

'Very kind of you but you'll strain your inside,' added Cortway. 'It's too hot for carryings this evening. You go along with Miss Steggles and see what a nice place in the train you've got. Good evening, Miss,' nodding and touching his cap to Margaret. 'You've got your hands full,' and he moved off into the crowd, obviously intending to sit over the evening paper for half an hour with a pot of tea.

It is not necessary to describe the hour and a half's journey – which included a change of train – in detail; those of our readers who are mothers will realize that it was made up of wrigglings, requests for food, drink, and excursions along the corridor, drawings in breath upon the windowpane, comments upon fellow passengers, promenades up and down the carriage and a brief fit of roaring from Jeremy. By the time Mrs Challis leaned across smilingly and said: 'It's the next station; cheer up!' Margaret was limp and irritable, and wondering if Zita were cross with her again, for she had not come to the door to see the party off (Oh, well I can't help it if she is, she thought with a sigh), and was becoming increasingly annoyed with Mrs Challis and Hebe, who only smiled or frowned absently at the children's behaviour and seemed to have resigned them entirely to herself.

In the bustle of alighting at Martlefield and keeping her charges close to her side, she received only a vague impression that the station was very small, with one or two shabby buildings of creamy weather-boarding and some others painted a faded brown; that white and red hollyhocks were growing outside the stationmaster's cottage at the far end of the platform, and that all was bathed in the radiant light of a cloudless summer evening, while beyond the station she caught glimpses of flat fields covered in the brilliant green of young wheat, with here and there a group of large elms. The air was full of sweet smells from warm grass and wild flowers, and as they came out of the tiny waiting-room on to the road, having exchanged greetings with the sturdy young woman who took their tickets, the first sight she saw was a field immediately opposite the station so thickly covered with buttercups that it really did look like a shining golden carpet. A placid white road wound away between the low hedges on either side of the station, and the only buildings in sight were a group of cottages at some distance along it. An aeroplane, alas, was passing overhead, but otherwise the scene was one of perfect tranquillity and she almost forgot her irritation in looking at it, while Seraphina exclaimed, 'How heavenly!' and Hebe silently removed her hat to let the faint breeze blow on her forehead.

They were the only passengers to alight here (indeed, the train had been getting steadily emptier for the last half-hour and had now gone ambling off into the flat green fields of Bedfordshire with apparently only the engine-driver and the guard and one or two children and old ladies aboard) and there had been no one to meet them on the platform, but now a voice exclaimed, ''Ullo! Evenin', Mrs Challis,' and they all turned to look at a smart governess-cart, drawn by a cob and driven by a large smiling boy with red hair, which was drawn up in the scanty shade afforded by the station buildings.

'Good evening, Bertie,' said Mrs Challis, going towards it. 'Have you come to meet us? How nice of you. In you get, children. How is Lady Challis?' she went on, handing up Barnabas and Emma into the trap, while Hebe took Jeremy from Margaret. 'Quite well? That's good. Oh – my dear,' she added winningly, turning to Margaret and putting her hand on her arm, 'it's *too* shattering for you but I *know* you'll be an angel and won't mind waiting until the governess-cart comes back to fetch my husband, will you? You see, there *isn't* room for everybody in this *minute* contraption. It's about three miles to the house from here so you can't possibly *walk* in this heat, but his train should be in in an hour or just over, and the trap will come back to meet it and take you along too. You don't *mind*, do you?'

'Not at all – I shall rather like it,' stammered Margaret, relieved at the prospect of some solitude and so thrilled at the prospect of a drive with Gerard Challis that she forgot that her answer might seem odd. But Mrs Challis only laughed sympathetically and, murmuring, 'I should think so, you poor lamb,' climbed gracefully into the now overladen vehicle, and took the wilting Emma upon her knee.

'Aren't you lucky!' said Hebe, making a face at Margaret, as the boy touched the pony with the whip and they drove off.

'I should sit on that bank if I were you – heavenly –' called Seraphina, turning her head above Emma's white sun-bonnet to smile at Margaret and pointing; and soon the governess-cart was getting steadily smaller and smaller, as it proceeded at a leisurely trot down the road between the bright green hedges under the blue evening sky, and presently it turned a gentle curve in the road and was lost to sight. The sturdy female ticket-collector had retired into her little office and Margaret was alone.

She crossed the road and sat down on the heavenly bank, where there were moon-daisies and buttercups growing in the long grass and a mosaic of yet flowerless green plants, ivy and ragged robin and goose-grass and many others, growing in the hedge; the main body of it appeared to be hawthorn, for there was white may-blossom showing among the rest and that faint scent, too fairylike to be completely pleasant, mingled with the scents breathed out by the other flowers and plants and just traced upon the warm air. She clasped her hands round her knees and sat in idle silence, rejoicing in the scene and the solitude, and wondering if it were possible ever to be so unhappy that such loveliness could fail to give delight. The hour passed like ten minutes, and she was almost sorry when the distant sound of a signal coming to attention, and the reappearance of the sturdy one carrying her clippers, and the arrival of an old man who was apparently going to travel by it, announced that the next train was due.

She thought it best to sit on the bank and await Gerard Challis's arrival, so she did not move when the train came leisurely into the station, although her heart beat faster and her calm delight in the beauty all about her had quite vanished. The train began to move slowly off, and the passengers came out of the little waiting-room and gave up their tickets; and there, a striking figure in thin grey summer clothes among the squat and undistinguished forms of the other passengers and looking indeed rather like Curdie among the Goblins, was he.

He removed his hat and stood glancing discontentedly about him; taking in the flat, uninteresting landscape, the shabby little station, the large form of the ticket-collector in her unfortunate trousers, and the plain, nervous young woman sitting (absurdly, he thought) among those dusty weeds on the other side of the road. In the distance the governess-cart was making its leisurely way towards them.

'Typical Home Counties scenery, isn't it?' he said abruptly, crossing the road to where Margaret sat. 'Is this your first visit here (but of course it is, how stupid of me), and why have you been abandoned by the rest of the party?' He stood looking down at her with a faint sarcastic smile, his long fingers gently swinging his hat and a black brief-case.

'There wasn't room in the governess-cart, so Mrs Challis said I had better – asked me if I would mind waiting until it came back for you,' answered Margaret, thinking how handsome he looked, as he stood there against the deep-blue sky, and colouring as she spoke.

'Do you mean to say that it isn't here?' he exclaimed. 'Surely we aren't expected to *walk*?'

'It's just coming, I think,' she said, and was preparing to struggle to her feet (this is never a graceful action and she was doubly handicapped by being very nervous) when she was surprised to see a fine white hand extended, which she accepted before she realized what was happening, and with unexpected strength he pulled her upright.

'Thank you,' she said.

'Your dress will be dusty,' he said gravely, and took out his handkerchief and held it out to her.

'It's all right – really – thank you,' she stammered, crimsoning, but accepted it and lightly dusted herself and gave him back the snowy object.

'It's a pity to spoil such a pretty dress,' said Mr Challis, who certainly would have won an All-Europe Championship for Philandering had such a contest existed, but this time he went too far; her dress was not pretty and she knew it, and she resented his sarcastic look, his grave tone, because she had been sitting on the grass by the roadside; she also felt a vague resentment at his obvious contempt for the landscape. You *couldn't* have anything lovelier than that field of buttercups, she thought rebelliously; what *does* he want?

What, indeed. Hilda and Kew, but both seemed very far from him at this moment, as he stood in Martlefield with Margaret, and, as he was like a spoilt child in the strength of his whims and his resentment when he could not gratify them, he felt really despairing at the prospect of the long, noisy, dull weekend stretching before him, and said no more, but waited in sulky silence until the governess-cart unhurriedly came to a standstill before them.

''Ullo. Good evenin', Mr Challis,' smiled the red-haired boy.

'Good evening, Bertie,' replied Mr Challis. ('Get in, will you,' to Margaret, again giving her his hand.) 'How is Lady Challis?'

Bertie, who seemed to have entered already into the Promised Land of the classless society, replied that she had seemed all right when he left and they hadn't waited supper, and then Mr Challis got into the governess-cart and off they went.

For some time there was silence. Margaret gazed nervously at the green hedges going slowly past and noticed how flat the country was, and wondered why Mr Challis seemed so unhappy (she was too loyal to use another word) and the boy Bertie whistled and occasionally flicked the whip at the flies hovering round the cob's neck, and Mr Challis sat with folded arms and brooded.

'A landscape without hills,' he suddenly pronounced, 'is like a woman without mystery.'

There simply was not any answer to this, especially as his unhappy audience realized that whatever she said would be wrong, so she replied feebly:

'Oh – do you think so?'

'The monotony of an endless plain,' continued Mr Challis, disparagingly surveying the mild meadows on every side, 'drives men mad. It produces –'

'Isn't Russia flat?' suddenly interrupted Bertie, to Margaret's amazement and horror.

After an affronted pause, intended to give Bertie the opportunity of realizing that he had offended, Mr Challis coldly replied that the greater part of Russia was, certainly, flat.

'Well, *they're* all right, any'ow,' said Bertie in a tone of satisfaction. '*They* know their onions. It hasn't driven *them* mad, living on a plain,' and he flicked the whip once more and whistled 'Mairzy Doats.'

Mr Challis did not propose to tell Bertie that he had had in mind the spiritual madness of confusion which tormented Dostoievsky, so he made no answer, and Margaret wondered what on earth she should say next, and suddenly decided (being slightly light-headed with the proximity of her hero and the beauty of the evening) that she must stand up a little for the Home Counties, though Bedfordshire could not strictly be called one of them.

'I – I rather like this country,' she said, turning her pleading brown eyes on Mr Challis. 'It's so peaceful.'

'Dull,' he corrected her gently, with his favourite smile.

'No,' she persisted daringly, 'I like all these little hedges, and the elms every now and then, and that little river over there –'

'The Martlet,' put in Bertie, flicking and whistling.

'And those willow trees growing all along it.'

'You may like it, but that does not make it less dull to people who have seen other landscapes, that ring and flash with beauty.'

'You mean my taste is dull,' she said, going crimson.

'I am sure that all your taste is not dull,' he said more kindly. 'No one whose taste was dull could care for the music of Beethoven.'

Bertie here whistled the first four notes of the Fifth Symphony, thus proving that culture was at last reaching the masses – and observed to himself, 'V for Victory.'

'Everybody can't see those landscapes,' Margaret blundered on, feeling so foolishly, hopelessly sorry for the fields and flowers that were being dismissed by Gerard Challis, 'and so they have to make the best of what they can see –'

'No one should accept a second-best in beauty.'

'But some people *have* to, Mr Challis!'

He only shook his head, studying her flushed cheeks and over-bright eyes. 'Never, my child.'

'Then if one cannot have the very best, shouldn't one have anything at all?' she asked, in a tone so despairing that it amused him and he gave a quite good-natured laugh, but all the same he answered firmly:

'No – nothing. In beauty, in art, in love, in spiritual integrity – the highest and best – or nothing!'

'That makes it very hard for some people,' she said at last in a low tone.

'Life is hard,' said Mr Challis, adjusting his tie. 'Very hard; for most people it is either a long starvation or a long surfeit upon the wrong sort of food.'

'Granted, but that'll all be put to rights, Mr Challis,' said Bertie tolerantly, turning the governess-cart down another mild little winding lane with fields of broad beans on either side which were already in the grip of blackfly. 'Give Us time, y'know. Come up, Maggie,' to the cob.

Mr Challis darted a glance of considerable irritation at Bertie and said deliberately to Margaret:

'I hope you have seen *Kattë*,' for he suddenly, wearily, longed for a great, satisfying chunk of warm-hearted, ungrudging praise, and he did not mind who handed it to him, and this girl's opinion of his work had always been obvious. But even as the muscles of his face relaxed to smile under the first reviving shower of enthusiasm, he was surprised to see the young woman go pale and become solemn as if under some mental distress, and not a word did she utter until a faint, 'Oh, yes, I was there on the first night,' which sounded chilling and guarded, came from her lips.

'Nearly there,' put in Bertie. 'Come up, Maggie,' and the cob quickened her pace to a trot.

Mr Challis turned his head away. He did not want to hear what she had to say – if she was going to say anything at all – he wished heartily that he had never asked her, for it was as plain as her face that she had not liked *Kattë*; did not admire it; hadn't been moved by it. But she might have had the feminine graceful-ness to *pretend* that she had. How he detested candid women!

'I thought –' faltered the miserable Margaret (oh, *why* did he have to mention *Kattë*?) 'it was very – parts of it were beautiful –'

His vanity compelled him to say *something* in response, or he would be branded as a fisher for compliments, a man avid for praise, and he murmured stiffly:

'So kind of you . . . I'm delighted you liked it —' hoping that she would at least have the tact to change the subject, but she, with a pale, set face, stumbled on:

'— but as a matter of fact I didn't like it as much as some of the earlier ones — it didn't seem so — I hope you won't mind my telling the truth about it because you did say that just now about never liking the second-rate' — she paused, horrified, with a tiny gasp — what had she said? — then rushed on, not looking at him but keeping her eyes fixed steadily, unseeingly, upon the row of cottages standing back from the lane under flowering apple trees which the governess-cart was now approaching:

'And I know *you* would rather I told the truth and I've always loved your work so much — I mean, I didn't mean —'

Her voice died wretchedly away as the governess-cart came to a standstill before a gate set in the wall which enclosed the row of cottages, and a tall old woman in a print overall, carrying a basket-full of cherries, opened the gate and came out to meet them. Gerard Challis had not said a word or once looked at Margaret while she was speaking, and he now opened the door of the cart and said quickly, 'Excuse me,' and climbed down.

'Hullo, Gerry, dear, how are you? How nice to see you,' said the woman with the cherries, and they exchanged a kiss.

'How are you, Mother?' he said, then, keeping his hand upon her arm, he turned to Margaret and said pleasantly:

'This is Margaret; I'm afraid I only know her as Margaret, but she is a friend of Zita's and has nobly offered to help Hebe with the children this week-end. Margaret, this is my mother.' The kind tone, and his use of her name (which she only now discovered that he even knew), coming immediately after what she had said, proved too much for Margaret's overladen feelings;

and to her unbearable shame, as she climbed out of the governess-cart murmuring, 'How do you do, Lady Challis,' her eyes were brimming with tears.

'How do you do,' replied Lady Challis. 'Gerry, go in and wash if you want to wash, and I'll look after Margaret. Then you go into supper; everybody's there and I won't be a minute. Bertie, turn Maggie into the paddock and then come in.'

Margaret, who was feeling for her handkerchief while Lady Challis turned away to give these instructions, did not see either Mr Challis or Bertie and Maggie go; and it was only while she was blowing her nose that she became aware how quiet everything had become all at once; with the pleasant sound of voices and laughter subdued by distance coming from the houses, and the soft movement of the evening breeze in the apple trees making the stillness seem more still.

'Would you like your supper upstairs in the attic? There's a sofa and plenty of books. Do you like cold rabbit pie? Good,' said Lady Challis, standing by her side and eating cherries.

Margaret answered in a muffled voice:

'Oh, thank you very much, but I ought to be with the children; isn't it time they were in bed?'

'It isn't seven yet, and the older ones always sit up to supper down here, so don't worry about them. Do you like beer or cider?'

'Cider, please,' answered Margaret, who was now following her down a path of narrow red bricks whose crevices were filled with bright green moss.

They were approaching a front door which stood open, revealing a long, low room which apparently ran the length of the five cottages and was used as a combined living- and dining-room, for as they entered Margaret heard a burst of laughter, and Seraphina's voice called, 'There she is, poor sweet!' Glancing confusedly towards the sound, she saw a large party (quite fifteen people, she thought) gathered about a supper-table at the far end of the hall. She could see Hebe seated between Emma and Jeremy, and then the sight of Gerard Challis's profile, gravely intent above a spoonful of something he was just raising to his lips, caused her to turn her eyes hastily away again, but not before she had noticed that there seemed to be a great many children of all ages in the party and a number of pretty young women who presumably were their mothers.

'This way. Mind your head!' said Lady Challis, and opened a door painted yellow, which led straight up a steep narrow staircase. Margaret's impression of the dining-hall had been pleasant, for the apartment had a wooden floor painted the same soft yellow as the door, and windows hung with glossy white material patterned by scarlet strawberries and their green leaves, and there must (she thought) have been literally thousands of books on shelves set high on the walls; but she was glad to be shown into a bathroom, which was not luxurious but whose appointments were solid and comfortable, and to bathe her eyes.

When she came out, Lady Challis was sitting at the head of the stairs, with a tray laden with food beside her, absorbed in a book. Margaret could see its title; it was Eddington's *The Nature of the Physical World*.

'Oh dear, I have been laughing so over this!' she exclaimed, putting the book into her overall pocket. 'It makes me think of what Raphael says to Adam in *Paradise Lost*:

> *He His fabric of the heavens*
> *Hath left to their disputes; perhaps to move*
> *His laughter at their quaint opinions wide*
> *Hereafter . . .*

'Are you ready?'

'There!' she said at last. (They had now climbed another perilous staircase.) 'You'll be all right here, won't you?' and she pulled out a table and set it near a window that looked across the orchard to some meadows.

'You are kind!' exclaimed Margaret fervently, putting the tray down on the table, and glancing round the large airy room with its sloping roof and shelves filled with worn, friendly-looking books.

'Not kind; selfish,' said Lady Challis oracularly, tucking a piece of silver hair into the coil at the back of her head. 'Good-bye; I'll see you later,' and she nodded and smiled and went out of the room.

As Margaret ate, she was thinking about nothing but her hostess, and trying to grasp the fact that she was Gerard Challis's mother; she, who was so completely, so utterly unlike what Margaret would have expected his mother to be. The worn loveliness of her features, certainly, was like her son's, and her faded blue eyes must once have had the depth and colour of his, but whereas (Margaret groped for words to express her impression) – he has made the best of his personality so that it is all in his face, she takes no notice of hers. She could have been strikingly beautiful, I should think, but she ignores her own beauty. Her hair is done anyhow and she hasn't even a pretty overall, and her hands are rough with gardening, and yet, all the same, she is beautiful. Oh, I do like her so much! I wish I could talk to her; I'm sure she could help me.

Lady Challis meanwhile wandered downstairs, still reading *The Nature of the Physical World*, and when she reached the head of the main staircase once more, which provided such a convenient seat, she was just absently sitting down to continue reading when a small voice cried warningly:

'Lady Challis! You're reading again and your supper will be beastly and cold,' and a little girl appeared at the bottom of the staircase, busily eating a mouthful of her own supper and gazing up at her.

'Thank you, Jane, I'm sorry,' murmured Lady Challis, and got up and continued her journey, slipping her hand into that of Jane as she reached the foot of the stairs, and going on reading. 'Did mother send you to find me?' she went on absently.

'No. Mr Challis, your son. He said, "Little girl" (I've *told* him my name when he was here before but he never *can* remember it), he said, "you go and look for Lady Challis and tell her to stop reading and come and eat her supper."'

'And so you did. Well, thank you very much, and now you run along and eat yours, or that will be beastly and cold too.'

24

The shadows of the apple trees were long upon the grass when Margaret at last decided that she must go down and find the children. She was now completely in command of herself, and could have wished that Lady Challis had let her go in to supper with the others, for she thought that everybody must have noticed her absence and commented upon it, but that the wish seemed ungrateful after such delicate kindness. It seemed strange not to be busily cooking an evening meal at this hour, so used had she become to going to Westwood-at-Brockdale, and in spite of the novelty and interest of this new household in which she temporarily found herself, she missed Dick and Linda. *There* she was needed; *there* her opinion was valued and her presence was indispensable to the comfort of the family, while *here*, though she had carelessly been called sweet and an angel for her pains, she was only being used as a convenience. She thought with real affection of the clumsy clasp of Linda's hand and of Dick's brief appreciation of the suppers she cooked, and returned again and again to the hope that Mrs Coates (whose large, slightly pop-eyes and loose mouth suggested a weakness for dramatic behaviour) would not make an unexpected return during the week-end.

I shall miss looking after them, she thought, as she stood by the window gazing out across the apple trees and the cooling meadows; and then she thought (poor Margaret), *if only I had someone who belonged only to me, and didn't always have to go into other people's homes and share with them; I want someone for my very own.* She had at first dreamt of letting her ideal love for Gerard

Challis so fill her life with selfless beauty that it should transform all her ways of feeling and thinking, but she had found, on a closer acquaintance with him, that her devotion did not blossom and enrich her existence as she had hoped. Now, at this moment, exactly eight months to a day since she had first spoken to him in the hall of Westwood, when she was to spend three nights under the same roof with him in his mother's home, she could not truthfully say that he meant as much to her as he had done on that first evening, when she had looked up into the eyes 'blue and meditative as the eyes of the Roman Augustus,' and felt that the greatest moment of her life had come.

'Margaret, are you dead or something?' exclaimed Hebe crossly, bursting into the room and startling her. 'Can you come down and cope with the brats? We want to go to the local.'

'Of course, I'm awfully sorry,' replied Margaret guiltily. 'I was just coming down, only I thought you wouldn't have finished supper yet.' She picked up her own supper-tray and followed Hebe out of the room.

Her tone seemed to have mollified Hebe slightly, for as they followed each other down the perilous staircase she said:

'I'm afraid it'll be a rigid bind for you, three days of it. It's angelic of you to do it, really; I'm blowed if I would.'

This was the pleasantest remark Margaret had received from Hebe since that first day at Lamb Cottage, when she had been charming and polite, with a manner modelled upon that of her mother, because she had wanted something; and it recalled to Margaret the fascinating creature who had sat on the sofa knitting and smiling at Earl's ingenuousness; the poetic figure gracing the stalls at the first night of *Kattë*; a personality so different from the sulky girl in the cotton frock she was used to seeing at Westwood that it was possible to show her something of one's feelings.

'I love the children, only I'm scared of them,' she answered simply. 'I'm not much good with kiddies, I'm afraid. And besides, I'm glad to be here because I wanted to be with all of you.'

Few people can resist a declaration of love which embraces their family and home and milieu and yet does not threaten to involve them in an embarrassing personal devotion. Hebe only said 'Blimey!' but the backward glance which she gave Margaret was almost good-humoured, and the latter was encouraged by it to continue eagerly:

'Isn't your grandmother – Lady Challis, I mean – absolutely *fascinating*?'

'Yes, she gets me down, though,' answered Hebe in one breath.

'*Does* she? I can't imagine her getting *anyone* down.'

'She's a saint, and saints do get you down. She makes me understand why the Romans were always giving the Early Christians the works.'

Margaret longed to hear more, but did not like to speak.

'If you'd known Grandpapa Challis, you'd see why my papa is like he is,' Hebe went on suddenly, pausing at a window to look out into the garden, where the children were playing in the evening light. 'Papa isn't a bit like Granny Challis, of course.'

'No,' murmured Margaret, enthralled.

'He *is* just like Grandpapa Challis was, though. He was Sir Edwin Challis, the physicist, you know. All he cared about was atoms. He had a house and a lot of land near here and Granny's pa looked after it for him. She must have been marvellous to look at – though I bet her hair never would keep up, even then. Grandpapa fell for her one morning when he saw her hanging out the washing; she was seventeen.'

'It's like a *fairy* story!'

'Not to notice it,' answered Hebe dryly. 'I don't think Granny had much fun and games after they were married. She always wanted swarms of brats (like me) and she only had my papa.'

Margaret was silent, fearing to break the spell.

'Grandpapa only died five years ago. He was eighty-seven and absolutely terrifying. He'd been so mad on atoms for years he was hardly there at all by that time, if you get me. The minute he'd had it, Granny rushed off and bought these cottages. They were going to be pulled down, but she had them all altered and made into one.'

'I *love* it here. It isn't a bit like anywhere else I've ever been.'

Hebe made one of her faces, and saying, 'Well, we'd better go down, I suppose,' moved away from the window.

'And all these young-marrieds hopping about the place are the granddaughters of her old friends,' she went on. 'She asks them all here with their brats and so she always has the house full of children. She likes children and books better than anything.'

'I noticed the books. There must be thousands.'

'Oh, she buys a book every time she goes out, and has done for years. I don't get it myself; I don't like all this reading; but if she's got a book in one hand and a brat hanging on to the other, she's all right. Coming!' she called suddenly, in response to a distant shout of 'Hebe!' 'Look, I must fly,' she said, turning to Margaret with a charming smile. 'It is angelic of you. You'll find them in the garden and mind you don't stand any nonsense from them,' and she ran off.

Margaret was in time to see the party leaving for the local, consisting of several young men in uniform (presumably the husbands of the pretty young women) and the young women themselves, looking weary at the end of a day spent in chasing their children, but cheerful and ready for the pleasures of the evening.

When they had gone, the hall seemed empty and quiet and shadowed by evening. *Now the day is over, night is drawing nigh*, thought Margaret, gazing dreamily about her, *Shadows of the evening steal across the sky* – and now was the moment for Gerard Challis to be discovered sitting quietly in one of those deep chairs at the far end of the hall, or for Lady Challis to enter by an unsuspected door and engage her in a long and wonderful talk.

But neither of these events took place, and after a pause she put down her tray on a table and went out into the garden through a passage with a stone floor. Sounds of washing-up and voices came from an apartment at the side of this passage, and, glancing in, she saw Lady Challis, Bertie, and a fair young woman who was going to have a baby, standing by the sink and all employed. A weedy young man in peculiar clothes was standing by an Aga cooker, stirring something in a saucepan.

'Hullo,' said Lady Challis, pushing back a lock of curly hair with one damp finger. 'Are you looking for Barnabas and Emma? She's here,' indicating a pile of miscellaneous cushions and rugs in a corner where lay Emma, fast asleep. 'He's outside with Jane and Dickon and the rest. He knows where he's to sleep. If I were you, I'd put Emma in first.'

'I shan't wake her to wash her,' whispered Margaret, lifting the warm, unexpectedly heavy little body from the cushions. Emma sighed and stirred but did not wake, and Margaret gathered her comfortably into her arms.

'My dear!' suddenly exclaimed the young man who was busy at the stove, 'it tastes madly strange! Do you think it's done?'

'I expect it's all right,' said Lady Challis. 'Try it on a plate. If it sticks it's ready.'

'I'll show you where Emma's to sleep,' said the fair young woman, and Margaret followed her upstairs, pursued by cries from the garden: 'Help! help! The grandfather's gone mad again! Where's the bicarbonate of soda?'

The fair young woman and Margaret exchanged glances and laughed.

'They're playing air-raids,' said the fair young woman, 'and Robert's the grandfather who's mad and keeps on having attacks.'

'Was that why he was lying on the grass and kicking?'

'I expect so. Jane and Claudia and my Edna are refugees from Norway, and they have to keep on taking the dolls into a shelter. Aren't they queer, wanting to play raids down here? I'm only too glad to forget them.'

'Do you live in London?' inquired Margaret – softly, so as not to awaken Emma.

The fair young woman explained that she and her Edna had been bombed out some months ago. Her husband was fighting in Italy. Her mother was an old school-friend of Lady Challis's, who was an absolute dear. 'I'm Irene,' she concluded, smiling.

'I'm Margaret,' said Margaret, smiling too. 'Oh, I *do* like this place!' she added suddenly. 'I'd like to live here for ever!'

'Well, there's nowhere like your own home, I always say,' said Irene, 'but I must say I never thought Edna and me would have settled down here the way we have. It's all Lady Challis, really. She isn't a bit like the rest of her family, though,' she added, lowering her voice. 'I don't know them awfully well. I was awfully thrilled to meet Hebe; I've seen her photo in *Home Chat*. She's not as pretty as I thought she'd be and not very *pleasant*, is she?'

Margaret agreed heartily that she was not, but added that she thought Hebe was nicer than she seemed, at which Irene (who was evidently one of those women living in a flowery little frame, from which life appears to be both miniature and manageable) looked her disagreement but was too polite to argue.

When Emma was comfortably bedded down, Margaret went in search of Barnabas, whom she found lying on his stomach on top of the derelict shelter at the far end of the garden with a purple face and threatening the party cowering inside.

'I'm a Messerschmitt!' he roared, waving his feet 'Unk-unk-unk-unk!'

'You've been shot down,' coldly said a tall child with long

brown hair, putting her head out for a minute. 'You're on the ground, so you must have been shot down and you oughtn't to be making that noise.'

'Oh, Mother, oh, Mother, be careful!' wailed a voice from the shelter.

'I *am* being careful, darling, don't worry,' said the tall child, turning her large green eyes towards the voice. 'How is the grandfather?'

'Very bad – e-r-r-r-r!' came a snarling voice from the darkness.

'One of the children is dead,' observed a fat younger voice with satisfaction.

'There's no time to bury it, no time to bury it,' said the tall child busily, drawing back into the shelter. 'Dear, have you made the bed?'

'Yes, dear, and supper's ready. Come along, children,' answered a little boy's voice, unusually pure in quality. 'Hurry up, the Alert will go again in a minute.'

Margaret peered into the shelter, where she could just make out the six children and a doll's pram huddled together on some old blankets. Twelve eyes were instantly fixed upon her, waiting.

'I'm sorry,' she said, 'but Barnabas must come to bed now.'

'Oh *no!*' howled everybody, but in a hopeless tone that seemed to express formal protest rather than active resentment, while Barnabas said flatly: 'I shan't. It's not my time.'

'Yes it is your time, Barnabas,' said the tall child sharply. 'You know we go in ages. The babies go at six; Jeremy first, because he's six months, and then William because he's nine months, and then Emma, and Peter at half-past six because he's four.'

'Emma stayed up till seven this evening,' interrupted Barnabas, 'so why should I go at my proper time if she doesn't?'

'The first evening doesn't count,' said the tall child. 'I'm the eldest; I'm nine and a month and I don't go until eight o'clock in the summer,' she added to Margaret, graciously.

'All right, I don't mind what time any of the rest of you go, you all seem to have got in a muddle with your times, anyway, but Barnabas must come *now*.'

'Go on, Barnabas,' said the little boy with the pure voice, who was named Dickon, and Barnabas unwillingly began to crawl out.

'Doesn't anyone else want to come?" asked Margaret, betraying her inexperience by this absurd question. 'Some of you *must* be getting sleepy. Who usually puts *you* to bed?' addressing the smallest girl, who had tiny fair pigtails and a pink and white check dress.

'Mummy, but she's gone to the local," said the little girl precisely. 'She said someone *else* would put me to bed.'

'Yes, Margaret would, she said,' nodded the tall child, who seemed to be named Claudia, and then Margaret realized what she was in for.

'Well, I am Margaret,' she said determinedly, 'and I've come to put you to bed. Come on, now. Youngest first. You —?' pointing at Jane. 'Are you youngest?'

'Yes!' shouted everybody, and Claudia added rapidly, waving her long fingers about, 'then Edna, then Barnabas, then Dickon, then Robert, then me.'

'All right, Edna, I think I see your mummy coming for you now, so Barnabas and Jane can come with me and surely Dickon and Robert and Claudia can put themselves to bed, can't they?'

'Of course,' said Dickon and Robert. Claudia looked haughty, and announced:

'I can put myself to bed but I *prefer* to be put to bed by my mummy.'

'Has your mummy gone to the local too?' inquired Margaret, giving Jane a hand (which Jane ignored) to help her out of the shelter.

'No, she's gone to say good-bye to my daddy,' answered Claudia, looking suddenly grave. 'He's going Abroad.'

'My daddy's Abroad,' said Edna, who was a cheerful little thing with bobbed hair and a missing front tooth, 'in Italy.'

'I'll give you a hand, Claudia,' said Margaret, wondering what time she herself would get to bed and if there would be any of the evening left after '*all were safely gathered in*.' 'If you'd like me to, that is?'

'Thank you very much, if you would kindly plait my hair, I can't manage it yet,' said Claudia, shaking back her mane.

The next hour was occupied in supervising the washing of faces, and hearing prayers and tucking people up and dealing firmly with Claudia, who tried to start a conversation on the difference between a Tory and a Conservative which was evidently intended to keep Margaret by her bed until Margaret's own hour for bed arrived. The latter found that her bedroom was in the middle of a nest of rooms where all the children slept, and as she tucked the last lot of bedclothes round the last child (who instantly thrust its feet out of bed, remarking, 'My feet are simply *burning*') she resigned herself to being aroused very early in the morning. As she came downstairs into the dining-hall an hour later, she was yawning, and wondering at what hour the household retired.

The hall was deserted and peaceful; the front door stood open, and through it there was a breath-taking glimpse of the orchard in the clear blue twilight, each tree spreading its white clouds of bloom above the dim green-blue grass, and all glimmering ethereally away in walks and dells wet with dew. There was not a sound; not a thrush singing, nor the last call of a blackbird, not even a cricket chirruping; and into the hall was stealing that chill, soaked in the scent of hidden dew, that comes on May evenings, and is the very touch of Spring's young hand.

There was a faint smell of burnt jam issuing from the

kitchen, but of the weedy young man, Irene, Lady Challis, and the rest, there was no sign. Margaret went over to the fireplace and saw that the mass of delicate ashes in it masked a red glow, and as she was shivering, she ventured to put on some forest-wood that was stacked in the hearth, and soon the flames were playing prettily.

While she was warming herself, lonely and content, she became aware of distant voices making remarks which suggested that someone was about to set out on a bicycle for Cambridge, and presently the sounds mounted to a crescendo of farewells, then died away. There was a brief silence; then out of the jam-perfumed passage Lady Challis appeared, dressed in an old house-coat, and came slowly across the hall towards the fire. Margaret's heart beat faster. Would the wonderful talk now take place? But somehow she only wanted Lady Challis to rest, because she looked so tired.

'That's right, I'm glad you put some wood on, it gets so cold in the evenings,' remarked Lady Challis absently, pulling up a chair and sitting down with a sigh. 'I've just been seeing him off to Cambridge, poor dear.'

After a respectful pause Margaret said:

'I hope he hasn't had bad news?' (The weedy young man, she presumed.)

'Oh, no. No worse than usual. There's always his father, of course – but we won't go into that. No, when I said *poor* dear, I only meant I was sorry for him as one is for a beetle, don't you know?'

Margaret said nothing, and Lady Challis leant back and shut her eyes. The twilight slowly deepened and the firelight began to throw shadows on the ceiling. Not a sound came from outside, and the house was still. Now and then Margaret quietly put a fresh stick on the fire and the fragrance of wood-smoke crept out on the air like the spirit of the house taking its evening walk.

She hoped very much that Lady Challis was resting, and then became so lost in her own vague dreams that she was startled when Lady Challis remarked from behind the fingers that were shading her face:

'In the five years that I have lived here, only two people of your age have sat in silence with me, and not started talking about themselves. One of them is you.'

Margaret glowed, and murmured something.

'And I know you've got lots to say,' went on Lady Challis sleepily, 'haven't you?'

'Masses!' answered Margaret, quietly but emphatically.

'Well, some day you shall. Not this time, I expect, because you'll be busy with the children, but you must come down by yourself one week-end later on, and then you shall talk and I will listen and try to help you.'

'Oh –!' breathed Margaret. '*Thank* you.'

'I mean it. You telephone one Friday and say you're coming, and I will be ready to listen. Now I don't expect I shall say another word to you while you're here, what with one thing and another, but don't go and get all hurt and disappointed, because I always keep my word; you ask the children. Ah, here are the others.'

And she sat up, looking like an ageless spirit that had chosen to live in a wrinkled skin under silver hair; and the rest of the party came in from the local, ready to crowd round the fire and remark on its pleasantness. Among them Margaret was surprised to see Gerard Challis; surely *he* had not been to the local too? But it transpired that he had, and had caused some respectful mirth among his juniors by bringing out a volume of Plato and reading it at a solitary table while he drank his one beer. He now lingered by the open door, apart from the gay group round the fire, gazing out into the orchard where it was almost dark, and the spell of his personal beauty so enchanted her that she found it difficult to keep from watching him.

At that moment he shut the door on the sweet darkness outside, and came over to the group beside the fire, where two of the more sophisticated young mothers made room for him, the ingenuous ones being too much in awe of his reputation to indicate that he should sit beside them. The rest of the evening passed pleasantly in gossip and laughter, and the drinking of tea, and Margaret was able to feel herself at home at least with one or two members of the party; but her only hope, so far as *he* was concerned, was a fervent one that he would not notice her any more during the week-end.

Mr Challis, as he sat nursing his teacup next to a reasonably intelligent and attractive young woman, was congratulating himself that the first evening was nearly over and that to-morrow morning he could shut himself up on the plea of work. He always found the active, cheerful atmosphere of his mother's home insipid, and the presence of so many young children, and of ungainly women who were about to have more children, affronted his aesthetic sense. There was never time at Yates Row for a leisurely conversation or for the development of subtle relationships, for every moment of the day seemed taken up with the toilet of the hordes of children and the preparation of the large, simple, commonplace meals; and in the winter there was wood to be hunted for and rehearsals for a play which always entertained the huge Christmas house-party, and Christmas presents to be made and reading aloud and sing-songs round the piano; and in the summer there was fruit-picking and picnics and haymaking and The Walk to be taken, and swimming excursions to the Martlet and tea in the garden; while in the autumn there was fruit-bottling and jam-making and nut-hunting; and in the spring everybody insanely gardened from morning till night, and looked forward to the summer.

No one seemed to take any interest in those questions, both eternal and temporary, which are the proper study of Man, and which mark him off, by his restless pursuit of them, from the beasts that perish.

The sight of his wife and daughter and grandchildren gathered about him under the matriarchal roof made him feel as involved in family life as a Chinese and he longed to be back in London, occupied with adult interests and dissatisfactions, while Hilda's face and form floated always before him with a faint, sweet pain.

Late that night Margaret went up to bed, making her way cautiously to her room through the other rooms where children lay asleep in varying stages of untidiness or cosy envelopment in the bedclothes. She paused to cover Jane's fat legs, which were bare almost to what would one day be her waist, and to smile at Robert, who was slumbering, with his long eyelashes sweeping his pale cheeks, in as neat a position as when she had tucked him in three hours ago.

It was strange to stand at her window and look out across the orchard, where the apple trees glimmered in the starlight and Mars flashed low and red upon the horizon, to feel herself surrounded by that sleeping childish loveliness, and to realize that far out across the meadows and little woods and darkened cities of England, beyond the calm spring sea, men were fighting; that the game the children had played in the garden was a pantomime of the horror in Europe and Asia. Half the world, she thought, is fighting to-night; and yet there are still people who are going to bed peacefully, with children asleep near them and candlelight making shadows on the walls and their beds looking comforting and quiet. And suddenly, for the first time in her life, she felt that she loved both the good and the wicked; she loved all her fellow-men.

25

She was awakened at six o'clock by Jane climbing into her bed and demanding to be made 'warmdy,' as her legs were cold; and in no time, it seemed, they were all seated at the breakfast-table, and spooning cereal and milk into their mouths. There was abundance of milk, for Lady Challis had a beautiful Jersey cow named Blossom, which was the admiration of all the babies, living in the paddock at the end of the garden, as well as a goat which was not quite so popular, and both were milked every morning and evening by Bertie. (There was some coffee for Mr Challis, which put him into a slightly better temper.)

Hebe looked even more placid than usual as she sat beside Emma and persistently directed the spoon, which the child was just learning to use, into her mouth. Although she professed to be bored in her grandmother's house and to long for the pleasures of London, the atmosphere suited her, especially when there were other young people staying there with whom she could go off to the local in the evening and be her age. As her children were her chief interest, this house where the routine revolved about children was the natural place for her to be, and she only occasionally became bored with a diet of Irish stew, macaroni cheese and semolina pudding, and a conversation consisting of riddles asked and answered, ancient jokes of which no one ever wearied, questions, and shrieks of laughter.

But she was still angry with Alex and resented his inability to be satisfied with the life that satisfied her. She had had a postcard, apparently from Dunster, saying, *Hope you are all quite well. I am quite well. Love from Alex*, but that had been a fortnight ago and that had been all. *The Shrapnel Hunters* had been called for and taken away in an ancient car by two of his painter friends, and by that she supposed that he was going to finish it in the friends' studio, and would not be home for some time, for it was only half-done. She had therefore decided that as soon as she got back to London she must try to find somewhere for them all to live. I've got all that money saved, she thought (for she was thrifty and had a good head for business) and that'll start us off comfortably, and this time I'll see that the house is big enough for all of us, blast him. She missed Alex every now and then, in painful bursts of feeling, but it is surprising how pain can be controlled if the sufferer refuses to give way to it and feels angry instead, and just now she was enjoying a relaxation from the cares of motherhood, while Margaret and the other women took some of her duties off her shoulders.

After her confidences to Margaret on the previous evening, she had decided that her debt had been paid and had said no more. *Struggles adored hearing about Grandpapa and Granny, with a bit about Pops thrown in*, she told her mother, *I thought it would do instead of thanking her, and I call it a cheap round*. She did not regard her family as sacrosanct, while poor old Struggles's earnest passion for Pops amused her. It was bad enough having to love somebody when they made you, let alone having a crush on somebody who didn't even try to make you, she thought, but Granny was always saying *People are so different, Hebe*, and she was too right.

Most of the day was spent by Margaret in the garden.

Her duties consisted chiefly in keeping an eye on the two babies who could just walk and carrying them off to 'see Blossom' when their interference with the games of the older ones became a nuisance. '*Will* you babies get out of the way!' in an exasperated shout was the signal for her to drop her book and go to the rescue. After a noisy and cheerful high tea in the paddock, she got her charges earlier to bed than on the previous night, and passed the remainder of the evening peacefully with a book by the dining-hall fire, now reading half a page and then looking up to exchange a smiling word with anyone who happened to come in from the garden.

The young people had again gone down to the local but this evening Mr Challis had not accompanied them, and Margaret had declined (for fear of being odd man out) an invitation which she afterwards wished she had accepted; for it was just a little dull in the hall with a book, when her spirits were exalted by the beauty of the spring weather and the change of scene and the society of new and interesting people. Already Linda and Dick Fletcher and the house at Brockdale seemed very far away. She now had Lady Challis's promise to think about, and its fulfilment to look forward to, and she watched her hostess admiringly as she moved lightly about, usually with a book, a gardening implement or a child in one hand, and marvelled that the mother should now mean as much to her as did the son, although they were such very different spirits. But it was the warmth of a tender heart and a loving nature that attracted her in Lady Challis, and she was already jealously sure that this spring, could she have the opportunity to drink from it, would never fail her.

She must give devotion to somebody, and as she was ashamed to indulge in those tender feelings for Gerard Challis's person which she had so readily given to his spirit and his work, she resolutely tried not to look at him and looked at his mother instead.

Sunday, the day on which the party was to go home, dawned not quite so fair as the previous two days, but it was judged sufficiently fine for Margaret to take Emma, Claudia, Dickon, Edna and Barnabas for The Walk.

This walk was so particularized because there was only one

345

true walk at Martlefield (as there usually is at any remote country place), and sooner or later everyone who stayed at Yates Row went on it, and surveyed the surrounding countryside from the fifty-foot hill, surmounted by a fine old oak tree, in which it terminated.

Meanwhile, in Highgate, Zita and Cortway were passing an alarming week-end.

On the Friday evening Grantey had seemed much as she had been for the last five weeks; maintaining a slow but steady improvement. The nurse no longer slept in the house, but came in every day, so that Zita and Cortway had no professional help when the latter was aroused in the small hours of Saturday morning by the prolonged ringing of the bell in his sister's room. Putting on his dressing-gown as he went, he hurried in to her, and found her blue and gasping and pointing to the tablets which had been left her to meet just such an emergency as this. While he was crushing them under her nostrils and observing with deep thankfulness that they were beginning to relieve her, Zita came stumbling upstairs, half awake and very alarmed, and loudly lamenting. Her anxiety and grief were genuine, but she was not of much practical use, as all she did was to hover distractedly round the bed exclaiming, 'Ach! mein Gott!' and make occasional dashes downstairs to fill a hot-water-bottle or brew some coffee to help Cortway through the watch he insisted on keeping, and then, forgetting what she had gone down for, return to the bedroom to see how Grantey was.

Cortway at last impatiently packed her back to bed, and sat grimly wakeful by his sister's side, trying to hear her breathing, and watching the darkness at the window slowly turn to the summer dawn. Every now and again he glanced at his sister's face. It looked very old amid the grey hair scattered on the pillow and yet in it he saw the likeness of the little girl who was one of his earliest memories.

Always together, he and Allie had been, and why she had ever wanted to marry that so-and-so Wally Grant beat him. *That* had all turned out wrong, and Allie had gone back into service again with the Braddons, where he himself was chauffeur; and that had been twenty years ago; and here she was, very bad, you could see that; and perhaps going for good this time.

His head nodded forward, and he dozed off, and when Zita came upstairs with a cup of tea at half-past seven he was asleep by his sister's side.

While Grantey was still dozing, they held a conference and discussed whether they should telephone to Mrs Challis, but as she seemed better and her colour was more normal, they decided to wait until they had heard what the doctor said.

When he came about nine o'clock, he told them that there was no more cause for alarm than there had been for the last five weeks, although he thought that they had better let Mrs Challis know how matters stood, and they decided to telephone when Grantey finally awoke. But when she did, she was apparently so much better that their fears receded, and after she had had some tea and bread and butter and nurse had come in and washed her and made a lot of jokes, they decided not to let Mrs Challis know just yet, as there was no point in alarming her unnecessarily. Grantey asked for the *Daily Mirror* and her knitting, and Cortway left her with them and went downstairs. It was a beautiful day and the house was full of sunlight and rang with music played by the wireless for Zita's entertainment. Grantey gently beat time with her spectacles, as she glanced through the pictures in the *Mirror*. Somehow she did not fancy putting them on this morning; they seemed to weigh kind of heavy on her face.

We must now return to Bedfordshire.

Jeremy had been added to Margaret's party, so that meant borrowing the big pram belonging to William, who would spend the afternoon crawling about the garden, and putting Emma and Jeremy at opposite ends. Thus burdened, and declining the offers of Barnabas and Edna to assist with the pushing, Margaret set out after lunch down the long lane which was the opening stage of The Walk. Claudia ranged so far ahead that she had to be called to, in the first five minutes, not to get out of sight; while Dickon, who had his own ideas about walks, speedily fell behind. Edna and Barnabas kept so close to the pram that they had to be told not to get in the way, and only Jeremy was in repose, full of milk and peaceful, and Emma actually sang to herself as they went along.

'Can we go in the woods?' demanded Barnabas suddenly. 'Gosh, this is a boring road!' and he swung on the pram and made it tilt.

'Can we go in the fields, Margaret?' demanded Edna, also swinging on the pram.

'Claudia!' called Margaret, waving to the long-legged figure straying a hundred yards away where the lane began to curve, 'don't get too far ahead!'

Claudia made elaborate signs, as of one who is anxious to hear what is being said, but cannot.

'We can't see Dickon now,' remarked Edna, in the satisfied tone she always used for disasters or ominous signs. 'Is he lost yet? Hadn't we better wait for him?'

'*Claudia!*' called Margaret, just as Claudia began to drift round the corner, and so loud was her voice that the sleepy Jeremy opened his eyes wide and Emma stopped her song and looked up in surprise.

'Sorry!' said Claudia charmingly, skimming down the road with her hair flying, 'Oh, didn't you want me to go so far away? Mummy always lets me.'

'No she doesn't, Claudia,' said Edna. 'Your mummy gets in a fuss if you do. My mummy thinks it's ever so silly.'

'My daddy's been in the Army longer than yours and so my mummy has had to bring me up by herself, and if you dare say she's silly I'll slap you down, so shut up,' retorted Claudia.

'That will do, now,' said Margaret, interrupting herself in her calling of Dickon, who had vanished. The long lane, bordered on either side by low hedges of brilliant green thorn, stretched away empty. Stories of children snatched up by gipsies went absurdly through her head.

'He always does this,' remarked Barnabas, bored. 'Let's go on and he'll catch us up.'

'Does his mother let him do it?' asked Margaret of Claudia.

'Oh no!' cried Claudia. 'She'd be in an awful flap if she knew!'

'No, she wouldn't, Claudia, she always lets him, you know she does,' said Edna.

'Oh *no*, she'd be *horrified*,' declared Claudia again, shaking all her hair round her face and smiling behind it.

'*There* he is!' yelled Barnabas, leaping about as a figure came leisurely into sight, swinging a bunch of wild flowers. 'Come on, can't you, we're going to the *woods*!'

Dickon, thus lured, broke into a slow run and presently came up with them. His delightful face was red as an apple under his thatch of dusty blond hair and when he smiled his tiny white teeth suggested a row of hazel nuts.

'Sorry,' he said cheerfuly, 'come on, let's go to the woods!'

'The woods, the woods!' cried Claudia, springing in the air.

'I'm afraid we can't go to the woods,' said Margaret. ('*Don't* hang on the pram, *please*, Edna.')

'Oh, *why* not?' roared Dickon, all his cheerfulness gone in a flash and replaced by utter despair; even his bunch of flowers fell forward in his hand and seemed to wilt.

'Because there aren't any near here,' said Margaret rather sharply. ('Barnabas, *don't* hang on the pram, *please*) and we're going to Sharps Hill.'

Several members of the party gave elaborate imitations of being sick.

'*Sharps Hill!* Enough to make you vomuate!' cried Claudia.

'I don't know why you're making all this fuss. You knew we were going to Sharps Hill,' said Margaret, steadily pushing the pram down the long lane. Big purple clouds were rolling up languidly in the east and there was not a breath of wind. 'It's going to rain,' she added.

'Oh, goody!' they all shouted, restored to good humour, and rushed ahead again, but soon the breathless heat and hush subdued them, and they gathered round the pram and walked beside it, complaining or silent. The Walk continued its unexciting course; curving round gentle bends into other lanes exactly like the last; passing gates opening on fields of young wheat or oats that looked startlingly green against the plum-blue thunder-clouds across the flat meadows; now crossing a stone bridge over the six-foot-wide Martlet with old willows growing along its banks and reflecting their yellow-green buds in the slowly gliding water; now including among its sights a completely flat and dry black-bird, the victim of a car, which threw Claudia into a passion of mourning; and at last providing a glimpse of the distant hill crowned by an oak which was the party's goal.

'There it is!' said Margaret cheerfully, and paused to wipe her face. Emma had fallen asleep and was lying back with her fair little limbs uncovered and a dew of heat on her forehead, and all the children looked limp and tired.

'Race you to it?' suggested Barnabas, but half-heartedly, and no one accepted his challenge.

'Now we've seen it, can't we go back?' suggested Dickon. 'I'm starving.'

'So am I,' said several voices.

'Can't we go home, Margaret?'

'Not until we've been up the hill. It's only half-past three.'

'I've got a stone in my sandal. It's absolute *agony*.'

'Take it out then, Claudia.'

'Where shall I sit?' and Claudia cast a scornful glance over the narrow grass banks of the ditches and the dusty road. 'The worst of the country is there are always cows.'

'There's a nice patch of grass; go over there.'

'*Beastly* country,' grumbled Claudia, crossing the road. 'How I hate it!'

'Hate the *country*?' cried Dickon, opening his eyes widely at Margaret. 'How can she? She must be mad.'

'Mad yourself,' said Claudia, without looking round.

'Hurry up, Claudia; I believe I felt a drop of rain.'

This led to much running up and down the road with uplifted faces to catch the first drops, but there was no increase in them until, Claudia having removed her stone, the party arrived at a stile which led across a meadow, covered in big daisies, to the hill.

'You can go up the hill, children, and I'll stay here; I can't take the pram over the stile,' said Margaret, glad of the chance to rest.

'Oh, need we? It's so boring.'

'Go and pick some moon-daisies, then.'

'I'm so hot.'

'I'm starving. I should like six glasses of iced orangeade and twelve sardine sandwiches.'

'The minute you've all been up the hill we'll turn round and go home. Hurry now, there's another drop of rain.'

They all climbed over the stile with much display of bare brown legs and shabby sandals, and struck out across the meadow; deep into the wilderness of delicate daisies and here and there a seven-branched buttercup, golden as rich candle-holders, among the silver and the green. Margaret arranged the pram under an elder bush, congratulating herself that Emma and

Jeremy were still asleep, and presently climbed the stile and strayed into the flowers, steadily picking the finest until a bunch began to grow in her hand, with endless trailing roots where she had pulled up a plant by mistake, and that faint scent breathing out from all the pretty, uplifted flower faces which seems to hold in itself the very life of the meadows. The daisies looked unearthly white in the lowering light and the grass was a lurid green, and suddenly there was a flash, followed by a long, distant rolling sound. The party climbing the hill immediately turned and began flying down again, spurred on by Claudia, whom Margaret could hear crying: 'Guns! Guns! I tell you it's guns!'

Margaret made angry signs to her to be quiet, but she took absolutely no notice, and soon they were all streaming through the daisies amid the first heavy drops of rain towards the stile, shrieking, 'Guns! Guns! It's guns!' At the same instant there came howls from the pram.

'There, there, s'sh, it's all right, Emma, Jeremy love, it's only rain,' soothed Margaret, hastily climbing over the stile. She helped the struggling Emma to sit up, and settled her comfortably, putting the bunch of daisies into her hand, and then patted Jeremy, who actually went off to sleep again.

'Pretty!' said Margaret, nodding and smiling at Emma as she put up the pram's double hoods against the increasing rain. From the stile came cries of, 'I'm soaking!' 'It's simply pouring!' 'We'll all get *frightful* colds!' and other encouraging prophecies.

'Oo, look a dat,' said Emma, holding up an unusually large flower to Margaret with a considering expression.

'Pretty flower, yes.'

'Oo, look a dat.'

'Come on, come on,' said Dickon, bustling up, followed by the others, 'it's going to pour, and we must get home as quickly as we can.'

'Claudia's sure to get a cold,' said Edna in a satisfied tone, 'she always does.'

Claudia gave a groan and Margaret sharply told her to hurry on with the others. She wheeled the pram out on to the road and hurried away through the rain which was now driving down in sheets. She glanced anxiously from side to side as she went, but it was useless; there was not a tree nor a thick shrub nor a barn in which they could shelter, and already Emma's face was screwed up distastefully over the rain which drove between the hoods and fell on her bare feet.

'No! Oh, no!' said Emma, moving her toes uneasily.

'It's all right, darling, it's only rain. It won't hurt Emma,' soothed Margaret, but when she tried putting the hoods closer together, Emma protested at being 'all dark,' and she had to open them again. The invaluable Jeremy continued to sleep.

'What? What?' Margaret shouted, in response to a distant yell from Claudia, who was lagging behind the boys with Edna, their grubby handkerchiefs spread over their heads in dismally inadequate protection against the wet.

'Her *legs* ache! She can't walk any *further*!' shrieked Claudia dramatically, hopping in the puddles which were rapidly accumulating.

'Oh, blow –' muttered Margaret, wiping rain out of her eyes. 'All right,' she shouted, 'come on, she can ride.'

This led to a halt while the pram came up with the party ahead, and much advice and confusion while the weeping Edna, whose hair hung in limp streaks, was put into the pram between Jeremy and Emma and covered with the mackintosh.

'No! Oh, no!' said Emma, frowning, but she was apparently so awed by the sight of an elder in tears that she said no more, only jealously drew her bunch of flowers away from Edna's feet.

'Now, perhaps we can get on,' sighed Margaret. 'Claudia, don't

do that! It will ruin your shoes. Come on, everybody, let's see
how soon we can be home.'

'Let's sing,' suggested Edna, somewhat comforted.

'All right, if you like. What shall we sing?'

'*He Who Would Valiant Be*,' from Claudia.

'*God Save the King*,' from Dickon.

'No, no, *Jesus Bids Us Shine*,' said Edna authoritatively, and
forthwith burst out in a tuneless pipe:

> *Jesus bids us shine with a clear pure light.*

None of the others knew the hymn, or if they did they
preferred their own choice and each sang it, while Barnabas
wandered from one song to another as the mood took him,
and Emma enchanted Margaret, amid all her discomfort, by
joining in with a tiny droning 'Ner-ner-ner' of her own.

On marched the dreary procession, with the rain soaking
through their summer dresses and their bare legs disagreeably
splashed, while every now and then a fresh shower of heavier
drops made everybody wriggle and shriek. Jeremy was now
awake and Margaret became alarmed at the loudness and passion
of his crying. As fast as she crowded Emma and Edna up into
one end of the pram to give him room, they slipped back and
upset him once more, Edna singing all the while and Emma
angrily trying to wipe the rain from her feet with the corner
of her blanket. Claudia, Barnabas and Dickon continued to sing,
pausing every now and then to compare notes on how wet
they were and to wring rain out of their garments, and Margaret
struggled on with the heavy pram, now seriously alarmed at
the prospect of pneumonia for all her charges.

'Here comes somebody!' suddenly shouted Dickon.

'Oh, where – is it a car?' cried Margaret, peering through
the rain in the hope of getting a lift for some of the party.

'No, it's a soldier with an umbrella and a pram,' said Barnabas.

'It's Daddy!' shrieked Claudia, and sprang away up the road towards the tall figure which Margaret could now see steadily coming towards them – only to falter, and pause, and turn slowly back again. 'I forgot,' she said in a quieter voice and hanging her head, 'he's gone by this time. Mummy said he was going last night.'

'It's an American soldier,' announced Barnabas. 'Has he come to meet us, Margaret? Can I go and ask him?'

The soldier was now quite close to them, and under the very large umbrella which he was holding over his head (while he competently guided with the other hand what Margaret saw was the second-largest pram at Yates Row) she recognized the cheerful face of Earl Swinger.

'Hullo therr!' he said pleasantly, as Barnabas dashed up to him. 'You'd better come under this right away, son. Margaret, please accept my aparlagies for not giving you a saloot, I am otherwise arccupied, as you see. Now how about putting Sister into this carriage right away? And you, too,' to Edna. 'Well, this certainly is vurry different from the last time I had the pleasure of meeting you, isn't it, Margaret? (Up you come, beautiful,' to Edna, as he lifted her gently out of one pram and settled her into the other.) 'Now, Sister.'

'Oh, Mr Swinger, I am so glad to see you!' cried Margaret, standing still and beginning to laugh. 'How very kind of you to come! We've been having the most *awful* time and we're nearly drowned, as you see.'

'Lady Challis suggested I should come and I thought it a vurry good notion,' he answered, settling the silent and staring Emma under the hood and tucking a mackintosh cover over her. 'Here are two more umbrellas,' getting them out from the side of the pram, 'and here's a waterproof for Margaret,' he ended, putting it round her and smiling down at her rain-wet face.

All this was very comforting, and as she rearranged Jeremy and had the satisfaction of hearing his cries cease, she was very glad that it was Earl who had come to their rescue and not Mr Challis; the very thought of *him* approaching them through the rain laden with prams and umbrellas sent her spirits down once more, and when the procession moved on again, now cheerfully employed in managing their umbrellas and calculating how far they were from home, she was wondering what use Mr Challis would be in an everyday dilemma in which integrity and austerity were not wanted but cheerfulness and common sense were?

'Is this your first visit to Yates Row, Margaret?' inquired Earl, marching along amidst the scurrying children and the gliding prams with their silent occupants as if he had been doing it all his life, and holding the umbrella steadily over Margaret's head.

'Oh, yes. I came down on Friday with Mrs Challis and Mrs Niland and the children. Is it your first visit?'

'No, I had the pleasure of visiting with Lady Challis six weeks ago and she kindly asked me to come again. There is a vurry delightful spirit in that house.'

'Isn't it lovely?' she answered eagerly. 'I've been simply longing to tell someone how much I love it.'

'Lady Challis is a lovely hostess. Vurry gracious.'

'Yes, isn't she,' but Margaret was conscious that he had used a word which did not at all express the impression made by Lady Challis upon herself.

'How is your friend, Mr – Levinsky, wasn't it?' she went on. ('Claudia, dear, *don't* do that; your shoes are soaking wet now.')

'Yes, but generally known to his friends as Lev. Lev is vurry well, thank you, but he has a grouch, as usual. Without wishing to tread on delicate ground, Margaret, I may say that Lev doesn't like England.'

'Oh dear, I'm sorry. Why is that?'

'Well, there are a number of reasons and perhaps it would be better if I did not mention them,' replied Earl, with a tact somewhat marred by the colour which came up into his fresh young face and the faintly wistful look in his eyes. For a little while they walked in silence, while Margaret wondered what could have so upset Lev as to cause his friend to blush, and Earl thought sadly about American girls; sweet-smelling, large-eyed, gay American girls, prettily dressed in frills and silk stockings, with tiny waists and little feet and shining hair. Certainly he was not going to confess to this pleasant British girl how desperately he and Lev, in common with all the other G.I.s, missed American girls and what a poor substitute he thought these little Britishers. In vain he had patiently explained to Lev that the British had already had nearly five years of war with the Germans less than a hundred miles from London; that their women couldn't get the right lipsticks and stuff because it wasn't being made in England any more, that all the good-lookers were in uniform (*and what uniforms*, groaned Lev) and the ones outside the Services couldn't get silk stockings unless they went to the Black Market. Lev had heard all these arguments without being impressed, and all he would say at the end of Earl's chivalrous defence was, 'Maybe, but it isn't what I've been used to.' Earl knew how he felt, for he suffered from the same painful loneliness, and some aspects of the problem horrified him, but being a simple, serious and domesticated character rather than a lover of the hot spots, he managed to enjoy England more than his friend did. It was a poor, small, badly arranged, dirty place, but personally he had found the people very kind and he was fascinated by the orderly peace in some of the British homes he had visited, and by the miniature loveliness of the countryside. And their wheat! that was wonderful; twice as heavy in the sheaf as the wheat in the hundred-acre fields of his own State of Kansas; drooping with its load of big, hard, weighty ears. When he had been helping to pile the stooks in a Gloucestershire farm last summer, he had had to stop and rest every now and then, and to admit that this British wheat certainly was heavy on the arm muscles. But peaceful homes, and kindness, and wonderful wheat did not make up for American girls and the *feeling*, comfortable and unthought-of as an old shoe, of his own country, and under that pleasant, earnest, polite manner he was a lonely and home-sick young American.

His admiration for Hebe had subsided with a shock on the first occasion that he had heard her be really rude to someone, and he now regarded her with bewilderment and some disapproval.

To relieve the tedium of the journey, Claudia and Barnabas (who seemed formed by nature to egg one another on) now set up an elaborate shivering and chattering of their teeth and demands for hot drinks when they got in, as they were sure they were starting colds.

'Oh, are you, do you think, Claudia?' said Margaret anxiously, having been warned that Claudia caught cold as easily as most people breathe. 'I do hope not.'

'Well, no, as a matter of fact,' confessed Claudia handsomely. 'I'm enjoying it; I like rain' (lifting a face like a wet pink flower to the dripping heavens). 'When me and Helen were coming home from games one day it was pouring, and we walked along *very* slowly drinking ginger-pop out of a bottle and having a good long *talk* and sucking Singers rolled in butter. It was *heavenly*.'

'Singers? What are they?'

'Little black sweets to do your voice good and make your breath smell nice. They aren't on points. *Your breath will smell like an angel*, it says on the packet. We were going to have a picnic in some bomb ruins, only it rained.'

'Who is Helen?' inquired Earl, looking down at her with amusement.

'She's my friend in *darling* London. Oh, if *only* I were there!' and she launched a kick at Bedfordshire.

'Don't you like the country?'

'*Like* it? My dear, I loathe and *abominate* it!' in an affected squeak. Margaret was wondering whether she ought to administer a mild snub when Claudia and Barnabas and Dickon rushed off down the road, shouting that they were nearly home. The rain had now nearly stopped and Earl smilingly furled his umbrella.

'I don't believe they're so very wet after all, thanks to you,' said Margaret, indicating Emma and Edna. Her earnest face, which was beginning to acquire a thoughtful, tender expression because of her constant longing for beauty, was framed in a scarlet handkerchief which showed her dark parted hair. That painfully acquired neatness, that straightforward yet gentler manner, that spirit in her eyes, were all in her favour; whereas a year ago she had looked an ordinary discontented young woman, she now looked an interesting one. To connoisseurs like Gerard Challis, she was still ordinary, but Earl Swinger liked her grave look and the gentle movements of her hands as she felt over Edna for possible dampness.

'It's kind of funny –' he said suddenly, as he watched her, 'when I came over here I was crazy about books and ideas. I was working on a theory of aesthetics of my own. Now, it all seems rather remote.'

'What did you teach in America?'

'Drawing and the History of European Art. Margaret,' he went on abruptly, 'do you like classical music?'

'Very much. It's one of my greatest pleasures.'

'That's grand, because I want you to come to a concert in London with me, soon.'

'It's awfully nice of you, Earl, I'd love to,' she answered quietly, beginning to push the pram once more.

'That's a date,' he said smiling. 'I'll call you up in a day or two.'

While they were making these arrangements they reached the house, and soon they were putting the prams into the shed where they were kept and carrying Emma and Jeremy into the living-room. But here they found a group clustered about Seraphina and Hebe, and the former was wiping her eyes while Lady Challis looked shocked and sad: they had just heard – Irene said in a low tone to Margaret as she took Edna in her arms – a telephone message had come from Highgate to say that the old nurse, Mrs Grant, had passed over that afternoon about an hour ago.

26

By three o'clock on the following day – what with the arrangements for the funeral, and Barnabas's questions, and the noisy grief of Zita and the silent grief of Cortway, and her mother's distress, and her father's scarcely hidden irritation, Hebe had had enough of it all; and she firmly parked the children upon Zita and, having previously stolen to the telephone and made the appointment as if with a clandestine lover, fled out of the house and away, away to the Maison Tel, to have her hair done.

A haughty, exhausted voice at the other end of the line had at first said that *It Was Impossible*, but had then discovered that someone had just cancelled their appointment. Madame could therefore have that appointment instead. Whom did Madame usually have? Mr Fidele or Mr Bonaventure? Mr Fidele, and Miss Gloria. Oh, very good then, would Madame please come at three o'clock.

Why do I come to this place, thought Hebe gloomily, at two minutes to three. It stinks like mad and all these little witches flipping about get me down, and she directed a glance at Miss Diana, who was floating past with a bottle of green stuff in one lily hand and her black curls cascading down her back, looking too beautiful to live. Honestly, they give me the sick, as Alex would say, thought Hebe, opening a door and entering a large, stiflingly hot apartment which smelt overpoweringly of green soft-soap solution, perfumed washes, scent and powder, and freshly washed hair. She looked about her at the patient seated figures; some with their wet heads, dripping and wretched, others slowly baking under vast metal hoods with no one paying attention to their cries, others merely huddled in corners, waiting, endlessly waiting, and turning over ragged copies of *Post*. At the reception desk was a lovely dark creature who kept pressing white fingers distractedly to her forehead, but doing little else. Fat little men in white coats with combs stuck in their pockets darted about; occasionally they tiptoed to one of the seated figures, lifted up the metal hood or carelessly pinched the waves under the net, and muttered, 'Who *did* your hair, madam?'

'Mr Fidele – or Mr Bonaventure,' would reply the victim, on which the little men nodded mysteriously and glided away for another hour or so, leaving the patient baking or dripping as before.

Hebe, having progressed so far as having her hair contemptuously washed by Miss Susan, who had a face like a very young pig that had managed to get hold of a lipstick, found herself dumped in a chair in an appalling draught, and waiting for a seat under a drier.

It's a hole, she thought, patiently dripping, but I must admit they do make your hair look all right.

Presently the inevitable little man came up and bent over her and whispered mysteriously.

'Who *did* your hair, madame?'

'Miss Susan,' announced Hebe, indicating the youthful porker, who had apparently gone to sleep in a corner.

'And who usually *sets* it, madame?'

'Mr Fidele.'

The little man nodded and went away. (These inquiries were apparently purely ritualistic survivals, like Jack-in-the-Green, and led nowhere.)

Upstairs, an alarming being who was very cross and all done up in a white jerkin like a doctor in an American film and who looked at your hair as if he hated it (which he probably did), prescribed for those whose locks needed rejuvenating, but Hebe had fortunately never had to penetrate so far.

Presently the woman sitting next to Hebe was done. The porker woke up and came over to Hebe, and moved her into the woman's place, and began to slam her hair into curls, but she had only done three of them when Mr Fidele, who actually looked and spoke like a human being, appeared in majesty and waved her away and began to do them himself. The drier was put over Hebe's head and began to whirr, and she became sleepier and sleepier in its warmth. She tried not to feel miserable about Grantey and Alex, and endeavoured to make her mind a blank.

Presently she became aware that someone was bending over her, and preparing (she supposed) to ask the inevitable question. She was just framing the answer, 'Miss Susan,' when a voice said, 'Hullo, darling,' and she opened her eyes and looked into the eyes of Alex.

He was bending down with his hands on his knees and peering at her under the drier, and he was chewing gum, and Miss Susan and the other Misses and the nymph in the reception desk and all the little comb-and-jacket men were staring at him with almost as much interest as if he had been a film star instead of a great painter.

'Hullo!' answered Hebe, beginning to smile in answer to his smile, and her happiness ran over her with warm delight because his eyes were full of love, 'however did you get here?'

''Phoned your mother. How are you, darling?'

'I'm all right. How are you?'

'I've had a cold, but it's nearly gone now. Hebe, *The Shrapnel Hunters* is finished.'

'Gosh! You must have been working like stink.'

'I have been. I'm dying for you to see it. Can you come along now? Get them to take this thing away, can't you?' and he tapped the drier with his finger-nail. 'How are the children? How's my Lady Hamilton?' (This was his pet name for Emma.)

'She's all right. Alex, isn't it bad about Grantey, poor old thing?'

'I know; I'm awfully sorry. *The Shrapnel Hunters* is at Morris Korrowitz's. I've got to get a frame for it. Can you come on afterwards when we've seen it and choose one?'

'Yes. (Oh, blast them; *will* they come and get me out of this thing?)' and she cast around her such a furious look out of her usually placid eyes that Mr Fidele himself glided forward and began to release her, protesting the while with an indulgent smile for love's impatience that her hair was not yet dry.

'It's blazing outside. She won't catch cold,' Alex assured him, but Mr Fidele murmured that the Effect would be spoiled by taking off the net and removing the pins before the hair was dry.

'It looks all right; it's beautiful,' said Alex earnestly, standing with his hands in the pockets of his corduroy trousers while Hebe paid her bill. She was carrying her soft little cap, and her brown curls, stiff and warm from the drier, shone like a spaniel's.

'Come on,' said Alex, taking her in his arms the moment he got her out into the passage and beginning to kiss her.

'How lovely you smell, I do love you, I've been so miserable this last week without you I didn't know what to do.'

'Why on earth didn't you telephone me then, you goat. I've been miserable too.'

'How could I? We were down in the depths of Wales at this place of Gilbert's and we were all drunk. I was sober once or twice, but as soon as I started to walk the five miles to the telephone we got as far as the local and all got drunk again.'

'Hadn't the local a telephone? It sounds quite a place. Never mind now, darling, let's get a taxi.'

On the way to Morris Korrowitz's they held hands and both talked at once; about *The Shrapnel Hunters* and Jeremy's new tooth; about the British Government's suggestion that Alex should go to Italy next month as the official chronicler in paint of the fighting there; about the large half-ruined house which Hebe had found in St John's Wood and which she proposed that they should buy and live in; and while they talked they lovingly, thirstily scanned each other's faces, and Hebe held Alex's massive, beautiful, dirty hands in her own.

In the large disorderly room with a skylight which was the studio of Morris Korrowitz, *The Shrapnel Hunters* stood against the wall and in silence they stood and looked at it; Alex critically, and Morris Korrowitz with a torturing mixture of homage and envy, and Hebe with delight; the simple delight that she felt when the sunlight warmed her face on a spring day.

After her first 'Oh!' she said no more until Alex said, frowning as he stooped to stare into the picture:

'I still don't feel quite right about this knee, Morris.'

'It's all *right*, Alex, do for God's sake lay off it,' said Morris exasperatedly, in a thin voice with a Cockney accent. He was a very tall young man with a shock of fair hair, who painted stiff pink flowers on vistas of sandy desert extending to an infinitely remote horizon, and he lived on an allowance from a widowed mother. Alex said that he had talent, but Hebe found his pink flowers in the desert tedious; this was the second time that she had met him.

'It's the best thing you've done, so far,' she said at last.

'Isn't it, isn't it, Mrs Niland?' said Morris eagerly. 'That's what we've all been telling him.'

'Do call me Hebe, won't you?' she said absently, still gazing at the picture. 'Alex, what sort of a frame?'

And they went off into a long discussion, only interrupted by their going out to have some food at a milk bar because

Morris had none in his flat. When Hebe went back to Westwood about six that evening, Alex and *The Shrapnel Hunters* were with her in the taxi, and he was telling her about the murals he had painted on the walls of a low café in Cardiff and how he wanted to do some more work of the same kind. 'Perhaps after all I'd better not take this Government job,' he ended vaguely, staring out of the window, 'unless they'd let me come back and paint Cassino and the Anzio beaches on the walls of the British Restaurants. Do you think they would?'

'Shouldn't think so. They said they wanted pictures, didn't they? Hangable ones.'

'I can't remember. Anyway, I haven't got to let them know for three weeks, so let's enjoy ourselves,' and he put his arm about her.

It required a strong effort for Margaret to give the necessary attention to her work on Monday morning, for she had an excited expectation that her services would be more in demand than ever now that poor Grantey was dead at Westwood-at-Highgate, while they were still needed at Westwood-at-Brockdale. Then, too, there was Earl's invitation to think about, and once or twice she had to reprove herself for romantic speculations.

However, she was learning to command her *self* (that one kingdom which is given to even the humblest of created human creatures) and she did succeed in giving her full attention to her work and at five o'clock, as she set her face homewards, she had the reward of re-entering the world of personal relationships with a pleasure which was the stronger because of her abstinence. She forgot the school as soon as she left it.

Her first duty on getting home was to get through some work which must be prepared for to-morrow, and when that was done, she telephoned Dick Fletcher. He seemed irritable, and admitted that he had had a trying week-end. The heat had been overpowering and Linda had missed Margaret.

'We both miss you,' he added laughing, and Margaret's heart suddenly felt full of happiness.

'And how is Mrs Coates?' she asked.

'Oh, I meant to tell you, she's had a slight relapse. Nothing much, but her temperature's up again and they don't think she'll be able to come home as soon as they thought.'

Margaret said that she was sorry, but actually felt glad, and promised him that she would be there as usual tomorrow evening.

As she dialled Zita's number she was guiltily conscious of her mother, sitting in the drawing-room with a stony look on her face as she knitted. Reg had gone; gone without being able to say good-bye to his sister, because she had been with 'those people' in the country, and all Mrs Steggles's grief and anxiety over his departure was expressing itself in bitter resentment against Margaret. Margaret herself had been touched by the fact that he had left a cheap lace collar and cuffs for her as a parting gift; all the more touched because it was the type of thing which she never wore; and she was vowing, even as she listened to the telephone-bell ringing in Westwood, that she would write to him every week, such letters as it would delight a soldier to receive; cheerful, affectionate, full of home news.

'Hullo!' said an unfamiliar masculine voice.

'May I speak to Zita, please, Miss Mandelbaum?' said Margaret, wondering who he might be.

'Hold on, I'll just get her,' answered the voice, and she heard him shouting 'Zita!' as if he were a familiar inmate of the house.

'Ach, Margaret,' said Zita's voice irritably, after a prolonged pause. 'I was with the children and Mr Niland' (with meaning emphasis) 'had to come all the way for me upstairs.'

'Oh was that Mr Niland? He's come back, then?'

'Yes. I will tell you about it later on. Now, how soon can you come roundt? The children are being so notty; Barnabas keeps on worrying about Grantey. I shall be glad of help.'

Margaret would have been glad to stay at home and do some necessary repairs to her wardrobe (which, like that of all the other women in England that summer, was rapidly and literally becoming a thing of shreds and patches), but she could not resist the temptation to go to Westwood; and, having told her mother where she was going and seen the information received in absolute silence and with no change of expression, she hurried out into the evening, where white may bloomed under the cloudless blue sky and the Heath was crowded with people walking idly with dog or lover through the long spring grass.

Grantey was dead, and had been taken away; and now Mr Challis did not want to think any more about her, and he was going out to play tennis with some friends. He came out of the side door in his white clothes just as Margaret was walking up to the house. She glanced timidly, imploringly at him, all the self-command and self-confidence so painfully won by her broadened interests vanishing at the sight of him and leaving her an awkward provincial schoolteacher once more, with inconveniently strong feelings and the recollection of their last interview to make her dumb with embarrassment.

But it was a beautiful evening, and there was another reason why Mr Challis felt almost kind towards the world. He smiled at her and said (remembering to keep his musical voice decently lowered because of the late Mrs Grant):

'Isn't this a wonderful evening? The light seems unwilling to leave the sky. Are you going in to see Zita?'

'Oh yes – just to help with the children –' said Margaret, her eyes fixed solemnly upon his face.

Mr Challis hesitated, and moved the rackets under his arm. She continued to gaze up at him, slowly colouring under his look.

'You mustn't let them wear you out, you know,' he said at last. 'It is more than kind of you to look after the children, but they can be very exhausting – who should know it better than I!' added Mr Challis, who encountered his grandchildren for perhaps ten minutes every evening, 'and your profession itself is an exhausting one. Do you like teaching?' he added abruptly, moved by a playwright's interest in character but with a feeling that he must not let himself be drawn into a lengthy conversation.

Margaret shook her head. She could not speak.

'Then get out of it, at all cost,' he said vehemently. 'It can be the most soul-destroying of all the professions. Have you private means?'

'Oh no, nothing –' she said, and a wild desire to laugh came over her. Private means! If he only knew! What sort of a home did he think she came from? But, of course, when she was not there, he never thought about her at all.

He shook his head. 'That's a pity. You are the type of woman who needs to ripen in the sun; do nothing for a few years; let your soul grow. But without money one can't do that.' He smiled and added kindly, 'It's a pity; money is a damned nuisance. Well – I shall be late. Good-bye,' and he hurried away.

She walked slowly on towards the house. It was the most human conversation that she had ever had with him, but it had only fanned the fire of her discontent, 'divine discontent,' as it was called. In all his plays there was no fulfilment or ripeness or satisfaction, only yearning and the subtle joys which flowered from renunciation.

She stopped for a moment by the door and stood looking down at a little bed of radishes, which had caught her eye by the bright purple of their globes embedded in the earth;

stout, large, juicy radishes, grown by Barnabas under the instructions of Cortway; each with a pair of rough astringent leaves and each with its rosiness fading away into succulent white flesh towards its tapering end. There's something satisfying about those, she thought dreamily. They give me the same feeling as Emma's cheeks and Dickon's voice and the rain on my face yesterday . . . it's silly, of course, compared with what he said.

Mr Challis's eldest grandson was kneeling up in bed in his pyjamas and asking questions about Grantey. Would she go straight to Heaven? Would she be able to see everything he and Emma and Jeremy did now she was in Heaven? Would her ghost come and haunt them? Could he and Emma go to the funeral? – and so on.

Margaret sat beside him and, subduing her own instinct to give indefinite answers to these questions, told him firmly that Grantey's spirit ('the mind-part of her') was met by an angel and taken straight to Heaven the minute she died. The angel was sent by God so that the soul should not feel lonely and surprised when it went away from the earth. No, Grantey would not be able to see everything that he and Emma and Jeremy did; she would be having a happy time, resting and being with all her friends and relations who were dead too. They would have lots to talk about, wouldn't they?

'Laughing?' asked Barnabas.

'Yes,' answered Margaret decidedly, beginning to straighten the bedclothes.

'And dancing about?'

'I expect so, later on, when she's used to it,' said Margaret, laughing herself. Emma was standing up naked in her cot and slowly, silently dropping the pillow, sheets, blankets and her nightgown over the side, one by one. Jeremy was asleep in the next room.

'Good night, Barnabas,' said Alex Niland, slouching into the room in slippers and smiling 'good evening' at Margaret.

'Dad!' exclaimed Emma with a radiant smile and dropped the last blanket over the side.

'Aren't you a shameless wench?' said her father, beginning to gather up the bedclothes. 'Come on now, put it on,' and he clumsily and tenderly drew the little nightgown over her head while Margaret finished tidying Barnabas's bed. She was not nervous of Alexander now, for his personality barely inspired respect, much less awe. She wondered what was the story behind his reconciliation with his wife.

'There! you notty boy,' said Zita crossly, entering with some Bovril and toast. 'Another time you will have a proper supper, I hope.'

'Co-co!' cried Emma with widening eyes, stretching out her arms towards the cup.

'No, no co-co to-night, Emma must go to sleep,' said Zita, trying to put her down on the pillow.

'No, oh no!' she cried, struggling up again and trying to pull off her nightgown.

'Better leave her, she'll go to sleep when she's tired,' suggested Alex, picking her up between his big hands and giving her a loud kiss, 'She can't get her nightie off; I've buttoned it up. Good night, Barnabas, my old companion,' and he gave his son another loud kiss. 'I want you to stay and read to me,' said Barnabas rather plaintively.

'Not to-night, I want to be with Mummy.'

'What are you going to do? Have a nice time?'

'We're going to the local.'

'Now?'

'No; first of all we're going to sit on the sofa together, and *then* go to the local.'

'Are you glad to be back?'

371

'Yes, very, in some ways.'

'Not in all ways? Zita says you're a great artist and very selfish. Are you?' asked Barnabas, not with complete ingenuousness.

'Zita's quite right,' said Alex, darting a look at Zita that completely altered his pale face and made her flush, and change the shocked protest she was beginning into an excited laugh. 'Now you go to sleep, I want to be off.'

After he had gone out of the room Margaret lingered, settling Emma and thinking about this little scene. That look had showed her that there was another side to his nature, a fact which she had been too inexperienced to realize. It disturbed her, for it had been – lawless? That was the word nearest to it. She was not surprised that Zita's disturbance had expressed itself in excited laughter, while she herself had strongly disliked the sense of adult impulses and behaviour that had suddenly invaded the nursery.

Barnabas consented to lie down with a picture-book until he felt sleepy, and Margaret was just going out of the room when he remarked:

'Grantey promised to take us to Kew. S'pose we shan't go now.'

'Did she, Barnabas? You and Emma? Well, I'll take you if you like. Would you like that?'

'Don't mind,' said Barnabas, shrugging his thin shoulders under the bedclothes, but Margaret knew that he was pleased.

'All right, then, and perhaps Zita and Jeremy could come too.'

'Not Jeremy.'

'Why ever not? Poor Jeremy.'

'I hate him. So does Emma hate him.'

'I'm sure she doesn't.'

'Yes, she does, don't you, Emma?' appealing to the cot, but the only answer was a murmur of 'Co-co'; Emma was playing with the wooden beads on the rail.

'Well, anyway, I'll see if we can all go next Saturday, if you'd like to. Good night. Go to sleep soon, like a good boy.'

And Margaret went downstairs to try to come unobtrusively across Seraphina or Hebe and ask if the children could go with her to Kew. She was apprehensive of seeing Alex and Hebe locked in an embrace on the great sofa in the hall, and was relieved to see them walking down the front garden hand-in-hand. Apparently the kisses were over and they were on their way to the local.

And now – on her way home with the arrangements for next Saturday's expedition settled, amid grateful thanks from the subdued Mrs Challis – her hero-worship for Mrs Challis's husband was all revived. How beautiful he had looked! How kindly he had spoken! How generously he had overlooked what she had said about his play! Perhaps there was another side to his nature, also; a warm, expansive side that she had never encountered until to-day. She would always remember those words – *You are the type of woman who needs to ripen in the sun.* Ah, how true that was! The sun of happiness, of warm, untroubled love!

Her mother's manner on her return was a little less stony; she had had a telephone call from a Lukeborough friend who was staying in London, and she wanted to talk over Lukeborough gossip; her daughter was better for this purpose than no one. Besides, she looked forward to telling one piece of news.

'Who do you think is married?' she asked suddenly, looking steadily at Margaret.

'Goodness knows. Someone we know?'

'Someone you used to know very well. Frank Kennett.'

'No! is he? Who to?' said Margaret, with a pang – of what feeling, it would be difficult to say.

'Pat Lacey. That blonde at the Luna. I wish him joy of her, that's all. I've always believed that child of hers wasn't legitimate.'

'Reg said she was married. I suppose she got a divorce or perhaps her husband was killed.'

'She was no more married than you are,' said Mrs Steggles, whose expression had become hard again at Reg's name.

'It's queer to think of Frank married to her, he used to say she wasn't his type,' said Margaret thoughtfully. Her mother's jibe passed her by, for marriage, as a way of achieving happiness, was no longer a state for which she longed. Love, yes; but not marriage.

'Oh well, I hope they'll be happy,' she said, as she went out of the room, and meant it, but Mrs Steggles only smiled bitterly as she answered. 'There's no harm in hoping.'

Margaret stood at her window for a moment, gazing out into the summer night and thinking how far away Lukeborough seemed now, with its mean ugly streets and commonplace people; the boys and girls whom she had watched growing up; the local characters who had done something wrong or unusual (the terms were identical in Lukeborough's eyes) and who drifted about the town, growing older; and all about it the flat, featureless countryside, so gentle as to be almost without character, as unnoticed as the green of grass or the grey of the sky on a spring day. Thank heaven, at least I've got out of that, she thought and then she remembered Hilda, of whom she had not thought for many days, and remorsefully decided that she really must ring her up.

Mr Challis was also thinking about Hilda, who had promised to go to Kew with him on the following Saturday afternoon. True, the beauty of the flowering trees would be practically over, but there would be *the rusted coverts of the may*, as Walter de la Mare beautifully calls the withering hawthorn flowers, and all that was Yellow-Bookish in Mr Challis was attracted by the perverse charm of dying blossoms; Hilda's youth would shine dazzlingly amidst the brown petals lying along the fresh spring grass, and I – he thought, leaning out of the window for a moment and gazing into the rich, dark trees standing motionless – I shall tell her, at last, that I love her.

He withdrew his head and retired – full of fluttering yet masterful anticipations – to bed.

27

The next evening Margaret went to Westwood-at-Brockdale. It seemed a long time since she had been there, but everything appeared to have gone well in her absence, except that Dick seemed worried and irritable. He kept these signs, of course, for Margaret, and did not display them too plainly before Linda, but when the child had gone to bed, and he and Margaret were washing-up, he became so moody and silent that she began to feel that she must make some comment, and at last said abruptly:

'Are you fed up with me about anything?'

'Of course not. Why should I be? You've been kindness itself.'

'Oh . . . that's all right then, I only wondered.'

He smiled faintly but said no more, and presently took up the evening paper. She had some mending to do for Linda, and sat down opposite to him with it. They were in the little drawing-room, which overlooked the garden, and there lingered a rich, fading glow in the sky by which they could see to read and sew. Margaret felt disturbed and uneasy; she was sure that something was the matter and gradually romantic suppositions began to fill her head and she became embarrassed; a deep flush came up in her cheeks and burned painfully there while her hands became moist and her heart beat heavily. In a quarter of an hour I will go home, she thought, there are all those books to be corrected. I'll just wait for the nine o'clock news.

Presently she felt his eyes fixed upon her, and finding this unbearable, she glanced up and found him staring moodily at her. He smiled at once, however, and put down the paper.

'You aren't engaged, are you?' he said.

Margaret's heart gave a great bound. Oh, what was coming? She shook her head and answered with schoolgirl clumsiness:

'No, worse luck,' and her hands began to tremble so that she had to put down her sewing and pretend to search for the scissors.

'It's a pity. You'd make a grand wife for somebody.'

'Oh, do you think so?' faintly.

'Don't you like the idea? Or haven't come across the right person, is that it?'

'I expect that's it,' she said, managing to regain some self-possession and even to smile. He did not return the smile, but continued to stare at her sombrely with a hangdog look. She glanced at the clock, and exclaiming, 'Oh, it's just on nine, shall I turn it on,' went over to the wireless cabinet and adjusted the dials. Big Ben began to strike faintly.

'I think I won't wait, if you don't mind, Dick; I've got a lot of correcting to do to-night,' she said, beginning to put Linda's clothes away.

'Just as you like,' he answered in a surprised, rather sulky tone, and she went upstairs to get her coat.

'Margaret?' called Linda's voice through an open door.

'Yes, darling. What's the matter? Can't you get to sleep?' and she went in to the curtained room, which was in the soft dusk of the lingering sunset, and bent over the bed. Linda's strange little face looked placidly up at her from the pillow and one hand crept out towards her own.

'Linda's cold, Margaret.'

'Poor girl, Margaret will make it better. We thought two blankets might not be enough, didn't we? Margaret will put on another one. There, is that better?'

'Margaret made it better for Linda,' Linda said, putting her unshapely arms under the bedclothes, and then she smiled, revealing her tiny teeth, pointed and white as a little cub's. Margaret looked down at her in a sudden passion of pity. There was much here of the elements of beauty; fine dark hair and firm flesh and smooth skin, yet behind these elements there was no controlling mind to fuse them into a whole; there was only a marred force that expressed itself in misshapenness. When Margaret remembered Claudia and Emma and Dickon, with their quick minds dancing behind their eyes, how could she help a faint, pitying shudder over Linda? And as she bent to kiss the child good night there drifted through her mind the disturbing thought – *the Nature of God may be completely different from what we imagine*, but she firmly pushed it aside, for she had enough problems to worry her, she felt, without starting on God.

In the hall she found Dick waiting.

'I'll walk up to the station with you,' he said. 'I'll just go up and tell Linda we're going.'

'You needn't bother, really, Dick.'

'I feel like a walk,' he said, and as she waited for him her embarrassment and apprehension were all renewed. Was he going to tell her that he loved her; perhaps ask her to marry him? Oh, what shall I say if he does? she thought.

'Ready?' said Dick. 'She'll be all right, she's nearly asleep.'

In the wide, quiet, shady road the masses of faded blossom on the may trees were lifted against the twilight sky and under Margaret's feet rustled the fallen acacia petals. Gusts of warmth came out from the dark hedges and shrubs, and the air was full of delicious faint scents.

They walked in silence. Margaret was only anxious to get to the station as soon as possible without a declaration from him, and yet she knew that if he said nothing she would be bitterly disappointed. But he continued to walk along in silence, with his head lowered and his hands in his pockets, and she was silent too, though she felt that she ought to say something; he would think this mutual silence so strange, and perhaps encouraging.

'Are you coming over to-morrow evening?' he asked at last.

'Of course, unless you'd rather I didn't? I mean, I took it for granted I should go on coming here every evening until Mrs Coates comes back. How is she, by the way?'

'About the same.'

She said no more, and in a few moments they reached the station. He saw her into the building and bought her ticket for her and then hesitated for a moment, looking away from her, and seeming unwilling to go.

'Well, good night,' she said, smiling. The danger was over now; and yet she felt disappointed. As she looked up at his thin face with the suffering that had eclipsed its youthful ardour lying upon it, she felt that she could easily love him.

'Good night,' he said suddenly. 'We'll see you to-morrow then.'

He made a vague farewell gesture and hurried away and Margaret descended into the tube and on the way back to Highgate thought seriously about the duties and responsibilities and sacrifices involved in marriage to a divorced man with a backward child. There's one thing, she thought heartily, as she walked up the road towards her own home, I'm sure I shouldn't mind him kissing me.

The next evening she arrived at Westwood-at-Brockdale to find Dick in the same mood as on the previous evening; so much so that, after supper, she announced her intention of putting Linda to bed instead of letting the child do it herself, as she had now learned to do; for she felt that she could not endure to sit in a meaningful silence downstairs with Linda's father until it was time to go home. If she did, it looked like giving him a chance – and yet, if she hid herself upstairs with Linda, would he not feel equally encouraged by such shyness and assume that she loved him? Oh dear, she thought, I wish I were more experienced in dealing with men.

But he made no attempt to bring her downstairs, even though she lingered, laughing with Linda and supervising her toilet and praising the progress she had made in tending herself, until nearly half-past eight. Downstairs all was silent; Dick was apparently reading through the three evening papers as he did every night, and Margaret was beginning to wonder whether she might get through the evening more comfortably than she had hoped, when she heard him calling at the foot of the stairs:

'Margaret? Nearly news-time!'

'All right, I'm just coming,' she answered, and went downstairs, remembering that out of the three marriages which she had had the opportunity of observing during the last year – her parents', the Challises' and the Nilands' – two were not happy. The Wilsons were happy, it was true, but the Wilsons were too suburban to be anything else, and Zita had said scornfully that Hebe and Mr Niland were 'All lovers again, my dear, but that will not last long,' and Margaret feared that this was true. Oh, marriage was the most solemn, the most important, act that a woman could undertake in this world!

'Going home early this evening?' asked Dick, looking sulkier than ever.

'I hadn't thought of it,' she stammered.

'I just wondered if you might have some work to do again; I don't want to keep you hanging about here if you're busy, you know.'

'I'm always busy, Dick, but I'd like to stay if you want me to,' she answered, bewildered.

'Oh – I don't know, I'm going to turn in early myself; I've had a hell of a day. I'll come with you to the station. Shan't keep you a minute.'

Trembling and by now slightly indignant, she waited until he had been upstairs to say good night to Linda, and then they set out together as on the previous evening, in silence. Margaret's instinct was to demand an explanation – 'have it out' – ask him what on earth was the matter and what she had done, and so on; but a wiser instinct, perhaps inherited from some sensitive ancestress, persuaded her to subdue this violent impulse and be silent, with as tranquil an expression as she knew how to assume. Her heart was beating hard and she felt instinctively that the situation was approaching a climax.

There was a quiet road to traverse where all the little houses were listening to the nine o'clock news, and luxuriant laburnums in blossom and thick, dark hedges made shady alcoves where lovers might linger unnoticed. They had almost reached the end of this road when Dick put his hand silently upon her arm, drew her aside into the shadows, and took her in his arms and kissed her with passion. She was too surprised at first to return his kisses, and her chief feeling was one of strangeness, but at last, as she began to kiss him warmly in return, he muttered something about 'a dear girl,' and released her. She was trembling and could not speak; she only stared in silence into the flushed face almost level with her own.

'Come on,' he said at last, and moved away, adding a remark which she did not clearly hear. She hurried along beside him, still so strongly remembering the touch of his mouth upon her own that she could not think clearly, but gradually she began to wonder if he were not going to say anything more, and while she was making up her mind to speak to him, she realized that there was now no time for him to say anything, for they were at the station. He came up to her with her ticket; he looked ill, and his thinning brown hair was ruffled as if he had been nervously rubbing his head.

'Here you are,' he said, holding up the ticket and smiling

painfully. 'Er – if you are coming over tomorrow will you 'phone me first. About six o'clock?'

'Yes, of course, if you want me to, but why –?'

'Just 'phone, there's a dear girl, will you? and then I'll explain –'

He gave her a quick kiss, warm and friendly, then seemed about to say something, but changed his mind and turned away.

Once more she went slowly down the steps and this time her thoughts were even more serious. He loved her; there was no doubt about that now; and to-morrow evening when she telephoned he would ask her to marry him. She did not like the idea of having such a momentous conversation over the telephone, but he was an odd man, angry and moody in spite of his warm heart, and she was prepared to give way to him because his life had been bitter and difficult; there was even sweetness in that thought.

Am I going to say 'yes' she thought, sitting in the train and gazing pensively out at the dusk. It will probably mean giving up all my new interests, for a time at any rate. No more going to my own Westwood, or seeing *him* (she was slightly disconcerted to find herself still thinking of Gerard Challis as *him*) or doing as I like in my spare time. Just looking after Dick and Linda and keeping that little house clean (a lot of stuff will *have* to go out of there; I really can't live with it; it would stifle me, all that sugary prettiness). But I shall have love. Dick loves me and I am growing to love him. A memory of his tired face rose before her and she smiled tenderly, alone as she was in the carriage. Happiness began to grow in her heart as she walked lightly homewards. I won't say a word about it to Mother until I've got my ring, she thought. I shan't let him get me anything expensive; I should like something very simple, and antique.

The following evening at exactly six o'clock, with heart beating heavily and dry mouth, she took off the receiver in the hall at home and dialled the number of Westwood-at-Brockdale. Her mother had gone out of London for the day to see some friends and her father would not be in until late, so she knew that she was safe from interruption.

She waited, while the bell rang steadily in the silent, airy sunlit house five miles away. Her own home had the same look of summer peace, and she thought vaguely, this may be the last time I shall see the hall, and that chair, and the staircase, as an unengaged girl. She wondered if everything would look different to her, when once the strange, transforming words had been said.

Suddenly the bell stopped ringing.

'Hullo!' said a woman's voice, carefully pretty and soft, 'who is that, please?'

'May I speak to Mr Fletcher, please,' answered Margaret, disconcerted that Dick had not answered it himself. Who could this be?

'I'm afraid he isn't in. Who wants him, please?'

'It's Miss Steggles,' answered Margaret, increasingly puzzled and beginning to feel dismayed. 'What time will he be in?'

'Oh, Miss *Steggles*! Margaret! (You must excuse me calling you that, I've got so used to hearing Dick talk about you as Margaret.) How sweet of you to 'phone. Was it about your coming over this evening? Because I've got some good news for you. I'm back!'

'You – you're –?'

'M – m!' the voice seemed to nod joyously. 'It's Mrs Coates – Elsie. I got back this afternoon in time for tea. Quite fit again and *ever* so grateful to you for having done all the dirty work while I was laid up.'

'I'm so glad,' answered Margaret, biting her lips while tears crowded into her eyes and fell on her hands as they grasped the receiver. 'Are you really quite all right again now?'

'All the better for the rest, between you and me, my dear. And Dick and I have got another piece of news for you, too. (He's had to go out on a story unexpectedly but I know he wouldn't mind my telling *you*.) Guess!'

'I couldn't possibly,' Margaret managed to answer.

'We're going to be mar-ried!' lilted Mrs Coates. 'Isn't it too thrilling? Next month. Very quietly, of course, but it will be no end of a rush getting my things together, even in these days of coupons.'

'I *am* so glad, Mrs Coates —'

'Elsie, please!'

'Elsie, then. It will be lovely for Linda to have — to have —' But she could not go on.

'Have you got a cold?' sweetly inquired Mrs Coates. 'There are a lot of these tiresome summer colds about, aren't there? I thought I was going to have one this morning but it seems to have gone off now. Well, I must go and start my hubby-to-be's supper. Bye-bye, Margaret, I'll tell him you 'phoned up, and thanks a million for being such a dear while I was away. You must come over and see us very soon. Bye-bye.'

'Good-bye,' answered Margaret, and slowly replaced the receiver. Then she sank down on the stairs, heedless of where she was, and burst into a passion, an agony of crying, while humiliation and defeated hopes and rage had their way with her.

Nearly an hour passed while she writhed and sobbed there; then suddenly she started up at the sound of the key in the front door and lifted her ravaged face to her mother, who stood looking at her in amazement.

'What on earth's the matter? Are you ill?' Mrs Steggles exclaimed, hurrying forward.

Margaret shook her head and stood up unsteadily.

'No, I'm all right. Sorry to be so silly. I've had a bit of a shock, that's all,' and she blew her nose.

'Have you lost your job?'

'Oh no, Mother,' laughing hysterically, 'it's all right, really; just leave me alone.'

'Well, let's shut the door, anyway, we don't want the neighbours seeing everything,' said Mrs Steggles giving her a rather anxious glance as she carried out the suggestion. 'I don't suppose you're going to tell me what's the matter but you may as well have a cup of tea. I'm going to, and it'll pull you round.'

'I'd sooner have a double whisky,' said Margaret – absurdly, she felt, even in the midst of her misery, and was not surprised when her mother said sharply, 'Don't talk such rubbish, Margaret. Where are you off to now?' as she began to go upstairs.

'Only to bathe my eyes.'

'You can do that in the kitchen. Come on, now.'

While Margaret sat with her head in her hands, Mrs Steggles bustled about, with her summer coat and hat flung aside, and made the tea and poured it out, and then sat down opposite Margaret at the table and pushed a cup towards her.

'Now you drink that up,' she said, and began to drink her own. In a moment Margaret tremulously sipped at the cup and for a while there was silence. The sunlight poured into the kitchen, and through the window the little garden dreamed in the heat.

Margaret's eyes were smarting and her head ached dully. She drank the tea with her eyes closed and tried not to think about anything, but presently her mother's voice broke sharply upon the blank which she was striving to create for herself.

'If you knew what a sight you look! Sitting there like a great baby with your lips stuck out! And you've been looking so nice lately. Spoiling all your looks, you silly girl.'

'I haven't got any looks,' and the tears started again.

'You used not to have, but lately you've got much better-looking. Some girls do. Do you want a biscuit?'

'Please, Mother,' said Margaret meekly.

Mrs Steggles gave her the biscuit and also an irritable kiss on the cheek, which made Margaret turn towards her with a sudden confiding movement.

'Mother, I am sorry to go on like this. It isn't anything serious and don't worry. I feel better now. It was only that I thought Dick Fletcher wanted to marry me and now he's going to marry Mrs Coates instead.'

'I told you so!' cried Mrs Steggles. 'Haven't I always said so?'

She had indeed; and Margaret's contempt for her 'suburban' outlook had prevented her from realizing that in nine cases out of ten it was based on drab experience and a knowledge of 'suburban' human nature. She now sighed heavily, and began to relate what had happened. Her heart had not been touched deeply enough for her to want to keep the pain to herself and it even occurred to her, in a new humble mood brought about by her mother having been proved right about Mrs Coates, that she might have some useful and bracing advice to give.

Mrs Steggles heard the story almost in silence, now and then dipping a biscuit in her tea while she stared thoughtfully at the kitchen table. She was secretly triumphing at being taken, after all, into Margaret's confidence, and she also felt an impatient pity, mingled with affection, for this daughter who was so highbrow and had such clever friends and yet could not get a husband for herself.

'The trouble with you, Margaret, is that you take these things too seriously,' she said decidedly, when the brief story was finished. 'Men don't always want to marry a girl when they kiss her, worse luck. They ought to, but they don't. Why, two men kissed me before your dad proposed.'

'Did they, Mother?' Margaret was too dejected to remind her mother how seriously *she* had taken the attentions of Frank Kennett.

'They did indeed, Margaret,' said Mrs Steggles, dryly, beginning to pack up the teacups. 'I was a very pretty girl, you know.'

'You're pretty now, Mother, only you don't look happy.'

'I haven't much to make me, have I? Reg gone away and p'raps never coming back, and you going your own way, and your Dad –' She did not finish the sentence but went across to the sink and started to rinse the cups.

'Then why do you think he kissed me?'

'You're young. Besides, you've been very kind to them. I expect he felt grateful and a bit ashamed, too, because he hadn't told you she was coming back to-day.'

'Oh! Do you think he knew?'

'Knew! Of course he knew, but he was afraid to tell you.'

'Do you think he meant to marry her all along?'

'I don't suppose he knew his own mind, Margaret, and she made it up for him. Or – anything may have been going on. She may be a bad woman. I don't know. Anyway, we've seen the last of him, I expect. She's the sort that'll never let him go; she's got too much sense.'

Margaret shuddered. It was horrible to think of that warm, loving nature, of which she had had a glimpse, made captive by its own longing for affection and kept under ceaseless supervision. But perhaps it would be worth it to him, she thought. *If she is very feminine and kind (so long as he doesn't try to have any life apart from her) she'll make him happy, poor Dick. I am selfish; I ought to want him to be happy in any way, so long as he is happy. It isn't as if I were in love with him; it's only that I can't get over his having kissed me like that, and somehow it's such a disappointment.*

She got up from the table and began helping her mother, with a little comfort from her brusque kindness. Yet how terrible it was that her mother should tacitly approve Mrs Coates's grip upon Dick! That was the life she would have made her own husband live, had she had the power, and when she saw another woman doing it she grudgingly admired that woman's success.

'That's what men are like, you know,' said Mrs Steggles suddenly. 'Weak as water. You'll have to get used to it.'

'All men, do you mean?'

'All of them where a pretty face is concerned. If they aren't, there's something funny about them – they're religious, or worse. What are you going to do this evening?'

'Oh – I hadn't thought,' sighed Margaret.

'Why don't you ring up Hilda? You haven't seen her for ages.'

'I don't feel like Hilda this evening. I'll do some work and go to bed early, I think.'

When she was at last alone, with books open on the table, and the evening light coming in mildly through the window, and the scent from some honeysuckle on her dressing-table filling the room, she experienced so strongly that relief which comes on escaping from human beings and their goings-on that she seriously wondered if she would end as a recluse. Flowers and solitude and Nature never fail one, she thought; they ask nothing and they are eternally comforting.

She passed the evening in preparing a lesson which must be given to-morrow, and in thinking of what she had lost: Dick's love, the opportunity of cherishing Linda and gradually strengthening her mind and body; a home of her own, perhaps children of her own. But after all, I didn't love him, she confessed to herself at last, and perhaps Mrs Coates does, so it's right that she, not I, should have all those things.

28

The rest of that week, which had promised to be so dreary, was agreeably relieved by a telephone call from Earl Swinger proposing that she should accompany him to a concert at the Phoenix Theatre, in which unexpected place concerts were being held since the destruction of the Queen's Hall by bombs.

She accepted the invitation with pleasure and was surprised to find how much she could look forward to it.

At the end of two days most of her disappointment had disappeared, and all that remained was bracing indignation and a contempt which now mingled with her affection for Dick. She did not resent being kissed, but she did resent his having been underhand with her; a shabby return for all that she had done for him and for Linda. For a day she wondered if she would get a letter from him, but it soon became clear that this was most unlikely, and she tried to get used to the idea that she would not be missed at Westwood-at-Brockdale and that the incident was over. Mr Steggles came in that same evening cheerfully announcing that he had been having one with old Dick, who was getting married to a damn pretty little woman, and Margaret and Mrs Steggles were able to damp him by saying that this was ancient news to them, but otherwise nothing more was said about the matter, and Margaret began to hope that by next month she might be able to attend the wedding, if invited, without a pang. It was Linda whom she missed most, and the quietness of the fairy house, broken by the sound of the wind-bells. She could not even comfort herself by thinking that Linda would miss her, for she knew that Linda would not; any more than, after a few days, she had missed Mrs Coates whom she had known for so much longer.

At least he did want to kiss me and that's something, she thought, moving her fingers over her firm throat as she gravely looked at herself in her mirror. I can't be so bad.

After a concert which she and Earl both described as glorious and which sent them home in an exalted yet dreamy mood, she was pleasantly surprised to find her hand being held by Earl and to hear him confess that he was vurry lonely and would be glad if he could date her up sometimes. She was touched and flattered by his assumption that she was a girl with many dates, and sought about for a date to give him as soon as possible. It was a pity, she said, that she was engaged on Saturday. Oh, nowhere exciting; she was only going to take Barnabas and Emma to Kew Gardens; there was so much more for Zita to do now that poor old Mrs Grant had gone and until Hebe found another nanny, and she, Margaret, loved the children, and liked helping with them. But, said Earl, couldn't he come along too? It would be quite a business for her, keeping those two in marching order, and when Emma got tired, he, Earl, could maybe carry her. Oh, but wouldn't Earl find that dull? Now, now, hadn't he just been telling Margaret that he had little brothers and sisters at home? They were a big family, the Swingers, going down in stages from twenty-two to five. He was used to kids, and he liked them fine. Well, it certainly would be a great help if he would come, and she was sure the children would love it. And how about Margaret, would she love it too? Margaret thought that it would be very nice.

When they said good night outside her house, it was arranged that he should meet them at the Archway tube station, whence they could get a bus direct to Kew, at one o'clock on Saturday, and then he gave her a boyish and rather brotherly good-night kiss; she thought that this was partly U.S. Army routine, but it was very pleasant, and she went into the house swinging the posy he had bought her and not thinking about Dick Fletcher or Gerard Challis or even about Margaret Steggles, but only feeling cheerful and slightly intoxicated with music.

At the same hour, Mr Challis was working late at the Ministry. All that week he had been doing so, which fact had caused him to have only a hazy idea about his family's social engagements. He always was vague about what his grandchildren were doing, partly from a natural lack of interest in such insipid activities and partly because he preferred to avoid thinking about them at all. He arrived home very late every evening, and dined in the library off an appetizing tray brought in by Cortway, then read for a little while and went to bed. In the morning he swallowed coffee with his nose in *The Times*, and only Seraphina opposite to him, and she read her letters and knew better than to talk to him. So he approached Saturday with a dim feeling that only he and Hilda were going to Kew; that the rest of the world would be miraculously absent from Kew on that day, and the glades and walks deserted.

He was in love. For the time being he had no creative work in hand and all his energies, fired and fanned by summer, were concentrated upon Hilda. He was in that state when a kind glance or word can act upon the senses like balm, giving a comfort to be treasured for days in secret, but as he was by now acutely aware of the incongruity between his fame, tastes and character and the abjectness of his love, he was at times both angry and unhappy. Seraphina resignedly supposed that there was Another One, and was slightly depressed by the fact. We are both getting older, she thought, sighing as she looked at herself in the glass. I do hope Gerry isn't going to be one of those *horrid* old men. If only he could take an interest in the boys, and the children! That would be the *natural* thing, at his age. Well, perhaps not *natural*, but *right*, and so much nicer.

The reconciliation between Hebe and Alex and their plans for the large half-ruined house in St John's Wood were her own chief sources of pleasure at present. Hebe had announced her intention of keeping a goat and bees in the vast shady garden, and when her mother had said how lovely the rooms would be for parties she had answered: 'There won't be any. What I'm going to do is to have some more children.'

Unfortunately, Saturday was a brilliantly fine day, and everybody in London seemed to be going to Kew. The buses and trains were crowded, as if it were a Bank Holiday, with women in light dresses and children who were steadily eating; every public seat was lined with old men enjoying the scene and the warm air, and every breadth of free grass in London was covered by picnickers, drunk with sunshine and successfully forgetting, for a few hours, the war.

'Lucky, aren't I?' said Hilda to Mr Challis, as she sat beside him in the taxi which he had managed to secure to take them in comfort to Kew. The excursion would cost (he reckoned in terms of money) a few pounds. How much it would cost him in other terms he had not thought. The humbleness of a true lover struggled with his confidence in himself, based upon years of success with women.

He turned to look at Hilda. She wore a thin blue silk dress that exactly matched her eyes, and carried a large white handbag. Her slender bare legs were expertly painted brown and on her small feet were white shoes. (We have described these objects from a masculine point of view; now, shifting our focus – or altering the Frame, as Professor Eddington might put it – we may say that the dress was of cheap rayon, and the shoes and handbag last year's; but they were all fresh and in perfect order, and Hilda wore them with such calm confidence that the effect could hardly have been improved.)

'I am lucky,' he answered, smiling, and took her hand in his cool one.

'You're telling me. I put off ever so many things to come to your old Kew to-day.'

'Did you?' bending towards her. 'What things?'

'Oh – tennis and going for a walk on the Heath; I nearly telephoned old Mutt to see'f she'd come too.'

Mr Challis was not interested in old Mutt. 'Did you want to come with me?' he asked, lowering his voice.

'I'll try anything once and I dare say it won't be so bad when we get there. Besides, you kept on about it so, I thought I'd better come and get it over.'

'Is that all you felt?' he asked, withdrawing his hand.

'Now, don't get all haughty. Of course I wanted to come; it's a nice day and I'm glad to be out of the or-fice. But I meant to tell you, I've got to be back early; I've got a date to-night.'

He was silent for a little while, then he said: 'Don't you think you might have kept the evening free for me? I've looked forward to this day for months.'

'Don't I know it! It was round about Boxing Day you started dating me up. Well, I would have, honestly, Marcus,' with a smile that pierced his heart – 'only someone rang me up this morning and' – she began to look in her handbag – 'I couldn't get out of it.'

'A man?'

'No, one of the crocodiles from the Zoo, as a matter of fact. Look, aren't we nearly there?' and she bent forward to gaze out at the streets of Hammersmith, through which they were now passing. He jealously stared at her face. Not a shade of consciousness touched its brightness, and slowly he removed his gaze and let it rest moodily upon her little shoes. Phew!

That was a near thing, thought Hilda, gaily surveying Hammersmith; and then, and only then, did a deeper pink begin to come into her face.

'I have brought a tea-basket,' he said presently, indicating an object in a corner. 'Tea at any of the usual places would be unendurable.'

'Is that what it is? What a bright idea; you are a dear, really,' and she gave him another smile. 'I thought it was papers or something.'

'Have you never seen a tea-basket before?' he asked, enchanted by such innocence.

'No. Is it only for tea? Couldn't you put lunch in it? Or do you have another kind for lunch? You do do yourself well, don't you? What's it got in it?'

'Er – sandwiches, I believe, and the usual things.'

He had, in fact, charged his secretary with the task of filling the tea-basket, and she had done her best, which was considerable, for she was an efficient woman.

The taxi was now traversing a wide, shady road bordered on one side by a long wall, and suddenly, through the foliage of the massive trees, there was a startling glimpse of red and gold, soaring into the heavens.

'Oh, what's that?' cried Hilda.

'The Pagoda. Isn't that a wonderful and exotic effect; that pure Chinese shape seen between the characteristically English shapes of the trees? I wanted you to see that.'

'It's so pretty against the blue sky.'

'Exactly,' he said, delighted by these evidences – or so he judged them – of the aesthetic faculty. 'England is full of such incongruities; the Pavilion at Brighton and the Mosque at Woking are two of the most striking. And in any English drawing-room you will find minor instances of the same sort; Chinese cabinets and Japanese cups, Zulu spears and Afghan knives. Incongruity; the power to startle with a sense of pleasure. For me, that is half the secret of art.'

'Come again?' said Hilda pleasantly, but he did not have to descend to explanations for at that moment the taxi stopped at the gates of Kew.

As they walked through the entrance, Mr Challis prepared himself to enter the realm of intense emotional and possibly sensuous experience. The day favoured him. The sunrays had a clear brilliance, and a light wind tempered their warmth, blowing it upon the dying or budding flowers and bringing their scents sweeping in waves now low, now high, over the grass. There were the rounded brown masses of the fading hawthorns; tree after tree of them, reared up against the divine deep blue; and there were the drifts of shrivelled acacia and laburnum petals blowing lazily along the walks. The glass roofs of the hothouses glittered in the sun (except where they were black and shattered by bombs) and the palms pressed spiked leaves against the panes of their prison. It seemed a special day. He gently put his fingers under Hilda's elbow and guided her into Kew.

His plan was to lead her gradually to some remote glade. He knew of one where bluebells stood thick in May, and would now be a host of brown seed-pods winding endlessly away, low among the bright green grass under the emerald beeches. He removed his hat and lifted his face to the sun, so that the delicious wind blew on his forehead, and moved eagerly onwards.

'It's quite nice,' said Hilda brightly, looking about her. She had no hat and her curls were only confined by a thick pale blue snood. 'Isn't there a crowd here to-day!'

There was indeed. The avenues and the brown may trees and the palms in their prison were shared by many thousands of people, and Mr Challis became slightly irritated by their presence. In and out he had to dodge; round laughing groups who had stopped to admire the water irises, and old people who preferred to saunter, while children darted under his nose and people stuck their feet out comfortably as they sat reading the newspaper.

'What time does your train go?' demanded Hilda at last, drawing back a little. 'You're in an awful hurry, aren't you?'

'I am sorry,' he said at once, slackening his pace, and repressing an impulse to wipe his forehead. 'I want to get you away from all these people.'

'Fat chance,' she answered gaily, glancing about her; and indeed, although they had now left the main walks and were proceeding across a grassy expanse which sloped to a lake over-hung by weeping willows, there were still far too many people about; people sitting on the grass; people sprawling under the trees; people obviously proposing and being proposed to; people proclaiming that they loved and were beloved by their silence; people sitting quite close to other people but obviously not seeing the other people or even knowing that they were there, and thereby demonstrating the marvellous truth that *The Kingdom of Heaven is within you.*

But Mr Challis did not wish to sit down in the middle of a lawn with Hilda and tell his love within twenty feet of another pair of lovers, and he hastened remorselessly on. Hilda had by now begun to cast glances at the tea-basket, but she said nothing, because after all it was his tea and to hint was not polite, for she combined a funny little set of conventional 'that's-Mum's-good-girl' manners with her native impertinence. All the same, she did begin to want her tea. However, so did he, she supposed, as otherwise what could account for his eagerness to find a suitable spot to sit down?

At last the bluebell glade came in sight, and certainly there were not quite so many people here. It was in a remote part of the gardens and was approached by a long broad avenue, mossy and shady and lined by magnificent trees, and too far away for little feet and tired old feet to make their way there.

However, there were plenty of feet at Kew that day that were neither little nor old; large strong feet clad in good U.S. Army boots, and here were their owners, rubber-necking respectfully at the vast, gentle, ancient trees and chewing gum as they strolled along. Up and down they went, and they all glanced approvingly at Hilda's snood and legs while Mr Challis doggedly urged her on, on, towards the bluebell glade.

'Here –' he said at last in a low tone, pausing amidst green shadows and sunny flickering rays. It was a space of rich grass, bent over by its own weight, with tiny twisted seed-sheaths, dried petals, the microscopic cast wing-cases of beetles, lying among the white roots. A few groups of people were in sight and the American soldiers still laughed in the broadwalk, but at least there was a *sense* of solitude.

'Nice,' pronounced Hilda, glancing round. 'Why can't they clear away all those dead bluebells?'

'Their richness sinks back into the earth,' he said. 'Let us sit down,' and he opened the tea-basket. Hilda saw this action with rising hope, but no; he only brought out a Shetland rug of fairy fineness, unfolded it, and spread it upon the ground.

'Thanks,' said Hilda, sitting down.

'May I sit down too?' he asked, still standing, looking yearningly down upon her sunny head.

'Well, I should hope so, you aren't going to have your tea standing up, I suppose?'

'I shall be . . . close to you,' he said a little unsteadily, seating himself.

'Yes, there isn't much room, is there? but it's a lovely quality,' and she respectfully fingered the rug. 'Look, you leave a place just *there*,' indicating some eight inches between them, 'and we can put the tea on it,' and she could not help a gleeful anticipatory glance towards the open basket.

There was a pause. Hilda, seeing her hint fall to the ground, gazed cheerfully about her and thought that it was nice to sit down for a bit, and Mr Challis, for all his experience, for all his fame and all his genius, gazed at her and swallowed convulsively, twice.

'Pardon?' she said, and turned her blue eyes upon him. 'Did you say something?'

Her look struck his heart with loneliness and pain.

'Hilda —' he burst forth urgently, bending towards her. 'I love you.'

'What?' exclaimed Hilda, going red. 'Pardon?' and in her confusion and surprise her pretty mouth opened and stayed open.

'I love you,' repeated Mr Challis recklessly, scrambling towards her across the eight inches. 'Oh, I didn't mean to tell you like this, I meant to lead up to it gently, but I can't — when you look at me like that — your eyes are so unutterably lovely —'

'Well, don't get so worked up,' she said soothingly, putting out her hand and taking his — an action which was intended to serve the double purpose of calming him down and preserving the *status quo* of the eight inches. 'It's very nice of you. I'm fond of you, too — in a way, and you've been ever so kind to me, only Mum and Dad do think it's funny the way you've never come to tea —'

'*Fond* of me!' he cried. 'Is that all? I *love* you, good God, I *love* you!'

'Yes, I heard you the first time, Marcus.' Hilda was used to dealing with this sort of thing, and had usually found that a bright, firm manner, like that of a nurse, was successful in the more violent and unwelcome cases; while the welcome ones were so enraptured at having their kisses returned that they did not demand those fervent protestations of love which she (at least up until last Wednesday evening at a quarter to ten) had never felt the wish to make. But it now struck her that the hospital manner was not going to work upon poor old Marcus.

'Don't you realize what that means?' He laid his hand upon her knee and she started away from him with a sharp 'Don't!'

'I want you, body and soul,' he said, withdrawing his hand and colouring sensitively as a boy, 'I want to take you away with me, to wonderful unknown places and strange lands, to South America. We could be so happy together – I would give you everything you wanted –'

'It's ever so kind of you,' interrupted Hilda firmly at this point, 'but I'd rather not. It *is* kind of you really, I do mean it,' she added, rather distressed by his stricken look, 'but what's the use of going on like that when I don't – er – don't feel like that about you? The fact is I – don't feel like that about anybody.' A pause. 'Not about *anybody*,' she repeated stoutly, as if reassuring herself.

'Listen,' he interrupted in a low persuasive tone, 'it has come as a shock to you, I can see that – I'm sorry – I was mistaken – I thought you *must* know, a little, how I've felt about you for months. Just think it over. Don't dismiss the whole idea at once. Oh, Daphne,' he pleaded pitifully, 'don't say "no." For God's sake, give me a chance!'

It was at this moment that an interruption occurred. Across the grass a small figure in grey came bounding, waving his arms, and followed more slowly by a smaller and stouter female form in a pink frock. And through the air, as they approached Mr Challis and Hilda with every sign of pleasure and excitement upon their broadly smiling faces, resounded their shrill cries:

'Grandpa! Grandpa! It's us! Grandpa! Grandpa!'

29

Mr Challis started to his feet and stood waiting for them to come up to him. He had turned pale, but after the one glance of amazement and fury which he had darted towards his grandchildren, he was immediately in control of himself and even managed to smile.

'Well, this *is* a surprise!' he said with stiff lips. 'What are you doing here? And Emma, too?' turning to the little girl who had now trotted into the group and stood silently gazing up at him.

'Margaret and Earl brought us. Did you know we were coming?' demanded Barnabas.

'I had an idea you might be,' returned Mr Challis, and dared to glance at Hilda, who was gazing from Barnabas to Emma and then at Margaret and Earl, who were coming over the grass towards them. Her face showed bewilderment, amusement, interest in the children, and then amazement as she recognized Margaret and scrambled to her feet. 'Hullo, look who's here!' she called, waving. 'Mutt, it's me!'

'Hullo, Hilda,' returned Margaret, who had also gone pale, even paler than Mr Challis. She was not in such command of herself, but she managed to smile. 'I didn't know you knew Mr Challis — this is a surprise, isn't it —' she ended unsteadily, and then, turning to Earl, who was looking at Hilda with surprised admiration: 'This is Earl Swinger, Hilda — Earl, meet Hilda Wilson, my best friend.'

Afterwards, she did not know why she had said that. Perhaps it was a desperate appeal to Hilda to stand by her, not to let her down, not to be angry with her, to comfort her in her bewilderment and pain. Whatever the reason, Hilda responded to the appeal. She could see that something was wrong. What, she simply could not imagine, but it was evident that Mutt knew Marcus, and knew him by another name too, the old deceiver. She felt her indignation growing as she smilingly acknowledged Earl's ceremonious greeting and then turned to the children, while Margaret recited their ages and names. So these were his grandchildren, were they? And how was it that Mutt knew him, and she had never known that Mutt knew him, while poor old Mutt was obviously struck all of a heap at seeing them sitting together on the grass? Oh well, it was plain that Marcus had been lying like fun and pretending he wasn't married when he was, and that was the sort of thing she, Hilda, was not going to stand for. The silly old fool, she thought, while asking Emma if she had seen the duck-ducks?

'There's the tea-basket,' said Barnabas meaningly, in the midst of the pause following the introduction, while Earl glanced from the pale Mr Challis to the paler Margaret and wondered just what was going on here. Everybody laughed, glad enough of the opportunity to do so, though Mr Challis's laugh was hollow.

'I want my tea,' said Barnabas, encouraged by this reception. 'We all want our tea, don't we, Emma?' ('Say yes,' in a fierce whisper, and nudging her.) 'We stood in a queue outside a place but when we got there it had all gone, so we didn't get any.'

'No teee!' suddenly exclaimed Emma, smiling brilliantly and showing all her baby teeth.

'No, poor Sister,' said Earl. 'We were just wondering what to do,' he added, turning with pleasant respect to Mr Challis.

Alas, for that famous and gifted man. The tea was fated to be eaten under circumstances very different from those of which he had dreamed; it was his painful task to invite his grandchildren and that dull girl and duller young man to partake of the paté sandwiches, the fresh rolls and home-made quince jam, the chocolate biscuits and the ginger biscuits and the flask of scalding delicately flavoured tea.

But he set his teeth, and amid his disappointment and humiliation courteously invited the party to share the tea-basket, and they (the younger members, at least) accepted with offensive haste and were ready to begin at once. However, first they must be taken to make some necessary toilet arrangements, and accordingly Margaret and Hilda, taking a hand of each child, led them away in the direction of a small building half-concealed amidst the trees, promising to rejoin the gentlemen in ten minutes. (We will assume that the gentlemen, left to their own devices, smoked and exchanged comments upon the weather and the landscape, though Mr Challis's only impulse was to bound away into the greenery like a stricken animal and never come out of it again.)

'Mutt!' burst forth Hilda the instant they were out of earshot. 'What's going on here, anyway? I didn't know you knew Marcus!'

'That isn't Marcus; it's Mr Challis.'

'Your playwriter, who lives at that big house? Boloney! It's my Mr Marcus; I've known him for ages.'

'Well, he's both of them, that's all.' Margaret had no desire to talk, or to hear any more; the shock was so great that she felt stunned.

'*And* married,' said Hilda, significantly. 'He told me he wasn't. (The old monkey!) Oh – p'raps he's a widower?'

'No, Mrs Challis is alive.'

'What's she like?'

'Lovely,' answered Margaret, and her tone and look increased Hilda's indignation.

'Lovely, is she? Then what right has he to go on like that, when he's got a "lovely" wife of his own?'

'Like what?' said Margaret faintly, shuddering.

'Oh – carrying on,' said Hilda vaguely, suddenly remembering that Mutt had a crush on this Mr Challis – Marcus – whatever he called himself. Poor old Mutt, she must be feeling awful; she took things so hard, and fancy having a crush on that phony old twister.

'Did he make love to you?' suddenly asked Margaret in a voice so full of anguish that Hilda instinctively bent down and urged Barnabas, who was holding her hand, to 'go on with Emma, son, we'll be there in a minute.' Barnabas, who was not yet at the stage when he took an interest in grown-up conversations, obediently went ahead with his mind busy with thoughts of tea, and Hilda turned to Margaret.

'Look here, Mutt, we must get this straight. I picked him up in the tube last autumn; he lent me a torch in that awful fog, and I've been going out with him ever since, off and on. And you say he's Mr Challis the playwriter, who lives at that house where Finkelwink lives? What's his other name?'

'Gerard. *Did he make love to you?*'

'He told me it was Marcus,' muttered Hilda. 'No, he didn't get the chance; he used to kiss me now and then, nothing much. I wish you wouldn't take it like this, ducky,' she added, distressed.

'I saw him holding your hand – he was – this afternoon – I did try to stop the children, but it was too late –'

'Well, this afternoon he *did* get rather worked up,' Hilda confessed. 'Wanted me to go to South Africa or somewhere with him. I never heard of such a thing; you could have knocked me down with a thousand-pounder.' She glanced at her friend. 'Look here, are you in love with him?' she demanded.

Margaret wildly shook her head. 'Oh no – it's not that – truly it isn't, but I looked up to him so – I thought he was so wonderful, and now –'

Hilda muttered something very rude about Mr Challis, but they had now reached the little building, and further conversation was impossible.

When they emerged again, some fifteen minutes later, the

children went hurrying across the grass in the direction of the tea-basket, while the two girls approached more slowly. Margaret was still very pale, but she had bathed her face and combed her hair and looked more her usual self. Hilda was already inclined to laugh over the situation.

'I can't get over it,' she repeated, 'neither of us knowing it was him.'

'I can understand him – caring – about you, of course, you're so pretty –' said Margaret in a low tone, but this was just what she could not understand. How could that lofty intellect, that rare spirit, chill yet fiery as the air that burns above a volcano, have stooped to Hilda? What intellectual companionship could possibly exist between them? What could that admirer of tragedy, that lover of integrity, have found in *Hilda*? Margaret felt as if she were going mad.

'I'm not objecting to his "caring" about me,' said Hilda. 'What I do think awful is him being married and with two grand-children. Such lovely kids, and you say his wife's lovely, too. How many children has *he* got, for heaven's sake?'

'Three. Two sons and a daughter.'

'Why, he's nothing but a dirty old man!' exclaimed Hilda indignantly, 'and you say he's always writing "beautiful" plays! I always did think there was something funny about him and so did Mum and Dad, but I never thought he was as bad as that. I shan't half give him the works!'

'Oh, Hilda, don't do that!'

'Why ever not? He deserves all he gets.'

'But if he cares about you – I know he's behaved badly – I can't ever feel the same about him again – it will hurt him so.'

'Good job, too. Teach him not to do it again. Two grand-children! I can't get over it!' And she began to giggle. 'Oh dear – wasn't it a scream! Him holding my hand and going on about

South Africa and then those two shrieking out "Grandpa!" I bet he felt like murdering them!'

'He has three grandchildren, actually,' said Margaret reluctantly. 'There is a baby boy of about eight months.'

'The more the merrier,' said Hilda, her cheerfulness now fully restored. 'All the same, I'm going to give him the works, and then I've done with him for good.'

Mr Challis, standing silently beside Earl and watching them come across the grass, might well feel, as he saw their faces, that the worst part of the afternoon was yet to come. Margaret was pale and grave and had a wounded, reproachful look in her eyes, and Hilda was all mischievous laughter with a sparkle of annoyance. Earl looked at the young ladies with interest and felt some sympathy with the famous elderly man standing at his side. The brilliant spring light showed up his silver hair and his wrinkles, and his dignified expression was clearly, to Earl, only a cloak for very unpleasant feelings. He was trying to make a date with her, thought Earl, and his grandchildren muscled in. But it certainly is a pity that men of his age can't keep to their own age-group in their affairs.

For the next half-hour outward harmony prevailed. The children loudly praised what there was to eat, although regretting that there was not more, and the grown-ups made a meagre meal in order that the children should be nourished, which was biologically sound but gastronomically unsatisfying for the grown-ups. Margaret continued to exchange remarks with Mr Challis; to pass him things and smile at his elaborate jokes, and gradually her inward self-control was restored and she was able to view the afternoon's events more calmly.

Her strongest feeling was one of incredulous disappointment. He was not the noble, austere soul she had believed him; he was a soul that assumed a false name and sat on the grass with pretty girls inviting them to go to South Africa with him. It was as if she had been reverencing someone who did not exist. How could she even go on admiring his plays when they expressed a philosophy which he did not follow in his own life? It was not as if they expressed a despairing admiration for integrity and tragedy and strength, obviously written *up* by a weak but aspiring soul; no, they were written *down*, as if by a lofty soul that already possessed integrity and the tragic sense and strength, and believed that everyone else should possess them too. What was he doing sniffing (yes, sniffing was the word which Margaret used to herself) at people with commonplace longings for happiness? What could be more commonplace than to want to take a pretty girl to South Africa? Most ordinary men would jump at the chance. But few ordinary men had so lovely a wife, such handsome children, and so ancient and beautiful a home as Mr Challis.

It seemed to her that he had been not only commonplace but extremely greedy.

Her heart was very sore, and she did not dare to look at his grave, handsome face, but devoted herself to waiting on the children.

As for Mr Challis, *he* hardly dared look at Hilda, but every time he did so he encountered a mischievous glance with a sparkle of anger in it, and he had no doubt that as soon as she was alone with him she would make a scene. As if this were not enough, there was Margaret's solemn, reproachful expression, and the American fellow looking knowing and amused, damn his impudence! Well, Hilda would not get the opportunity to make her scene. He would at least keep what was left of his dignity.

Accordingly, as the last crumbs were being wiped from Emma, he stood up and said, addressing the company at large but looking at Hilda:

'I am sorry to leave you so abruptly, but I have just remembered that I have left some work at the Ministry which I must take home to study this week-end, and if I go now, I shall just get there before the building is closed. I am so very sorry,' pleasantly to Hilda, 'but I leave you in good hands, I know.'

'G'anpa?' said Emma, glancing inquiringly at Hilda, next to whom she was seated.

'Yes, Grandpa, ducks,' repeated Hilda, wiping Emma's fingers. 'Poor Grandpa's got to go back to the office. Emma, say "Good-bye, Grandpa." I shall be all right, really,' she added, smiling at Margaret and Earl, 'You run along, or you'll miss the 'bus. Bye-bye,' and − for the last time, he knew − she smiled at him.

For a moment he stood looking at her, as she sat on the grass with her blue dress spread about her. Her beauty still struck his heart; he still desired her, but he would never see her again. I shall suffer, but it is by suffering that we live, he thought, and out of my suffering I shall create.

'Good-bye,' he answered, and then he walked away; across the grass, through the withered bluebells that marked the end of spring.

Hilda watched him go. Some natural wounded vanity mingled with her other feelings. She had supposed him to be a wealthy and respectable bachelor whose offer of marriage she might one day have the satisfaction of refusing, and he had turned out to be a married celebrity who had tried to make her go wrong. But she was not deeply resentful; her strongest feeling was disapproval that a man with all those lovely grandchildren should have wanted to run after a girl half his age.

The rest of the afternoon passed pleasantly for everybody except Margaret. Earl and Hilda naturally got on well together, and nothing more was said about the oddness of her being alone at Kew with Mr Challis, while her suppressed laughter added to the gaiety of the party's mood, and Margaret did her best not to let her own pain spoil everyone's pleasure. It was a comfort at least to have Hilda's affectionate sympathy. The one person she could not endure to find out the situation was Zita, although she knew that Zita would understand her own feelings for Mr Challis in a way that Hilda could never do. What she needed was not Zita's eager comprehension of her hero-worship for a man whom she had thought a great artist; it was Hilda's schoolgirlish squeeze of her arm and rueful giggles that would comfort her as they had comforted her when she took things hard at school.

By the time they reached Highgate about half-past six, they were all very tired of bumping up and down on buses and pushing their way through crowded streets. Emma was asleep in Earl's arms with her fair little cheek pillowed on his khaki shoulder, and Barnabas, pale and weary, held a hand of each of the girls as he dragged his feet along. Earl and Emma received many smiling glances and murmurs of 'Sweet!' and although the comments of such of his fellow G.I.s as they happened to pass were less idyllic, they were good-natured and good-naturedly received, and when he passed two Snowdrops (or Military Police) they looked the other way.

He saw the party to the door of Westwood, and then, having thanked the girls for a delightful afternoon, he excused himself; he had a date, he said. Hilda told Margaret that she would probably come round and see her at her home after supper and hurried away. Margaret was left on the doorstep with Barnabas, who was almost weeping with tiredness, and the sleeping Emma, warm and heavy in her arms.

'Ach!' exclaimed Zita, flinging open the door with a beaming smile, '*Willkommen!* I haf some good broth for you, Barnabas, and into your bath you go. Margaret, I will take her – you must be tired.'

'I am rather,' confessed Margaret, thankfully handing over her burden. 'But we've had a lovely time,' she added. 'I did wish you had been there.'

This was the kind of thing one had to remember to say to Zita or she became hurt. In this case, it was even less accurate than usual.

'Where's Mummy?' demanded Barnabas.

'Here, here,' observed Hebe soothingly, emerging from a doorway with ruffled head and a copy of *Vogue* in one hand. She was followed by Alex, eating something. 'My poor son, are you nearly dead? Never mind, Mummy'll soon have you in bed. (We won't wash Emma; sling her in as she is.) Come along.'

As she went upstairs hand-in-hand with Barnabas and followed by Zita carrying Emma, she smiled over her shoulder at Margaret and said:

'You ought to have a medal. Have they worn you out?'

'I loved it,' answered the incurable Westwood worshipper eagerly. Hebe shook her head as if such devotion was beyond her.

Left alone, Margaret lingered in the hall for a moment, looking wistfully about her. The marble staircase was illuminated by a ray of sunlight striking through the garden trees and making delicate reflections, like the dance of water, over the cool white stone. The fragile chairs shaped like harps or ladders, the dim colours of the Eastern carpets, the splendour of a flower painting which she now knew with some satisfaction to be by Matthew Smith, all breathed the same serenity and beauty. O Westwood, she thought, how could he betray you?

'Can I make a drawing of your head some time?' mumbled Alex pleasantly, coming out from behind a cabinet.

'Yes, of course,' she answered mechanically, so surprised that she hardly realized what she was saying. 'I work all day. Would the evening do?' she went on, still hardly taking his question in.

'Oh yes. Look here, I'll tell you what, I can't fix it up now because I'm going to be away all next week fixing up about my picture. I'm going to have a show.'

'How exciting,' she murmured.

'At Mallock's in Leicester Square. (Better than Bond Street; more people will see it.) Well, the week after that, on the day the show opens, there's going to be a party here; I expect you'll come, won't you?'

'I will if I'm asked, Mr Niland, but I don't expect I shall be.'

'Oh, yes you will, Hebe said so. She wants you to come.'

'How lovely. Then I will,' she answered, smiling too, but more faintly. To have had this invitation only a month – only a week – ago! And now it brought nothing but pain.

'All right then. We'll fix things up at the party. Have one?' and he held out a bag of toffees.

'Thank you. Is the picture *The Shrapnel Hunters*?' she asked shyly, accepting a sweet. But she was wondering why he wanted to draw *her*.

'Yes. Have you seen it?'

She shook her head.

'That's a pity. It isn't here now or I'd have shown it to you. Why I want to do *your* head,' he went on confidentially, 'is because I'm going to see if the Government will let me do some murals on the walls of the Council Schools and places like that – in the Underground too, if they'll let me – and they're to be people. Rather the sort of thing Canaletto and Breughal did. Just ordinary people doing everyday things. I thought you would do for one. I've always wanted to draw you, from the first time I saw you.'

'Have you?' she murmured.

'Yes. Would you like me to pay you at the ordinary model's rates?'

'Oh *no*!' she cried, horrified.

'I don't see why not. It's all taking up your time.'

'I'd much rather have just the honour, Mr Niland.'

'If you go on being as green as you are now,' pronounced

Alex, giving her one of his disturbing looks, 'you'll have a hell of a time. Honestly, I mean it. Go on, you let me pay you. You can buy something special and keep it to remind you.'

'Yes – well, that would be nice,' she admitted. 'All right then, you'll tell me at the party when I can come. Mr Niland –' and then she paused.

'Don't be so *bourgeois*,' he said, grinning. 'Just call me Alex.'

But this she was not capable of doing. 'Am I green?' she blurted.

'Green as grass,' he said cheerfully, patting her on the back and opening the front door. 'Only I have seen grass look pink, *and* purple. You run along now. Your name's Margaret, isn't it? Try calling yourself Maggie. Good-bye,' and he laughed and shut the door.

She walked slowly homewards, glad of the evening coolness and thinking about him a little before letting her thoughts return to her grief. She was not sure that she liked him. He had no dignity, and his manner was mocking – no, perhaps teasing was a better word – and *never* had she imagined that a genius could be so unlike the conventional idea of one. Of course, there was Oliver Goldsmith, she thought vaguely, who *wrote like an angel and talked like poor Poll*. But I am glad that he is going to draw my head.

Then her thoughts returned sadly to the events of the afternoon. She remembered every detail with painful vividness; her first glimpse of the couple seated upon the grass, her startled recognition of them, her incredulous feelings and her pang at the sight of his hand clasped in Hilda's; the expression upon his face (ah! that she would never forget), her vain attempt to prevent the children, who had recognized him at the same time, from running towards him; and then the look of rage he had darted towards them, which had so shocked her.

In that moment the disillusionment which (she now realized) had been gradually approaching, was completed. She had reluctantly suspected the value and genuineness of his philosophy for some time, and now she saw with her own eyes that he was as other men; a disloyal husband, a weak admirer of pretty faces. He could even stoop to carrying on his flirtation under a false name; that was actually sordid, like some story in the evening papers, and it sickened her more than all the rest.

She was not angry or disgusted with Hilda. In the brief moments of privacy when they had been able to talk, she had understood that Hilda had been deceived, and was blameless. She had only been impatiently kind to him (oh, the pain of that thought!) and believed him to be dull but respectable. But how could she have resisted him, thought poor Margaret, as she opened the gate of her home. I suppose it wasn't until this afternoon that he *came out into the open*. As if he were tracking something! Ugh!

And then she remembered his attempt to be dignified and to carry the situation off smoothly, and suddenly she felt sorry for him; as she would have been for anything weak and unhappy. Sorry for Gerard Challis! If anyone had told me eight months ago that I should ever be that, she thought.

30

The harvest of suffering which Mr Challis had enthusiastically anticipated did not ripen. He went home feeling not full of tortured romantic yearnings, but very cross; in fact, he began to feel cross as soon as he was out of sight of the party on the grass and all the way home in the bus (he was unable to get a taxi) he got crosser and crosser. Stupid little fool! Sitting there with her mouth open when he declared his love, and then refusing such an offer; the chance of her narrow suburban lifetime; the one opportunity she would ever get to broaden her horizon and enjoy luxury and the society, the devotion, of an educated (and gifted, thought Mr Challis modestly) man!

I was mistaken in her, he thought, gazing at the woman seated opposite to him with such a bitter expression that she felt quite uneasy. Lovely as she is (the memory of that loveliness came with its familiar pain), she is shallow. She is an Undine, lacking a soul.

But how did it come about that she was apparently an intimate friend of this Margaret girl's? Was it a conspiracy? (women were always plotting). Had he been the victim of a plot? And if so, what was its object? No, it was probably not a plot; it was just the ironical way in which events shaped themselves. Now Hilda would endlessly discuss him with that other young woman, and the latter would be shocked. She was shocked already. He had seen it in her eyes, that afternoon; a shocked wounded look which caused him to make literary comparisons with trapped fauns, rabbits in gins, etc. Every time she came to the house she would look at him like that. He would no longer have upon her character the – er – the refining and civilizing influence which he had hitherto possessed. He hoped she would not come to the house often if she was going to look at him like that. He might drop a hint to Seraphina that she was an undesirable influence on the children; and so forth.

Even if I had taken Daphne to South America, he thought, I doubt if the experience would have deepened her nature. Later on she will become a shrew. It is as well, perhaps, that the affair has ended as it has.

But that same evening, about half-past nine, when he was sitting in his study alternately glancing over a history of the French Romantic Movement and gazing apathetically out of the window, he heard the telephone-bell in the hall begin to ring. He waited, assuming that Cortway or Zita would answer it, for Seraphina and Hebe were out, but it continued to ring, and at last with an impatient exclamation he got up and went out into the hall.

'Hullo?' he said – being one of the many who refuse to announce their telephone number on lifting the receiver.

'Marcus? Is that you?' said Hilda's voice. 'Aren't you ashamed of yourself? And you with all those lovely grandchildren?'

He was very angry with her, but her voice revived his passion.

'That has nothing to do with it,' he answered coldly, his heart beating fast; he was already hoping to arrange a meeting.

'Oh, hasn't it? Well, if that's the way you feel, that's the way you feel. Only I made up my mind to give you the works and here we go. You buck up, and make the best of what you've got. I don't like to think of it being wasted and –' she hesitated, her voice grew softer, 'good things are scarce in this world, you know –' her voice became indistinct and he thought he heard her murmur, 'I've been so lucky,' but the next thing he heard was a cheerful 'Bye-bye,' and then the click of the receiver being replaced.

'Daphne,' he exclaimed, actually moving closer to the tele-phone as if to clasp her to him, but she had gone. He got up with a sigh, and went back moodily to the study. Silly, imper-tinent, shallow little girl! common as a daisy or a blade of grass. How humiliating it was that in spite of all he still desired this daisy, this child, who had given him back his youth!

The next week passed quietly. Alex was busy arranging the details of his show; giving an interview to the Press at the Dorchester for which some space was found even in the miniature news-papers of war-time England; superintending the lighting and the arrangement of the room in which *The Shrapnel Hunters* and other pictures were to be displayed; and taking the bus to St John's Wood, where Hebe was wandering contentedly among blackened timbers and fallen bricks with a tape measure in one hand, accompanied by a local builder. It seemed possible, in spite of enormous difficulties, that the house might be sufficiently repaired within the next three months for them to live in. 'After all, we are bombed out,' she kept reminding the builder.

'Is there a studio?' shouted Alex to his wife, as he stepped over the fallen gate and walked up the uneven stone path, where tiny purple horns of fading lilac were scattered. He had not previously seen the house.

'You bet,' shouted Hebe from somewhere inside the blackened shell. 'In the garden, round the back. I did tell you.'

Presently she heard him shouting, 'My God, this is splendid,' and then there was silence. She smiled, and continued her conference with the builder. It would be enough for her if the place were warm and watertight, with room for plenty of chil-dren, but some of the velvet curtains had been salvaged from Lamb Cottage and when they were joined together and put at the large windows, they would look magnificent − when there was glass in the windows. I expect he will go away again, she thought, but this time at least he won't – she glanced up at the exposed laths of the ceiling fifteen feet above her head – he won't be able to say there wasn't enough room.

Margaret actually went back to the school on Monday morning with some relief. It was the first time in her experience that she had done so, and she supposed the dullness of the routine was welcome because it supplied an anodyne for pain. The faces of her colleagues, usually half-noticed by her as she went through her day's work, now appeared those of individual women not without interest, who were mostly well-disposed towards her and had their own problems and satisfactions, while the members of her form, now that she could give them an attention not bemused with day-dreams and memories, even seemed attractive. It struck her that all this youth, expressed in smooth cheeks and bright eyes, could be helped by her to avoid the worship of false gods. She pitied them. They were so young, and they did not know. But what she herself came to know, after a few days of this sentimentalizing over the twelve- and thirteen-year-olds, was that they were not likely to worship false gods because they would not worship any gods at all. Not one of them possessed imagination of the dreaming, intense, yearning type that was her own, and so far as she could discover, there had only once been a pupil of the Anna Bonner who had possessed imaginative fire; the famous writer Amy Lee, from whose brain had trooped the series of strange, Poe-like tales that had ceased abruptly after her marriage. Miss Lathom often talked of her, and regaled the staff with anecdotes about her, and Margaret thought how wonderful it would be to discover another Amy Lee in her own form. But if there were one, she thought, I probably shouldn't discover her. No one noticed that Amy Lee was any different from the others; they just seem to have thought she was rather dull.

Well, if I can't teach them not to worship false gods, I can at least teach them how to add up their change quickly when they're shopping, and the geography of the British Isles, she thought impatiently, and I will. She began to take more pleasure in her teaching, and to feel satisfied when her classes showed clearly that they were learning from her lessons and enjoying them. To her embarrassment, one skinny little creature, who had long been looking at her solemnly from corners, took to bringing her posies of flowers and loitering outside the school, waiting to walk down the road with her. I must be getting nicer, thought Margaret.

But life seemed dull now that she was no longer needed at the one Westwood and the romantic glow had departed from the other. Zita, who of course did not know of any change in her friend's feelings, continued to ring her up every two or three days whenever she was unusually hard-pressed with the children or there was a concert on the air which she wanted Margaret to hear, and sometimes Margaret would go, but sometimes she excused herself (to Zita's indignation) and went for a walk with Hilda instead.

Hilda's behaviour was rather mysterious lately; she was irritable, a most unusual mood with her, and sometimes absent-minded, an even more unusual mood – and on two occasions she telephoned Margaret at the last minute and broke an appointment without giving a reason. Margaret resignedly supposed that her friend had altered during the months of their estrangement, and thought that it was only just that she, who had for so long shut Hilda out from her confidence, should now be shut out from Hilda's. Nevertheless, she was hurt.

She saw and heard nothing of Earl Swinger during the fort-night following on their expedition to Kew, and altogether it was a time with her of sober reflection and the making of good resolutions, more suitable to the end of December than the end of June.

A few days before the end of the fortnight, she received her invitiation to the party at Westwood. It was to be on Saturday evening at nine o'clock, and as she stood in the hall, holding the card carefully between her fingers which still felt dry from blackboard chalk, she almost decided that she would not go. It will be so hot, she thought, and sighed. I did tell Mr Niland I would, though. I'd forgotten that.

A blackbird was singing and the lilies in the garden next door gave out their rich scent, and a stir and murmur of pleasure seemed to hover over London, full though it was of tired people and ruined buildings. It was no more than the spirit of summer, but it was delightful. I am too tired to enjoy a party, anyway, she thought. And I don't want to see him. I can't bear it.

Nevertheless, on the evening of the party Margaret, carefully dressed and even perfumed, stepped out of her own gate at a quarter to nine, and began to walk slowly up the hill. (. . . We know well that nowadays it is not the done thing to give descriptions in novels of what women are wearing. It is assumed that either the reader knows, or can guess, or will derive more insight into the heroine's character from a casual reference to some grubby mackintosh or holey vest; and, being slavishly willing to bow to literary fashion, we have endeavoured to suppress our natural inclination to describe our female characters' clothes; with varying success, we admit, but nevertheless we *have tried*. However, this evening we intend to describe *all* the women's clothes and hang the done thing.)

She was painfully excited. A fornight is not long in which to learn philosophy, resignation, devotion to duty and all the other qualities which are necessary in order to bear life's pains, and she was twenty-four and owned a warm heart. Her one hope, stronger than all other feelings, was that she would not feel a return of her former devotion when she again saw Mr Challis.

She dreaded this, for she knew that she could not admire what she did not respect; she *needs must love the highest* when she saw it; and if her feelings did return, they would do so in a debased form of which she must be ashamed.

There was more than one taxi drawing away from Westwood as she came near to the house, and even a private car or two, with dark foreign faces inside, waiting their turn to go into the drive. The delicate iron gates were set wide open and on either side of them, in tubs, were blue hydrangea shrubs in flower. Margaret shyly dropped behind a group of people who had just alighted from a taxi and followed them towards the house.

It was a calm evening, grey and still. Soft plumes of violet cloud lay along the west, where a little golden light broke through, wave on wave of cloud lying beyond the clear reaches of the light. Not a leaf stirred, and the pansies and roses, lifting their motionless faces in the flower-beds, looked as if their eyes were shut. There was a sweet cool smell in the air of freshly mown grass. A trail of blades and severed daisies had escaped as Cortway was carrying the heaped bin over the paths and lay along the ground; his sight was not so good as it used to be, and he had overlooked them when he was sweeping.

She glanced up at the goddess above the portico, with full lips set in their pensive line and her face turned towards the west. A soft glow illuminated it, like a reflection of light rather than light itself. The door of Westwood was open and she could see massive jars filled with flowers, the glitter of lights, people standing about talking and laughing. She could hear a piano being softly played; it was a childish-sounding versioin of 'Lili-Marlene,' rendered with an expert touch, and she saw that the grand piano from the drawing-room had been brought into the hall. Some people were gathered about it, singing softly, and she recognized Hebe, in a white dress of net with a wonderful necklace of green stones which looked like emeralds (but surely, thought Margaret, they can't be). In her brown hair, which to-night was dressed high on her head in a top-knot of curls, there was a quaint little tiara of the same green gems and in the low bosom of her dress there were pink roses, a stiff bunch stuck down her neck in such a way that the beholder felt that their thorns must be scratching her. She looked like a little girl dressed up. Oh, what an hour of careful consideration had been bestowed upon that little-girl look, those ungraceful roses! All the young men there were dying of love for her.

Margaret came into the house in the wake of a large woman in a fur cape who looked as if she must be Somebody and who was talking loudly in French to the men who accompanied her. Margaret's own intention was to slip away to Zita's room and leave her coat there before she looked about for Gerard Challis and got over the first shock of seeing him, but before she could even move across the hall, he suddenly came forward from the crowd, tall and slender in evening dress, with his hands held out to the large lady whom he smilingly greeted in French. Margaret's heart leapt, her throat grew dry, but it was with shame for him. How could he look so dignified and at ease, when all his life was a lie? No; she was saved. Her feeling for him had not returned; she felt nothing but shame and pity. But her heart was empty as she turned away and she already wished that she had not come.

'Hullo, Struggles, ducky, I'm tight!' whispered a gurgling voice in her ear and she turned quickly to see Hebe at her shoulder, hand-in-hand with a young man. 'I wish you wouldn't always try to shock me, as if I were about fifty!' Margaret was moved to retort tartly, and Hebe looked surprised and amused as she drifted away. The front door was now shut by Cortway, looking unfamiliar in a white jacket, and Margaret was making her way across the hall to the staircase when Seraphina, who was passing, stopped and put a kind hand upon her arm.

'So glad you could come, my dear,' she said. 'Did you have *too* shattering a time at Kew? We've been *wondering* about you. Zita *did* say you had been in once or twice, but I couldn't believe you'd really *recovered*. Go and leave your things and then come and have a *drink*.'

She moved away smiling before Margaret could answer. The latter, who was already regretting what she had said to Hebe and wondering if she had been rude, thought how lovely she looked in a white lace dress, showing arms and shoulders which were only slightly too heavy and setting off the delicacy of her complexion. She had a necklace and bracelets of garnets set in gold.

Zita's room was untidy and silent. A letter of some twelve pages was flung down upon the bed, covered with exclamation-marks and green writing. It was apparent that Zita was having another love affair and that, as usual, it was leading to complications. Margaret took off her coat, tidied her hair, and stood looking at herself in the glass.

'I don't look too bad,' she murmured at last.

She had taken to heart some of Zita's scornful remarks about young English misses who dressed in bright colours which 'did make themselves seem dim,' and had managed to get herself a dress of dark-grey lace. With this she wore black net gloves and kept her black velvet bow at the nape of her neck, and carried an outsize glittering gold sequin handbag. Her hair was brushed very smoothly and she wore much brilliant red lipstick. No ear-rings, no necklace, no bracelets or rings, for Zita said that young English misses hung themselves with these things as if Christmas-trees they had been.

I look distinguished, she thought sadly, but what's the use of that? I look so hopelessly serious, so earnest and thoughtful. I look as if I sat on committees all day or made pendants with a hammer. I should like to look like a kitten.

With which reflection, she went downstairs feeling subdued and remote from the rest of the cheerful company, with the intention of finding Zita.

However, Seraphina was agreeably surprised at her appearance, which Margaret had indeed rated too low. She looked elegant, as well as distinguished, and Seraphina thought that any young man who was not hopelessly spoiled by a surfeit of beauties ought to be pleased to talk to her. Accordingly, she presented to her a young man in naval uniform who asked her if she were Angela Britton? He was so bad at names. As Angela Britton was a gifted young repertory actress, Margaret was gratified at the implied resemblance, the young man assuring her that it was striking. But after they had thoroughly discussed this, and exchanged some remarks about one another's jobs, and had each had a drink, silence began to fall between them, and even while Margaret was searching for something to say, the young man exclaimed, 'Oh, I say – Nicky! – do excuse me, there's Nicky Mallison,' and darted away into the crowd.

She sipped her drink and watched the people. She was standing at the foot of the staircase, on which people were sitting, in groups and in twos, talking – talking – talking. Some of the girls were in Service dress, including a Pole, with the languid eyes of a harem beauty gleaming above her stiff soldierly collar. Many distinguished elderly men in evening clothes were there, and younger ones in uniform, and Hebe's friends were recognizable by their youth, their air of abundant health, and their wedding-rings; they stood together in corners talking about their children. But there was plenty going on besides talking, for someone was usually at the piano improvising a gay tune or a dreamy one, while the large drawing-room had been cleared for dancing and Margaret could hear the medley of squeaky and metallic noises made by a small swing band. The smoke of many cigarettes wreathed slowly up into the air and the noise of conversation grew steadily louder but the room did not become disagreeably hot, for all the windows and the front door stood open and cool air floated in from the garden.

Presently Margaret saw Zita working a way towards her between the chattering groups, looking very cross and very smart in a dress of thinnest black lawn with wide ruffles round its hem, sleeves and neck. She had brilliant blue delphiniums made into a tight posy, fastened to a black band on one wrist and a tiny watch shimmering with diamonds on the other. Margaret, while admiring her toilette, did not feel quite pleased about it, for her own appearance slightly resembled Zita's; both might have been dressed by the same House – as indeed they had, for the taste of one had moulded that of the other. We look like two plain women making the very best of ourselves, she thought.

'Ach! such an evening!' began Zita in a low, furious tone. She cast a glance over Margaret's dress and snapped: 'Good. You look *chic*.' Then she viciously wound the diamond watch.

'What's the matter? I love your dress; did you make it? And what a lovely watch!' said Margaret soothingly.

'Of course I made it and much trouble it was. Ach! those children, I thought never should I come away. You like my watch?' more complacently. 'My new boy friend gave it to me.'

After the watch had been admired and Margaret had suppressed some disloyal reflections on Zita's capacity for attracting boy friends who could afford to buy her miniature diamond watches, they chatted for a little while and then Zita darted away to speak to Mrs Challis and did not return and Margaret was once more left alone, but not so isolated as to be conspicuous. One or two people glanced at her with vague smiles but no one addressed her, and after some time she began to think that most of these people knew each other, for she heard many nicknames exchanged and caught shreds of gossip which argued intimacy between the gossipers. To her, everyone whom she studied seemed distinguished, interesting, beautiful, and she recognized several celebrities, while the soft continuous music, the warm air filled with perfume and cigarette smoke and the scent of dying roses, the brilliant lights and the continuous babble of lively voices, presented such an entertaining spectacle that after a while she ceased to wish to take an active part herself and was content to listen and look on.

In a little while she thought: I am enjoying it. Here I am, at a brilliant party that I would have given ten years of my life to go to when we lived in Lukeborough, but I'm not taking any part in it; I'm just looking on as if I were at a play; and yet I'm enjoying it. I *am* more content than I was a year ago; yes, I really am.

'There's *the* most wonderful view from the roof,' suddenly said a girl's voice above her head. '*Too* impressive. *You* go up and look at it, darling. You can see absolutely to the *Ruhr*!'

Margaret glanced up as the speaker came down the marble staircase, picking her way between the guests seated upon the steps, and saw that people were going along the corridor at the head of the stairs as if on their way to the roof. She suddenly felt that a breath of evening air would be delicious.

A few minutes later she stood breathing the faint breeze and gazing out across London, that beloved city, that wounded, unmartial group of villages, lying spread for mile upon mile, east and west and north and south, as far as the eye could reach, under the darkening summer sky. For the clouds had drifted away, and now every tower and dome and factory, every palace and church and stadium, stood out ghostly clear in the soft afterglow. Sometimes the myriad grey and cream tints were broken into by a dark-green mass of summer trees and occasionally, like bones, white or yellow ruins reared up. A few lights sparkled here and there amid the miles of buildings and smoke from the trains spread itself rollingly along the dark-blue or brown façades. It was the minute yet clear detail of the whole colossal expanse of masonry which gave it an irresistible fascination to the eye: the vastness of it awed the heart, and the pride and splendour of its history awed the mind, but these tiny rose-pink walls and dwarfed houses of tea-colour or livid white, each with its very windows distinct and each unlike its fellow, were – in the sense that they excited the imagination of the beholder and set it soaring – wonderful.

Margaret leant upon a parapet and gazed, her thoughts moving on from dream to dream. A few people were on the roof when she first came up, pointing out landmarks to one another and exclaiming at the clearness of the air, but soon they went away and she was alone. She had not thought to bring her coat, and presently she shivered.

'Cold or miserable?' asked Alex Niland's voice, and she turned and saw him coming towards her across the leads. His evening clothes were rumpled and his hair was disarranged and under one arm he carried a bottle.

'Which?' he repeated, and put his arm, which was pleasantly warm, about her shoulders.

'Having a nice little brood, eh? *What are we here for? What does it all mean? Where are we all going and why?* I know. Have some,' and he unscrewed the bottle, putting both arms tightly round her in order to do so, and invitingly held out the foaming neck.

'No, thank you – oh – all right – thanks, I will –' and she drank some foam, hoping that he would not spill it over her dress and wondering what was coming next.

'That's better,' he said, and carefully wiped the neck of the bottle with a large, grubby handkerchief and drank himself.

'You miserable?' he went on earnestly, putting his face close to hers and gazing intently into her eyes with his own large ones, that looked dark and strange in the fading light. 'Yes. Worrying about Gerry, aren't you? Poor old Gerry, he's had it. You don't want to worry, you know.' He waved his arm at the wonderful panorama spread below and around them and then at Venus, flashing above them through air so clear that an infinitely thin fiery net made of her own light seemed flung about her. 'Look at that. Always something to look at. Minute you open your eyes in the morning. Have some more.'

'I will, but I don't like it much. I like you, though,' said Margaret, in what she felt was a reckless manner, and she leant closer against the warmth of his shoulder. She drank some more foam and Alex carefully wiped her mouth with the handkerchief and then kissed her with a long friendly kiss.

'I've taken all the paint off your mouth,' and he wiped his own with the handkerchief. 'You put on some more. That's right. Now about my drawing your head. You come here next Saturday afternoon. About four o'clock.'

'All right. What shall I wear? Will my hair do like this?'

'Wear anything. Anything you like. Yes, keep your hair like that.' He kissed her again. 'That better?'

'Yes – oh, yes, thank you – Alex. This' – she tried to regain control over a situation which was rapidly becoming dreamlike – 'this is awfully unexpected, isn't it – I mean –'

'No, no,' he interrupted, shaking his head. 'I've always noticed you and liked the shape of your head and your mouth, and I could see you were worried about Gerry. You shouldn't, it's a waste. He isn't the right person for you to love, you want somebody who can love too, not a stuffed shirt; you stop worrying about him, Maggie.'

'All right, I will,' she said, beginning to laugh. 'Oh, you are kind!'

'Drink,' said Alex, waving the bottle, 'drink and kissing. That's what you like, isn't it? And you go and look at things, like I said. (You can see things anywhere; you needn't go into the country or anything.) I wish there was some more.' He turned the bottle upside down and shook it. 'Damn. Never mind; it's cold. Let's walk up and down.'

'Won't people be wondering where you are?' she asked, feeling it her duty thus to remind him, but hoping that he would not think it his duty to go back to his guests.

'They'll think I'm necking with someone somewhere. Doesn't matter.' He put her arm round her waist and arranged her arm round his, and thus entwined they began to pace up and down. She wished that Mr Challis and all the celebrities downstairs could see her, alone upon the roof with, and amiably enlaced about, the lion of the evening, and yet, on second thoughts, she was rather glad that they could not.

'You don't want to take things *seriously*,' Alex was beginning, when a voice exclaimed, 'Hullo there!' and the soldier Lev came out of the attic window which led on to the roof, and over towards them. Though not exactly untidy, his appearance was not completely orderly; his hair was ruffled and – Margaret began to have a faintly nightmarish feeling – under one arm he carried a bottle.

'Uh – huh,' he said, nodding at Margaret as if he had always suspected that this was the sort of thing she did. 'They're asking for you downstairs,' to Alex. He unscrewed his bottle and held it out to Margaret. 'Thusty, Gorgeous?'

'I'll keep you company,' she answered, and this time she drank some. It was rather good. Lev nodded as if satisfied.

'I've been telling her she mustn't worry,' said Alex, taking the bottle from Lev and drinking. 'She mustn't, must she?'

'Certainly not,' said Lev, and his dark eyes, which glowed with melancholy fires, turned upon Margaret a sardonic smile that was not unkind. 'Believe me, it's a mistake.' He took the bottle from Alex and drank.

'We were walking up and down. To keep warm. *You* come and walk up and down,' said Alex. 'Here –' he tried to put Lev's arm round Margaret's waist. 'We all walk up and down, see?'

'I get the idea,' said Lev, arranging his arm round Margaret and hers about him. 'Now, where do we go from here?'

'Up and down,' said Alex, beginning to march. 'Just go up and down. I've been telling her – here, you kiss her,' he interrupted himself. 'You kiss her, too. That's what she likes.'

'I didn't –' began Margaret.

'Maybe she doesn't want me to,' said Lev, peering down into her face.

'If you would like to, I don't –'

'O.K. by me,' said Lev, and gave her a kiss that was expert but not offensively so. They then resumed their march. It was beginning to get dark.

'She's a nice girl,' Alex assured Lev, speaking over Margaret's head. 'Loving, I mean. She's all right.'

'I told you she was, didn't I?'

'You did.' It struck Margaret that Lev had had more than Alex but carried it better. He walked a little unsteadily, but his voice was not so solemn.

'I knew what she was like the first time I saw her,' said Lev suddenly, 'I thought, it's just too bad I can't fall for that dame but that's my luck. I always fall for the other sort. She'll be all right, though.'

'Which dame do you mean?' said Alex.

'Why, this one. Which is it?' peering into Margaret's face. 'Yes, that's the one. Dress is different, but it's the same one,' and he kissed her again.

Margaret was now divided between a dreamy and slightly intoxicated pleasure in this regular promenade under the stars supported by their arms while their voices solemnly discussed her (they were both tall men) above her head, and a growing conviction that Alex should go downstairs and entertain his guests. I am alone on a roof with two drunken men at night and they keep kissing me, she thought. Doesn't it sound awful? But it isn't awful at all. Things are very often different, thought Margaret, from what they sound in words.

'Don't you think you ought to go down?' she said gently to Alex.

'What for? Oh yes, I suppose so. Lev, you tell her she mustn't worry.'

'You mustn't worry, sister,' said Lev's deep voice out of the dusk. 'It's bad, but it's not *so* bad.'

'That's it,' said Alex, dreamily. 'Bad but not so bad.'

'Bad, but not so bad,' repeated Margaret. 'All right, I'll try not to worry, and thank you both very much.'

'What was she worrying about?' asked Lev, drinking again.

'Everything,' said Alex.

'You shouldn't,' said Lev to Margaret. 'Earl likes you; he thinks you're swell. He's gotten himself engaged to a British girl; what do you know about that?'

'Oh, I am so glad!' exclaimed Margaret, and as the last of her eligible admirers thus left the lists, she heard him go without a pang.

'You like me?' demanded Lev suddenly, diving at her.

'Very much,' she answered.

'You like me too,' said Alex, 'and I like you and I like Lev —'

How much longer this would have lasted was a question Margaret often pondered afterwards, but at this moment a figure in white appeared at the attic window, and Hebe's voice called: 'You three lunatics. Come on downstairs!'

Chapter The Last

In the autumn, Margaret paid that visit to Lady Challis to which she had long looked forward.

When she had nervously telephoned to propose herself, she had been unable to speak to Lady Challis and had made the arrangements with a cheerful voice calling itself Mary, against the customary background of other voices and barking dogs, while there seemed a doubt whether Bertie (who was described as being Busy With The Plums) could meet her at the station. Oh, that did not matter; she knew the way; she could walk, Margaret eagerly assured Mary's voice, and so it was decided that she should go down on the morning of the following Saturday.

When she set out, it was in the full and glorious type of an autumn day; with a wind rolling white and golden clouds across a sky whose sunny blue gulfs seemed to lead on and on into Heaven. Her heart was light; she pressed forward eagerly into the wind and looked every now and again at the sky, thinking it resembled that in Alex's great painting, *The Shrapnel Hunters*. All England was talking of the picture that autumn. It showed three children searching for fragments of steel that had fallen overnight among the willow-herb and dock-plants of a bombed site, and the critics were comparing it with Millais's *Autumn Leaves*, some of them insisting that this was the greater painting because in it there were pity and terror, as well as beauty, whereas in the older master's picture there was *only beauty*. Margaret had no opinions about that, but she had been many times to see *The Shrapnel Hunters* and had taken its shapes and colours into her mind's eye, finding comfort in them amid the picture's grim strength.

It was now difficult for her to realize that the man who had painted this picture should once have kissed her and advised her about her attitude towards life, for after the drawing of her head had been made, she had seen no more of him. He had gone to Italy on his official mission, leaving Hebe to make the house in St John's Wood habitable against his return, and he had already been away for nearly three months. While he was making the drawing he had barely spoken to Margaret, and when he had said good-bye to her, all that he had given her with her model's fee was an absent smile and a pat on the shoulder and a 'Thank you, Maggie dear.'

She was disappointed, but not so disappointed as she would have been some months ago. She told herself that if she intended to follow the advice which he had bestowed upon her at the party (and she did) the best way to begin was not to take his own casualness to heart. It was natural, she told herself, that the Nilands and the Challises should mean more to her than she did to them, because their lives were full, while her life, in all that human beings most desire, was empty.

When once we begin to make the best of circumstances, the task becomes easier as we proceed. Change of heart, conversion, seeing the light, are all names for the quick or gradual turning of our faces towards that ancient Way, worn by the tired feet of millions of ordinary people who 'tried to make the best of it' as well as by the bleeding feet of the Saints. During that autumn, Margaret also resolutely turned her mind away from the great tragedians, the great philosophers, the great wrestlers and strugglers and questioners, and listened instead to music and poetry. Occasionally some strong-minded acquaintance suggested that she was being weak, cowardly and escapist (that blessed word), and then Margaret would think of Lev, who would have demanded 'So what?' and continue in her habits, strengthened. (Lev had been sent abroad, Zita informed her, and the family at Westwood had heard no more of him. Zita naturally assumed him to be dead, and was aggrieved when Margaret received a card from him at Christmas.)

The holiday which the two girls had spent together had proved a success. Margaret had set out upon it with apprehensions concerning Zita's talkativeness and touchiness, to say nothing of other qualities which might well come to light after sharing existence with her for a week, but most of her fears proved unfounded. The fresh scenes and new faces and sense of freedom acted upon Zita like a tonic; her Jewish liveliness and warmth expanded in them; and she also possessed the invaluable quality of making an occasion *go*; at least there was never dullness where Zita was.

Margaret became protectively fond of her. In many ways she seemed the elder and Zita turned to her for advice and comfort. This (though tiresome when leading to sessions prolonged into the small hours) was flattering.

It was as well that she had become true friends with Zita, for when she returned to London she found that Hilda was engaged.

And never was anyone so engaged as Hilda; she might as well, thought Margaret, have worn a label; so dreamy, so silent, so solemn was she. Sometimes Margaret would see her in the evening, setting out for a walk with the young petty officer in the Navy who had brought about this transformation. They walked in silence, looking at one another, with Hilda's arm passed through his in defiance of Regulations, and to Margaret he seemed a pleasant, ordinary young man enough. They were to be married soon, and would share his leaves in the very small flat which Hilda had been fortunate enough to find until his ship was ordered abroad. It would then be lonely for Hilda, but

Mrs Wilson hoped that she would quickly have a baby and then there would be plenty to do.

So the skimmer over the surface was caught; the dancer trapped and bound and made to undergo those feelings at which she had so often smiled in others. Margaret was glad that her friend was to be so happily settled, and looked forward to being bridesmaid at the large and elaborate wedding which was being planned; she thought that the change in Hilda was poetic justice.

Mrs Steggles said that Hilda had gone downright soppy over that boy, and refrained from mentioning Margaret's own unengaged state. Mother and daughter found it easier to get on together than they had at one time, and when the inevitable estrangement with her dear friend, Mrs Piper, occurred, rather later than Margaret had anticipated, it was to Margaret that Mrs Steggles vented her indignation and turned for comfort.

The Steggleses attended Dick Fletcher's wedding, and saw Mrs Coates looking indeed damn' pretty in a pink dress and a flowery hat with floating veil. She pressed Margaret's hand effusively and studied her with eyes in which the expression did not soften except when she glanced at Dick. During the reception at Westwood-at-Brockdale afterwards, Margaret thought how completely the installation of its new mistress had destroyed the fairy-tale feeling in the little house. It was still pretty; still so clean as to seem unreal amid the shabbiness and dirt of war-worn London, but the hush through which the wind-bells sounded had gone for ever.

She saw Linda once more, dressed suitably and with obvious care, but the child did not seem to recognize her until Margaret asked her if she had 'forgotten Margaret?' and then Linda smiled and put out her hand, but it was not clear if she did remember. It seemed to Margaret that her manner had returned to the apathy from which she herself had once taken pride in leading her, and once she overheard the bride speak to her somewhat sharply, but perhaps it was healthier that the child should be treated with normal impatience when the occasion demanded and, in any case, Margaret herself could do nothing about it.

When Dick accepted her congratulations, she could detect no trace of consciousness in his manner. If he had once suspected that there was a wealth of love in herself which could have enriched his life, he had forgotten it; and if her own satisfaction in his happiness was tempered by a wonder at his being content with a Mrs Coates, she was prepared to admit that she still knew but little about men.

Sometimes when she went to Westwood-at-Highgate she caught glimpses of Gerard Challis. According to the theatrical gossip writers, he was working upon a new play, but the theme was being kept a secret, and Zita had not been able to glean from Seraphina or Hebe what it was.

In case the reader should like to be better informed than the theatrical gossip writers, we will reveal that the play was called *In Autumn*; it was about a woman who was described by her friends as 'corrupt yet fiery' – a sort of compost heap and bonfire in one, but not so useful as either – married to a man who was a mystic. She had been philandering for years, cheerful in the belief that when she wanted to Go Back to him he would Understand, but when she did want to Go Back to him (in the middle of the Blitz, of all inconvenient times) he did not Understand, and so she was compelled to return, broken-hearted, to her latest lover. The husband went off to India and lived with a yogi in a cave, which (except for the yogi) was exactly what he would have had to do if he had stayed in London.

This gem was to be flashed upon the British public in February, about the same time as the new issue of clothing coupons, but as *Kattë* was still playing to packed houses, perhaps the British public deserved what it got. Mr Challis was paying very large sums in Income Tax and complaining bitterly about them. (He was fond of money, as we know; not in a cheerful, greedy way but in a solemn contemptuous way that we, for our part, think far worse.)

Margaret no longer felt a strong interest in him or his plays. When her respect for him as a human being had been destroyed, her admiration for him as an artist had been destroyed also. For Alex Niland, who deserted his wife at intervals and approached young women with kisses on his lips and drink in his hands, yet painted pictures breathing goodness and beauty, she made excuses. At least, she thought, he doesn't pretend to be better than he is; he doesn't pretend to be anything; he's just himself. But then, she liked Alex Niland.

All that now remains to be said of Mr Challis is that late in life he himself Went Back to Seraphina with what remained of his heart, and was received by her with the unfailing loving-kindness she had always shown towards him. And so, farewell to this gifted man.

Margaret had more than once, in response to an abrupt invitation thrown out by Hebe, visited the house at St John's Wood. She found it as full of charm for her as the house at Highgate. Hebe was gradually filling her home with large, solid pieces of Victorian furniture against which the children could bump without any damage to themselves and – which was almost as important at that time – without any to the furniture. She bought big dishes wreathed with red and blue flowers which had once held the noble joints of Victorian days, and served meat and vegetables together upon them in order to reduce the washing-up; and she invited her friends to sit with her and make patch-work in the evenings and refresh themselves with bowls of soup, afterwards using the coverings thus made to adorn their shabby chairs and beds. She had her bees in the garden and had planted the flowers which bees prefer, but she was now engaged in a struggle with her neighbours about her right to keep chickens, and she had been reluctantly compelled to abandon altogether the scheme of the goat. *Vogue* had already approached her with the object of chronicling some of these activities, with photographs, in its pages.

When Margaret alighted at Martlefield, her ticket was taken by the same sturdy young woman whose costume had aroused the distaste of Gerard Challis in the summer, and when she came out of the station she saw that the field which had then impressed her with its sheet of gold buttercups was now scattered with leaves flying past from the elms, while the foliage lingering upon the more distant trees resembled a bloom of yellow plush.

The weather was so splendid that she was a little disappointed to see the dog-cart, the cob and Bertie coming towards her; she would have enjoyed the three-mile walk. She wondered if Bertie had been compelled to abandon his Business with the Plums in order to meet herself and would be sulky in consequence? Indeed, he did look rather severe, but she knew that this was his usual expression and was due to his opinion of the British Empire rather than to any more personal grief.

After greetings of a suitably casual nature had been exchanged, Margaret inquired how everybody was, and if there were many people staying at Yates Row.

'Bung full, that's what we are,' replied Bertie briefly, thereby casting the first shade over her hopes of uninterrupted and lengthy conversations with her hostess. 'Everybody's all right down here. My gran died, though.'

Margaret expressed regret and as soon as was delicately possible inquired if Irene were still at Yates Row.

'Oh yes. She's a permanency, seemingly. That Edna of hers goes to the village school. This week-end there's a whole lot of kids down from London supposed to be helping with the plums. *Supposed* is right. Then all last week there was my sister.'

'Oh, how nice for you. How old is she?'

'Ten. Regular nuisance, she is. Can't think how I ever put up with her when I was at home.'

'You come from London, don't you?'

'Walthamstow, E.17. I was evacuated here in 1939. Got me education down here and all and haven't never gone back again. Catch me going back.'

'Don't you like London?'

'Not after the country, I don't. Mechanized farming; that's going to be my line. There's nothing really doing for my class in London; it's all right for your class.'

While Margaret was getting over this one, the governess-cart arrived at the well-remembered row of houses, looking different in their autumnal setting, and she alighted and walked slowly up the path, glancing about her. There were still some red apples amongst the highest branches of the orchard trees, and a few dahlias and sunflowers that had escaped the frosts were swinging their massive rich heads in the wind above the mossy paths.

'They were all out nutting yesterday,' observed Bertie, beginning to lead Maggie the cob away. 'Didn't get any, of course. Squirrels had them all weeks ago. Lady Challis was ever so amused, she says it was just the same when she was a kid. That's your room, up there,' pointing to a gabled attic window where a white curtain was streaming forth, 'Lady Challis says you're to go on down the meadow when you've put your things away, they're all down there.'

Voices and laughter came towards Margaret on the wind as she walked through the garden at the back of the houses a little later, and soon she could distinguish figures moving about among the plum trees at the far end of the wide meadow, which extended for the whole length of Yates Row at the end of the gardens. The trees were of all heights, bearing many different varieties of plum, and this was convenient for the pickers, whose ages were as widely diverse as the fruit they were gathering. The children carefully pulled down the bloomy, hard, dark-purple globes from small trees yielding late fruit for jam, and high above their heads, perched on ladders resting against the trees rocking ceaselessly in the wind, worked the grown-ups, laughing and calling to one another in gasps as the gusts snatched their breath away. High above them all, in the tallest veteran tree, with one foot on the last step of a ladder and the other planted in a crotch of boughs, was Lady Challis.

Margaret recognized her from afar, and shyly approached the foot of the ladder. She stood there unnoticed for a few moments, alternately glancing up at her hostess and endeavouring to reconcile with her conception of the latter's poetic dignity a glimpse of thin limbs clad in laddered grey stockings and other very utilitarian garments; and looking at the children, who seemed as mixed in age and class as the plums themselves but who were all rosy with rushing about in the wind and all carrying on that pompous, slightly self-righteous running commentary with which children always accompany any useful work.

'I say, they do need picking here, there are simply thousands of them, absolutely choking up the boughs, there wouldn't be any room for new ones next year if I didn't pick them.'

'I *know*. It's a very useful job of work. Don't say *thousands*, Claudia. My mummy says you exag-erate.'

'Exag-gerate, not exag-erate. Oh well, there are twelve on this branch, anyway. Look, Edna, you want to put them *gently* into the basket, not drop them in, you'll spoil the *bloom* if you do. My mummy says half the joy of a plum is the *bloom*. I say, this one is *super*! As big as a shell-egg!'

'Not a very large egg.'

'Oh yes, an enormous egg. Look, I'll put it very gently in the basket so as not to spoil the *bloom* . . . oh, go *away*, Maggie!' in a terrified shriek.

Margaret ran over and led away the cob, who had trotted up and put her nose into the plum-basket, and Claudia came out from behind a tree.

'Hullo, Claudia. Do you remember me?' Margaret asked, smiling.

'Of course. You were here in the summer,' replied Claudia graciously, smoothing her long ruffled tresses.

'Hullo, Margaret,' said Edna, who had continued picking unperturbed, 'We're helping with the Plum Harvest. It's a very useful job of work. Lady Challis is going to make fifty pounds of jam to-morrow' (oh dear, thought Margaret) 'and Frank and me are going to have the scum for our tea if we watch it and see it doesn't *catch*.'

'Which is Frank?'

'My cousin. Over there.' She pointed to three small boys who, apparently bored by the method of hand-picking, were violently shaking the tree upon which they were engaged. 'He's the one in the pixie-hood. He's had a bad ear. M-something.'

'Mastoid,' put in Claudia.

'Boys! No!' cried Lady Challis's voice so close to Margaret's ear that the latter started. She turned round and saw her hostess standing at her elbow, frowning and shaking her head at the group who were agitating their tree. 'Bad for the plums! You do it by hand or not at all!'

Then she turned smilingly to Margaret:

'Here you are then. I'm so glad that you could come. Are you hungry?'

'A little, but not very,' Margaret answered, smiling too as she remembered that almost the first remark Lady Challis had ever addressed to her had been about food.

'Quite sure? There's an enormous stew in a pot on the range, but we don't have lunch until half-past one on Saturdays.'

'I saw it as I came through the kitchen. It smells heavenly.'

'It's got prunes in it,' confided Lady Challis. Then she gazed at Margaret for a moment, while her large eyes, now faded by age, took on an inquiring, and then a faintly apologetic, expression.

'Do forgive my being so absent-minded,' she said at last, 'but did I ask you to come down for any special reason (apart from liking to see you again, of course), or was it just to help with the plums?'

'Well –' began Margaret, slightly taken aback, 'as a matter of fact, when I was here in the summer you did say that I – I might talk to you, if it wouldn't take up too much of your time, that is.'

'Of course. How stupid of me not to remember.' Her tone was relieved and brisk. 'Did I *promise*?'

'Well, you did, actually.'

'Then we'll get another ladder (there's one over there they've just finished with) and we'll go up the plum tree together and start talking right away. I always keep my promises, don't I, young ladies?' appealing to Edna and Claudia, but the appeal received no more than an 'Of *course* you do, Lady Challis,' from Claudia which was obviously merely polite, and a robustly sarcastic, 'Oh, of *course*!' from Edna, which made Lady Challis burst out laughing and cast a glance at Margaret that banished the latter's slight disappointment.

As she climbed the second ladder, carried to the tree by Bertie and an elderly countryman who helped about the grounds, and gradually mounted into an unfamiliar world of mossy branches and rustling clusters of dark-green leaves through which blew faint scents of bark and sunned fruit, Margaret felt her spirits rising to meet the immense clouds hurrying across the sky. Balancing herself against the seamed trunk, she gazed upwards through the pattern of leaves, which suddenly seemed black against the sunny blue vault overhead, and saw that where there was a large gap in the intricate pattern, the sky thus revealed resembled a fathomlessly deep pool, calm despite the buffeting wind that made the whole tree, from hidden roots to sun-nourished leaves, rock and sway without rest.

She lowered her eyes, and met Lady Challis's smile, as the latter confronted her from the summit of a ladder on the opposite side. She was enclosed by leaves; her head was thrust right amongst them and some were touching her thin cheek as she glanced about in search of the large, ripe fruits, the Emperors among plums, that had lingered on week after week, escaping the long (but not quite long enough) hooked stick of the gatherer.

'There are lots up here,' she called to Irene, who was waiting below beside a basket and who now looked up at Margaret with a smiling greeting. 'We'll have them down in no time. Have you got your stick?' (to Margaret, who had an unresentful suspicion that her hostess had forgotten her name, if indeed she had ever known it). 'Hook it over a branch when you aren't using it and mind you're careful not to drop it. Now!' She reached out energetically across a branch with her stick towards a cluster of plums. 'Talk!'

Of course Margaret was instantly silenced. She smiled confusedly but could not find a word with which to begin. It was of her spiritual and mental future that she had wished to talk to Lady Challis, but how could such important subjects be discussed up a plum tree in a high wind?

'You look happier than you did in the summer,' began Lady Challis, helping her out. ('Oh, just let them fall anywhere and Irene will collect them but don't send down too many at a time or they'll get lost in the grass.) *Are* you happier?'

'Oh, yes, I am.' This was a question that Margaret did not have to consider before answering.

'Any special reason, or just – (whew! there's a gust! – hang on tight – and there goes my handkerchief!' as a large grey object sailed away across the trees), 'just everything?'

'No special reason,' answered Margaret, colouring. She leant out along a bough and manœuvred with her stick for a plum half-hidden in leaves. 'Nothing much has happened to me this last year, except getting to know all of you and seeing some pictures and hearing a lot of lovely music.'

'Are you fond of music? (Claudia, get my handkerchief, will you, my dear?' in a prolonged shout, 'Look, there, on that bush.)'

'I like it better than anything except poetry.'

'Ah, poetry. I can't enjoy that as I used to. You'll find that, too, I expect, as you get old. I've heard other old people say so. *This* is what I like now.' She put her hand upon the trunk of the tree and lifted her face into the wind. 'Let's rest a minute, shall we?'

She hooked her stick over a branch and Margaret did likewise. Lady Challis took out her cigarette-case, but put it away again, for no light could have lasted for an instant in that wind.

'And I've been thinking a lot about the Past,' Margaret continued, finding it easier to talk as she went on. 'There's an old hunting-lodge that belonged to Odo of Bayeux, the tradition goes, close to where I live in London – or rather, the site of it is quite close; there's nothing left of it now but a low hill that you can see from the Underground railway station. I went specially to look at it. It was a sort of pilgrimage.'

> *'All the horrors dimmed with age*
> *Like demons in a missal page,'*

said Lady Challis absently, linking her hands round a bough as if to enjoy the roughness of the bark. 'I am not sure if a passion for the past is altogether satisfying. And sometimes it produces a horror of the present.'

'That's exactly what it is producing in me! I'm getting to hate everything contemporary. I expect you will say that the poor suffered horribly in the past; I know that, and I don't care. It was all beautiful; that's all that matters to me.'

'I am glad to hear you speak with such feeling; it shows enjoyment. Nevertheless, a passion for the past is a form of yearning. It is doomed never to be satisfied, and therefore it can never be satisfying.'

'I am used to not being satisfied.' Margaret's tone was a little tart, for it seemed to her that Lady Challis was easily placed for giving advice about satisfaction; she had been beautiful, had married, had borne a child, and now in old age possessed money to buy the objects and experiences which gave her delight. 'I have to get my happiness out of wanting things.'

'You are very young to realize that happiness can come from wanting things. I expect that God will get hold of you one of these days. By the way, has Hebe spoken to you yet?'

'What about?' Margaret's tone was too startled to sound perfectly polite.

'Perhaps I am being indiscreet, if she hasn't, but she is thinking of asking you to go to her to look after the children.'

'As a job, do you mean, Lady Challis?'

'Yes. She thinks you are wonderful with them.'

Margaret was silent, employed in attending to her nose, which the wind had caused to become disagreeably active, with her handkerchief. A slight resentment mingled with her flattered surprise. They seem to take it for granted, she thought, that I would be only too pleased to give up teaching and accept a far lower salary just for the reward of living under the same roof with Nilands and getting occasional glimpses of Challises. Really, their arrogance – (relishing the word) – their arrogance is unbelievable! I suppose even *she* (darting a glance at Lady Challis, who had climbed a little way down her ladder to take the handkerchief from Claudia, who was delightedly climbing up) takes my saying 'yes' for granted.

'Do you think it would be a good thing for me to do?' she asked timidly in a moment, her mood suddenly humbled by a glimpse of Lady Challis's beautiful head, silver and worn amidst the crowding leaves.

'No.' Lady Challis surprised her by decidedly replying. 'You ought to get free of people for a time. If you go to Hebe, you will be swamped.'

'That's what I feel, too,' murmured Margaret, 'but it seems so ungrateful.'

'Ungrateful! Nonsense. Hebe has always had a Faithful Dog Tray, and every now and then one dies or rebels or gets married and she has to find another. She has just lost poor Grantey and now she is after you.'

Margaret had such a clear conception of Hebe as the hunted rather than the huntress that this novel idea of her being 'after' herself left her for a moment with nothing to say.

'Do you think she likes me at *all*?' she burst out at last. 'It isn't that I'm so fond of *her*, if it comes to that, but no one likes to be thought of *entirely* as a convenience.'

'She thinks that you would be overjoyed at the chance of living with the family and that it might possibly be doing you a good turn, too. Oh yes, she likes you up to a point, I expect. Hebe doesn't like anyone much except Alex and the children and her mother. She will always be protected from life because she is not sensitive. You are. So, if I were you I would say, "No, thank you." I don't think there are any more plums up here, do you? Shall we go down?'

'Oh, please do let's stay up here a little longer,' Margaret implored. 'You'll be making jam all to-morrow and I shan't get a chance to talk to you.'

'That's true. Fifty pounds of it. I made all the grown-ups go without sugar in their tea for weeks. Well, what else is troubling you?'

'You said I was sensitive. I am, I'm afraid. I don't feel things quite as badly as I did when I first came to London, but I still feel them very much. Is there any cure for it? The headmistress at the first school I taught in said that I needed a tragedy to make me grow up and bring out the best in me, and people do seem to think — in Mr Challis's plays — I mean, some people think that it's silly and weak to want to be happy and that one ought to take the tragic view of life —'

Her words poured out eagerly and her eyes were fixed earnestly upon Lady Challis as she leant forward among the leaves with her hands locked together.

'Not for you,' Lady Challis interrupted her. 'I don't think that you are one of the people who need tragedy. You need what I call the Gentle Powers.'

'Oh, *please* tell me what they are!'

'Beauty, and Time, and the Past and Pity (their names sound like a band of angels, don't they?) Laughter, too — you need calming and lifting into the light, not plunging into darkness and struggle.'

She began to dust her hands upon her hessian overall, which was belted in at the waist like the voluminous robe of a medieval nun. While she was uttering the vast tranquil names of her band of angels, Margaret's imagination, by one of those flights which it sometimes sustained, seemed to see passing before her eyes the earthly shapes which those angels had worn for her during the past year; Westwood, music, Bishop Odo's Lodge, Linda, the children and Alex Niland; and she realized how far she had already been 'calmed and lifted into

445

the light.' The Gentle Powers! *That* is why I am happier, she thought.

'Coming?' Lady Challis began to descend the ladder. Irene had left her basket at the foot of the tree and gone to collect the fruit from another band of workers at the far end of the meadow. Some of the children had lit a bonfire of withered weeds and prunings at the far end, and the azure smoke was blowing flat across the grass, racing away into the hedge, where some late honeysuckles lingered upon the sunlit summit.

'Oh – just two questions more!'

Lady Challis paused, lifting a slightly smiling, slightly impatient face.

'Do you think it likely that I shall marry?' Margaret asked in a low hurried tone, coming down her own ladder.

'Now what a thing to ask me! How should I know? I hope so, my dear, but if you don't, the Gentle Powers will still help you to do the hardest thing in the world.'

'What is that?' asked Margaret. But she knew.

'To live without earthly love.'

For a moment neither spoke. Lady Challis attempted to lift the basket of plums and, finding it beyond her strength, set it down again with a little sigh; Margaret stared, lost in a dream, down into the rich dark grass threaded with yellowing leaves. Lady Challis rested herself against a ladder and took out her cigarette-case.

'You said,' Margaret began again, suddenly looking up, 'that God would probably get hold of me one day. What did you mean, please? I never go to church or think about God much – if there is one, that is. I'm not even sure of that.'

'I think you look what a man I once knew called "a God-struggler." I can't tell you why I think it, but I do, and what you said about getting your satisfaction out of wanting things made me sure of it. You see, the only "thing" that a human being can go on wanting all their life, *and* be satisfied with just wanting, is God.'

'I don't like the idea of wanting God,' said Margaret decidedly.

Lady Challis laughed.

'My poor dear, that won't help you or make any difference. Have you read *The Hound of Heaven*?'

'Yes. To me it seems technically beautiful but emotionally it doesn't mean a thing.'

'I wouldn't let that worry you. There's plenty of time.'

'I'm not letting it, Lady Challis. I *wish*,' rebelliously, 'I could make you *see* how I *hate* the idea of getting religious!'

Lady Challis only laughed again and stood upright. The wind blew the tip of her cigarette into a little fire which occasionally gave off minute sparks.

'We shall have to get Maggie to carry this load in for us,' she said, indicating the basket, 'and there's another one ready over there. I'll go and ask Bertie to put the panniers on her,' and before Margaret could offer to go in her stead, she walked rapidly away with the hands in the pockets of her nun-like robe.

Margaret stood in the shade of the sighing tree, watching the figures moving about the bonfire and gathering round the baskets piled high with pale red and golden and dark purple fruit, while the leaves drifted past them in showers:

> *From all the woods that autumn*
> *Bereaves in all the world,*

she thought. *Bereaves*; that's a beautiful word. But the leaves do come back again in the spring, and there will be the wallflowers and the narcissus again, and the long evenings. I shall never tire of them; I shall love nature and art until I am an old, old woman, and the Gentle Powers too. But I will never love God, even if

God exists. I am not naturally religious. I do not feel the need of God.

And she stood there, with the struggle that was to last for so many years already beginning in her heart.

A procession now made its way out from the stable near the hedge. It consisted of Bertie leading Maggie, Lady Challis walking at the cob's head with a crown of honeysuckle upon her own, and Edna, Claudia, Frank, some other children, and finally the odd-job man bringing up the rear. They came through the blue smoke, that swirled low and straight about their knees.

'We've just time to take a load up to the house before lunch,' called Lady Challis, looking like a prophetess with the smoke floating about her and the wreath of honeysuckle on her hair, 'Margaret, come and help.'

So Margaret left the shade of the tree and went out to meet the procession, and joined it, and helped.